BLOOD, GUTS, AND GLORY

BLOOD, GUTS, AND GLORY
SMOKE JENSEN, AMERICAN LEGEND

WILLIAM W. JOHNSTONE

PINNACLE BOOKS
Kensington Publishing Corp.
www.kensingtonbooks.com

PINNACLE BOOKS are published by

Kensington Publishing Corp.
119 West 40th Street
New York, NY 10018

Copyright © 2021 J. A. Johnstone

Revenge of the Mountain Man copyright © 1988 William W. Johnstone
Vengeance of the Mountain Man copyright © 1997 William W. Johnstone

ISBN-13: 978-0-7860-4788-8
ISBN-10: 0-7860-4788-7

First Pinnacle paperback printing: April 2021

10 9 8 7 6 5 4 3 2 1
Printed in the United States of America

Electronic edition:

ISBN-13: 978-0-7860-4789-5 (e-book)
ISBN-10: 0-7860-4789-5 (e-book)

CONTENTS

REVENGE OF THE
MOUNTAIN MAN

I am the wound and the knife!
I am the blow and the cheek!
I am the limbs and the wheel
—the victim and the executioner.

—BAUDELAIRE

CHAPTER ONE

They had struck as cowards usually do, in a pack and at night. And when the man of the house was not at home. They had come skulking like thieving foot-padders; but instead of robbery on their minds, their thoughts were of a much darker nature.

Murder.

And they had tried to kill Smoke Jensen's wife, Sally. When Smoke and Sally had married, just after Smoke almost totally wiped out the small town of Bury, Idaho, Smoke had used another name; but later, during the valley war around Big Rock and Fontana, he had once more picked up his real name, and be damned to all who didn't like the fact that he had once been a gunfighter.

It had never been a reputation that he had sought out; rather, it had seemed to seek him out. Left alone as a boy, raised by an old mountain man called Preacher, the young man had become one of the most feared and legended gunslingers in all the West. Some say he was the fastest gun alive. Some say that Smoke Jensen had killed fifty, one hundred, two hundred men.

No one really knew for certain.

All anyone really knew was that Smoke had never been an outlaw, never ridden the hoot-owl trail, had no warrants out on him, and was a quiet sort of man. Now married, for several years he had been a farmer/rancher/horse breeder. A peaceful man who got along well with his neighbors and wished only to be left alone.

The night riders had shattered all that.

Smoke had been a hundred miles away, buying cattle, just starting the drive back to his ranch, called the Sugarloaf, when he heard the news. He had cut two horses out of his remuda and tossed a saddle on one. He would ride one, change saddles, and ride the other. They were mountain horses, tough as leather, and they stood up to the hard test.

Smoke did not ruin his horses on the long lonely ride back to the Sugarloaf, did not destroy them as some men might. But he rode steadily. He was torn inside, but above it all Smoke remained a realist, as old Preacher had taught him to be. He knew he would either make it in time, or he would not.

When he saw the snug little cabin in the valley of the high lonesome, the vastness of the high mountains all around it, Smoke knew, somehow, he had made it in time.

Smoke was just swinging down from the saddle when Dr. Colton Spalding stepped out of the cabin, smiling broadly when he spied Smoke. The doctor stopped the gunfighter before Smoke could push open the cabin door.

"She's going to make it, Smoke. But it was a close thing. If Bountiful had not awakened when she did and convinced Ralph that something was the matter . . ." The doctor shrugged his shoulders. "Well, it would have been all over here."

"I'm in their debt. But Sally is going to make it?"

"Yes. I have her sedated heavily with laudanum, to help her cope with the pain."

"Is she awake?"

"No. Smoke, they shot her three times. Shoulder, chest, and side. They left her for dead. She was not raped."

"Why did they do it? And who were they?"

"No one knows, except possibly Sally. And so far, the sheriff has not been able to question her about it."

"Bounty hunters, maybe. But there is no bounty on my head. I'm not wanted anywhere that I'm aware of."

"Nevertheless, Sheriff Carson believes it was bounty hunters. Someone paid to kill you. Or to draw you out, to come after them. The sheriff is with the posse now, trying to track the men."

"I'll just look in on her, Colton."

The doctor nodded and pushed open the cabin door. Smoke stepped past him.

The doctor's wife, Mona, a nurse, was sitting with several other women in the big main room of the cabin. They smiled at Smoke as he removed his hat and hung it on a peg by the door. He took off his gunbelt and hung it on another peg.

"Doc said it was all right for me to look in on her."

Mona nodded her head.

Smoke pushed open the bedroom door and stepped quietly inside, his spurs jingling faintly with each step. A big man, with a massive barrel chest and arms and shoulders packed with muscle, he could move as silently as his nickname implied.

Smoke felt a dozen different emotions as he looked at the pale face of his wife. Her dark hair seemed to make her face look paler. In his mind, there was love and hate and fury and black-tinged thoughts of revenge, all intermingled with sorrow and compassion. Darker emotions filled the tall young man as he sat down in a chair beside the bed and gently placed one big rough hand on his wife's smaller and softer hand.

Did she stir slightly under his touch? Smoke could not be sure. But he was sure that somehow, in her pain-filled mind, Sally knew that he was there, beside her.

Now, alone, Smoke could allow emotions to change his usually stoic expression. His eyes mirrored his emotions. He wished he could somehow take her pain and let it fill his own body. He took the damp cloth from her head, refreshed it with water, wrung it out, and softly replaced it on her brow.

All through the rest of that day and the long, lonely night that followed, the young man sat by his wife's bed. Mona Spalding would enter hourly, sometimes shooing Smoke out of the room, tending to Sally's needs. Doc Spalding slept in a chair, the two other women, Belle North and Bountiful Morrow, Smoke and Sally's closest neighbors, slept in the spare bedroom.

Outside, the foreman, Pearlie, and the other hands had gathered, war talk on their lips and in the way they stood. Bothering a woman, good or bad, in this time in the West, was a hangin' matter . . . or just an outright killin'.

Little Billy, Smoke and Sally's adopted son, sat on a bench outside the house.

Just as the dawn was breaking golden over the high mountains around the Sugarloaf, Sally opened her eyes and smiled at her husband.

"You look tired," she said. "Have you had anything to eat?"

"No."

"Have you been here long?"

"Stop worrying about me. How do you feel?"

"Washed out."

He smiled at her. "I don't know what I'm going to do with you," he said gently. "I go off for a time and you get into a gunfight. That isn't very ladylike, you know? What would your folks back east think?"

She winked at him.

"Doc says you're going to be all right, Sally, But you're going to need lots of rest."

"Three of them," she whispered. "I heard them talking. I guess they thought I was dead. One was called Dagget . . ."

"Hush now."

"No. Let me say it while I still remember it. I heard one call another Lapeer. He said that if this doesn't bring you out, nothing will."

She closed her eyes. Smoke waited while she gathered strength.

Doc Spalding had entered the room, standing in the doorway, listening.

He met Smoke's eyes and inwardly cringed at the raw savagery he witnessed in the young man's cold gaze. Spalding had seen firsthand the lightning speed of Smoke's draw. Had witnessed the coldness of the man when angered. Fresh from the ordered world back east, the doctor was still somewhat appalled at the swiftness of frontier justice. But deep inside him, he would reluctantly agree that it was oftentimes better than the ponderousness of lawyers jabbering and arguing.

Sally said. "The third one was called Moore. Glen Moore. South Colorado, I think. I'm tired, honey."

Spalding stepped forward. "That's all, Smoke. Let her sleep. I want to show you something out in the living room."

In the big room that served as kitchen, dining, and sitting area, the doctor dropped three slugs into Smoke's callused palm.

He had dug enough lead out of men since his arrival to be able to tell one slug from another. ".44s, aren't they?"

"Two of them," Smoke said, fingering the off-slug. "This is a .44-40, I believe."

"The one that isn't mangled up?"

"Yes."

"That's the one I dug out of her chest. It came close to killing her, Smoke." He opened his mouth to say something, sighed, and then obviously thought better of it.

"You got something else to say, Doc?"

He shook his head. "Later. Perhaps Sally will tell you herself; that would be better, I'm thinking. And no, she isn't going to die. Smoke, you haven't eaten and you need rest. Mona agrees. She's fixing you something now. Please. You've got to eat."

"You will eat, and then you will rest," Belle said, a note of command in her voice. "Johnny is with the posse, Smoke. Velvet is looking after the kids. You'll eat, and then sleep. So come sit down at the table, Smoke Jensen."

"Yes, ma'am," Smoke said with a smile.

* * *

"I was waiting to be certain," Sally told him the next morning. "Dr. Spalding confirmed it the day before those men came. I'm pregnant, Smoke."

A smile creased his lips. He waited, knowing, sensing there was more to come.

Sally's eyes were serious. "Colton is leaving it all up to me, isn't he?"

"I reckon, Sally. I don't know. I do know that your voice is much stronger."

"I feel much better."

Smoke waited.

"You're not going to like what I have to say, Smoke. Not . . . in one way, that is."

"No way of knowing that, Sally. Not until you say what's on your mind."

She sighed, and the movement hurt her; pain crossed her face. "I'm probably going to have to go back east, Smoke."

Smoke's expression did not change. "I think that might be best, Sally. For a time."

She visibly relaxed. She did not ask why he had said that. She knew. He was going after the men who attacked her. She expected that of him. "You're not even going to ask why I might have to go back east?"

"I would think it's because the doctor told you to. But you won't be going anywhere for weeks. You were hard hit." He smiled. "I've been there, too." He kissed her mouth. "Now, you rest."

Mona and Belle stayed for three days; Bountiful lived just over the hill and could come and go with ease. On the morning of the fourth day, Sally was sitting up in bed, her color back. She was still in some pain and very weak, and would be for several more weeks.

Smoke finally brought up the subject. "The Doc is sure that you're with child?"

"Both of us are," she smiled with her reply. "I knew before the doctor."

Discussion of women's inner workings embarrassed Smoke. He dropped that part of it. "Now tell me why you think you might have to go back east."

"I have several pieces of lead in me, Smoke. Colton could not get them all. And he does not have the expertise nor the facilities to perform the next operation. And also, I have a small pelvis; the birth might be a difficult one. There is a new—well, a more highly refined procedure that is being used back east. I won't go into detail about that."

"Thank you," Smoke said dryly. "'Cause so far I don't have much idea of what you're talking about."

She laughed softly at her husband. A loving laugh and a knowing laugh. Smoke knew perfectly well what she was saying. He was, for the most part, until they had married, a self-taught man. And over the past few years, she had been tutoring him. He was widely read, and to her delight and surprise, although few others knew it, Smoke was a very good actor, with a surprising range of voices and inflections. She was continually drawing out that side of him.

"Mona's from back east, isn't she?"

"I'm way ahead of you, Smoke. Yes, she is. And if I have to go—and I'm thinking it might be best, and you know why, and it doesn't have anything to do with the baby or the operation—Mona will make all the arrangements and travel most of the way with me."

"That'll be good, Sally. Yes. I think you should plan on traveling east." She knew the set of that chin. Her leaving was settled; her husband had things to do. "You haven't seen your folks in almost five years. It's time to visit. Tell you what I'll do. I'll come out for you when it's time for you and the baby to return."

This time her laugh was hearty, despite her injuries. "Smoke, do you know the furor your presence would arouse in Keene, New Hampshire?"

"If *fu-ror* means what I think it does, why should people get all in a sweat about me coming east?"

"For sure, bands would play, you would be a celebrity, and the police would be upset."

"Why? I ain't wanted back there, or anywhere else for that matter."

She could but smile at him. If he knew, he had dismissed the fact that he was the most famous gunfighter in all of the West; that books—penny dreadfuls—had been and still were being written about his exploits—some of them fact, many of them fiction. That he had been written up in tabloids all over the world, and not just in the English-speaking countries. Her mother and father had sent Sally articles about her husband from all over the world. To say that they had been a little concerned about her safety—for a while—would be putting it mildly.

"People don't really believe all that crap that's been written about me, do they? Hell, Sally, I've been reported at fourteen different places at once, according to those stories."

"If they just believed the real things you've done, Smoke, that is enough to make people very afraid of you."

"That's silly! I never hurt anybody who wasn't trying to hurt me. People don't have any reason to be afraid of me."

"Well, I'm not afraid of you, Smoke. You're sort of special to me."

He smiled. "Oh, yeah? Well, I'd have to give it a lot of thought if someone was to offer to trade me a spotted pony for you, Sally."

CHAPTER TWO

Smoke Jensen and Sally Reynolds, gunfighter and schoolteacher, had met several years back, in Idaho. Just before Smoke had very nearly wiped out a town and all the people in it for killing his first wife and their child, Nicole and Baby Arthur; the boy named after Smoke's friend and mentor, the old mountain man, Preacher.

Smoke and Sally had married, living in peace for several years in the high lonesome, vast and beautiful mountains of Colorado. Then a man named Tilden Franklin had wanted to be king of the entire valley . . . and he had coveted Smoke's wife, making it public news.

Gold had been discovered in the valley, and a bitter, bloody war had ensued.

And in the end, all Tilden Franklin got was a half-a-dozen slugs in the belly, from the guns of Smoke Jensen, and six feet of hard cold ground.

That had been almost two years back; two years of peace in the valley and in Smoke and Sally's high-up ranch called the Sugarloaf.

Now that had been shattered.

On the morning of the first full week after the assault

on Sally, Smoke sat on the bench outside the snug cabin and sipped his coffee.

Late spring in the mountains.

1880, and the West was slowly changing. There would be another full decade of lawlessness, of wild and woolly days and nights; but the law was making its mark felt all over the area. And Smoke, like so many other western men, knew that was both good and bad. For years, a commonsense type of justice had prevailed, for the most part, in the West, and usually—not always, but usually—it worked. Swiftly and oftentimes brutally, but it worked. Now, things were changing. Lawyers with big words and fancy tongues were twisting facts, hiding the guilt to win a case. And Smoke, like most thinking people, thought that to be wrong.

The coming of courts and laws and lawyers would prove to be both a blessing and a curse.

Smoke, like most western men, just figured that if someone tried to do you a harm or a meanness, just shoot the son of a bitch and have done with it. 'Cause odds were, the guilty party wasn't worth a damn to begin with. And damn few were ever going to miss them.

Smoke, like so many western men, judged other men by what they gave to society as opposed to what they took away from it. If your neighbor's house or barn burned down or was blown down in a storm, you helped him rebuild. If his crops were bad or his herd destroyed, you helped him out until next season or loaned him some cows and a few bulls. If he and his family were hungry through no fault of their own, you helped out with food and clothing.

And so on down the line of doing things right.

And if a man wouldn't help out, chances were he was trash, and the sooner you got rid of him, the better.

Western justice and common sense.

And if people back east couldn't see that—well, Smoke thought . . . Well, he really didn't know what to think about people like that. He'd reserve judgment until he got to know a few of them.

He sipped his coffee and let his eyes drift over that part of his land that he could see from his front yard. And that was a lot of land, but just a small portion of all that he and Sally owned . . . free and clear.

There was a lot to do before Smoke put Sally on the steam trains and saw her off to the East—and before he started after those who had attacked her like rabid human beasts in the night.

And there was only one thing you could do with a rabid beast.

Kill it.

Billy stepped out of the house and took a seat on the bench beside his adopted father. The boy had been legally adopted by the Jensens; Judge Proctor had seen to that. Billy was pushing hard at his teen years, soon turning thirteen. Already he was a top hand and, even though Smoke discouraged it, a good hand with a gun. Uncommon quick. Smoke and Sally had adopted the boy shortly after the shoot-out in Fontana, and now Billy pulled his weight and then some around the Sugarloaf.

"You and Miss Sally both gonna go away?" Billy asked, his voice full of gloom.

"For a time, Billy. Sally thought about taking you back east with her, but you're in school here, and doing well. So Reverend Ralph and Bountiful are going to look after you. You'll stay here at the ranch with Pearlie and the hands. We might be gone for the better part of a year, Billy, so it's going to be up to you to be the man around the place."

Pearlie was leaning up against a hitch rail and Smoke winked at his friend and foreman.

"If I hadn't a-been out with the hands the other night . . ." Billy said.

Smoke cut him off. "And if your aunt had wheels, she'd have been a tea cart, Billy. You and the hands were doing what I asked you to do—pushing cattle up to the high grass. Can't any of you blame yourselves for what happened."

"I don't think my aunt had no wheels, Smoke," Billy said solemnly. Then he realized that Smoke was funning with him and he smiled. "That would be a sight to see though, wouldn't it?"

Pearlie walked up to the man and boy. "We'll be all right here, Billy. I don't know what I'd do without you. You're a top hand."

Billy grinned at the high compliment.

When the foreman and the boy had walked away, Smoke stepped back into the house and fixed breakfast for Sally, taking it to her on a tray. He positioned pillows behind her shoulders and gently eased her to an upright position in the bed.

He sat by the bed and watched her eat; slowly she was regaining her strength and appetite. But she was still very weak and had to be handled with caution.

She would eat a few bites and then rest for a moment, gathering strength.

"I'm getting better, Smoke," she told him with a smile. "And the food is beginning to taste good."

"I can tell. At first I thought it was my cooking," he kidded her. "Your color is almost back to normal. Feel like telling me more about what happened?"

She ate a few more bites and then pushed the tray from her. "It's all come back to me. The doctor said it would. He said that sometimes severe traumas can produce temporary memory loss."

Colton had told Smoke the same thing.

She looked at him. "It was close, wasn't it?"

"You almost died, honey."

She closed her eyes for a moment and then opened them, saying, "I remember the time. Nine o'clock. I was just getting ready for bed. I remember glancing at the clock. I was in my gown." Her brow furrowed in painful remembrance, physically and mentally. "I heard a noise outside, or so I thought. But when it wasn't repeated, I ignored it. I walked in here, to the bedroom, and then I heard the noise again. I remember feeling a bit frightened. . . ."

"Why?" he interrupted. He was curious, for Sally was not the spooky or flighty kind. She had used a rifle and pistol several times since settling here, and had killed or wounded several outlaws.

"Because it was not a natural sound. It was raining, and I had asked Billy, when he came in to get lunch packets for the crew, to move the horses into the barn, to their stalls for the night. Bad move, I guess. If Seven or Drifter had been in the corral, they would have warned me."

"I would have done the same thing, Sally. Stop blaming yourself. Too much of that going on around here. It was nobody's fault. It happened, it's over, and it's not going to happen again. Believe me, I will see to that."

And she knew he would.

"When the noise came again, it was much closer, like someone brushing up against the side of the house. I was just reaching for a pistol when the front door burst open. Three men; at least three men. I got the impression there was more, but I saw only three. I heard three names. I did tell you the names, didn't I? That part is hazy."

"Yes."

"Dagget, Lapeer, and Moore. Yes. Now I remember telling you. The one called Dagget smiled at me. Then he said"—she struggled to remember—"'Too bad we don't have more time. I'd like to see what's under that gown.' Then he lifted his pistol and shot me. No warning. No time at all to do anything. He just lifted his gun and shot me. As I was falling, the other two shot me."

Smoke waited, his face expressionless. But his inner thoughts were murderous.

Sally closed her eyes, resting for a moment before once more reliving the horrible night. "Just as I was falling into darkness, losing consciousness, I heard one say, 'Now the son of a bitch has us all to deal with.'"

And I will deal with you, Smoke thought. One by one, on a very personal basis. I will be the judge, the jury, and the executioner.

Smoke started to roll and light one of his rare cigarettes, then thought better of it. The smoke might cause Sally to cough and he knew that would be harmful.

"Do you know any of the men I mentioned, Smoke?"

"No. I can't say that I've even heard of them." There was a deep and dangerous anger within him. But he kept his voice and his emotions well in check. He hated night riders, of any kind. He knew those types of people were, basically, cowards.

He kept his face bland. He did not want Sally to get alarmed, although he knew that she knew exactly what he was going to do once she was safely on the train heading east. He also knew that when she did mention it—probably only one time—she would not attempt to stop him.

That was not her way. She had known the kind of man he was when she married him.

He met her eyes, conscious of her staring at him, and smiled at her. She held out a hand and Smoke took it, holding it gently.

"It's a mystery to me, honey," she said. "I just don't understand it. The valley has been so peaceful for so many months. Not a shot fired in anger. Now this."

Smoke hushed her, taking the lap tray. He had never even heard of a lap tray until Sally had sent off for one from somewhere back east. "You rest now. Sleep. You want some more laudanum?"

She minutely shook her head. "No. Not now. The pain's not too bad. That stuff makes my head feel funny."

She was sleeping even before Smoke had closed the door.

He scraped the dishes and washed them in hot water taken from the stove, then pumped a pot full of fresh water and put that on the stove, checking the wood level that heated the back plate and checking the draft. He peeled potatoes for lunch and dropped them into cold water. Then he swept the floor and tidied up the main room, opening all the windows to let the house cool.

Then the most famous and feared gunfighter in all the west washed clothes, wrung them out, and hung them up to dry on the clothesline out back, the slight breeze and the warm sun freshening them naturally.

He walked around to the front of the cabin and sat beside the bedroom window, open just a crack, so he could hear Sally if she needed anything.

Lapeer, Moore, and Dagget. He rolled those names around in his mind as his fingers skillfully rolled a cigarette. He had never heard of any of them. But he knew one thing for certain.

They were damn sure going to hear from him.

CHAPTER THREE

Smoke did not leave the Sugarloaf range for weeks. If supplies were needed, one of the hands went into town for them. Smoke did not want to stray very far from Sally's side.

The days passed slowly, each one bringing another hint of the summer that lay lazily before them. And Sally grew stronger. Two weeks after the shooting, she was able to walk outside, with help, and sit for a time, taking the sun, taking it easy, growing stronger each day.

Smoke had spoken with Sheriff Monte Carson several times since the posse's return from a frustrating and fruitless pursuit. But Monte was just as baffled as Smoke as to the why of Sally's attack and the identity of the attackers.

Judge Proctor had been queried, as well as most of the other people around the valley. No one had ever heard of the men.

It was baffling and irritating.

Not even the legended Smoke could fight an enemy he could not name and did not know and could not find.

Yet.

But he was going to find them, and when he did, he was going to make some sense out of this.

Then he would kill them.

It was midsummer before Dr. Colton Spalding finally gave Sally the okay to travel. During that time, he had wired the hospital in Boston several times, setting up Sally's operation. The doctor would use a rather risky procedure called a caesarean to take the baby—if it came to that. But the Boston doctor wanted to examine Sally himself before he elected to use that drastic a procedure. And according to Dr. Spalding, the Boston doctor was convinced a caesarean was necessary.

"What's this operation all about?" Smoke asked Dr. Spalding.

"It's a surgical procedure used to take the baby if the mother can't delivery normally."

"I don't understand, but I'll take your word for it. Is it dangerous?"

Colton hesitated. With Smoke, it was hard to tell exactly what he knew about any given topic. When they had first met, the doctor thought the young man to be no more than an ignorant brute, a cold-blooded killer. It didn't take Colton long to realize that while Smoke had little formal education, he was widely read and quite knowledgeable.

And Colton also knew that Smoke was one of those rare individuals one simply could not lie to. Smoke's unblinking eyes never left the face of the person who was speaking. Until you grew accustomed to it, it was quite unnerving.

Before Colton could speak, Smoke said, "Caesar's mother died from this sort of thing, didn't she?"

The doctor smiled, shaking his head. Many of the men of the West were fascinating with what they knew and how they had learned it. It never ceased to amaze the man to see some down-at-the-heels puncher, standing up in a bar-room quoting Shakespeare or dissertating on some subject as outrageous as astrology.

And knowing what he was talking about!

"Yes, it is dangerous, Smoke. But not nearly so dangerous as when Caesar was born."

"Let's hope not. What happens if Sally decides not to have this operation?"

"One of two things, Smoke. You will decide whether you want Sally saved, or the baby."

"I won't be there, Doc. So I'm telling you now—save my wife. You pass the word along to this doctor friend of yours in Boston town. Save Sally at all costs. You'll do that, right?"

"You know I will. I'll wire him first thing in the morning."

"Thank you."

Colton watched as Smoke helped Sally back to bed. He had not fully leveled with the young man about the surgical procedure. Colton knew that sometimes the attending physician had very little choice as to who would be saved. And sometimes, mother and child both died.

He sighed. They had come so far in medicine, soaring as high as eagles in such a short time. But doctors still knew so very little . . . and were expected to perform miracles at all times.

"Would that it were so," Colton muttered, getting into his buggy and clucking at the mare.

As the weather grew warmer and the days grew longer, Sally grew stronger . . . and was beginning to show her pregnancy. Several of the women who lived nearby would come over almost daily, to sew and talk and giggle about the damndest things.

Smoke left the scene when all that gabble commenced.

And he was still no closer to finding out anything about the men who attacked his wife.

Leaving Sally and the women, with two hands always on guard near the cabin, Smoke saddled the midnight-black horse with the cold, killer eyes, and he and Drifter went to town.

The town of Fontana, once called No Name, which had been Tilden Franklin's town, was dying just as surely as Tilden had died under Smoke's guns. Only a few stores remained open, and they did very little business.

It was to the town of Big Rock that Smoke rode, his .44s belted around his lean waist and tied down, the Henry rifle in his saddle boot.

Big Rock was growing as Fontana was dying. A couple of nice cafés, a small hotel, one saloon, with no games and no hurdy-gurdy girls. There was a lawyer, Hunt Brook, and his wife, Willow, and a newspaper, the *Big Rock Guardian,* run by Haywood and Dana Arden. Judge Proctor, the reformed wino, was the district judge and he made his home in Big Rock, taking his supper at the hotel every evening he was in town. Big Rock had a church and a schoolhouse.

It was a nice quiet little town; but as some men who had tried to tree it found out, Big Rock was best left alone.

Johnny North, who had married the widow Belle Colby after her husband's death, was—or had been—one of the West's more feared and notorious gunfighters. A farmer/rancher now, Johnny would, if the situation called for it, strap on and tie down his guns and step back into his gunfighter's boots. Sheriff Monte Carson, another ex-gunfighter, was yet another gunhawk to marry a grass widow and settle in Big Rock. Pearlie, Smoke's foreman, had married and settled down; but Pearlie had also been, at one point in his young life, a much-feared and respected fast gun. The minister, Ralph Morrow, was an ex-prizefighter from back east, having entered the ministry after killing a man with his fists. Ralph preached on Sundays and farmed and ranched during the week. Ralph would also pick up a gun and fight, although most would rather he wouldn't. Ralph couldn't shoot a short gun worth a damn!

Big Rock and the area surrounding it was filled with men and women who would fight for their families, their homes, and their lands.

The dozen or so outlaws who rode into town with the thought of taking over and having their way with the women some months back soon found that they had made a horrible and deadly mistake. At least half of them died in their saddles, their guns in their hands. Two more were shot down in the street. Two died in the town's small clinic. The rest were hanged.

The word soon went out along the hoot-owl trail: Stay away from Big Rock. The town is pure poison. Folks there will shoot you quicker than a cat can scat.

Smoke caught up with Johnny North, who was in town

for supplies. The two of them found Sheriff Carson and went to the Big Rock saloon for a couple of beers and some conversation. The men sipped their beers in silence for a time. Finally, after their mugs had been refilled, Johnny broke the silence.

"I been thinkin' on it some, Smoke. I knew I'd heard that name Dagget somewheres before, but I couldn't drag it out of my head and catch no handle on it. It come to me last night. I come up on that name down near the Sangre de Cristo range a few years back. It might not be the same fellow, but I'm bettin' it is. Sally's description of him fits what I heard. If it is, he's a bad one. Bounty hunter and bodyguard to somebody. I don't know who. I ain't never heard of the two other men with him."

"I ain't never heard of any of them," Monte said sourly. "And I thought I knew every gunslick west of the Big Muddy. That was any good, that is."

"Dagget don't ride the rim much," Johnny explained. "And he only takes jobs his boss wants him to take. If this is the same fellow, he's from back east somewheres. Came out here about ten years ago. Supposed to be from a real good family back there. Got in trouble with the law and had to run. But his family seen to it that he had plenty of money. What he done, so I'm told, is link up with some other fellow and set them up an outlaw stronghold; sort of like the Hole-In-The-Wall. All this is just talk; I ain't never been there."

Smoke nodded his head. Something else had jumped into his mind; something the old mountain man, Preacher, had said one time. Something about the time he'd had to put lead into a fellow who lived down near the Sangre de Cristo range. But what was the man's name? Was it Davidson? Yes. Rex Davidson.

"Rex Davidson," Smoke said it aloud.

Both Monte and Johnny stiffened at the name, both men turning their heads to look at Smoke.

When Johnny spoke, his voice was soft. "What'd you say, Smoke?"

Smoke repeated the name.

Monte whistled softly. "I really hope he ain't got nothing to do with the attack agin Sally."

Smoke looked at him. "Why?"

Monte finished his beer and motioned the two men outside, to the boardwalk. He looked up and down the street and then sat down on the wooden bench in front of the saloon, off to the side from the batwing entrance. Johnny and Smoke joined him.

"That name you just mentioned, Smoke . . . what do you know about him?"

"Absolutely nothing. I heard Preacher mention it one time, and one time only. That was years back, when I was just a kid. The name is all I know except that Preacher told me he had to put lead into him one time."

Monte nodded his head. "So that's it. Well, that clears it up right smart. Finishes the tale I been hearin' for years. I'll just be damned, boys!"

The men waited until Monte had rolled and licked a cigarette into shape and lighted it.

"Must have been . . . oh, at least twenty years back, so the story goes. Rex Davidson was about twenty, I guess. Might have been a year or two younger than that. I don't know the whole story; just bits and pieces. But this Davidson had just come into the area from somewheres.

California, I think it was. And he though he was castin' a mighty big shadow wherever it was he walked. He was good with a gun, and a mighty handsome man, too. I seen him once, and he is a lady killer. What's the word I'm lookin' for? Vain, that's it. Pretties himself up all the time.

"There was a tradin' post down on the Purgatoire called Slim's. Run by a Frenchman. It's still there, and the same guy runs it. Only now it's a general store. It sits east and some north of Trinidad, where the Francisco branches off from the Purgatoire.

"This Davidson was there, braggin' about how he was gettin' rich diggin' gold and running cattle up between the Isabel and the Sangre de Cristos. Said he was gonna build hisself a town. Done it, too."

Monte dragged on his cigarette and Johnny said, "Dead River."

"You got it."

"Damn good place to stay shut of."

"Sure is," Monte ground out his smoke under the heel of his boot. "Whole damn town is owned by this Davidson and maybe by this Dagget, too. Anyways, this was back . . . oh, 'bout '60, I reckon, and this mountain man come into the tradin' post with some pelts he'd taken up near the Apishapa and the Arkansas. Him and Slim was jawin' over the price when this Rex Davidson decided he'd stick his nose into the affair. He made some crack about the mountain man's weapons and the way he was talkin'. This mountain man wasn't no big fellow; but size don't amount to a hill of beans when you start gettin' smart-lipped with them people—as you well know, Smoke."

Smoke nodded his head. He knew all too well the truth in that statement. Mountain men, for the most part, stayed away from people and civilization, keeping mostly to themselves, but God have mercy on your soul if you started trouble with them.

Oh, yes, Smoke knew. He had been raised up during his formative years by the most legended of all mountain men—old Preacher.

"Well, that mountain man's name was Preacher," Monte continued. "Slim told me that Preacher didn't say nothin' to Davidson; just ignored him. And that made Davidson hot under the collar. He called out, "Hey, you greasy old bastard. I'm talking to you, old man!"'

"He shouldn't have done that," Smoke said softly.

And in his mind's eye, as Monte told his tale, Smoke could see what had happened. Smoke smiled as he visualized the long-ago day. . . .

Preacher turned slowly, looking at the young man with the twin Colt Navy .36s belted around his waist and tied down low. The fast draw was new to the West, and some that thought they were fast weren't. The mountain man, slim and lean-waisted, had a faint smile on his lips.

"What'd you want, Tadpole?"

"Davidson flushed red, hot and unreasonable anger flashing in his eyes.

The kid is crazy, Preacher guessed accurately. And he's a killer.

"The name is Rex Davidson, old man."

"Do tell? Is that 'pposed to mean something to me, Tadpole?"

"Yeah. I'm a gunfighter."

"Is that right?" Preacher drawled. "Well, now, how

come it is I ain't never seen none of your graveyards, Tadpole?"

"Well, old man, maybe you just haven't been in the right towns, standing in the right boot hill. I got 'em scattered around, here and there."

"My, my! I 'spect I should be im-pressed." He smiled. "But I ain't," he added softly.

"I thought you mountain men was supposed to be so damn tough!" Rex sneered. "You sound like you're scared to visit a graveyard."

"Oh . . . well, now, I tend to shy away from graveyards, Tadpole. They can be mighty spooky places. Some Injuns believe a man can lose his soul by wanderin' around in a graveyard. Mayhaps that's what happened to you, Tadpole."

"What the hell are you babbling about, you old bastard? I think you're silly!"

"Tadpole, I think you've prowled around so many old boneyards, lookin' up names on markers so's you could lie about how bad you want people to think you is . . . why, hell, Tadpole, I think you lost your soul."

"You calling me a liar, old man?" Rex fairly screamed the question, his hands dropping to his sides to hover over the butts of his Navy Colts.

"Could be, Tadpole," Preacher spoke softly. "But if I was you, I wouldn't take no of-fense. Not if you want to go on livin' healthy."

Slim Dugas got the hell out of the line of fire. He didn't know this punk-faced kid from Adam's Off Ox, but he sure as hell knew all about Preacher and that wild breed of men called mountain men. There just wasn't no back-up in a mountain man. Not none at all.

"No man calls me a liar and lives, you greasy old fart!"
Rex *screamed.*

*"Well, now, Tadpole. It shore 'ppears like I done it,
though, don't it?"*

*"Damn your eyes! Draw!" Davidson shouted, his palms
slapping the butts of his guns.*

*Preacher lifted his Sharps and pulled the trigger. He
had cocked it while Davidson was running off at the
mouth about how bad he was. The .52 slug struck the
young man in the side, exactly where Preacher intended
it to go; he didn't want to kill the punk. But in later years
he would realize that he should have. The force of the
slug turned Davidson around and spun him like a top,
knocking him against a wall and to the floor. He had not
even cleared leather.*

Monte chuckled and that brought Smoke back from
years past in his mind.

"Slim told me that Preacher collected his money for
his pelts, picked up his bacon and beans, and walked out
the door; didn't even look at Davidson. There was four or
five others in the room, drinking rotgut, and they spread
the story around about Davidson. Smoke, Davidson has
hated Preacher and anyone connected with him for years.
And one more thing: All them men in that room, they
was all back-shot, one at a time over the years. Only one
left alive was Slim."

"That tells me that this Davidson is crazy as a bessie-
bug."

"Damn shore is," Johnny agreed. "What kind of man
would hate like that, and for so long? It ain't as if Smoke

was any actual kin of Preacher's. Why wait this long to do something about it?"

"You askin' me questions I ain't got no answers for," Monte replied.

Smoke stood up. "Well, you can all bet one thing. I'm damn sure going to find out!"

CHAPTER FOUR

Smoke could tell that Sally was getting anxious to travel east and see her folks. She tried to hide her growing excitement, but finally she gave in and admitted she was ready to go.

Some men—perhaps many men—would have been reluctant to let their wives travel so far away from the hearth of home, especially when taking into consideration the often terrible hardships that the women of the West had to endure when compared with the lifestyle of women comfortably back east, with their orderly, structured society and policemen walking the beat.

Why, Sally had even told of indoor plumbing, complete with relief stations, not just bathing tubs. Smoke couldn't even imagine how something like that might work. He reckoned it would take a hell of a lot of digging, but it sure would be smelly if the pipes were to clog.

"You real sure you're up to this thing?" Smoke asked her.

"I feel fine, honey. And the doctor says I'm one hundred percent healed."

He patted her swelling belly and grinned. "Getting a little chubby, though."

She playfully slapped at his hand. "What are you going to do if it's twins?"

He put a fake serious look on his face. "Well, I might just take off for the mountains!"

She put her arms around him. "Mona says all the travel arrangements are complete. She says we'll be leaving the last part of next week."

"She told me. The Doc and me will ride down to Denver with you and see you both off."

"I'll like that. And then, Smoke? . . ."

"You know what I have to do, Sally. And it isn't a question of wanting to do it. It's something I have to do."

She lay her head on his chest. "I know. When will they ever leave us alone?"

"Maybe never, honey. Accept that. Not as long as there is some punk kid who fancies himself a gunslick and is looking to make a rep for himself. Not as long as there are bounty hunters who work for jackasses like this Rex Davidson and his kind. And not as long as there are Rex Davidsons in the world."

"It's all so simple for you, isn't it, Smoke?"

He knew what she was talking about. "Yes. If we could get rid of the scum of the earth, it would be such a very nice place to live."

With her arms still around him, feeling the awesome physical strength of the man, she said, "Didn't you tell me that this Dagget person came from back east?"

"Yeah. That's what Johnny told me and the sheriff. Came out here about ten years ago. Are you thinking that you know this fellow?"

"It might be the same person. Maybe. It was a long

time ago, Smoke. And not an experience that I wanted to remember. I've tried very hard to put it out of my mind."

"Put what out of your mind?"

She pulled away from him and walked to the open window, the curtains ruffling with the slight breeze. "It was a long time ago. I was . . . oh, I guess nine or ten." She paused for a time, Smoke waiting patiently. "I finally forced myself to remember something else Dagget said that night. He said that he . . . had wanted to see me naked for a long time. Then he grinned. Nasty. Evil. Perverted. Then I recalled that . . . experience so long ago."

She turned to face him.

"I was . . . molested as a child. I was not raped, but molested. By a man whom I believe to be this Dagget person. I screamed and it frightened him away. But before he left me, he slapped me and told me that if I ever told, he would kill my parents." She shrugged her shoulders. "I never told anyone before this."

"And you believe this Dagget is the same man?"

"I'm sure of it now. Shortly after my . . . incident, the man was forced to leave town; he killed a man in a lover's quarrel."

"All the more reason to kill the man."

"I was not the only little girl he molested. Some were actually raped. It's the same man," she said flatly. "That is not something a woman ever forgets."

"They still have warrants out for him in New Hampshire, you reckon?"

"I'm sure they do. Why do you ask?"

"Maybe I'll bring his head back in a bag. Give it to the police."

She shuddered. "Smoke, you don't do things like that in New Hampshire."

"Why? He's worse than a rabid beast. What's the matter with the people back east?"

"It's called civilization, honey."

"Is that right? Sounds to me like they got a yellow streak running up their backs."

She shook her head and fought to hide a smile.

"If I take him alive, you want me to wrap him up in a fresh deer hide and stake him out in the sun?"

Sally sighed and looked at her man. "Smoke . . . no! How gruesome! What would that accomplish?"

"Pay back, Sally. Sun dries the hide around them; kills them slow. Helps to tie a fresh cut strip of green rawhide around their heads. That really lets them know they've done wrong; that someone is right displeased with them."

She shuddered. "I think they would get that message, all right."

"Almost always, Sally. Your folks back east, Sally, they've got this notion about treating bad men humanely. That's what I've been reading. But the bad men don't treat their victims humanely. Seems like to me, your folks got things all screwed up in their heads. You won't have crime, Sally, if you don't have criminals."

She sighed, knowing there was really no argument against what he was saying. It was a hard land, this frontier, and it took a hard breed to survive. They were good to good people. Terribly brutal to those who sought the evil way.

And who was to say that the hard way was not the right way?

She smiled at her man. "I guess that's why I love you

so much, Smoke. You are so direct and straightforward in your thinking. I think you are going to be a most refreshing cool breeze to my family and friends back in New Hampshire."

"Maybe."

"Smoke, I am going to say this once, and I will not bring it up again. I married you, knowing full well what kind of man you are. And you are a good man, but hard. I have never tried to change you. I don't believe that is what marriage is all about."

"And I thank you for that, Sally."

"I know you are going man-hunting, Smoke. And I know, like you, that it is something you have to do. I don't always understand; but in this case, I do. My parents and brothers and sisters will not. Nor will my friends. But I do."

"And you're going to tell them what I'm doing?"

"Certainly. And you'll probably be written up in the local newspaper."

"Seems to me they ought to have more important things to write about than that."

Sally laughed at his expression. How could she explain to him that the people back in Keene didn't carry guns; that most had never seen a fast draw; that many of them didn't believe high noon shoot-outs ever occurred?

He probably wouldn't believe her. He'd have to see for himself.

"Smoke, I know that you take chances that many other men would not take. You're a special breed. I learned early on why many people call you the last mountain man. Perhaps that is yet another of the many reasons I love you like I do. So do this for me: When you put me on that train and see me off, put me out of your mind. Concentrate solely on the job facing you. I know you have that quality about you; you do it. I will leave messages at the wire offices for you, telling you how I am and where I can be reached at all times. You try to do the same for me, whenever you can."

"I will, Sally. And that's a promise. But I'm going to be out-of-pocket for a couple of months, maybe longer."

"I know. That's all I ask, Smoke. We'll say no more about it." She came to him and pulled his head down, kissing him.

"I have an idea, Sally."

"What?"

"All the hands are gone. The place is all ours. But it might hurt the baby."

"I bet it won't." She smiled impishly at him.

She was right.

Smoke stood watching until the caboose was out of sight. Dr. Spalding had walked back into the station house. Spalding and his wife, Mona, along with Sally, had ridden the stage into Denver. Smoke had ridden Drifter. He had not brought a pack animal; he'd buy one in the city.

There were already laws in parts of Denver about carrying guns, so Smoke had left his twin Colts back in the hotel room. He carried a short-barreled Colt, tucked behind his belt, covered by his coat.

Smoke turned away from the now-silent twin ribbons of steel that linked the nation. "See you soon, Sally," he muttered. He walked back into the station house.

"Are you going to stay in town for a time and see some of the shows?" Colton asked.

Smoke shook his head. "No. I'm going to gear up and pull out." He held out his right hand and Colton shook it. "You'll stay in touch with the doctors in Boston?"

"Yes. I'll have progress reports for you whenever you wire Big Rock."

"Check on Billy every now and then."

Colton nodded. "Don't worry about him. He'll be fine. You take care, Smoke."

"I'll be in touch." Smoke turned and walked away.

He bought three hundred rounds of .44s. The ammo was interchangeable between rifle and pistols. He bought a tent and a ground sheet, a coffee pot and a skillet. Coffee and beans and flour and a small jug of lard. Bacon. He walked around the store, carefully selecting his articles, choosing ones he felt a back-east dandy come west might pick up to take on his first excursion into the wilds.

He bought lace-up boots and a cap, not a hat. He bought a shoulder holster for his short-barreled Colt. He bought a sawed-off 12-gauge shotgun and several boxes of buck-shot shells.

"Have this gear out back on the loading dock in two hours," Smoke instructed the clerk. "That's when I'll be coming for it. And I'll pay you then."

"Yes, sir. That will be satisfactory. I shall see you in two hours."

"Fine."

Smoke inspected several packhorses and chose one that

seemed to have a lot of bottom. Then he took a hansom to a fancy art-house and bought a dozen sketch pads and several boxes of charcoal pencils.

He had not shaved that morning at the hotel and did not plan on doing anything other than trimming his beard for a long time to come.

At a hardware store, he picked up a pair of scissors to keep his beard neat. An artist's beard. He would cut off his beard when it came time to reveal his true identity.

When it came time for the killing.

Smoke had a natural talent for drawing, although he had never done much with it. Now, he thought with a smile, it was going to come in handy.

At the art store, the clerk was a dandy if Smoke had ever seen one, prissing around like a peacock, fussing about this and that and prancing up one aisle and down the other.

Smoke told him what he wanted and let the prissy little feller fill the bill.

Smoke studied the way the clerk walked. Wasn't no damn way in hell he was gonna try to walk like that. Some bear might think he was in heat.

He went to a barbershop and told the barber he wanted his hair cut just like the dandies back east were wearing theirs. Just like he'd seen in a magazine. Parted down the middle and greased back. The barber looked at him like he thought Smoke had lost his mind, but other than to give him a queer look, he made no comment. Just commenced to whacking and shaping.

Smoke did feel rather like a fop when he left the barber chair, and he hoped that he would not run into anyone he knew until his beard grew out. But in a big city like Denver—must have been four or five thousand people in the city—that was unlikely.

Smoke checked out of the hotel and got Drifter and his packhorse from the stable, riding around to the rear of the store, picking up and lashing down his supplies. His guns were rolled up and stored in a spare blanket, along with the sawed-off express gun.

He was ready.

But he waited until he got outside of the city before he stuck that damn cap on his head.

He rode southeast out of Denver, taking his time, seeing the country—again. He and old Preacher had ridden these trails, back when Smoke was just a boy. There were mighty few trails and places in Colorado that Smoke had not been; but oddly enough, down south of Canon City, down between the Isabels and the Sangre de Cristo range, was one area where Preacher had not taken him.

And now Smoke knew why that was. The old man had been protecting him.

But why so much hate on the part of this Rex Davidson? And was Sally right? Was this Dagget the same man who had molested her as a child? And how were he and Davidson connected—and why?

He didn't know.

But he was sure going to find out.

And then he would kill them.

Smoke spent a week camped along the West Bijou, letting his beard grow out and sketching various scenes, improving upon his natural talent. He still didn't like the silly cap he was wearing, but he stuck with it, getting used to the damned thing. And each day he combed and brushed his hair, slicking it down with goop, retraining it.

Damned if he really wasn't beginning to look like a dandy. Except for his eyes; those cold, expressionless, and emotionless eyes. And there wasn't a damn thing he could do about that.

Or was there? he pondered, smiling.

Oh, yes, there was.

Allowing himself a chuckle, he swiftly broke camp and packed it all up, carefully dousing his fire and then scattering the ashes and dousing them again. He mounted up and swung Drifter's head toward the south and slightly west. If he couldn't find what he was looking for in Colorado City, he'd head on down to Jim Beckworth's town of Pueblo—although some folks tended to spell it Beckwourth.

Smoke stopped in at the fanciest store in town and browsed some, feeling silly and foppish in his high-top lace-up boots and his city britches tucked into the tops like some of them explorer people he'd seen pictures of. But if he was gonna act and look like a sissy, he might as well learn the part—except for the walk—cause he damn sure was gonna look mighty funny if he could find him a pair of those tinted eyeglasses.

He found several pairs—one blue-tinted, one yellow-tinted, and one rose-tinted.

"Oh, what the hell," he muttered.

He bought all three pairs and a little hard case to hold them in, to keep them from getting broken.

Smoke put on his red-tinted eyeglasses and walked outside, thinking that they sure gave a fellow a different outlook on things.

"Well, well," a cowboy said, stepping back and eye-balling Smoke and his fancy getup. "If you jist ain't the purtiest thing I ever did see." Then he started laughing.

Smoke gritted his teeth and started to brush past the half-drunk puncher.

The puncher grabbed Smoke by the upper arm and spun him around, a startled look on his face as his fingers gripped the thick, powerful muscles of Smoke's upper arm.

Smoke shook his arm loose. Remembering all the grammar lessons Sally had given him, and the lessons that the urbane and highly educated gambler, Louis Longmont, had taught him, Smoke said, "I say, my good fellow, unhand me, please!"

The cowboy wasn't quite sure just exactly what he'd grabbed hold of. That arm felt like it was made of pure oak, but the speech sounded plumb goofy.

"What the hell is you, anyways?"

Smoke drew himself erect and looked down at the smaller man. "I, my good man, am an ar-tist!"

"Ar-tist? You paint pitchers?"

"I sketch pic-tures!" Smoke said haughtily.

"Do tell? How much you charge for one of them sketchies?"

"Of whom?"

"Huh?"

Smoke sighed. "Whom do you wish me to sketch?"

"Why, hell . . . me, o' course!"

"I'm really in a hurry, my good fellow. Perhaps some other time."

"I'll give you twenty dollars."

That brought Smoke up short. Twenty dollars was just about two thirds of what the average puncher made a month, and it was hard-earned wages. Smoke stepped back, taking a closer look at the man. This was no puncher. His boots were too fancy and too highly shined. His dress was too neat and too expensive. And his guns—two of them, worn low and tied down—marked him.

"Well . . . I might be persuaded to do a quick sketch. But not here in the middle of the street, for goodness sake!"

"Which way you headin', pardner?"

Smoke gestured with his arm, taking in the entire expanse. "I am but a free spirit, a wanderer, traveling where the wind takes me, enjoying the blessing of this wild and magnificent land."

Preacher, Smoke thought, *wherever you are, you are probably rolling on the ground, cackling at this performance.*

Smoke had no idea if Preacher were dead or alive; but he preferred to believe him alive, although he would be a very old man by now. But still? . . .

The gunfighter looked at Smoke, squinting his eyes. "You shore do talk funny. I'm camped on the edge of town. You kin sketch me there."

"Certainly, my good man. Let us be off."

Before leaving town, Smoke bought a jug of whiskey and gave it to the man, explaining, "Sometimes subjects tend to get a bit stiff and they appear unnatural on the paper. For the money, I want to do this right."

The man was falling-down drunk by the time they got to his campsite.

Smoke helped him off his horse and propped him up against a tree. Then he began to sketch and chat as he worked.

"I am very interested in the range of mountains known as the Sangre de Cristos. Are you familiar with them?"

"Damn sure am. What you wanna know about them? You just ax me and I'll tell you."

"I am told there is a plethora of unsurpassed beauty in the range."

"Huh?"

"Lots of pretty sights."

"Oh. Why didn't you say so in the first place? Damn shore is that."

"My cousin came through here several years ago, on his way to California. Maurice DeBeers. Perhaps you've heard of him?"

"Cain't say as I have, pardner."

"He stopped by a quaint little place for a moment or two. In the Sangre de Cristos. He didn't stay, but he said it was . . . well, odd."

"A town?"

"That's what he said."

"There ain't no towns in there."

"Oh, but I beg to differ. My cousin wrote me about it. Oh . . . pity! What was the name? Dead something-or-the-other."

The man looked at him, an odd shift to his eyes. "Dead River?"

"Yes! That's it! Thank you!"

Drunk as he was, the man was quick in snaking out a pistol. He eased back the hammer and pointed the muzzle at Smoke's belly.

CHAPTER FIVE

Smoke dropped his sketch pad and threw his hands into the air. He started running around and around in a little circle. "Oh, my heavens!" he screamed, putting as much fright in his voice as he could. Then he started making little whimpering sounds.

The outlaw—and Smoke was now sure that he was—smiled and lowered his gun, easing down the hammer. "All right, all right! Calm down 'fore you have a heart attack, pilgrim. Hell, I ain't gonna shoot you."

Smoke kept his hands high in the air and forced his knees to shake. He felt like a total fool but knew his life depended on his making the act real. And so far, it was working.

"Take all my possessions! Take all my meager earnings! But please don't shoot me, mister. Please. I simply abhor guns and violence."

The outlaw blinked. "You does what to 'em?"

"I hate them!"

"Why didn't you just say that? Well, hell, relax. Don't pee your fancy britches, sissy-boy. I ain't gonna shoot you. I just had to check you out, that's all."

"I'm terribly sorry, but I don't understand. May I please lower my hands?"

"Yeah, yeah. Don't start beggin'. You really is who you say you is, ain't you?" His brow furrowed in whiskey-soaked rumination. "Come to think of it, just who in the hell is you, anyways?"

"I am an artist."

"Not that! What's your name, sissy-britches?" He lifted the jug and took a long, deep pull, then opened his throat to swallow.

"Shirley DeBeers," Smoke said.

The outlaw spat out the rotgut and coughed for several minutes. He pounded his chest and lifted red-rimmed eyes, disbelieving eyes to Smoke.

"Shirley! That there ain't no real man's name!"

Smoke managed to look offended. What he really wanted to do was take the jerk's guns away from him and shove both of them down his throat. Or into another part of the outlaw's anatomy.

"I will have you know, sir, that Shirley is really a very distinguished name."

"I'll take your word for that. Get to sketching, Shirley."

"Oh, I simply couldn't!" Smoke fanned his face with both hands. "I feel flushed. I'm so distraught!"

"Shore named you right," the outlaw muttered. "All right, Shirley. If you ain't gonna draw my pitcher, sit down and lets us palaver."

Smoke sat down. "I've never played palaver; you'll have to teach me."

The outlaw put his forehead into a hand and muttered under his breath for a moment. "It means we'll talk, Shirley."

"Very well. What do you wish to talk about?"

"You. I can't figure you. You big as a house and strong as a mule. But if you're a pansy, you keep your hands to yourself, you understand that?"

"Unwashed boorish types have never appealed to me," Smoke said stiffly.

"Whatever that means," the gunhawk said. "My name's Cahoon."

"Pleased, I'm sure."

"What's your interest in Dead River, Shirley?"

"I really have no interest there, as I told you, other than to sketch the scenery, which I was told was simply breath-takingly lovely."

Cahoon stared at him. "You got to be tellin' the truth. You the goofiest-lookin' and the silliest-talkin' person I ever did see. What I can't figure out is how you got this far west without somebody pluggin' you full of holes."

"Why should they do that? I hold no malice toward anyone who treats me with any respect at all."

"You been lucky, boy, I shore tell you that. You been lucky. Now then, you over the vapors yet?"

"I am calmed somewhat, yes."

"Git to sketchin', Shirley."

When Smoke tossed off his blankets the next morning, the outlaw, Cahoon, was gone. Smoke had pretended sleep during the night as the outlaw had swiftly gone through his pack, finding nothing that seemed to interest him. Cahoon had searched one side of the pack carefully, then only glanced at the other side, which held supplies. Had he searched a bit closer and longer, he would have found Smoke's twin Colts and the shotgun.

Smoke felt he had passed inspection. At least for this time. But he was going to have to come up with some plan for stashing his weapons close to Dead River.

And so far, he hadn't worked that out.

Cahoon had left the coffee pot on the blackened stones around the fire and Smoke poured a cup. He was careful in his movements, not knowing how far Cahoon might have gone; he might well be laying out a few hundred yards, watching to see what Smoke did next.

Smoke cut strips of bacon from the slab and peeled and cut up a large potato, dropping the slices into the bacon grease as it fried. He cut off several slices of bread from the thick loaf and then settled down to eat.

He cut his eyes to a large stone and saw his sketch pad, a double eagle on the top page, shining in the rays of the early morning sun.

Cahoon had printed him a note: YOU DO FARLY GOOD DRAWINS. I PASS THE WORD THAT YOU OK. MAYBE SEE YOU IN DEAD RIVER. KEEP THIS NOTE TO HEP YOU GIT IN. CAHOON.

Smoke smiled. Yes, he thought, he had indeed passed the first hurdle.

Smoke drifted south, taking his time and riding easy. He had stopped at a general store and bought a bonnet for Drifter and the packhorse. The packhorse didn't seem to mind. Drifter didn't like it worth a damn. The big yellow-eyed devil horse finally accepted the bonnet, but only after biting Smoke twice and kicking him once. Hard.

Smoke's beard was now fully grown out, carefully trimmed into a fuller Vandyke but not as pointed. The beard had completely altered his appearance. And the news was spreading throughout the region about the goofy-talking and sissy-acting fellow who rode a horse with a bonnet and drew pictures. The rider, not the horse. The word was, so Smoke had overheard, that Shirley DeBeers was sorta silly, but harmless. And done right good drawin's, too.

And Cahoon, so Smoke had learned by listening and mostly keeping his mouth shut, was an outlaw of the worst kind. He fronted a gang that would do anything, including murder for hire and kidnapping—mostly women, to sell to whoremongers.

And they lived in Dead River, paying a man called Rex Davidson for security and sanctuary. And he learned that a man named Danvers was the Sheriff of Dead River. Smoke had heard of Danvers, but their trails had never crossed. The title of Sheriff was a figurehead title, for outside of Dead River he had no authority and would have been arrested on the spot.

Or shot.

And if Smoke had his way, it was going to be the latter.

Smoke and Drifter went from town to town, community to community, always drifting south toward the southernmost bend of the Purgatoire.

Smoke continued to play his part as the city fop, getting it down so well it now was second nature for him to act the fool.

At a general store not far from Quarreling Creek— so named because a band of Cheyenne had quarreled violently over the election of a new chief—Smoke picked up a few dollars by sketching a man and his wife and child, also picking up yet more information about Dead River and its outlaw inhabitants.

"Outlaws hit the stage outside Walensburg last week," he heard the rancher say to the clerk. "Beat it back past Old Tom's place and then cut up into the Sangre de Cristos."

The clerk looked up. There was no malice in his voice when he said, "And the posse stopped right there, hey?"

"Shore did. I reckon it's gonna take the Army to clean out that den of outlaws at Dead River. The law just don't wanna head up in there. Not that I blame them a bit for that," he was quick to add.

"Nobody wants to die," the clerk said, in a matter of agreeing.

"I have heard so much about this Dead River place," Smoke said, handing the finished sketch to the woman, who looked at it and smiled.

"You do very nice work, young man," she complimented him.

"Thank you. And I have also heard that around Dead River is some of the most beautiful scenery to be found anywhere."

The rancher put a couple of dollars into Smoke's hand and said, "You stay out of that place, mister. It just ain't no place for any decent person. And you seem to be a nice sort of person."

"Surely they wouldn't harm an unarmed man?" Smoke asked, holding on to his act. He managed to look offended at the thought. "I am an artist, not a troublemaker."

The clerk and the rancher exchanged knowing glances and smiles, the clerk saying, "Mister, them are bad apples in that place. They'd as soon shoot you as look at you. And that's just if you're lucky. I'd tell you more, but not in front of the woman and child."

"Mabel" the rancher spoke to his wife. "You take Jenny and wait outside on the boardwalk. We got some man-talking to do." He glanced at Smoke. "Well . . . some talking to do, at least."

Smoke contained his smile. He could just imagine Sally's reaction if he were to tell her to leave the room so the men could talk. A lady through and through, she would have nevertheless told Smoke where to put his suggestion.

Sideways.

The woman and child waiting on the boardwalk of the store, under the awning, the rancher looked at Smoke and shook his head in disbelief. Smoke was wearing a ruffle-front shirt, pink in color, tight-fitting lavender britches—he had paid a rancher's wife to make him several pairs in various colors—tucked into the tops of his lace-up hiking boots, tinted eyeglasses, and that silly cap on his head.

Foppish was not the word.

"Mr. DeBeers," the rancher said, "Dead River is the dumping grounds for all the scum and trash and bad hombres in the West. Some of the best and the bravest lawmen anywhere won't go in there, no matter how big the posse. And for good reason. The town of Dead River sits in a valley between two of the biggest mountains in the range. Only one way in and one way out."

The clerk said, "And the east pass—the only way in—is always guarded. Three men with rifles and plenty of ammunition could stand off any army forever."

Smoke knew that one-way-in and one-way-out business was nonsense. If he could find some Indians, he'd discover a dozen ways in and out. When he got close to the range of mountains, he'd seek out some band and talk with them.

The rancher said, "There've been reports of them outlaws gettin' all drunked up and draggin' people to death just for the fun of doin' it, up and down the main street. Some men from the Pinkerton agency, I think it was, got in there a couple of years ago, disguised as outlaws. When it was discovered what they really was, the outlaws stripped 'em nekkid and nailed 'em up on crosses, left the men there to die, and they died hard."

"Sometimes," the clerk added, "they'll hang people up on meathooks and leave them to die slow. Takes 'em days. And it just ain't fittin' to speak aloud what they do to women they kidnap and haul in there. Makes me sick to just think about it."

"Barbaric!" Smoke said.

"So you just stay out of that place, mister," the rancher said.

"But Mr. Cahoon said I would be welcome," Smoke dropped that in.

"You know Cahoon?" The clerk was bug-eyed.

"I sketched him once."

"You must have done it right. Cause if you hadn't, Cahoon would have sure killed you. He's one of the worst. Likes to torture people—especially Indians and women; he ain't got no use for neither of them."

"Well, why doesn't someone do something about it?" Smoke demanded. "They sound like perfectly horrid people to me."

"It'd take the Army to get them out," the rancher explained. "At least five hundred men—maybe more than that; probably more than that. But here's the rub, mister:

No one has ever come out of there to file no complaints. When a prisoner goes in there, he or she is dead. And dead people don't file no legal complaints. So look, buddy . . . eh, fellow, whatever, the day'll come when the Army goes in. But that day ain't here yet. So you best keep your butt outta there."

Smoke drifted on, and his reputation as a good artist went before him. He cut east, until he found a town with a telegraph office and sent a wire to Boston. He and Sally had worked out a code. He was S.B. and she was S.J. He waited in the town for a night and a day before receiving a reply.

Sally was fine. The doctors had removed the lead from her and her doctor in Boston did not think an operation would be necessary for child-birthing.

Smoke drifted on, crossing the Timpas and then following the Purgatoire down to Slim's General Store. A little settlement had been built around the old trading post, but it was fast dying, with only a few ramshackle buildings remaining. Smoke stabled his horses and stepped into the old store.

An old man sat on a stool behind the article-littered counter. He lifted his eyes as Smoke walked in.

"I ain't real sure just perxactly what you might be, son," the old man said, taking in Smoke's wild get-up. "But if you got any fresh news worth talkin' 'bout, you shore welcome, whether you buy anything or not."

Smoke looked around him. The store was empty of customers. Silent, except for what must have been years of memories, crouching in every corner. "Your name Slim?"

"Has been for nigh on seventy years. Kinda late to be changin' it now. What can I do you out of, stranger?"

Smoke bought some supplies, chatting with Slim while he shopped. He then sat down at the offer of a cup of coffee.

"I am an artist," he announced. "I have traveled all the way from New York City, wandering the West, recreating famous gunfights on paper. For posterity. I intend to become quite famous through my sketchings."

Slim looked at the outfit that Smoke had selected for that morning. It was all the old man could do to keep a straight face. Purple britches and flame-red silk shirt and colored glasses.

"Is that right?" Slim asked.

"It certainly is. And I would just imagine that you are a veritable well of knowledge concerning famous gunfighters and mountain men, are you not?"

Slim nodded his head. "I ain't real sure what it is you just said, partner. Are you askin' me if I knowed any gun-fighters or mountain men?"

"That is quite correct, Mr. Slim."

"And your name be? . . ."

"Shirley DeBeers."

"Lord have mercy. Well, Shirley, yeah, I've seen my share of gunfights. I personal planted six or eight right back yonder." He pointed. "What is it you want to know about, pilgrim?"

Smoke got the impression that he wasn't fooling this old man, not one little bit. And he was curious as to the why of that.

"I have come from New York," he said. "In search of any information about the most famous mountain man of all time. And I was told in Denver that you, and you alone, could give me some information about him. Can you?"

Slim looked at Smoke, then his eyes began to twinkle. "Boy, I come out here in '35, and I knowed 'em all. Little Kit Carson—you know he wasn't much over five feet tall—Fremont, Smith, Big Jim, Caleb Greenwood, John Jacobs; hell, son, you just name some and I bet I knew 'em and traded with 'em."

"But from what I have learned, you did not name the most famous of them all!"

Slim smiled. "Yeah, that's right. I sure didn't—Mr. Smoke Jensen."

CHAPTER SIX

Over a lunch of beef and beans and canned peaches, Smoke and Slim sat and talked.

"How'd you know me, Slim? I've never laid eyes on you in my life."

"Just a guess. I'd heard people describe you 'fore. And I knowed what went on up on the Sugarloaf, with them gunnies and your wife; I figured you'd be comin' on along 'fore long. But what give you away was your accent. I've had folks from New York town in here 'fore. Your accent is all wrong."

"Then I guess I'd better start working on that, right?"

"Wrong. What you'd better do is shift locations. You ain't never gonna talk like them folks. You best say you're from Pennsylvannie. From a little farm outside Pittsburgh on the river. That ought to do it. If you're just bounded and swore to go off and get shot full of holes."

Smoke let that last bit slide. "How's Preacher?" He dropped that in without warning.

Slim studied him for a moment, then nodded his head. "Gettin' on in years. But he's all right, last I heard. He's livin' with some half-breed kids of hisn up in Wyoming. Up close to the Montanie line."

"It's good to know that he's still alive. But I can't figure why he won't come live with me and Sally up on the Sugarloaf."

"That ain't his way, Smoke, and you know it. He's happy, boy. That's what's important. Why, hell, Smoke!" he grinned, exposing nearly toothless gums. "They's a whole passel of them ol' boys up yonder. They's Phew, Lobo, Audie, Nighthawk, Dupre, Greybull—two/three more. Couple of 'em has died since they hepped you out three/four years back."

Smoke remembered them all and smiled with that remembrance.

"Yeah," Slim said. "I'm thinkin' hard on sellin' out and headin' up that way to join them. Gettin' on in years myself. I'd like to have me a woman to rub my back ever now and then. But," he sighed, "I prob'ly won't do that. Stay right here until I keel over daid. But Preacher and them? They happy, boy. They got their memories and they got each other. And when it's time for them to go, they'll turn their faces to the sky and sing their death songs. Don't worry none 'bout Preacher, Smoke. He raised you better than that."

"You're right, Slim." Smoke grinned. "As much as I'd like to see him, I'm glad he can't see me in this get-up today."

Slim laughed and slapped his knee. "He'd prob'ly laugh so hard he'd have a heart attack, for sure. I got to tell you, Smoke, you do look . . . well . . . odd!"

"But it's working."

"So far, I reckon it is. Let's talk about that. You got a plan, Smoke?"

"About getting into Dead River?" Slim nodded. "No. Not really. But for sure, I'm going in like this."

Smoke did not hesitate about talking about his plans to Slim. He could be trusted. Preacher had told him that.

"Might work," Slim said.

"The outlaws think they've got everybody convinced there is only one way in and one way out. I don't believe that."

"That's a pile of buffalo chips! You get on with the Utes, don't you?"

"Stayed with them many times."

"White Wolf and a bunch of his people is camped over just west of Cordova Pass. The word is, from old-timers that I talked to, White Wolf's braves make a game out of slippin' in and out of Dead River. White Wolf ain't got no use for none of them people in there. They been hard on Injuns. You talk to White Wolf. He's an old friend and enemy of Preacher."

Smoke knew what he meant. You might spend a summer with the Indians and the winter fighting them. That's just the way it was. Nearly anyone could ride into an Indian camp and eat and spend the night and not be bothered. 'Course they might kill you when you tried to leave. But at least you'd die after a good night's sleep and a full stomach.

Indians were notional folks.

"I did meet and sketch and convince some outlaw name of Cahoon." He showed Slim the note.

The old man whistled. "He's a bad one; 'bout half

crazy. Hates Injuns and women; ain't got but one use for a woman and you know what that is. Then he tortures them to death. How'd you meet him?"

Smoke told him, leaving nothing out. Slim laughed and wiped his eyes.

"Well, you can bet that Cahoon has told his buddies 'bout you plannin' on comin' in. And you can bet somebody is right now checkin' on your back trail. And they'll be here 'fore long. So you best draw me two or three of them pitchers of yourn and I'll stick 'em up on the wall."

Smoke spent several days at Slim's, relaxing and learning all that the old man knew about Dead River, Rex Davidson, and the man who called himself Dagget.

And Slim knew plenty.

They were the scum of the earth, Slim said, reinforcing what Smoke had already guessed. There was nothing they would not do for money, or had not already done. Every man in Dead River had at least one murder warrant out on his head.

That was going to make Smoke's job a lot easier.

"Smoke, if you do get inside that outlaw stronghold," Slim warned him, "don't you for one second ever drop that act of yourn. 'Cause ifn you do, sure as hell, someone'll pick up on it and you'll be a long time dyin'.

"Now, listen to me, boy: Don't trust nobody in there. Not one solitary soul. You cain't afford to do that.

"Now personal, Smoke, I think you're a damn fool for tryin' this. But I can see Preacher's invisible hand writ all over you. He'd do the same thing." He eyeballed Smoke's foppish get-up and grinned. "Well, he'd go in there; let's put it that way! I ain't gonna try to turn you around. You a growed-up man."

"But they have people being held as slaves in there, or so I'm told."

"Yeah, that's right. But some of them would just as soon turn you in as look at you, for favor's sake. You know what I mean?"

Smoke knew. It sickened him, but he knew. "How many you figure are in there, Slim? Or do you have any way of knowing that?"

"Ain't no way of really tellin' 'til you git in there," Slim said. "Them outlaws come and go so much. Might be as many as three hundred. Might be as low as fifty. But that's just the real bad ones, Smoke. That ain't countin' the shop owners and clerks and whores and sich. Like the minister."

"Minister! Wait a minute. We'll get back to him. What about the clerks and shop owners and those types of people?"

"What about them? Oh, I get you. Don't concern yourself with them. They're just as bad, in their own way, as them that ride out, robbin' and killin'. The clerks and shopkeepers are all on the run for crimes they done. There ain't no decent people in that town. Let me tell you something, boy: When a baby is borned to them shady gals in there, they either kill it outright or tote it into the closest town and toss it in the street."

Smoke grimaced in disgust. "I can't understand why this town hasn't attracted more attention."

"It has, boy! But lak I done tole you, can't no legal

thing be done 'cause no decent person that goes in there ever comes out. Now, I hear tell there's a federal marshal over to Trinidad that might be convinced to git a posse together if somebody would go in and clear a path for them. His name's Wilde."

Smoke made a mental note of that. "Tell me about this so-called minister in Dead River."

"Name is Tustin. And he's a real college-educated minister, too. Got him a church and all that goes with it."

"But you said there wasn't any decent people in the town!"

"There ain't, boy. Tustin is on the run jist lak all the rest. Killed his wife and kids back east somewheres. He's also a horse thief, a bank robber, and a whoremonger. But he still claims to be a Christian. Damndest thing I ever did hear of."

"And he has a church and preaches?"

"Damn shore does. And don't go to sleep durin' his sermons, neither. If you do, he'll shoot you!"

Smoke leaned back in his chair and stared at Slim. "You're really serious!"

"You bet your boots I am. You git in that place, Smoke, and you're gonna see sights like the which you ain't never seen."

"And you've never been in there?"

"Hell, no!"

Smoke rose from his chair to walk around the table a few times, stretching his legs. "It's time to put an end to Dead River."

"Way past time, boy."

"You think my wife was attacked just because of a twenty-year-old hate this Davidson has for Preacher?"

"I'd bet on it. Davidson lay right over there in that corner," he pointed, "and swore he'd get Preacher and anyone else who was a friend of hisn. That's why them outlaws is so hard on Injuns. 'Specially the Utes. Preacher was adopted into the Ute tribe, you know."

Smoke nodded. "Yeah. So was I."

"All the more reason for him to hate you. Law and order is closin' in on the West, Smoke. And," he sighed, "I reckon, for the most part, that's a good thing. Them lak that scum that's over to Dead River don't have that many more places to run to . . . and it's time to wipe that rattler's nest out. Sam Bass was killed 'bout two years ago. Billy the Kid's 'bout run out his string, so I hear. John Wesley Hardin is in jail down in Texas. The law is hot on the trail of the James gang. Bill Longley was hanged a couple of years back. The list is just gettin' longer and longer of so-called bad men that finally got they due. You know what I mean, Smoke?"

"Yes. And I can add some to the list you just named. You heard about Clay Allison?"

"Different stories about how he died. You know the truth of it?"

"Louis Longmont told me that Clay got drunk and fell out of his wagon back in '77. A wheel ran over his head and killed him."

Slim laughed and refilled their coffee cups. "I hear Curly Bill is goin' 'round talkin' bad about the Earp boys. He don't close that mouth, he's gonna join that list, too, and you can believe that."

Smoke sipped his coffee. "Three hundred bad ones," he said softly. "Looks like I just may have bitten off more than I can chew up and spit out."

"That's one of the few things you've said about this adventure of yourn that makes any sense, boy."

Smoke smiled at the old man. "But don't mean I'm gonna give it up, Slim."

"I's afeared you'd say that. Boy, I don't lak that grin on your face. Now, what the hell have you got up that sleeve of yourn?"

"Where is the nearest wire office, Slim?"

"Trinidad. It's a real big city. Near'bouts three thousand people in there. All jammed up lak apples in a crate. Gives me the willies."

"That U.S. Marshal might be in town."

"Could be. I know he comes and goes out of there a whole lot. What's on your mind, boy?"

Smoke just grinned at him. "Can you get a message to Preacher?"

"Shore. Good God, boy! You ain't figurin' on dealing Preacher in on this, are you?"

"Oh, no. Just tell him I'm all right and I'm glad to hear that he's doing okay."

"I'll do it. You keep in touch, boy."

Smoke rose to leave. "See you around, Slim."

"Luck to you, boy."

After the U.S. Marshal got over his initial shock of seeing the red and lavender-clad Shirley DeBeers introduce himself, he looked at the young man as if he had taken leave of his senses.

He finally said, "Have you got a death wish, boy? Or are you as goofy as you look?"

"My name is not really Shirley DeBeers, Marshal."

"That's a relief. I think. What is your handle—Sue?"

"Smoke Jensen."

The U.S. Marshal fell out of his chair.

CHAPTER SEVEN

"The reason I wanted us to talk out here," Marshal Jim Wilde said, standing with Smoke in the livery stable, "is 'cause I don't trust nobody when it comes to that lousy damn bunch of crud over at Dead River."

Smoke nodded his agreement. "You don't suspect the sheriff of this county of being in cahoots with them, do you?"

"Oh, no. Not at all. He's a good man. We've been working together, trying to come up with a plan to clean out that mess for months. It's just that you never really know who might be listening. Are you really Smoke Jensen?" He looked at Smoke's outfit and shuddered.

Smoke assured him that he was, despite the way he was dressed.

"And you want to be a U.S. Marshal?"

"Yes. To protect myself legally."

"That's good thinkin'. But this plan of yours ain't too bright, the way I see it. Let me get this straight. You're goin' to act as point man for a posse to clean up Dead River?"

"That is my intention. At my signal, the posse will come in."

"Uh-huh."

"You, of course, will lead the posse."

"Uh-huh." The marshal's expression was hound-dog mournful. "I was just afraid you was gonna say something 'bout like that."

U.S. Marshal Wilde checked his dodgers to see if there were any wanted flyers out on Smoke. There were not. Then he sent some wires out to get approval on Smoke's federal commission. Smoke lounged around the town, waiting for the marshal's reply wires.

Trinidad was built at the foot of Raton Pass, on a foothill chain of the Culebra Range. The streets of the town twisted and turned deviously, giving it a curiously foreign look. The Purgatoire River separated the residential area from the business district.

Trinidad was known as a tough place, full of rowdies, and due to its relative closeness to Dead River, Smoke kept a close eye on his back trail.

On his third day in town, sensing someone was following him, he picked up his pursuers. They were three rough-looking men. Inwardly, he sighed, wanting nothing so much as to shed his role as Shirley DeBeers, foppish artist, and strap on his guns.

But he knew he had to endure what he'd started for a while longer.

He had deliberately avoided any contact with any lawmen, especially Jim Wilde. He had spent his time sketching various buildings of the town and some of the more colorfully dressed Mexicans.

But the three hard-looking gunhawks who were always

following him began to get on his nerves. He decided to bring it to a head, but to do it in such a way as to reinforce his sissy, foppish act.

With his sketch pad in hand, Smoke turned to face the three men, who were standing across a plaza from him. He began sketching them.

And he could tell very quickly that his actions were not being received good-naturedly. One of the men made that perfectly clear in a hurry.

The man, wearing his guns low and tied down, walked across the plaza and jerked the sketch pad out of Smoke's hands, throwing it to the street.

"Jist what in the hell do you think you're doin', boy?"

Smoke put a frightened look on his face. "I was sketching you and your friends. I didn't think you would mind. I'm sorry if I offended you."

Smoke was conscious of the sheriff of the county and of Jim Wilde watching from across the plaza, standing under the awning of a cantina.

The outlaw—Smoke assumed he was an outlaw—pointed to the sketch pad on the ground and grinned at Smoke. "Well, you shored did o-fend me, sissy-pants. Now pick that there pitcher book up offen the ground and gimme that drawin' you just done of us."

Smoke drew himself up. "I most certainly will do no such thing . . . you ruffian."

The man slapped him.

It was all Smoke could do to contain his wild urge to tear the man's head off and hand it to him.

Smoke fought back his urge and put a hand to his reddened cheek. "You struck me!" he cried. "How dare you strike me, you—you animal!"

The man laughed as his friends walked across the plaza to join him. "What you got here, Jake?" one of them asked. "Looks to me like you done treed a girl dressed up in britches."

"I don't know what the hell it is, Red. But he shore talks funny."

"Le's see if he'll fight, Shorty," Jake said.

The three of them began pushing Smoke back and forth between them, roughing him up but doing no real physical damage; just bruising his dignity some. A crowd had gathered around, most of the men drinking, and they were getting a big laugh out of the sissy being shoved back and forth.

"Now, you all stop this immediately!" Smoke protested, putting a high note of fear into his voice. "I want you to stop this now . . . you hooligans!"

"Oh, my!" the outlaw called Red said, prancing around, one hand on his hip. "We hooligans, boys!"

Shorty reached out and, with a hard jerk, sent Smoke's trousers down around his ankles. Red shoved Smoke, who hit the ground hard and stayed there.

"I guess Cahoon was right, Shorty," Red said. "He ain't got a bit of sand in him." Then he turned and gave Smoke a vicious kick in the side, bringing a grunt of pain from him.

Forcing himself to do it, Smoke rolled himself up in a ball and hid his face in his hands. "Oh, don't hurt me anymore. I can't stand pain."

The crowd laughed. "Hell, Jake," Red said. "We wastin' our time. Sissy-boy ain't gonna fight."

Not yet, Smoke thought.

"Le's make him eat some horseshit!" Shorty suggested.

"Naw, I got a better idee. 'Sides, there ain't fresh piles around. We done found out what we come to find out: He's yeller."

"That shore was funny the time we made that drummer eat a pile of it, though!"

Shorty then unbuttoned his pants and urinated on Smoke's legs. The crowd fell silent; only Jake and Red thought that was funny.

Smoke's thoughts were savage.

The three hardcases then left and the crowd broke up, with no one offering to help Smoke to his feet.

Smoke hauled up his britches, found his sketch pad, and brushed himself off, then, with as much dignity as he could muster, he walked across the plaza. As he passed by the sheriff and the U.S. Marshal, Smoke whispered, "I think I'm in."

He stopped to brush dirt off his shirt.

"Picked a hard way to do it," the sheriff said. "I'd a never been able to lay there and take that."

"Let's just say it's going to be interesting when I come out of this costume," Smoke whispered.

"We'll be there," Wilde whispered. "There is a packet for you in your room. Good luck."

The packet contained a U.S. Marshal's badge, his written federal commission, and a letter.

On the night of Smoke's seventh day in Trinidad, two hours after dusk, unless Smoke could get a signal out to tell them differently, the U.S. Marshals, and various sheriffs and deputies from a four-county area, beefed up with volunteers from throughout the area, would strike at

Dead River. They would begin getting into position just at dusk. It would be up to Smoke to take out the guards at the pass. Do it any way he saw fit.

And to Smoke's surprise, the marshal had a plant inside Dead River, one that had been there for about six months.

A woman. Hope Farris.

It would be up to Smoke to contact her. The marshal had no way of knowing whether she was dead or alive; they had received no word from her in several months.

They feared she might have been taken prisoner. Or worse.

Good luck.

"Yeah," Smoke muttered, burning the note in the cut-off tin can that served as an ashtray. "I am sure going to need that."

He pulled out of Trinidad before dawn the next morning, after resupplying the night before. He headed west, avoiding the tiny settlements for the most part. But a threatening storm forced him to pull up and seek shelter in the small town of Stonewall.

And Stonewall was not a place Smoke cared to linger long. The town and the area around it was torn in a bitter war between cattlemen and the lumber industry on one side and the homesteaders on the other side, over grazing and lumber interests.

Smoke knew he would have to be very careful which saloon he entered that night, if any, for each side would have their own watering holes in this war. Finally he said to hell with having a drink and sketching anyone. He got him a room and stayed put.

He pulled out before daylight, before the café even opened, and made his way to Lost Lake. There he caught some trout for breakfast, broiling them. Looking around, far above the timberline, Smoke could see the tough and hardy alpine vegetation: kinnikinnick, creeping phlox, and stunted grass.

After a tasty breakfast and several cups of strong hot coffee, Smoke bathed quickly—very quickly—in the cold blue waters of Lost Lake.

Shivering, even though it was the middle of summer, he dressed and had one more cup of coffee. He was still a good three days hard ride from the outlaw town, but he wanted to sort out all his options, and considering where he was going, they were damn few.

And once again, the question entered his mind: Was he being a fool for doing this?

And the answer was still the same: yes, he was. But if he didn't settle it now, it would just happen again and again, and with a child coming, Smoke did not want to run the risk of losing another family.

So it had to be settled now; there was no question about that.

And, if the truth be told—and Smoke was a truthful man—there was yet another reason for his challenging the seemingly impossible. He wanted to do it.

He followed an old Indian trail that cut between Cordova Pass to the east and Cucharas Pass to the west. He found what he hoped was White Wolf's Ute camp and approached it cautiously. They seemed curious about this big strong-looking white man who dressed and behaved like a fool.

Smoke asked them if they would like to share his food in return for his spending the night. They agreed, and over the meal, he explained where he was going but not why.

The Ute chief, White Wolf, told him he was a silly man to even consider going into the outlaw town.

And Smoke could not understand the twinkle in the chief's eyes.

He asked them what they could tell him about the town called Dead River.

Smoke was stunned when White Wolf said, "What does the adopted son of my brother Preacher wish to know about that evil place?"

When he again found his voice, Smoke said, "For one thing, how did you know I was not who I claimed to be, White Wolf?"

Dark eyes twinkling, the chief of the small band of Utes said, "Many things give you away, to us, but probably not to the white man. The white man looks at many things but sees little. Your hands are as hard as stones. And while you draw well, that is not what you are."

Smoke did not offer to sketch the Indians, for many tribes believe it is not good medicine to have their pictures taken or their images recreated.

Smoke told them of his true plans.

They told him he was a very brave man, like Preacher.

"Few are as brave and noble as Preacher."

"That is true," White Wolf agreed. "And is my brother well?"

"Slim Dugas just told me that Preacher and a few other mountain men are well and living up near Montana."

"Thank you. That is also truth. Preacher is living with the children of my sister, Woman-Who-Speaks-With-Soft-Voice. Because she married Preacher, the children are recognized as pure and are not called Apples."

Red on the outside, white on the inside. Indians practiced their own form of discrimination.

"It is good to know they are true Human Beings."

"As you are, Smoke Jensen."

"Thank you. I have a joke for you."

"A good laugh makes a good meal even better."

"I was told that most people believe there is but one way in and one way out of Dead River."

The Indians, including the squaws, all found that richly amusing. After the laughter, White Wolf said, "There are many ways in and out of that evil place. There are ways in and out that the white man have not now and never will know, not in our lifetime."

Smoke agreed and finished his meal, belching loudly and patting his full belly. The Indians all belched loudly and smiled, the sign of a good meal. And the squaws were very pleased.

Smoke passed around several tobacco sacks, and the Indians packed small clay pipes and smoked in contentment. Smoke rolled a cigarette and joined them.

"You still have not told me how you knew I was the adopted son of Preacher, White Wolf."

The chief thought on that for a moment. "If I told you that, Smoke, then you would know as much as I know, and I think that would not be a good thing for one as young as you."

"It is true that too much knowledge, learned before one is ready, is not a good thing."

White Wolf smiled and agreed.

Smoke waited. The chief would get to the matter of Dead River when he was damn good and ready.

White Wolf smoked his pipe down to coals and carefully tapped out the ashes, then handed the pipe to his woman. "It has been a fine game for us to slip up on the outlaw town and watch them. All without their knowing, of course," he added proudly.

"Of course," Smoke agreed. "Anyone who does not know the Ute is as brave as the bear, cunning as the wolf, and sharp-eyed as the eagle is ignorant."

The braves all nodded their heads in agreement. This white man was no fool. But they all wished he would do something about his manner of dress.

"A plan has come to me, White Wolf. But it is a very dangerous plan, if you and your braves agree to it."

"I am listening, Smoke."

"I met with a man in Trinidad. I believe he can be trusted. He is a government man. His name is Jim Wilde."

"I know this man Wilde," White Wolf said. "He carries Indian blood in his veins. Co-manche from Texas place. He is to be trusted."

"I think so, too. Could you get a message to him?"

"Does the wind sigh?"

Smoke smiled. Getting his sketch pad, he sketched the campfire scene, leaving the faces of the Utes blank but drawing himself whole. On the bottom of the sketch, he wrote a note to Wilde.

"If you agree to my plan, have this delivered to Wilde, White Wolf."

"If we agree, it will be done. What is this thing that you have planned?"

"Times have not been good for you and your people."

"They have been both good and bad."

"Winter is not that far away."

"It is closer tonight than it was last night, but not as close as it will be in the morning."

"There are guns and much food and clothing and warm blankets in the outlaw town."

"But not as many as in the town of Trinidad."

"But the people of Trinidad are better than the people in Dead River."

"A matter of opinion. But I see your point. I think that I also see what you have in mind."

"If you agree, some of your people will surely die, White Wolf."

"Far better to die fighting like a man than to grovel and beg for scraps of food from a nonperson."

Only the Indians felt they were real people. Most whites had no soul. That is the best way they could find to explain it.

"I know some of how you feel. I do not think you want the buildings of the town."

White Wolf made an obscene gesture. "I spit on the buildings of the outlaw town."

"When the battle is over, you may do with them as you see fit."

"Wait by the fire," Smoke was told. "I will talk this over with my people."

Smoke sat alone for more than an hour. Then White Wolf returned with his braves and they took their places.

"We have agreed to your plan, Smoke."

They shook hands solemnly.

"Now it depends on the government man, Jim Wilde."

"I will send a brave to see him at first light. Once he has agreed, then we will make our final plans."

"Agreed."

They once more stuffed their pipes and smoked, with no one talking.

White Wolf finally said, "There is a young squaw, Rising Star. She does not have a man. She is very hard to please. I have thought of beating her for her stubbornness. Do you want her to share your robes this night?"

"I am honored, White Wolf, but I have a woman and I am faithful to her only."

"That is good. You are an honorable man."

"I'll pull out at first light. I'll be camped at the head of Sangre de Cristo creek, waiting to hear from you."

White Wolf smiled. "It will be interesting to see if the white men at the outlaw town die well."

"I think they will not."

"I think you are right," White Wolf agreed.

CHAPTER EIGHT

Smoke angled down the slopes and onto the flats, then cut northwest, reaching his campsite by late afternoon. He made his camp and waited.

And waited.

It was three full days before a brave from White Wolf's band made an appearance.

He handed Smoke a note, on U.S. Marshal's stationery. Jim Wilde had agreed to the plan and complimented Smoke on enlisting the Utes.

He told the brave what the scratchings on the paper meant.

"Yes," the brave said. "The Co-manche lawman told me the same thing. All the rest of your plan is to remain the same. Now I must return and tell him when you plan to enter the outlaw town."

Smoke had calculated the distance; about a day and a half of riding over rough country. "Tell Wilde I will enter the town day after tomorrow, at late afternoon. Do you know a place near the town where you could hide some guns for me?"

The brave thought for a moment, and then smiled.

"Yes. Behind the saloon with an ugly picture of a bucket on the front of it. The bucket is filled with what I think is supposed to be blood."

"The bloody bucket?" Smoke guessed.

"Yes! Behind the little building where the men go to relieve themselves there is a rotting pile of lumber. I will put them under the lumber."

"Good. What is your name?"

"Lone Eagle."

"Be very careful, Lone Eagle. If you're caught, you will die hard."

The Ute nodded. "I know. The Co-manche lawman says that two hours after dark, on the seventh day of your entering the outlaw place, we shall attack. And White Wolf says that you need not worry about the guards. Concern yourself only with the town. It might take the main body of men an hour to fight their way to your location."

"Tell White Wolf thank you. It will be a good coup for you all."

The brave nodded. "The outlaws in the town have not been kind to my people. They have seized and raped some of our young girls. Twice, they have taken young braves and have been cruel beyond any reason. One they cut off his feet and left him to die, slowly. They called it sport. On the night of the seventh day, we shall have our sport with the outlaws."

Smoke nodded, repeating what he had said to the chief, "They shall not die well, I am thinking."

The Ute smiled, very unpleasantly. "We are counting on that."

Then he was gone, back to his pony hidden in the deep timber.

The outlaws of Dead River had had their way for years, torturing, raping, robbing and looting, enslaving the innocent and ravaging the unsuspecting for several hundred miles, or more, in any direction. Now they were about to have the tables turned on them. And Smoke knew the more fortunate ones would die under his guns or the guns of the posse.

It would be very unpleasant for those taken alive by the Utes.

For the Utes knew ways of torture that would make the Spanish Inquisitioners green with envy. Dying well was an honor for the Indians, and if a prisoner died well, enduring hours and sometimes days of torture, they would sing songs about that person for years, praising his courage. That person who died well would not be forgotten.

The Indians had nothing but contempt for a man who begged and cried and died in dishonor.

They had their own code of honor and justice, and the whites had theirs. There were those who said the red man was nothing but a barbaric savage. But he had learned to scalp from the European white man. The Indians were different; but they would not steal from within their own tribe. The white man could not say that. War was a game to the Indians—until the white man entered the picture and began killing in war. For the Indians, for centuries, counting coup by striking with a club or stick was preferable to killing.

So it is very questionable who was the savage and who was the instructor in barbarism.

Smoke had lived with the Indians and, in many ways, preferred their lifestyle to the white ways. Smoke, as did nearly anyone who learned their ways, found the Indians to be honest, extremely gentle, and patient with their children or any captured children, of any color. The Indians lived a hard life in a hard land, so it was foolish to think their ways to be barbaric. They were, Smoke felt, just different.

Smoke felt nothing for the outlaws in the town. He knew the truth in the statement that whatever befalls a man, that man usually brought the bad onto himself. Every person comes, eventually, to a fork in the road. The direction that person takes comes from within, not from without, as many uninformed choose to believe when slavering pity on some criminal. The outlaw trail is one that a person can leave at any time; they are not chained to it.

An outlaw is, in many ways, like an ignorant person, who knows he is ignorant and is proud of it, enjoying wallowing in blind unenlightenment, knowing that he is is wrong but too lazy to climb the ladder of knowledge. Too inwardly slovenly to make the effort of reaching out and working to better himself.

To hell with them!

"It's a different world for me," Sally said, sitting in her parents' fine home in New Hampshire. "And a world, I fear, that I no longer belong in."

"What an odd thing to say, dear," her mother said, looking up from her knitting.

Sally smiled, glancing at her. She shifted her gaze to her brothers and sisters and father, all of them seated in the elegant sitting room of the mansion. And all of them, including her father, not quite sure they believed anything Sally had told them about her husband, this seemingly wild man called Smoke.

"Odd, Mother? Oh, I think not. It's just what a person wants; what that person becomes accustomed to, that's all. You would consider our life hard; we just consider it living free."

"Dear," her father spoke, "I am sure you find it quite amusing to entertain us with your wild stories about the West and this . . . person you married. But really now, Sally, don't you think it a bit much to ask us to believe all these wild yarns?"

"Wild yarns, Father?"

Jordan, Sally's oldest brother, and a bore and stuffed shirt if there ever were one, took some snuff gentlemanly and said, "All that dribble-drabble about the wild West is just a bunch of flapdoodle as far as I'm concerned."

Sally laughed at him. She had not, as yet, shown her family the many newspapers she had brought back to New Hampshire with her; but that time was not far off.

"Oh, Jordan! You'll never change. And don't ever come west to where I live. You wouldn't last fifteen minutes before someone would slap you flat on your backside."

Jordan scowled at her but kept his mouth closed.

For a change.

Sally said, "You're all so safe and secure and comfortable

here in Keene, in all your nice homes. If you had trouble, you'd shout for a constable to handle it. There must be more than a dozen police officers here in this town alone. Where I live in Colorado, there aren't a dozen deputies within a two-thousand-square-mile radius."

"I will accept that, Sally," her father, John, said. "I have heard the horror stories about law and order in the West. But what amazes me is how you handle the business of law and order."

"We handle it, Father, usually ourselves."

"I don't understand, Sally," her sister Penny said. "Do you mean that where you live women are allowed to sit on juries?"

Sally laughed merrily. "No, you silly goose!" She kidded her sister. "Most of the time there isn't even any trial."

Her mother, Abigal, put her knitting aside and looked at her daughter. "Dear, now I'm confused. All civilized places have due process. Don't you have due process where you live?"

"We damn sure do!" Sally shocked them all into silence with the cuss word.

Her mother began fanning herself vigorously. Her sisters momentarily swooned. Her brothers looked shocked, as did her brothers-in-law, Chris and Robert. Her father frowned.

"Whatever in the world do you mean, dear?" Abigal asked.

"Most of the time it's from a Henry," Sally attempted to explain, but only added to the confusion.

"Ah-hah!" John exclaimed. "Now we're getting to it. This Henry person—he's a judge, I gather."

"No, a Henry is a rifle. Why, last year, when those TF riders roped and dragged Pearlie and then attacked the house, I knocked two of them out of the saddle from the front window of the house."

"You struck two men?" Betsy asked, shocked. "While they were stealing your pearls?"

Sally sighed. "Pearlie is our foreman at the ranch. Some TF riders slung a loop on him and tried to drag him to death. And, hell, no, I didn't strike them. When they attacked the house, I shot them!"

"Good Lord," Chris blurted. "Where was your husband while this tragedy was unfolding?"

Sally thought about that. "Well, I think he was in Fontana, in the middle of a gunfight. I believe that's where he was."

They all looked at her as if she had suddenly grown horns and a tail.

Smiling, Sally reached into her bag and brought out a newspaper, a copy of Haywood's paper, which detailed the incident at the Sugarloaf, where she and young Bob Colby had fought off the attackers.

"Incredible!" her father muttered. "My own daughter in a gunfight. And at the trial, dear, you were, of course, acquitted, were you not?"

Sally laughed and shook her head. They still did not understand. "Father, there was no trial."

"An inquest, then?" John asked hopefully, leaning forward in his chair.

Sally shook her head. "No, we just hauled off the bodies and buried them on the range."

John blinked. He was speechless. And for an attorney, as he and his sons were, that was tantamount to a phenomenon.

"Hauled off the . . . bodies," Robert spoke slowly. "How utterly grotesque."

"What would you have us do?" Sally asked him. "Leave them in the front yard? They would have attracted coyotes and wolves and buzzards. And smelled bad, too." Might as well have a little fun with them, she concluded.

Robert turned an ill-looking shade of green.

And Sally was shocked to find herself thinking: what a lily-livered bunch of pansies.

Abigal covered her mouth with a handkerchief.

"Did the sheriff even come out to the house?" Walter inquired.

"No. If he had, we'd have shot him. At that time, he was in Tilden Franklin's pocket."

John sighed with a parent's patience.

Penny was reading another copy of Haywood's newspaper. "My God!" she suddenly shrieked in horror. "According to this account, there were ten people shot down in the streets of Fontana in one week."

"Yes, Sister. Fontana was rather a rowdy place until Smoke and the gunfighters cleaned it up. You've heard of Louis Longmont, Father?"

He nodded numbly, not trusting his voice to speak. He wondered if, twenty-odd years ago, the doctor had handed him the wrong baby. Sally had always been a bit . . . well, free-spirited.

"Louis was there, his hands full of Colts."

Sally's nieces and nephews were standing in the archway,

listening, their mouths open in fascination. This was stuff you only read about in the dime novels. But Aunt Sally—and this was the first time most of them could remember seeing her—had actually lived it! This was exciting stuff.

Sally grinned, knowing she had a captive audience. "There was Charlie Starr, Luke Nations, Dan Greentree, Leo Wood, Cary Webb, Pistol LeRoux, Bill Foley, Sunset Hatfield, Toot Tooner, Sutter Cordova, Red Shingletown, Bill Flagler, Ol' Buttermilk, Jay Church, The Apache Kid, Silver Jim, Dad Weaver, Hardrock, Linch—they all stayed at our ranch, the Sugarloaf. They were really very nice gentlemen. Courtly in manner."

"But those men you just named!" Jordan said, his voice filled with shock and indignation. "I've read about them all. They're killers!"

"No, Jordan," Sally tried to patiently explain, all the while knowing that he, and the rest of her family, would never truly understand. "They're gunfighters. Like my Smoke. A gunfighter. They have killed, yes; but always because they were pushed into it, or they killed for right and reason and law and order."

"Killed for right and reason," John muttered. His attorney's mind was having a most difficult time comprehending that last bit.

Abigal looked like she might, at any moment, fall over from a case of the vapors. "And . . . your husband, this Smoke person, he's killed men?"

"Oh, yes. About a hundred or so. That's not counting Indians on the warpath. But not very many of them. You see, Smoke was raised by the mountain man, Preacher. And we get along well with the Indians."

"Preacher," John murmured. "The most famous, or infamous, mountain man of the West."

"That's him!" Sally said cheerfully. "And," she pulled an old wanted poster out of her bag and passed it over to her father, "that's my Smoke. Handsome, isn't he?"

Under the drawing of Smoke's likeness, was the lettering:

WANTED
DEAD OR ALIVE
THE OUTLAW AND MURDERER
SMOKE JENSEN
$10,000.00 REWARD

"Ye, Gods!" her father yelled, "the man is wanted by the authorities!"

Sally laughed at his expression. "No, Father, That was a put-up job. Smoke is not wanted by the law. He never has been on the dodge."

"Thank God for small favors." John wiped his sweaty face with a handkerchief.

Walter said, "And your husband has killed a hundred men, you say?"

"Well, thereabouts, yes. But they were all fair fights."

The kids slipped away into the foyer and silently opened the front door, stepping out onto the large porch. Then they were racing away to tell all their friends that their uncle, Smoke Jensen, the most famous gunfighter in all the world, was coming to Keene for a visit.

Really!

Sally passed around the newspapers she had saved over the months, from both Fontana and Big Rock. The family read them, disbelief in their eyes.

"Monte Carson is your sheriff?" John questioned. "But

I have seen legal papers that stated he was a notorious gunfighter."

"He was. But he wasn't an outlaw. And Johnny North is now a farmer/rancher and one of our neighbors and close friends."

They had all heard of Johnny North. He was almost as famous as Smoke Jensen.

"Louis Longmont is a man of great wealth," Jordan muttered, reading a paper. "His holdings are quite vast. Newspaper, hotels, a casino in Europe, and a major stockholder in a railroad."

"He's also a famous gunfighter and gambler," Sally informed them all. "And a highly educated man and quite the gentleman."

Shaking his head, John laid the paper aside. "When is your husband coming out for a visit, Sally?"

"As soon as he finishes with his work."

"His work being with his guns." It was not put as a question.

"That is correct. Why do you ask, Father?"

"I'm just wondering if I should alert the governor so he can call out the militia!"

CHAPTER NINE

On the morning he set out for Dead River, Smoke dressed in his most outlandish clothing. He even found a long hawk feather and stuck that in his silly cap. He knew he would probably be searched once inside, or maybe outside the outlaw town, and what to do with his short-barreled .44 worried him. He finally decided to roll it up in some dirty longhandles and stick it in his dirty clothes bag, storing it in his pack. He was reasonably sure it would go undetected there. It was the best idea he could come up with.

He adjusted the bonnets on Drifter and his packhorse, with Drifter giving him a look that promised trouble if this crap went on much longer. Smoke swung into the saddle, pointing Drifter's nose north. A few more miles and he would cut west, into the Sangre de Cristo range and into the unknown.

About two hours later, he sensed unfriendly eyes watching him as he rode. He made no effort to search out his watchers, for a foppish gent from back east would not have developed that sixth sense. But White Wolf had told him that there were guards all along the trail, long before one ever reached the road that would take him to Dead River.

Smoke rode on, singing at the top of his lungs, stopping occasionally to admire the beautiful scenery and to make a quick sketch. To ooh and aah at some spectacular wonder of nature. He was just about oohed and aahed out, and Drifter looked like he was about ready to throw Smoke and stomp on him, when he came to a road. He had no idea what to expect, but this startled him with its openness.

A sign with an arrow pointing west, and under the arrow: DEAD RIVER. Under that: IF YOU DON'T HAVE BUSINESS IN DEAD RIVER, STAY OUT!

Smoke dismounted and looked around him. There was no sign of life. Raising his voice, he called, "I say! Yoo, hoo! Oh, yoo hoo! Is anyone there who might possibly assist me?"

Drifter swung his big bonneted head around and looked at Smoke through those cold yellow eyes. Eyes that seemed to say: Have you lost your damn mind!

"Just bear with me, boy," Smoke muttered. "It won't be long now. I promise you."

Drifter tried to step on his foot.

Smoke mounted up and rode on. He had huge mountains on either side of him. To the north, one reared up over fourteen thousand feet. To the south, the towering peaks rammed into the sky more than thirteen thousand feet, snow-capped year-round.

The road he was on twisted and climbed and narrowed dramatically.

The road was just wide enough for a wagon and maybe a horse to meet it, coming from the other direction. Another wagon, and somebody would have to give. But where? Then Smoke began to notice yellow flags every few hundred yards. A signal for wagon masters, he supposed, but whether they meant stop or go, he had no idea.

He had ridden a couple of miles, always west and always climbing, when a voice stopped him.

"Just hold it right there, fancy-pants. And keep your hands where I can see them. You get itchy, and I'll blow your butt out of the saddle."

Smoke reined up. Putting fear into his voice, he called, "I mean you no harm. I am Shirley DeBeers, the artist."

"What you gonna be is dead if you don't shut that goddamn mouth."

Smoke shut up.

The faint sounds of mumbling voices reached him, but he could not make out the words.

"All right, fancy-britches," the same voice called out. "Git off that horse and stand still."

Smoke dismounted and stood in the roadway. Then he heard the sounds of bootsteps all around him: There was Hart, the backshooter; Gridley, who murdered his best friend and partner, and then raped and killed the man's wife; Nappy, a killer for hire. There were others, but Smoke did not immediately recognize them, except for the fact that they were hardcases.

"Take off that coat," he was ordered, "and toss it to me. Frisk 'im, Nappy."

Smoke was searched and searched professionally; even his boots were removed and inspected. His pack ropes were untied and his belongings dumped in the middle of the road.

"Oh, I say now! Is that necessary, gentlemen?"

"Shut up!"

Smoke shut up.

His belongings were inspected, but his bag of dirty underwear was tossed to one side after only a glance. Luckily the bag landed on a pile of clean clothes and the weight of the .44 did not make a sound.

So far, so good, Smoke thought.

Finally, the search was over and the men stared at him for a moment. One said, "I reckon Cahoon and them others was right. He ain't got nothing but a pocket knife. And it's dull."

"Is my good friend Cahoon in town? Oh, I hope so. He's such a nice man."

"Shut your mouth!"

"What about it, Hart?"

"I reckon some of us can take silly-boy on in."

"I say," Smoke looked around him at the mess in the road. "Are some of you good fellows going to help me gather up and repack my possessions?"

The outlaws thought that was very funny. They told him in very blunt language that they were not. And to make their point better understood, one of them kicked Smoke in the butt. Smoke yelled and fell to the ground. Drifter swung his head and his yellow eyes were killer-cold. Smoke quickly crawled to the horse and grabbed a stirrup, using that to help pull himself up, all the while murmuring to Drifter, calming him.

Rubbing his butt, Smoke faced the outlaws. "You don't have to be so rough!"

"Oh, my goodness!" Gridley cried, prancing about to the laughter of the others. "We hurt his feelin's, boys. We got to stop bein' so rough!"

And right then and there, Smoke began to wonder if he would be able to last a week.

He calmed himself and waved his hand at his pile of belongings. "I say, as you men can see from your trashing of my possessions, I am low on supplies. Might I be allowed to continue on to Dead River and resupply?" He had left most of his supplies at the head of the Sangre de Cristo creek.

"Cahoon was supposed to have given you a note," a man said. A hardcase Smoke did not know. "Lemme see the note, sissy-pants."

"I am not a sissy! I am merely a man of great sensibilities."

"Gimme the goddamn note!"

The note was handed over and passed around.

"That's Cahoon's writin' all right. What about it, Hart, it's up to you?"

"Yeah, let him go on in. He can draw us all, and then we'll have some fun with him."

Smoke caught the wink.

"Yeah. That's a good idee. And I know just the person to give him to."

"Who?" Nappy asked.

"Brute!"

That drew quite a laugh and narrowed Smoke's eyes. He had heard of Brute Pitman. A huge man, three hundred pounds or more of savage perversions. He was wanted all over the eastern half of the nation for the most disgusting crimes against humanity. But oddly enough, Smoke had never heard of a warrant against him west of the Mississippi River. Bounty hunters had tried to take him, but Brute was hard to kill.

It was rumored that Brute had preyed on the miners in the gold camps for years, stashing away a fortune. And he had lived in Dead River for a long time, keeping mostly to himself.

But, Smoke thought, if these cruds think Brute is going to have his way with me, I'll start this dance with or without the rest of the band.

Smoke looked from outlaw to outlaw. "This Brute fellow sounds absolutely fascinating!"

The outlaws laughed.

"Oh, he is, sweetie," Hart told him. "You two gonna get along just fine, I'm thinkin'."

Uh-huh, Smoke thought. We'll get along until I stick a .44 down his throat and doctor his innards with lead.

"Oh, I'm so excited!" Smoke cried. "May we proceed onward?"

"Son of a bitch shore talks funny!" Gridley grumbled.

Smoke had killed his first man back on the plains, back when he was fifteen or sixteen; he wasn't quite sure. And he had killed many times since then. But as accustomed as he was to the sights of brutality, he had to struggle to keep his lunch down when they passed by a line of poles and platforms and wooden crosses sunk into the ground. Men and women in various stages of death and dying were nailed to the crosses; some were hung from chains by their ankles and left to rot; some had been horsewhipped until their flesh hung in strips, and they had been left to slowly die under the sun.

Smoke had never seen anything like it in his life. He

did not have to force the gasp of horror that escaped from his lips. He turned his face away from the sight.

The outlaws thought it was funny, Hart saying, "That's what happens to people who try to cross the boss, Shirley. Or to people who come in here pretendin' to be something they ain't."

Gridley pointed to a woman, blackened in rotting death, hanging by chains. "She was a slave who tried to escape. Keep that in mind, sissy-boy."

"How hideous!" Smoke found his voice. "What kind of place is this?"

"He really don't know," Nappy said with a laugh. "The silly sod really don't know. Boy, are we gonna have some fun with this dude."

"I don't wish to stay here!" Smoke said, putting fear and panic in his voice. "This place is disgusting!" He tried to turn Drifter.

The outlaws escorting him boxed him in, none of them noticing the firm grip Smoke held on Drifter's reins, steadying the killer horse, preventing him from rearing up and crushing a skull or breaking a back with his steel-shod hooves.

The bonnet had worked in disguising Drifter for what he really was. Worked, so far.

"You just hold on, fancy-pants," Hart told him. "You wanted to come in here, remember?"

"But now I want to leave! I want to leave right this instant!"

"Sorry, sweets. You're here to stay."

* * *

Jim Wilde looked at the late afternoon sunlight outside his office window. He sighed and returned to his chair. "He ought to be in there by now. God have mercy on his soul; I guess I got to say it."

"Yeah," Sheriff Mike Larsen agreed. "He's got more guts than I got, and I'll stand out in the middle of the damn street and admit that."

Jim sipped his coffee. "You told your boys not a word about this to anybody, right?"

"Damn well bet I did. I told 'em if they even thought hard on it, I'd catch the vibrations and lock 'em up."

And the marshal knew the sheriff would do just that. Mike ran a good solid straight office in a tough town.

"You got the final tally sheet of all that's goin' in, Mike?"

"Yep. The boys is gearin' up now. Quietly. Three sheriffs, including myself. Twenty regular deputies. Twenty volunteers—all of them top riders and good with short gun and rifle—and you and ten marshals."

"The other marshals will be comin' in by train two at a time, staring tomorrow at noon. They're goin' to stay low. I just wish we had some way of findin' out how many hardcases we're gonna be up against."

"I think that's impossible, Jim. But if I had to make a guess on it . . . I'd say two hundred at the low end. We all gonna tie a white handkerchief on our left arm so's the Injuns won't mistake us for outlaws . . . that is still the plan, ain't it?"

"Yeah. Best I can come up with. I've already contracted for horses to be stashed along the way. So when we start ridin', we ain't gonna stop until it's over and done with. One way or the other," he added grimly.

Mike Larsen chose not to elaborate on that last bit. He would tell his wife only at the last moment, just before he stepped into the saddle. It was not a job he looked forward to doing, but he knew it was a job that had to be done. "Where you got the horses?"

"We'll switch to fresh at Spanish Peaks, then again at La Veta Pass. The last stop will be at Red Davis's place. I ain't gonna kill no good horse on that final run. Most of that is gonna be uphill."

Both men knew the fastest way to tire a horse was riding uphill.

"Red is givin' us the best of his line and wanted to go in with us. I thanked him but told him no. Told him he was doin' enough by loanin' us fresh horses."

"He's a tough old man. But you was right in refusin' him. You think he took offense?"

"No. He understands. White Wolf says he'll have at least thirty braves around that town when Jensen opens the dance. And Jensen is goin' to start the music as soon as White Wolf signals him that we've left the trail and entered the pass. White Wolf says the guards along the road will be taken care of. Them Utes ain't got no use for anybody in Dead River. And I told the boys that volunteered that the reward money will be split up amongst 'em."

"That's good, but I don't like Smoke openin' the show by hisself." Larsen frowned. "We're gonna be a good forty-five minutes of hard ridin' away from the town when he starts draggin' iron and lettin' it bang."

"I know it. But he was by hisself when he met them ol' boys up there on the Uncompahgre. And he killed ever' damn one of them."

"Yep," the sheriff agreed. "He damn shore did that, didn't he?"

"Unhand me, you beast!" Smoke shrilled his protest, struggling against the hands that held him in front of the saloon.

"My, my." A man stepped out of the Bloody Bucket and onto the boardwalk. "What manner of creature do we have here, boys?"

"It's that sissy-boy that draws them pitchers, Mr. Davidson. The one that Cahoon told us about."

"Where is my friend, Cahoon?" Smoke asked.

No one from the gathering crowd of thugs and hard-cases replied.

"Well, well," Davidson said with a smile, his eyes taking in Smoke's outlandish dress. "So it is. And how do you like our little town, Mr. DeBeers?"

"I think it is appalling and disgusting and most offensive. And I do not like being manhandled by thugs. Tell your henchmen to unhand me this instant!"

Rex Davidson stepped from the boardwalk, faced Smoke and then backhanded him viciously across the face. He slapped him again. Smoke allowed his knees to buckle and he slumped to the ground, whimpering.

"You, silly boy," Rex said, standing over Smoke, "do not give me orders. Around here, I give the orders, and you obey. I say who lives and dies, and who comes and goes. Do you understand that, Shirley?"

"Yes, sir," Smoke gasped. The blows from Davidson had hurt. The man was no lightweight; he was big and muscled. Smoke decided to remain on the ground, on his hands and knees, until ordered to rise.

"Here, silly-boy," Rex continued, "I am king. You are nothing. However, if I decide you may live—and that is a big if—I might elect to make you my court jester. Would you like that, silly-boy?"

"Yes, sir." *Until I shed this costume and put lead in you, you overbearing jackass!*

King Rex kicked Smoke in the belly, knocking him flat on the ground. "When you address me, silly-boy, you will address me as Your Majesty. Now, say it, you foppish-looking fool!"

"Yes, Your Majesty." and Smoke knew it was going to take a miracle for him to last out the entire seven days. Maybe two or three miracles.

"That's better, Jester. Some of you men get this fool on his feet and drag him inside the saloon. I wish to talk with him about doing my portrait."

Smoke started to tell him that he didn't do portraits, then decided it would be best if he'd just keep his mouth shut for the moment. He let the hardcases drag him to his feet and shove him up the steps, onto the boardwalk, and through the batwings. And it was all done with a lot of unnecessary roughness and very crude language.

What the hell did you expect, Jensen? Smoke silently questioned. *A tea party?*

The saloon—and from what Smoke had been able to glean, the only one in town—was a huge affair, capable of seating several hundred people. There was a large stage on one end of the building. The stage had red velvet curtains. Smoke wondered who did the acting and singing.

He was shoved roughly into a chair and then, looking up, got his first good look at Rex Davidson.

The man was a handsome rascal, no doubt about that. And a big man, in his mid-forties, Smoke guessed, solid, with heavily muscled arms and shoulders, thick wrists. Big hands. His eyes were cruel but not tinged with any sign of madness that Smoke could readily detect.

Rex leaned against the polished bar and smiled at Smoke; but the smile did not reach the man's eyes. "Talk to me, Jester."

"About what, Your Majesty?" Smoke promptly responded as instructed.

"Good, good!" Rex shouted to the hardcases gathered in the saloon. "You all see how quickly he learns? I think this one will do just fine. Oh, my, yes. Where are you from, Jester?"

"I am originally from Pennsylvania, Your Majesty."

"What city?"

"I am not from a city, Your Majesty."

"Oh? You certainly don't speak like a hick."

"Thank you, Your Majesty." You royal pain in the ass! "I was born on a small farm. Both my mother and father were highly educated people. They taught us at home." And I'm going to teach you a thing or two, King Jackass! "There were no schools nearby."

"Thank you, Jester. And where did you learn to draw, Jester?"

"I suppose I was born with the talent, Your Majesty." Just like I was born good with a gun, which you shall certainly get the chance to see . . . briefly. "My brother, Maurice, has the ability to write quite eloquently."

"Ah, yes, Maurice. Did you tell Cahoon that this Maurice person had stopped by here?"

"That is what he wrote and told me. But I have no way of knowing if he did stop or not. Maurice, ah, tends to story a bit."

"I see. In other words, he's nothing more than a god-damned liar?"

"Ah, yes, Your Majesty."

"Where is he now, Jester?"

"I have no idea, Your Majesty."

"I see. Does he look like you, Jester?"

"No, Your Majesty. Maurice was adopted, you see. While my hair is—"

Rex waved him silent as a man carrying a tray of drinks stumbled and went crashing to the floor. The glasses shattered and the smell of raw whiskey and beer filled the huge room.

"Incompetent fool!" Rex yelled at the fallen man.

"I'm sorry, sir. It was an accident."

"Your services will no longer be needed here, idiot."

The man tried to crawl to his feet just as Rex pulled out a .44. "I cannot tolerate clumsiness." He eased back the hammer and shot the man in the chest, knocking him back to the floor. The man began screaming in pain. Rex calmly shot him in the head. The screaming stopped.

Smoke watched it all, then remembered to put a shocked look on his face. Just in time, for Rex had cut his eyes and was watching Smoke carefully.

"Oh, my goodness!" Smoke gasped, putting a hand over his mouth. "That poor fellow."

"Drag him out of here and sprinkle some sawdust over the blood spots," Rex ordered. He punched out the empty brass in the cylinder and replaced the spent cartridges, then cut his eyes to Smoke. "Life is the cheapest commodity on the market around here, Jester. Bear that in mind at all times. Now then, how long were you planning on staying in my town?"

"My original plans were to spend about a week, sketching the scenery, which I was told was lovely. Then I was going to resupply and move on."

"A week, hey?"

"Yes, Your Majesty."

"Give me all your money."

"Sir?"

King Rex slapped Smoke out of the chair. And as he hit the floor, Smoke was really beginning to question his own sanity for getting himself into this snakepit. And wondering if he were going to get out of it alive.

Smoke was jerked up from the floor and slammed into his chair. The side of his face ached and he tasted blood in his mouth. And if Rex, king of Dead River, could just read Smoke's thoughts . . .

"Never, never question me, Jester," Rex told him. "You will obey instantly, or you will die. Very slowly and very painfully. Do you understand me, Jester?"

"Yes, Your Majesty. Just don't hurt me. I can't stand pain. It makes me ill."

"Stop your goddamned babblings, you fool. Give me your money!"

Smoke dug in his trousers and handed the man his slim roll of greenbacks.

Rex counted the money. "Sixty dollars. I charge ten dollars a day to stay here, Jester, unless you work for me, which you don't. What are you going to do at the end of six days, Jester?"

A woman began screaming from one of the rooms upstairs. Then the sounds of a whip striking flesh overrode the screaming. A man's ugly laughter followed the sounds of the lashing.

"A slave being punished, Jester," Rex told him. "We have many slaves in this town. Some live a long, long time. Others last only a few weeks. How long do you think you would last, Jester?"

"I don't know, Your Majesty."

"An honest answer. Now answer my original question, Jester."

"Well, I suppose after my six days are up, I'll just leave, sir." *After I kill you, Davidson.*

From the depths of the crowd, a man laughed, and it was not a very nice laugh. Smoke looked around him; all the hardcases were grinning at him.

"So you think you'll leave, hey, Jester?" Davidson smiled at him.

"Yes, sir. I hope to do that."

"Well, we'll see. If you behave yourself, I'll let you leave."

Sure you will, Smoke thought. *Right. And Drifter is going to suddenly start reciting poetry at any moment.*

Davidson shook the greenbacks at Smoke. "This money only allows you to stay in this protected town. You pay for your own food and lodgings. You may leave now, Jester."

Smoke stood up.

"Welcome to Dead River, Mr. DeBeers," Rex said with a smile.

Smoke began walking toward the batwings, half expecting to get a bullet in his back. But it was a pleasant surprise when none came. He pushed open the batwings and stepped out onto the boardwalk. He mounted up, packhorse rope in his hand, and swung Drifter's bonneted head toward the far end of town, away from the sights and sounds and smells of the dead and slowly dying men and women at the other end of the town. He got the impression that hell must be very much like what he had witnessed coming in.

One thing for sure, he knew he would never forget that sight as long as he lived. He didn't have to sketch it to remember it; it was burned into his brain.

He wondered what had finally happened to that slave woman he had heard being beaten back at the Bloody Bucket. He thought he knew.

How in the name of God could a place like this have existed for so long, without somebody escaping and telling the horrors that were going on?

He had no answers for that question either.

But he knew that this place must be destroyed. And he also knew that when Marshal Jim Wilde and Sheriff Larsen and the posse members saw this chamber of horrors, there would never be any due process of law. No courts with judge and jury would decide the fate of the outlaws of Dead River. It would be decided on the seventh night, with gunsmoke and lead.

If the posse could help it, no outlaw would leave this valley alive.

Smoke pushed those thoughts out of his mind and concentrated on his own predicament: He did not have a cent to his name and had very few supplies left. Maybe enough to last a couple of days, if he was careful.

Smoke Jensen, the most famous and feared gunfighter in all the West, didn't know what in the hell he was going to do.

CHAPTER TEN

"So that's it." Sally's father's voice was filled with ill-disguised disgust. "What a wretched excuse for a human being."

Abigal's face mirrored her shock and horror.

Sally sat with her mother and father in the book-lined study of the mansion. Her father's room, which few of them had dared enter when they were children. But Sally had never been afraid of doing so. She used to love to sit in her father's chair and look at all the books about law and justice.

The three of them were alone; her brothers and sisters had left for the evening. And the town was fairly buzzing about the news of the famous gunfighter who was soon to be arriving.

"Why didn't you tell us when it happened, dear?" her mother asked.

"Because he told me he would kill you both. Then, after he left town, after killing that man, I just did my best to put the incident out of my mind, as much as possible. As the years went by, the memory became dimmer and dimmer. But there is no doubt in my mind that Dagget is the same man who tried to molest me years ago."

John rose from his chair to pace the room, his anger very evident. Wife and daughter watched him until he composed himself and returned to his leather chair. "The first thing in the morning, I shall inform the authorities as to this scoundrel's whereabouts. Then we shall begin extradition proceedings to have him returned to New Hampshire to stand trial."

Sally could not contain the smile that curved her lips. "Father, by the time you do all that legal mumbojumbo, the matter will most probably be taken care of—if it isn't already tended to. However, Smoke did suggest he cut off Dagget's head and bring it back here in a sack."

Abigal turned a bit green around the mouth and began fanning herself. "For heaven's sake!" she finally blurted. "He was joking, of course?"

"Oh, no, Mother. He wasn't joking a bit."

"Just exactly what is your husband doing while you are visiting here, Sally?" John asked.

Sally then explained to her parents what her husband was doing.

"Are you telling us, expecting us to believe," John said, astonishment in his voice, "that your husband . . . ah . . . Smoke, one man, is going to . . . ah . . . attack and destroy an entire town of thugs and hooligans and ne'er-do-wells— all by himself? Now, really, Sally!"

"Oh, he's found some help. And I think you will approve of his methods, Father, or what you think his methods will be—in your New England straight-by-the book mind."

"You disapprove of law and order, Sally?"

"Of course not, Father. Your way works here; our way

works for us in the West. This will not be the first time Smoke has taken on an entire town." Then she told them about the shoot-out at the silver camp and what had happened in Bury, Idaho.

Her parents sat in silence and stared at her.

"And you can believe what I say, the both of you. I was in Bury. I saw it all. When Smoke gets his back up, you better get out of the way. 'Cause he's going to haul it out, cock it back, and let her bang."

"The finest schools in the country and Europe," John muttered. "And she hauls it out and lets her bang. Incredible."

Sally laughed openly at the expression on her father's face. "It's just a western expression, father."

"It's just that it is terribly difficult for us, here in the long-settled East, to fully understand the ways of the West, Sally," Abigal said. "But we don't doubt for a moment what you've told us. Sally, when Smoke comes out here for a visit, will he be armed?"

"If he's got his pants on."

John looked heavenward, shook his head, and sighed. "Yet another delightful colloquialism."

Sally reached into a pocket of her dress—she was getting too large to wear jeans, but she would have loved to do so, just to see the expression on her parents' faces—and took out a piece of paper. "This wire came this morning, while you both were out. It's from Smoke."

"Shall I contact the governor and have him call out the militia?" John asked his daughter, only half-joking. He wanted to meet his son-in-law, certainly; but he had absolutely no idea what to expect. And just the thought of an armed western gunfighter riding into the town made him slightly nauseous.

Sally laughed at him. "You're both thinking my husband to be some sort of savage. Well," she shrugged her shoulders, "when he has to be, he is, to your way of thinking. Yet, he is a fine artist, well-read, and highly intelligent. He knows the social graces; certainly knows what fork and spoon to use. But we don't go in for much of that where we live. In the West, eating is serious business, and not much chitchat goes on at the table. But I really think you'll like Smoke if you'll give him just half a chance."

Abigal reached over and patted Sally's hand. "I know we will, dear. And of course he'll be welcomed here. Now please tell us what is in the wire. I'm fairly bursting with excitement." She looked at her husband. "This is the most exhilarating thing that's happened in Keene in twenty years, John!"

"Not yet, dear," John said. "Smoke hasn't yet arrived in town, remember."

Sally laughed so hard she had to wipe her eyes with a handkerchief. She read from the wire. "Smoke has been appointed a deputy U.S. Marshal. This is from the marshal's office in Denver. He has entered the outlaw town in disguise. They'll wire me when the operation has been concluded."

"Well!" John said, obviously pleased, "I'm happy to hear that your husband has chosen the legal way, Sally. He'll properly arrest the criminals and bring them to trial the way it's supposed to be, according to the laws of this land."

Sally smiled. "Father, do you believe pigs can fly like birds?"

"What! Of course not."

"Father, the only law Smoke is going to hand out to those outlaws will be coming out of the muzzles of his .44s. And you can believe that."

"But he's an officer of the law!" the man protested. "More than that, he is operating under a federal badge. He must see to due process. That is his sworn duty!"

Sally's smile was grim. "Oh, he'll see that the outlaws get their due, Father. Trust me."

Smoke made his camp at the very edge of town, pitching his tent and unrolling his blankets. He gathered and stacked wood for a fire. Saving his meager supplies, he cut a pole and rigged it for fishing, walking to a little stream not far away. There he caught his supper, all the while letting his eyes stay busy, checking out the terrain. The stream had to come from somewhere; it didn't just come out of the ground here. For it was full of trout.

He had deliberately made his camp far enough away so he could not hear the terrible cries and the begging of those men and women at the far end of town, being tortured to death. He wished desperately to help, but he knew for the moment, he was powerless to do so.

Huge peaks rose stately and protectively all around the little valley that housed Dead River. Smoke wondered where and how it had gotten its name. At first glance, he could understand why a lot of people would believe the myth of one way in and one way out. But Smoke knew that was crap, and he felt that most of the outlaws knew it as well. But those who would try to seek escape, when the attack came, would be in for a very ugly surprise when they tried those secret trails. White Wolf and his braves would be in hiding, waiting for them.

As Smoke had ridden to his camp, he had seen the compound where some prisoners were being held; but mostly the town itself was a prison, and he had noticed many slaves had free access to the town.

They obviously had been convinced, probably very brutally, that there was no way out except for the road, so why lock them up? But they were probably locked up at night. The compound, then, must be for any newcomers to the town. Or perhaps those were people being punished for some infraction of the rules.

Or waiting to die.

He wondered if the marshal's plant, Hope Farris, was in the compound.

Or had she been discovered and killed?

He cleaned his fish and cooked his supper, all the while watching the comings and goings of the outlaws. So far, few had paid any attention to him.

Smoke judged the number of outlaws in the town at right around two hundred, and that was not counting the shopkeepers and clerks and whores. Rex Davidson had himself a profitable operation going here, Smoke concluded, and he was sure King Rex got his slice of the pie from every store in town and from every whore who worked.

Not that there were that many stores; Smoke had counted six. But they were all huge stores. By far, the biggest place in town was the livery stable and barns, a half dozen of them, all connected by walkways. And during bad weather, many men, Smoke guessed, would live and sleep in those barns. He knew that this high up the winters would be brutal ones.

And so far, Smoke had not seen the man called Dagget. He felt sure he would recognize him from Sally's description. Already he had seen a dozen or more hardcases he had brushed trails with years back; but his disguise had worked. They had paid him no mind, other than a quick glance and equally quick dismissal as being nothing more than a fop and totally harmless.

He wondered if Lone Eagle had hidden his guns behind the privy yet, then decided he had not. Not enough time had gone by since Smoke had met with the brave at the head of the creek.

Smoke heard a harsh shriek of pain from a shack across the wide road. Then a man's voice begging somebody not to do something again. Wild cursing followed by more shrieks of pain.

The door to the cabin was flung open and Smoke watched as a naked man ran out into the road. He was screaming. Then the obscene bulk of Brute Pitman appeared in the door of the shack. He was shirtless, his galluses hanging down to his knees. Brute held a long-barreled pistol in his hand.

The face of the running man was a mask of terror and pain. His body bore the bruises and markings of the many beatings he had endured until he could no longer take any more of it. And because he was naked, Smoke knew that beatings were not the only thing the man had been forced to endure.

But the man's agony was about to end, Smoke noted,

watching as Brute lifted the pistol and jacked the hammer back, shooting the man in the back. The naked man stumbled, screamed, and fell forward, sliding on his face in the dirt and the gravel. The bullet had gone clear through the man, tearing a hole in his chest as it exited. The man kicked once, and then was still.

"How shocking!" Smoke said.

Brute turned, looking at him. "You, come here!" he commanded.

"Not on your life, you obscene tub of lard!"

A dozen outlaws had stopped what they were doing and they were motioning for others to come join them; come listen and watch. For sure, they thought, the fop was about to get mauled.

Brute stepped away from his shack. "What'd you call me, sissy-boy?"

Smoke could see Rex Davidson and another man, dressed all in black from his boots to his hat, walking up the dirt street to join the crowd.

Dagget.

And he wore his guns as Smoke preferred to wear his: the left hand Colt high and butt-forward, using a cross draw.

It was going to be a very interesting match when it came, Smoke thought. For no man wore his guns like that and lived very long, unless he was very, very quick.

Smoke turned his attention back to Brute. The man had moved closer to him. And, Jesus God, was he big and ugly! He was so ugly he could make a buzzard puke.

"Is aid you were a fat tub of lard, blubber-butt!" Smoke shouted, his voice high-pitched.

"I'll tear your damn head off!" Brute shouted, and began lumbering toward Smoke.

"Only if you can catch me!" Smoke shouted. "Can't catch me, can't catch me!"

He began running around in circles, taunting the huge man.

The outlaws thought it funny, for few among them liked Brute and all could just barely tolerate his aberrant appetites. He lived in Dead River because there he could do as he pleased with slaves, and because he could afford the high rent, paying yearly in gold. He left the place only once a year, for one month to the day. Those who tried to follow him, to find and steal his cache of stolen gold, were never seen again.

Smoke knew that he could never hope to best Brute in any type of rough and tumble fight—not if he stayed within the limits of his foppish charade—for Brute was over three hundred pounds and about six and a half feet tall. But he was out of shape, with a huge pus-gut, and if Smoke could keep the ugly bastard running around after him for several minutes, then he might stand a chance of besting him and staying known as a sissy.

It was either that or getting killed by the huge man, and the odds of Smoke getting killed were strong enough without adding to it.

Smoke stopped and danced around, his fists held in the classic fighter's stance. He knew he looked like a fool in his fancy-colored britches and silk shirt and stupid cap with a feather stuck in it.

"I warn you!" Smoke yelled, his voice shrill. "I am an expert pugilist!"

"I'm gonna pugile you!" Brute panted, trying to grab Smoke.

"First you have to catch me!" Smoke taunted. "Can't catch me!"

The outlaws were all laughing and making bets as to how long Smoke would last when Brute got his hands on him, and some were making suggestions as to how much they would pay to see Brute do his other trick, with Smoke on the receiving end of it.

"No way, hombre!" Smoke muttered, darting around Brute. But this time he got a little too close, and Brute got a piece of Smoke's silk shirt and spun him around.

Jerking him closer, Brute grinned, exposing yellowed and rotted teeth. "Got ya!"

Smoke could smell the stink of Brute's unwashed body and the fetid animal smell of his breath.

Before Brute could better his hold on Smoke, Smoke balled his right hand into a hard fist and, with a wild yell, gave Brute five, right on his big bulbous nose.

Brute hollered and the blood dripped. Smoke tore free and once more began running around and around the man, teasing and taunting him. The crowd roared their approval, but the laughter ceased as Smoke lost his footing, slipping to the ground, and Brute was on him, his massive hands closing around Smoke's throat, clamping off his supply of air.

"I'll not kill you this way," Brute panted, slobber from his lips dripping onto Smoke's face. "I have other plans for you, pretty-boy."

Smoke twisted his head and bit Brute on the arm, bringing blood. With a roaring curse, Brute's hand left his throat and Smoke twisted from beneath him, rolling and coming to his feet. He looked wildly around him, spotting a broken two-by-four and grabbing it. The wood was old and somewhat rotten, but it would still make a dandy club.

Brute was shouting curses and advancing toward him.

Smoke tried the club, right on the side of Brute's head. The club shattered and the blood flew, but still the big man would not go down.

He shook his head and grinned at Smoke.

"All right, you nasty ne'er-do-well," Smoke trilled at him. "I hate violence, but you asked for this."

Then he hit Brute with everything he had, starting the punch chest-high and connecting with Brute's jaw. This time when Brute hit the ground, he stayed there.

Smoke began shaking his right hand and moaning as if in pain, which he was not.

He heard Davidson say, "Doc, look at DeBeers's hand. See if it's broken. Sheriff Danvers? If DeBeers's hand is broken and he can't draw, shoot Brute."

"Yes, sir," the so-called sheriff said.

An old whiskey-breathed and unshaven man checked Smoke's hand and pronounced it unbroken.

Smoke turned to Rex Davidson. "I am sorry about this incident, sir. I came in peace. I will leave others alone if they do the same for me."

Davidson looked first at the unconscious Brute, then at Smoke. "You start drawing me first thing in the morning. Sheriff Danvers?"

"Yes, sir?"

"When Brute comes out of it, advise him I said to leave Mr. DeBeers alone. Tell him he may practice his sickening perversions on the slaves, but not on paying guests."

"Yes, sir."

He once more looked at Smoke. "Breakfast at my house. Eight o'clock in the morning. Be there."

"Yes, sir," Smoke replied, and did not add the "Majesty" bit.

"Does this place offend your delicate sensibilities, Mr. DeBeers?" Davidson asked.

"Since you inquired, yes, it does."

It was after breakfast, and Davidson was posing for the first of many drawings.

"Why, Mr. DeBeers?" For some reason, Davidson had dropped the "Jester" bit.

"Because of the barbarous way those unfortunate people at the edge of town are treated. That's the main reason."

"I see. Interesting. But in England, Mr. DeBeers, drawing and quartering people in public was only stopped a few years ago. And is not England supposed to be the bastion of civilized law and order . . . more or less?"

"Yes, sir, it is."

"Well, this is still a young country, so it's going to take us a while to catch up."

What an idiotic rationalization, Smoke thought. Louis Longmont would be appalled. "Yes, sir, I suppose you're right."

"Don't pander to me, Mr. DeBeers. You most certainly do not think I am right."

"But when I do speak my mind, I get slapped or struck down."

"Only in public, Mr. DeBeers. When we are alone, you may speak your mind."

"Thank you, sir. In that case, I find this entire community

the most appalling nest of human filth I have ever had the misfortune to encounter!"

Davidson threw back his head and laughed. "Of course, you do! But after a time, one becomes accustomed to it. You'll see."

"I don't plan on staying that long, sir." Smoke looked at King Rex, checking for any signs of annoyance. He could see none.

Instead, the man only smiled. "Why would you want to leave here?"

Smoke stopped sketching for a moment, to see if the man was really serious. He was. "To continue on with my journey, sir. To visit and sketch the West."

"Ah! But you have some of the most beautiful scenery in the world right around you. Plus many of the most famous outlaws and gunfighters in the West. You could spend a lifetime here and not sketch it all, could you not?"

"That is true, but two of the people I want to meet and sketch are not here."

"Oh? And who might those be?"

"The mountain man, Preacher, and the gunfighter, Smoke Jensen."

The only sign of emotion from the man was a nervous tic under his right eye. "Then you should wait here, Mr. DeBeers, for I believe Jensen is on his way."

"Oh, really, sir! Then I certainly shall wait. Oh, I'm so excited."

"Control yourself, Shirley."

"Oh, yes, sir. Sorry. Sir?"

"Yes?"

"Getting back to this place . . . The west, from what I

have been able to see, is changing almost daily. Settling. Surely this town is known for what it really is?"

Davidson met his eyes. "So?"

"Do you think this will go on forever and ever? As the town becomes known outside of this immediate area, the citizens will eventually grow weary of it and demand that the Army storm the place."

"Ummm. Yes, you're probably right. And I have given that much thought of late. But, young man,"—he smiled and held up a finger, breaking his pose—"this town has been here for twenty years and still going. How do you account for that?"

"Well, when you first came here, I suppose there were no others towns nearby. Now all that has changed. Civilization is all around you and closing in. That, sir, is why I wanted to come west now, before the wild West is finally tamed."

"Ummm. Well, you are a thinking man, Mr. DeBeers, and I like that. There is so little intellectual stimulation to be found around here." He abruptly stood up. "I am weary of posing." He walked around to look at the sketch. "Good. Very good. Excellent, as a matter of fact. I thought it would be. I have arranged for you to take your meals at the Bon Ton Café. I will want at least a hundred of your sketches of me. Some with an outside setting. When that is done, to my satisfaction, then you may leave. Good day, Mr. DeBeers."

Gathering up his pencils and sketch pads, Smoke left the house, which was situated on a flat that sat slightly above the town, allowing Rex a commanding view. As he walked back to his tent, Smoke pondered his situation.

Surely, Rex Davidson was insane; but if he was, would that not make all the others in this place mad as well?

And Smoke did not believe that for a moment.

More than likely, Davidson and Dagget and all the others who voluntarily resided in Dead River were not insane. Perhaps they were just the personification of evil, and the place was a human snake pit.

He chose that explanation. Already, people who had committed the most terrible of crimes were saying they were not responsible for their actions because they had been crazy, at the time, before the time, whatever. And courts, mostly back east in the big cities, were accepting that more and more, allowing guilty people to be set free without punishment. Smoke did not doubt for one minute that there were people who were truly insane and could not help their actions.

But he also felt that those types were in the minority of cases; the rest were shamming. If a person were truly crazy, Smoke did not believe that malady could be turned off and on like a valve. If a person were truly insane, they would perform irrational acts on a steady basis, not just whenever the mood struck them.

He knew for an ironclad fact that many criminals were of a high intelligence, and that many were convincing actors and actresses. Certainly smart enough to fool this new thing he'd heard about called psychiatry. Smoke Jensen was a straight-ahead, right-was-right and wrong-was-wrong man, with damn little gray in between. You didn't lie, you didn't cheat, you didn't steal, and you treated your neighbor like you would want to be treated.

And if you didn't subscribe to that philosophy, you best get clear of men like Smoke Jensen.

As for the scum and filth and perverts in this town of Dead River, Smoke felt he had the cure for what ailed them.

The pills were made of lead.

And the doctor's name was Smoke Jensen.

CHAPTER ELEVEN

For one hour each day, Smoke sketched Rex Davidson; the rest of the time was his to spend as he pleased. He took his meals at the Bon Ton—the man who owned the place was wanted for murder back in Illinois, having killed several people by poisoning them—and spent the rest of his time wandering the town, sketching this and that and picking up quite a bit of money by drawing the outlaws who came and went. He made friends with none of them, having found no one whom he felt possessed any qualities that he wished to share. Although he felt sure there must be one or two in the town who could be saved from a life of crime with just a little bit of help.

Smoke put that out of his mind and, for the most part, kept it out. He wanted nothing on his conscience when the lead started flying.

He was not physically bothered by any outlaw. But the taunts and insults continued from many of the men and from a lot of the women who chose to live in the town. Smoke would smile and tip his cap at them, but if they could have read his thoughts, they would have grabbed the nearest horse and gotten the hell out of Dead River.

Brute saw Smoke several times a day but refused to speak to him. He would only grin nastily and make the most obscene gestures.

Smoke saw the three who had shoved him around in Trinidad—Jake, Shorty, and Red—but they paid him no mind.

What did worry Smoke was that the town seemed to be filling up with outlaws. Many more were coming in, and damn few were leaving.

They were not all famous gunfighters and famous outlaws, of course. As a matter of fact, many were no more than two-bit punks who had gotten caught in the act of whatever crimes they were committing and, in a dark moment of fear and fury, had killed when surprised. But that did not make them any less guilty in Smoke's mind. And then as criminals are prone to do, they grabbed a horse or an empty boxcar and ran, eventually joining up with a gang.

It was the gang leaders and lone-wolf hired guns who worried Smoke the most. For here in Dead River were the worst of the lot of bad ones in a three state area.

LaHogue, called the Hog behind his back, and his gang of cutthroats lived in Dead River. Natick and his bunch were in town, as was the Studs Woodenhouse gang and Bill Wilson's bunch of crap. And just that morning, Paul Rycroft and Slim Bothwell and their men had ridden in.

The place was filling up with hardcases.

And to make matters worse, Smoke knew a lot of the men who were coming in. He had never ridden any hoot-owl trails with any of them, but their paths had crossed now and then. The West was a large place but relatively small in population, so people who roamed were apt to meet, now and then.

Cat Ventura and the Hog had both given Smoke some curious glances and not just one look but several, and that made Smoke uneasy. He wanted desperately to check to see if his guns were behind the privy. But he knew it would only bring unnecessary attention to himself, and that was something he could do without. He had stayed alive so far by playing the part of a foolish fop and by maintaining a very high visibility. And with only a few days to go, he did not want to break that routine. He spent the rest of the day sketching various outlaws—picking up about a hundred dollars doing so—and checking out the town of Dead River. But there was not that much more to be learned about the place. Since he was loosely watched every waking moment, Smoke had had very little opportunity to do much exploring.

He was sitting before his small fire that evening, enjoying a final cup of coffee before rolling up in his blankets, for the nights were very cool this high up in the mountains, when he heard spurs jingling, coming toward him. He waited, curious, for up to this point he had been left strictly alone.

"Hello, the fire!" the voice came out of the campfire-lit gloom.

"If you're friendly, come on in," Smoke called. "I will share my coffee with you."

"Nice of you." A young man, fresh-faced with youth, perhaps twenty years old at the most and wearing a grin, walked up and squatted down, pouring a tin cup full of dark, strong cowboy coffee. He glanced over the hat-sized fire at Smoke, his eyes twinkling with good humor.

He's out of place, Smoke accurately pegged the young cowboy. *He's not an outlaw.* There was just something about the young man; something clean and vital and open. That little intangible that set the innocent apart from the lawless.

"My first time to this place," the young man said. "It's quite a sight to see, ain't it?"

Smoke had noticed that the cowboy wore his six-gun low and tied down, and the gun seemed to be a living extension of the man.

He knows how to use it, Smoke thought. "It is all of that, young man, to be sure."

"Name's York."

"Shirley DeBeers."

York almost spilled his coffee down his shirtfront at that. He lifted his eyes. "You funnin' me?"

Smoke smiled at his expression. "Actually, no. It's a fine old family name. Is York your first or last name?" he inquired, knowing that it was not a question one asked in the West.

York looked at him closely. "You new out here, ain't you?"

"Why, yes, as a matter of fact, I am. How did you know that Mr. York?"

The cowboy's smile was quick. "Just a guess. And it's just York."

"Very well." Smoke noticed that the young man's eyes kept drifting to the pan of bacon and bread he had fixed for his supper. There were a few strips of bacon left, and about half a loaf of bread. "If you're hungry, please help yourself. I have eaten my fill and I hate to throw away good food."

"Thanks," York said quickly and with a grin. "That's right big of you. You don't never have to worry 'bout tossin' out no food when I'm around." He fixed a huge sandwich and then used another piece of bread to sop up the grease in the pan.

Smoke guessed he had not eaten in several days.

When York had finished and not a crumb was left, he settled back and poured another cup of coffee. Smoke tossed him a sack of tobacco and papers.

York caught the sack and rolled and lit. "Thanks. That was good grub. Hit the spot, let me tell you. Anything I can do for you, you just let me know. Most"—he cut his eyes suspiciously—"most of the hombres around here wouldn't give a man the time of day if they had a watch in every pocket. Sorry bastards."

"I agree with you. But you be careful where you say things like that, York."

York nodded his agreement. "Ain't that the truth. Say, you don't neither talk like nor look like a man that's on the dodge, DeBeers."

"On the dodge?" Smoke kept up his act. "Oh! Yes, I see what you mean now. Oh, no. I can assure you, I am not wanted by the authorities."

York studied him across the small fire, confusion on his young face. "Then . . . what in the hell are you doin' in a place like this?"

"Working. Sketching the West and some of its most infamous people. Mr. Davidson was kind enough to give me sanctuary and the run of the place."

"And you believed him?"

Smoke only smiled.

"Yeah. You might look sorta silly—and I don't mean

no o-fence by that, it's just that you dress different—but I got a hunch you ain't dumb."

"Thank you." Smoke was not going to fall into any verbal traps, not knowing if York was a plant to sound him out.

The cowboy sipped his coffee and smoked for a moment. "You really come in here without havin' to, huh?"

"That is correct."

"Weird. But," he shrugged, "I reckon you have your reasons. Me, now, I didn't have no choice at all in the matter."

"We all have choices, young man. But sometimes they are disguised and hard to make."

"Whatever that means. Anyways, I'm on the hard dodge, I am."

He tried to sound proud about that statement, but to Smoke, it came across flat and with a definite note of sadness.

"I'm very sorry to hear that, York. Is it too personal to talk about?"

"Naw. I killed a man in Utah."

Smoke studied him. "You don't sound like a man who would cold-bloodedly kill another man."

"Huh? Oh, no. It wasn't nothin' like that. It was a stand-up-and-face-him-down fight. But the law didn't see it thataway. I guess near'bouts all these people in this lousy town would claim they was framed, but I really was." He poured another cup of coffee and settled back against a stump, apparently anxious to talk and have somebody hear him out. "You see, I bought a horse from this feller. It was a good horse for fifty dollars. Too good, as it turned out. I had me a bill of sale and all that. Then these folks come ridin' up to me about a week later and claimed I stole the horse. They had 'em a rope all ready to stretch my neck. I showed 'em my bill of sale and that backed 'em down some. But they was still gonna take the horse and leave me afoot in the Uintahs. Well, I told 'em that they wasn't gonna do no such a thing. I told 'em that if the horse was rightfully theirs, well, I was wrong and they was right. But let me get to a town 'fore they took the horse; don't leave me in the big middle of nowheres on foot."

He sighed and took a swallow of coffee. "They allowed as to how I could just by God walk out of there. I told them they'd better drag iron if that's what they had in mind, 'cause I damn sure wasn't gonna hoof it outta there.

"Well, they dragged iron, but I was quicker. I kilt one and put lead in the other. The third one, he turned yeller and run off.

"I got the hell outta there and drifted. Then I learned that I had a murder charge hangin' over my head. That third man who run off? He told a pack of lies about what really happened.

"Well, bounty hunters come up on me about two or three months later. I buried one of them and toted the other one into a little town to the doc's office. The marshal, he come up all blustered-up and I told him what happened and added that if he didn't like my version of it, he could just clear leather and we'd settle it that way."

He grinned boyishly. "The marshal didn't like it, and I'll admit I had my back up some. But he liked livin' moreun gunfightin'. So I drifted on and things just kept gettin' worser and worser. I couldn't get no job 'cause of them posters out on me. I heard about this place and sort of drifted in. I ain't no outlaw, but I don't know what else to do with all them charges hangin' over my head."

Smoke thought on it. He believed the young man; believed him to be leveling as to the facts of it all. "Might I make a suggestion?"

"You shore could. I'd rather live in hell with rattlesnakes than in heaven with this bunch around here."

Smoke couldn't help it. He laughed at the young man's expression. "York, why don't you just change your name and drift. And by the way, do you still have the horse in question?"

"Naw. I turned him loose and caught me up a wild horse and broke him. He's a good horse."

"Well then, York, drift. Change your name and drift. Chances are that you'll never be caught."

"I thought of that. But damn it, DeBeers, I ain't done nothin' wrong. At least, not yet. And York is my family name. By God, I'm gonna stick with it. I'm doin' some thinkin' 'bout linkin' up with Slim Bothwell's bunch. They asked me to. I guess I ain't got no choice. I don't wanna hurt nobody or steal nothin' from nobody. But, hell, I gotta eat!"

"York, you are not cut out for the outlaw life," Smoke told him.

"Don't I know it! Look, DeBeers, I listened to some of the men talk 'bout all they've done, in here and out there." He jerked his thumb. "Damn near made me puke." He sighed heavily. "I just don't know what to do."

Could this entire thing be a setup? Smoke wondered, and concluded that it certainly could be. But something about the young cowboy was awfully convincing. He decided to take a chance, but to do it without York knowing of it.

"Perhaps something will come up to change your mind, York."

The cowboy looked up across the fire, trust in his eyes. "What?"

"I really have no idea. But hope springs eternal, York. You must always keep that in mind. Where are you staying while you're here?"

"I ain't got no place. Give that Dagget feller my last fifty dollars. He told me that give me five days in here." He shook his head. "After that . . . I don't know."

"You're welcome to stay here. I don't have much, but you're welcome to share with me."

"That's mighty white of you, DeBeers. And I'll take you up on that." He grinned at Smoke. "There is them that say you're goofy. But I don't think so. I think you're just a pretty nice guy in a bad spot."

"Thank you, York. And have you ever thought that might fit you as well?"

The grin faded. "Yeah, I reckon it might. I ain't never done a dishonest thing in my life. Only difference is, you ain't got no warrants hangin' over your head. You can ride out of this hellhole anytime you take a notion. Me? I'm stuck, lookin' at the wrong side of society!"

The next morning Smoke left the still-sleeping York a full pot of coffee, then took his sketch pad and went walking, as was his custom every morning. As the saloon came into view, Smoke noticed a large crowd gathered out front, in the street. And it was far too early for that many drinkers to have gathered.

"Let's have some fun!" Smoke could hear the excited shout.

"Yeah. Let's skin the son of a bitch!"

"Naw. Let's give him to Brute."

"Brute don't want no dirty Injun."

"Not unless it's a young boy," someone shouted with hard laugh.

"Hold it down!" a man hollered. "Mr. Davidson's got a plan, and it's a good one."

Smoke stepped up to a man standing in the center of the street. "What on earth has happened here?"

The outlaw glanced at him. "The guards caught them an Injun about dawn. He was tryin' to slip out over the mountains. No one knows what he was doin' in town." The man shut up, appraising Smoke through cool eyes, aware that he might have said too much.

"He must have slipped in on the road," Smoke said quickly, noting the coolness in the man's eyes fading. "It would be impossible to come in through those terribly high mountains around the town."

The outlaw smiled. "Yeah. That's what he done, all right. And there ain't no tellin' how long he's been tryin' to get out, right?"

"Oh, absolutely. I think the savage should be hanged immediately." Smoke forced indignation into his voice.

The outlaw grinned. His teeth were blackened, rotted stubs. "You all right, Shirley. You're beginnin' to fit right in here. Yeah, the Injun's gonna die. But it's gonna be slow."

"Why?" Smoke asked innocently.

"Why, hell's fire, Shirley! So's we can all have some fun, that's why."

"Oh. Of course."

A man ran past Smoke and the outlaw, running in that odd bowlegged manner of one who has spent all his life on a horse.

"What's happenin', Jeff?" the outlaw asked.

"Mr. Davidson tole me to get the kid, York. Says we gotta test him. You know why?"

"Yeah."

Neither man would elaborate.

Smoke felt he knew what the test was going to involve, and he also felt that York would not pass it. There was a sick feeling in the pit of his stomach. Smoke wandered on down to the large crowd gathered in front of the saloon and tried to blend in.

The crowd of hardcases and thugs and guns-for-hire ignored him, but Smoke was very conscious of Rex Davidson's eyes on him. He met the man's steady gaze and smiled at him.

Davidson waved the crowd silent. "I have decided on a better plan," he said as the crowd fell quiet. "Forget York; we know he's a wanted man. There are some of you who claim that our artist friend is not what he professes to be. Well, let's settle that issue right now. Bring that damned Indian out here."

Smoke felt sure it would be Lone Eagle, and it was. He was dragged out of the saloon and onto the boardwalk. He had been badly beaten, his nose and mouth dripping blood. But his face remained impassive and he deliberately did not look at Smoke.

"Drag that damned savage to the shooting post," Davidson ordered. He looked at Smoke and smiled, an evil curving of the lips. "And you, Mr. Artist, you come along, too."

"Do I have to? I hate violence. It makes me ill. I'd be upset for days."

"Yes, damn it, you have to. Now get moving."

Smoke allowed himself to be pushed and shoved along, not putting up any resistance. He wondered if any Indians were watching from the cliffs that surrounded the outlaw town and concluded they probably were.

And he also had a pretty good hunch what the test was going to entail.

The crowd stopped in a large clearing. In the center of the clearing, a bullet-scarred and blood-stained post was set into the ground.

Lone Eagle turned to face the crowd, and when he spoke, his voice was strong. "I do not need to be tied like a coward. I face death with a strong heart, and I shall die well. I will show the white man how to die with honor. Which is something that few of you know anything about."

The crowd of hardcases booed him.

Lone Eagle spat at them in contempt.

He had not as yet looked at Smoke.

Smoke was shoved to the front of the crowd and a pistol placed into his hand.

"What am I supposed to do with this weapon, Mr. Davidson?"

"Kill the Indian," Rex told him.

"Oh, I say now!" Smoke protested shrilly. "I haven't fired a gun in years. I detest guns. I'm afraid of them. I won't be able to hit the savage."

Lone Eagle laughed at Smoke, looking at him. "The white man is a woman!" Lone Eagle shouted. And Smoke knew he was deliberately goading him. Lone Eagle knew he was going to die and preferred his death to be quick rather than slow torture, torture for the amusement of the white men gathered around. He might have chosen the slow way had he been captured by another tribe, for to die slowly and with much pain was an honor—if at the hands of other Indians. But not at the hands of the white men. "The silly-looking white man is a coward."

"You gonna take that from a damned Injun, Shirley?" a man shouted.

"What am I supposed to do?"

"Hell, sissy-boy. Kill the bastard!"

Smoke lifted the pistol and pretended to have trouble cocking it. He deliberately let it fire, the slug almost hitting an outlaw in the foot. Smoke shrieked as if in fright and the outlaw cussed him.

The others thought it wildly funny.

"Watch it there, Black!" an outlaw yelled. "He lift that muzzle up some you liable to be ridin' side-saddle!"

The man whose foot was just missed by the slug stepped back into the crowd and gave Smoke some dirty looks.

"Shoot the goddamn Indian, DeBeers!" Davidson ordered.

Smoke lifted the pistol and cocked it, taking careful aim and pulling the trigger. The slug missed Lone Eagle by several yards, digging up dirt. The outlaws hooted and laughed and began making bets as to how many rounds it would take for Smoke to hit his target.

"Try again, Shirley," Davidson told him, disgust in his voice.

"What a silly, silly man you are!" Lone Eagle shouted. "If you had two pistols and a rifle and shotgun beside you, you still would not be able to hit me. It is good they are out of your sight. You might hurt yourself, foolish man."

Lone Eagle was telling Smoke that his weapons had been hidden as planned.

"Shoot the damned Injun, Shirley!" Dagget hollered in Smoke's ear.

"All right! All right!" Smoke put a hurt expression on his face. "You don't have to be so ugly about it!"

Smoke fired again. The slug missed Lone Eagle by a good two feet.

"Jesus Christ, DeBeers!" Dagget said, scorn thick in his voice.

"The pistol was fully loaded, Shirley," Davidson told him. "You have four rounds left."

Lone Eagle turned his back to Smoke and hiked up his loincloth, exposing his bare buttocks; the height of insult to a man.

Facing the crowd, Lone Eagle shouted, "There are little girls in my village who are better shots than the white man. Your shots are nothing more than farts in the wind."

"If you don't kill him," Davidson warned, "you shall be the one to gouge out his eyes. And if you refuse, I'll personally kill you. After I let Brute have his way with you."

Smoke cocked the pistol.

Lone Eagle began chanting, and Smoke knew he was singing his death song.

He fired again. This time, the slug came much closer. Lone Eagle's words changed slightly. Smoke listened while he fumbled with the gun. Lone Eagle was telling him to miss him again, and then he would charge and make the outlaws kill him; it was too much to ask a friend to do so. He told him that his death could not be avoided, that it was necessary for the plan to work. That for years it would be sung around the campfires about how well Lone Eagle had died, charging the many white men with only his bare hands for a weapon.

And it was a good way to die. The Gods had allowed a beautiful day, warm and pleasant.

Smoke cocked the pistol and lifted it, taking aim.

Lone Eagle sang of his own death, then abruptly he screamed and charged the line of outlaws and gunslingers. Using the scream as a ruse to miss him, Smoke emptied the pistol and fell to the ground just as Lone Eagle, with a final scream, jumped at the line and a dozen guns barked and roared, stopping him in midair, flinging him to the ground, bloody and dead.

Rex helped Smoke up. "You'll never change, Shirley," he said disgustedly. "Do us all a favor and don't ever carry a gun. You'd be too dangerous. Hell, you might accidentally hit something!"

Smoke fanned himself. "I feel faint!"

"If you pass out, DeBeers," Dagget told him, contempt in his eyes and his voice, "you'll damn well lie where you fall."

"I can probably make it back to the camp before I collapse," Smoke trilled.

"Stand aside, boys!" an outlaw said with a laugh. "Shirley's got the vapors!"

"Come on, boys! The drinks are on me."

As they passed by him, several hardcases jokingly complimented Smoke on his fine shooting.

Smoke looked first at Davidson and Dagget, standing by his side, and then at the bullet-riddled and bloody body of Lone Eagle. "Isn't anyone going to bury the savage?"

Dagget laughed, cutting his eyes to Davidson. "I think that'd be a fine job for Shirley, don't you, Rex?"

"Yes." That was said with a laugh. "I do. There is a shovel right over there, DeBeers." He pointed. "Now get to it."

It took Smoke more than a hour to dig out a hole in the rocky soil, even though he dug it shallow, knowing the chief would take the body from the ground and give it a proper Indian burial.

When he got back to his camp, York was laying on his blankets, looking at him, disgust in his eyes.

Smoke flopped down on his own blankets. "What a horrible experience."

"They wasn't no call to kill that Injun. He wasn't even armed and probably was lookin' for food. You was missin' him deliberate, wasn't you?"

Smoke made up his mind and took the chance. "Yes, York, I was."

"I figured as much. Can't nobody shoot that bad. 'Specially a man who was raised up on a farm the way you claim to be. You puttin' on some sort of act, DeBeers. But you best be damn careful around here. This is a hell-hole, and they ain't nothin' but scum livin' here."

"I know. Davidson at first said if I didn't kill the Indian, he was going to give me to Brute Pitman and then have me gouge out the Indian's eyes." Smoke let the mention of his putting on an act fade away into nothing, hoping York would not bring it up again.

York lay on the ground and gazed at him. "I heard of Brute; seen him around a couple of times. He's a bad one.

If they'd a tried that, I'd have been forced to deal myself in and help you out."

"You'd have gotten yourself killed."

"You befriended me. Man don't stand by his friends when they in trouble ain't much of a man or a friend. That's just the way I am."

And Smoke felt the young cowboy was sincere when he said it. "I agree with you. You know, at first, they were going to make you kill the Indian."

"I'd a not done it," he said flatly. "My ma was part Nez Percé. And I'm damn proud of that blood in my veins. And I don't make no effort to hide that fact, neither."

And judging by the scars on his flat-knuckled hands, York had been battling over that very fact most of his life, Smoke noted.

York followed Smoke's eyes. "Yeah. I'm just as quick with my fists as I am with my guns." His eyes dropped to Smoke's big hands. "And you ain't no pilgrim, neither, Mr. Shirley DeBeers. Or whatever the hell your name might be."

"Let's just leave it DeBeers for the time being, shall we?"

"'Kay." York took off his battered hat and ran fingers through his tousled hair. "DeBeers?"

"Yes, York?"

"Let's you and me get the hell gone from this damn place!"

CHAPTER TWELVE

There was no doubt in Smoke's mind that York was serious and was no part of Davidson's scheme of things in or around Dead River. The young cowboy was no outlaw and had made up his mind never to become one. But Smoke had three days to go before the deadline was up and the posse would strike. He had a hunch that would be the longest three days of his life. He looked at York for a moment before replying.

"I'm just about through sketching Davidson. He has indicated that he would allow me to leave after that."

"Like I said before—and you believed him?"

"I have no choice in the matter."

"I guess not. But I still think you're draggin' your boots for some reason. But I'll stick around just to see what you're up to. Don't worry, DeBeers. I'll keep my suspicions to myself."

Again, Smoke had nothing to say on that subject. "What are you going to do on the outside, York?"

York shook his head. "I don't know. Drift, I reckon. I just ain't cut out for this kind of life. I think I knowed that all along. But I think I owe it to you for pointin' it out."

"Stay out of sight, York." Smoke picked up his sketch pad. "I have to go sketch Davidson. Even though I certainly don't feel up to it."

"What if Davidson won't let you leave here like he says he will?"

"I don't know. Let's cross that bridge when we come to it."

"Bridges don't worry me," York said glumly. "It's that damn guarded pass that's got me concerned."

The next two days passed without incident. York stayed at Smoke's camp—and stayed close. Smoke continued his sketching of Rex Davidson, and his opinion that the man was a conceited and arrogant tyrant was confirmed. The man remained friendly enough—as friendly as he had ever been to Smoke—but Smoke could detect a change in him. He appeared tense and sometimes nervous. And there was distance between them now, a distance that had not been there before. Smoke knew that Davidson had never really intended to let him leave. He did not think that Rex suspected he was anything except the part he was playing, what he claimed to be. It was, Smoke felt, that Rex had been playing a game with him all along; a cat with a cornered mouse. A little torture before the death bite.

"I'm becoming a bit weary of all this," Davidson suddenly announced, breaking his pose. The afternoon of the sixth day.

"Of what, sir?" Smoke lifted his eyes, meeting the hard gaze of the man.

"Of posing, fool!" Davidson said sharply. "I have

enough pictures. But as for you, I don't know what to do about you."

"Whatever in the world are you talking about, Mr. Davidson?"

Rex stared at him for a long moment. Then, rising from the stool where he'd been sitting, posing, he walked to a window and looked out, staring down at his outlaw town. He turned and said, "I first thought it was you; that you were the front man, the spy sent in here. Then I realized that no one except a professional actor could play the part of a fool as convincingly as you've done . . . and no actor has that much courage. Not to come in here and lay his life on the line. So you are what you claim to be. A silly fop. But I still don't know what to do with you. I do know that you are beginning to bore me. It was the Indian. Had to be. The marshals hired the Indian to come in here and check on us."

"Sir, I have no idea what you're talking about." But Smoke knew. Somewhere in the ranks of the marshals or the sheriffs or the deputies, there was a turncoat. Now he had to find out just how much Rex Davidson knew about the plan just twenty-four hours away from bloody reality.

And stay alive long enough to do something about it, if he could.

"That damn woman almost had me fooled," Davidson said, more to himself than to Smoke. He had turned his back again, not paying any attention to Smoke. "It was good fun torturing her, DeBeers; I wish you had been here to see it. Yes, indeed. I outdid myself with inventiveness. I kept her alive for a long time. I finally broke her, of course. But by the time I did, she was no more than a broken, babbling idiot. The only thing we learned was that the marshals were planning on coming in here at some time or the other. She didn't know when."

"Sir, I—"

Davidson whirled around, his face hard with anger. "Shut your goddamn mouth, DeBeers!" He shouted. "And never interrupt me when I'm speaking."

"Yes, sir."

"Of course, she was raped—among other things. The men enjoyed taking their perversions upon her." He was pacing the room. "Repeatedly. I enjoyed listening to her beg for mercy. Dagget can be quite inventive, too. But finally I wearied of it, just as I am rapidly wearying of you, DeBeers. You're really a Milquetoast, Shirley. I think I'll put you in a dress and parade you around. Yes. That is a thought."

Smoke kept his mouth shut.

Davidson turned back to the window, gazing out over his town of scum and filth and perversion. "I have not left this place in years. I stay aware of what is going on outside, of course. But I have not left this valley in years. It's mine, and no one is going to take it from me. I will not permit it. I know an attack is coming. But I don't know when."

Smoke knew then why the sudden influx of outlaws. Somehow, probably through outriders, Davidson had gotten the word out to them: If you want to save your refuge, you'd better be prepared to fight for it.

Or something like that.

With King Rex, however, it had probably been put in a much more flowery way.

"Ah, sir, Your Majesty?" Smoke verbally groveled, something he was getting weary of.

"What do you want, Shirley?"

"May I take my leave now, Your Magesty?"

"Yes, you silly twit!" Davidson did not turn from the window. "And stay out of my sight, goofy. I haven't made up my mind exactly what I'm going to do with you. Get out, fool!"

I've made up my mind what to do with you, King Rex, Smoke thought, on his way out. And about this time tomorrow, you're going to be in for a very large surprise. One that I'm going to enjoy handing you.

He gently closed the door behind him. He was smiling as he walked down the hill from the King's house. He had to work to get the smile off his lips before he entered the long main street of Dead River.

In twenty-four hours, he would finally and forever shed his foppish costume and strap on his guns.

And then Dr. Jenson would begin administering to a very sick town.

With gunsmoke and lead.

Smoke was conscious of York staring at him. He had been sliding furtive glances his way for several hours now, and Smoke knew the reason for the looks. He could feel the change coming over him. He would have to be very careful the remainder of this day, for he was in no mood to continue much longer with his Shirley DeBeers act.

York had just returned from town and had been unusually quiet since getting back. He finally broke his silence.

"DeBeers?"

"Yes, York?"

"I gotta tell you. The word is out that come the morning, you're gonna be tossed to the wolves. Davidson is gonna declare you fair game for anybody. And you know what that means."

Mid-afternoon of the seventh day.

"Brute Pitman."

"Among other things," York said.

"What size boots do you wear, York?"

"Huh! Man, didn't you hear me? We got to get the hell gone from this place. And I mean we got to plan on how to do it right now!"

"I heard you, York. Just relax. What size boots do you wear?"

The cowboy signed. "Ten."

"That's my size. How about that?" Smoke grinned at him.

"Wonderful!" The comment was dryly given. "You lookin' at gettin' kilt, and you all het up about us wearin' the same size boots. You weird, DeBeers."

With a laugh, Smoke handed York some money. "Go to the store and buy me a good pair of boots. Black. Get me some spurs. Small stars, not the big California rowels. Don't say a word about who you're buying them for. We'll let that come as a surprise for them. Think you can do that for me, York?"

"Why, hell, yes, I can! What do you think I am, some sort of dummy? Boots? 'Kay. But I best get you some walkin' heels."

"Riding heels, York," Smoke corrected, enjoying the look of bewilderment on his new friend's face. "And how many boxes of shells do you have?"

"One and what's in my belt. Now why in the hell are you askin' that?"

"Buy at least three more boxes. When you get back, I'll explain. Now then, what else have you heard about me, York?"

"You ain't gonna like it."

"Oh, I don't know. It might give me more incentive to better do the job that faces me."

York shook his head. "Weird, DeBeers. That's you. Well, that Jake feller? He's been makin' his brags about how he's gonna make you hunker down in the street and eat a pile of horse-droppin's."

"Oh, is he now?"

"Yeah. He likes to be-little folks. That Jake, he's cruel mean, DeBeers. That one and them that run with him is just plain no-good. He makes ever' slave that comes in here do that. I've had half a dozen or more men tell me that. All the men here, they think it's funny watchin' Jake force folks to eat that mess."

"I wonder how Jake would like to eat a poke of it himself?"

York grinned. "Now that'd be a sight to see!"

"Don't give up hope, York. Would you please go get my stuff for me?"

"Sure." He turned, then stopped and whirled around to face Smoke. "I can't figure you, DeBeers. You've changed. I noticed that this morning."

"We'll talk when you get back, York. Be careful down in town. I think things are getting a bit tense."

"That ain't exactly the way I'd put it, but whatever you say." He walked off toward town, mumbling to himself and shaking his head. Smoke smiled at the young man and then set about preparing himself mentally for what the night held in store.

And he knew only too well what lay before him when the dusk settled into darkness in the outlaw town.

There was no fear in Smoke; no sweaty palms or pounding heart. He was deathly calm, inside and out. And he did not know if that was an asset or liability. He knew caution, for no man lived by the gun without knowing what was about him at all times. But Smoke, since age sixteen, had seldom if ever at all experienced anything even remotely akin to fear.

He sat down on his ground sheet and blankets and calmly set about making a pot of coffee. He looked up at the sound of boots striking the gravel. Brute Pitman stopped a few yards away, grinning at him.

"Go away, Bruce. The smell of you would stop a buzzard in flight."

Brute cussed him.

Smoke smiled at him.

"I'm gonna enjoy hearin' you holler, pretty-boy," Brute told him, slobber leaking past his fat lips. "With you, I'm gonna make it las' a long time."

Smoke made no reply, just sat on the ground and stared at the hulking mass of perversion. He allowed his eyes to do the talking, and they silently spoke volumes to the big slob.

Brute met the gaze and Smoke's smile was wider still as something shifted in the hulk's eyes. Was it fear touching Brute's dark eyes? Smoke felt sure that it was, and that thought amused him. Brute Pitman was like so many men his size, a bully from boyhood. He had bulled and heavy-shouldered his way through life, knowing his sheer size would keep most from fighting back. But like most bullies, Brute was a coward at heart.

"Something the matter, Brute?"

That took him by surprise. "Huh! Naw, they ain't nothin' the matter with me, sissy-boy. Nothin'," he added, "that come night won't clear."

"You best watch the night, Brute," Smoke cautioned. "Night is a time when death lays close to a man."

"Huh! Whatda you talkin' 'bout now, pretty boy. I don't think you even know. I think you so scared you peein' your drawers."

Smoke laughed at him. Now he didn't care. It was too close to the deadline to matter. By now, the men from the posse would be approaching the ranch and would be changing horses for the last time before entering the mountain pass. Already, the Utes would be slipping into place, waiting for the guards to change.

Everything was in motion; it could not be stopped now.

"Get out of my sight, Brute. You sickin' me."

Brute hesitated, then mumbled something obscene under his breath and walked down the small hill. Twice he stopped and looked back at Smoke. Smoke gave him the finger, jabbing the air with his middle finger.

"Crazy!" Brute said. "The bassard's crazy! Done took leave of his senses."

Smoke heard the comment and smiled.

Brute met Cat Ventura on his way down. The men did not speak to each other. Cat stood over Smoke, staring down at him.

"I would wish you a good afternoon," Smoke told him, "but with you here, it is anything but that."

Cat stared at him, ignoring the remark; Smoke was not

sure the man even knew what he meant by it. "I seen you somewheres before, artist," the gunfighter, outlaw, and murderer said. "And you wasn't drawin' no pitchers on paper, neither."

"Perhaps if you dwell on it long enough, it will come to you in time, Mister-whatever-your-name is. Not that I particularly care at this juncture."

"Huh! Boy, you got a damn smart mouth on you, ain't you? I'm Cat Ventura."

"Not a pleasure, I'm sure. Very well, Mr. Meow. If you came up here to ask me to sketch you, my studio is closed for the time being. Perhaps some other time; like in the next century."

"You piss-headed smart ass! When the time comes, I think I'll jist stomp your guts out; see what color they is. How 'bout that, sissy-pants?"

"Oh, I don't think so, Mr. Purr. I really have my doubts about you doin' that."

Before he turned away to walk back down the hill, Cat said, "I know you from somewheres. It'll come to me. I'll be back."

"I'll certainly be here."

Smoke lay on his ground sheet and watched a passing parade of outlaws visit him during the next few minutes. Some walked up and stared at him. A few made open threats on his life.

He would have liked to ask why the sudden shift in their attitude toward him, but he really wasn't all that interested in the why of it.

Smoke checked the mountain sky. About three hours until dusk. He rose from the ground and got his fishing pole, checking the line and hook. Jake and Shorty and

Red had been watching him, hunkered down at the base of the hill. Out of the corner of his eyes, Smoke saw them all relax and reach for the makings, rolling and lighting cigarettes. He stepped back into the timber behind his camp, as if heading for the little creek to fish and catch his supper. Smoke assumed his line of credit at the Bon Ton Café had been cut off. The food hadn't been all that good anyway.

Out of sight of the trio of outlaws, Smoke dropped his pole and walked toward the center of town, staying inside the thin timber line until he was opposite the privy and the pile of lumber behind the saloon. He quickly stepped to the lumber, moved a couple of boards, and spotted the rolled-up packet.

The back door to the saloon opened, a man stepping out. "What you doin', boy? Sneakin' around here. You tryin' to slip out, pretty-pants?"

Smoke looked up as the man closed the door behind him and walked toward him. His hand closed around a sturdy two-by-four, about three feet long and solid. "Just borrowing a few boards, sir. I thought I might build a board floor for my tent. Is that all right with you?"

The outlaw stepped closer, Smoke recognizing him as a wanted murderer. "No, it ain't all right with me. You jist git your butt on out of here."

Smoke could smell the odor of rotting human flesh from those unfortunates hanging from the meat hooks at the edge of town. Those few still alive were moaning and crying out in pain.

Smoke looked around him. They were alone. He smiled at the outlaw. "Playtime is all over, you bastard."

"What'd you say to me, fancy-pants?" The man stepped

closer, almost within swinging distance. Just a few feet more and Smoke would turn out the man's lights. Forever.

"I said you stink like sheep-shit and look like the ass end of a donkey."

Cursing, growling deep in his throat, the outlaw charged Smoke. Smoke jerked up the two-by-four and laid the lumber up against the man's head. The outlaw stopped, as if he had run into a stone wall. His skull popped under the impact. He dropped to the earth, dying, blood leaking from his ears and nose and mouth.

Smoke dropped the two-by-four and quickly dragged the man behind the privy, stretching him out full length behind the two-holer. He could only be seen from the timber.

Smoke took the man's two .44s and punched out the shells from the loops of his belt. He grabbed up his own guns and walked back into the timber, heading for his campsite.

He was smiling, humming softly.

They had said their good-byes to their wives and kids and girlfriends and swung into the saddle, pointing the noses of their horses north, toward the outlaw town.

One deputy from an adjoining county had been caught trying to make it alone to Dead River. He had been brought back to face Jim Wilde. It turned out his brother was one of the outlaws living in Dead River. The deputy was now locked down hard in his own jail, under heavy guard.

The members of the posse were, to a man, hard-faced and grim. All knew that some of them would not live through the night that lay before them. And while none of them wanted to die, they knew that what lay ahead of them was something that had to be done, should have been done a long time back. The outlaw town had been a blight on society for years, and the time had come to destroy it and all who chose to reside within its confines.

The riders each carried at least two pistols belted around their waists. Most had two more six-guns, either tucked behind their belts or carried in holsters, tied to their saddles. All carried a rifle in the boot; some had added a shotgun, the express guns loaded with buckshot. The men had stuffed their pockets full of .44s, .45s, and shotgun shells.

The posse rode at a steady, distance-covering gait; already they had changed horses and were now approaching Red Davis's place. While the hands switched saddles, the men of the posse grabbed and wolfed down a sandwich and coffee, then refilled canteens. All checked their guns, wiping them free of dust and checking the action.

"Wish I was goin' with you," Davis said. "I'd give a thousand dollars to see that damn town burned slap to the ground."

Wilde nodded his head. "Red, there'll be doctors and the like comin' out here and settin' up shop 'bout dark. Some of us are gonna be hard-hit and the slaves in that town are gonna be in bad shape. You got your wagon ready to meet us at the mouth of the pass?"

"All hitched up." He spat on the ground. "And me and my boys will take care of any stragglers that happen to wander out when the shootin' starts."

Jim Wilde smiled grimly. Between the Utes and Red Davis's hard-bitten hands, any outlaws who happened to escape were going to be in for a very rough time of it.

Red's ranch had been the first in the area, and the old man was as tough as leather—and so were his hands.

Red clasped Jim on the shoulder. "Luck to you, boy. And I wanna meet this Smoke Jensen. That there is my kind of man."

Jim nodded and turned, facing the sixty-odd men of the posse. The U.S. Marshal wore twin .44s, tied down. He carried another .44 in his shoulder holster and a rifle and a shotgun in the boots, on his horse. "All right, boys. This is the last jumpin'-off place. From here on in, they's no turnin' back. You gotta go to the outhouse, get it done now. When we get back into the saddle, we ain't stoppin' until we're inside Dead River." He glanced at the sinking sun. "Smoke's gonna open up the dance in about an hour—if he's still alive," he added grimly. "And knowin' him he is. Anybody wanna back out of this?"

No one did.

"Let's ride!"

The guards along the pass road had just changed, the new guards settling in for a long and boring watch. Nothing ever happened; a lot of the time many of them dozed off. They would all sleep this dusky evening. Forever.

One guard listened for a few seconds. Was that a noise behind him? He thought it was. He turned, brought his rifle up, and came face to face with a war-painted Indian. He froze, opening his mouth to yell a warning. The shout was forever locked in his throat as an axe split his skull. The Ute caught the bloody body before it could fall to the ground and lowered it to the earth. The body would never be found; time and wind and rain and the elements and animals would dispose of the flesh and scatter the bones. A hundred years later, small boys playing would discover the gold coins the outlaw had had in his pockets and would wonder how the money came to be in this lonely spot.

His job done, for the moment, the brave slipped back into the timber and waited.

Up and down the heavily guarded narrow road, the guards were meeting an end just as violent as the life they had chosen to live. And they had chosen it; no one had forced them into it. One outlaw guard, who enjoyed torturing Indians, especially children, and raping squaws, was taken deep into the timber, gagged, stripped, and staked out. Then he was skinned—alive.

Their first job done, the Indians quietly slipped back and took their positions around the outlaw town of Dead River. With the patience bred into them, they waited and watched, expressionless.

York looked up and blinked, at first not recognizing the tall muscular man who was walking toward him, out of the timber. Then he recognized him.

"Damn, DeBeers. I didn't know you at first. How come you shaved off your beard?"

"It was time. And my name is not DeBeers."

"Yeah. I kinda figured it was a phony. And I didn't believe that Shirley bit, neither."

"That's right. You get my boots and spurs?"

York pointed to a bag on the ground. He had never seen such a change in any man. The man standing in front of him looked . . . awesome!

Smoke was dressed all in black, from his boots to his

shirt. His belt was black with inlaid silver that caught the last glows of the setting sun. He wore a red bandana around his neck. He had buckled on twin .44s, the left handgun worn butt-forward, cross-draw style. He had shoved two more .44s behind his belt.

"Ah . . . man, you best be careful with them guns," York cautioned. "You packin' enough for an army. Are you fixin' to start a war around here?"

"That is my hope, York."

"Yeah?" Somehow, that did not come as any surprise to York. There was something about this tall man that was just . . . well, unsettling. He poured a cup of coffee and sipped it, hot, strong, and black. He looked at the tall man. Naw, he thought, it couldn't be. But he sure looked like all the descriptions York had ever heard about the gun-fighter. "Who are you, man?"

Smoke pulled a badge from his pocket and pinned it to his shirt. "I'm a United States Deputy Marshal. And as far as I'm concerned, York, all those warrants against you are not valid. And when we get out of here, I'll see that they are recalled. How does that sound to you?"

York took a sip of coffee. Oddly, to Smoke, he had shown no surprise. "Sounds good to me, Marshal." He stood up and pulled a gold badge out of his pocket and pinned it on his shirt. "Buddy York is the name. Arizona Rangers. I was wonderin' if you plan on corralin' this town all by your lonesome."

"That's a good cover story of yours, Ranger," Smoke complimented him.

"Well, took us six months to set it up. The dodgers that are out are real. Had to be that way."

"I gather you have warrants for some people in here?"

"A whole passel of them, including some on Dagget."

"There is a large posse on the way in. They'll be here just at dusk. The Utes have taken care of the guards along the road."

York looked up at the sky. "That's a good hour and a half away, Marshal." He was grinning broadly.

"That's the way I got it figured, Ranger. Of course, you do know that you have no jurisdiction in this area?"

"I'll worry about that later."

"Consider yourself deputized with full government authority."

"I do thank you, Marshal."

"You ready to open this dance, Ranger?" Smoke sat down on a log and buckled on his spurs. He looked up as York opened another bag and tossed him a black hat, low crowned and flat brimmed. "Thanks. I am ever so glad to be rid of that damned silly cap." He tried the hat. A perfect fit.

"You did look a tad goofy. But I got to hand it to you. You're one hell of a fine actor."

Both men stuffed their pockets full of shells.

Rifle in hand, York said, "What is your handle, anyways?"

"Smoke Jensen," the tall, heavily muscled man said with a smile.

York's knees seemed to buckle and he sat down heavily on a log. When he found his voice, he said, "Holy jumpin' Jesus Christ!"

"I'm new to the marshaling business, Ranger. I just took this on a temporary basis." Then he explained what had happened at his ranch, to his wife.

"Takes a low-life SOB to attack a lone woman. I gather you want Davidson and Dagget and them others all to yourself, right?"

"I would appreciate it, Ranger."

"They're all yours."

Smoke checked his guns, slipping them both in and out of leather a few times. He filled both cylinders and every loop on his gunbelt, then checked the short-barreled pistol he carried in his shoulder holster. Breaking open the sawed-off shotgun, he filled both barrels with buckshot loads. Smoke looked on with approval as the ranger pulled two spare .44s out of his warbag and loaded them full. He tucked them behind his belt and picked up a Henry repeating rifle, loading it full and levering in a round, then replacing that round in the magazine.

"I'll tell you how I see this thing, Ranger. You don't have to play this way, but I'm going to."

"I'm listenin', Smoke."

"I'm not taking any prisoners."

"I hadn't planned on it myself."

The men smiled at each other, knowing then exactly where the other stood.

Their pockets bulging with extra cartridges, York carrying a Henry and Smoke carrying the sawed-off express gun, they looked at each other.

"You ready to strike up the band, Ranger?"

"Damn right!" York said with a grin.

"Let's do it!"

CHAPTER THIRTEEN

Marshal Jim Wilde's posse had an hour to go before reaching Dead River when Smoke and York stepped into the back of the saloon. Inside, the piano player was banging out and singing a bawdy song.

"How do we do this?" York asked.

"We walk in together," Smoke whispered.

The men slipped the thongs off their six-guns and eased them out of leather a time or two, making certain the oiled interiors of the holsters were free.

York eased back the hammer on his Henry and Smoke jacked back the hammers on the express gun.

They stepped inside the noisy and beer-stinking saloon. The piano player noticed them first. He stopped playing and singing and stared at them, his face chalk-white. Then he scrambled under the lip of the piano.

"Well, well!" an outlaw said, laughing. "Would you boys just take a look at Shirley. He's done shaven offen his beard and taken to packin' iron. Boy, you bes' git shut of them guns, 'fore you hurt yourself."

Gridley stood up from a table where he'd been drinking and playing poker—and losing. "Or I decide to take 'em off you and shove 'em up your butt, lead and all, pretty-boy. Matter of fact, I think I'll jist do that, right now."

Smoke and York had surveyed the scene as they had stepped in. The barroom was not nearly filled to capacity . . . but it was full enough.

"The name isn't pretty-boy, Gridley," Smoke informed him.

"Oh, yeah? Well, mayhaps you right. I'll jist call you shit! How about that?"

"Why don't you call him by his real name?" York said, a smile on his lips.

"And what might that be, punk?" Gridley sneered the question. "Alice?"

"First off," York said. "I'll tell you I'm an Arizona Ranger. Note the badges we're wearing? And his name, you blowholes, is Smoke Jensen!"

The name was dropped like a bomb. The outlaws in the room sat stunned, their eyes finally observing the gold badges on the chests of the men.

Smoke and York both knew one thing for an ironclad fact: The men in the room might all be scoundrels and thieves and murderers, and some might be bullies and cowards, but when it came down to it, they were going to fight.

"Then draw, you son of a bitch!" Gridley hollered, his hands dropping to his guns.

Smoke pulled the trigger on the express gun. From a distance of no more than twenty feet, the buckshot almost tore the outlaw in two.

York leveled the Henry and dusted an outlaw from side to side. Dropping to one knee, he levered the empty out and a fresh round in and shot a fat punk in the belly.

Shifting the sawed-off shotgun, Smoke blew the head off

another outlaw. The force of the buckshot lifted the headless outlaw out of one boot and flung him to the sawdust-covered floor.

York and his Henry had put half a dozen outlaws on the floor, dead, dying, or badly hurt.

The huge saloon was filled with gunsmoke, the crying and moaning of the wounded, and the stink or relaxed bladders from the dead. Dark gray smoke from the black powder cartridges stung the eyes and obscured the vision of all in the room.

The outlaws had recovered from their initial shock and had overturned tables, crouching behind them, returning the deadly hail of fire from Smoke and Arizona Ranger York.

Smoke had slipped to the end of the bar closest to the batwing doors, and York had worked his way to the side of the big stage, crouching behind a second piano in the small orchestra pit. Between the two of them, Smoke and York were laying down a deadly field of fire. Both men had grabbed up the guns of the dead and dying men as they slipped to their new positions and they now had a pile of .44s, .45s, and several shotguns and rifles in front of them.

A half-dozen outlaws tried to rush the batwings in a frantic attempt to escape and were met by a half-dozen other outlaws attempting to enter the saloon from the outside. It created a massive pileup at the batwings, a pileup that was too good for Smoke to resist.

Slipping to the very end of the long bar, Smoke emptied a pair of .45s taken from a dead man into the panicked knot of outlaws. Screaming from the men as the hot slugs tore into their flesh added to the earsplitting cacophony of confusion in the saloon.

Smoke grabbed up an armload of weapons and ran to the end of the bar closest to the rear of the saloon. He caught York's attention and motioned to the storeroom where they had entered. York nodded and left his position at a run. The men ran through the darkened storeroom to the back door.

Just as they reached the back door it opened and two outlaws stepped inside, guns drawn. Smoke and York fired simultaneously, their guns booming and crashing in the darkness, lancing smoke and fire, splitting the heavy gloom of the storeroom. The outlaws were flung backward, outside. They lay on the ground, on their backs, dying from wounds to the chest and belly.

"York, you take the north end of town," Smoke said. "I'll take the south end." He was speaking as he was stripping the weapons from the dead men.

York nodded his agreement and tossed Smoke one of two cloth sacks he'd picked up in the storeroom. The men began dumping in the many guns they'd picked up along the way.

"Find and destroy the heathens!" a man's strong voice cut the night. "The Philistines are upon us!"

"Who the hell is that?" York whispered.

"That's Tustin, the preacher. Has to be."

"A preacher? Here?" The ranger's voice was filled with disbelief.

The gunfire had almost ceased, as the outlaws in the saloon could not find Smoke or York.

"Oh, Lord!" Tustin's voice filled the night. "Take these poor unfortunate bastards into the gates of Heaven and give us the strength and the wherewithal to find and shoot the piss outta them that's attackin' us!"

"I ain't believin' this," York muttered.

Smoke smiled, his strong white teeth flashing in the night. "Good luck, York."

"Same to you, partner."

Carrying their heavy sacks of weapons and cartridge-filled belts, the men parted, one heading north, the other heading south.

York and Smoke both held to the edge of the timber as they made their way north and south. The town's inhabitants had adopted a panicked siege mentality, with outlaws filling the streets, running in every direction. No one among them knew how many men were attacking the town. Both York and Smoke had heard the shouts that hundreds of lawmen were attacking.

Just before Smoke slipped past the point where he could look up and see the fine home of Davidson, he saw the lamps in the house being turned off, the home on the hill growing dark.

And Smoke would have made a bet that Davidson and Dagget had a rabbit hole out of Dead River, and that both of them, and probably a dozen or more of their most trusted henchmen, were busy packing up and getting out.

Just for a moment, Smoke studied the darkened outline of the home on the hill. And then it came to him. A cave. He would be a hundred dollars that King Rex had built his home in front of a cave, a cave that wound through the mountain and exited out in the timbered range behind Dead River. And he would also bet that White Wolf and his braves knew nothing of it. It might exit out into a little valley where horses and gear could be stored.

Cursing in disgust for not thinking of that sooner, Smoke

slipped on into the night, seeking a good spot to set up a defensive position.

He paused for a moment, until York had opened fire, showing Smoke where the ranger had chosen to make his stand. And it was a good one, high up on the right side of the ridge overlooking the town, as Smoke stood looking north. With a smile, Smoke chose his position on the opposite side of the street, above the first store one encountered upon entering the outlaw town.

Below him, the outlaws had settled down, taking up positions around the town. Smoke could see several bodies sprawled in the street, evidence of York's marksmanship with his Henry.

A handful of outlaws tried to rush the ranger's position. Hard gunfire broke out on either side and above York's position. White Wolf's Utes were making their presence known in a very lethal manner. For years, the outlaws had made life miserable for the Utes, and now it was payback time. With a vengeance.

A horseman came galloping up the street, toward the curve that exited the town. The man was riding low in the saddle, the reins in his teeth and both hands full of six-guns. Smoke took careful aim with a rifle he'd picked up in the saloon and knocked the man out of the saddle. The rider hit the ground hard and rolled, coming up on his feet. A dozen rifles spat lead. The man was hit a dozen times, shot to bloody rags. He dropped to the roadway, his blood leaking into the dirt.

The horse, reins trailing, trotted off into an alley.

Smoke hit the ground, behind a series of boulders, as his position was found and rifles began barking and spitting in the night, the lead ricocheting and whining off the huge rocks, spinning into the night.

A Ute came rolling down the hill crashing against the boulder behind which Smoke was hiding. Smoke rolled the brave over and checked his wound—a nasty wound in the brave's side. Smoke plugged it with moss and stretched the Indian out, safe from fire. The Ute's dark eyes had never left Smoke's face, and he endured the pain without a sound.

Smoke made the sign for brother and the Indian, flat on his back returned the gesture. Gunfighter and Indian smiled at each other in the gunfire-filled night above the outlaw town.

Smoke picked up his rifle as the Indian, who had never let go of his rifle, crawled to a position on the other end of the line of boulders. Smoke tossed him a bag of cartridges and the men began lacing the town with .44 rifle fire. The .44s, which could punch through a good three inches of pine, began bringing shouts and yells of panic from the outlaws in the town below.

Several tried to run; they were knocked down in the street. One outlaw, his leg twisted grotesquely, tried to crawl to safety. A slug to the head stopped his strugglings.

Smoke spoke to the Ute in his own language. "If they ever discover how few we are up here, we're in trouble, brother."

The Ute laughed in the night and said, "My people have always fought outnumbered, gunfighter. It is nothing new to us."

Smoke returned the laugh and began working the lever on his Henry, laying a line of lead into a building below their position. The sudden hard fire brought several screams of pain from inside the building. One man fell through a shattered window to hang there, half in and half out of the building.

The Ute shouted a warning as a dozen outlaws charged their position, the men slipping from tree to tree, rock to rock, working closer.

Smoke quickly reloaded the Henry and laid two .44s on the ground beside him, one by each leg. There was no doubt in his mind that the outlaws would certainly breach their position, and then the fighting would be hand to hand.

Smoke heard the ugly sound of a bullet striking flesh and bone, and turning his head, he saw the Ute fall backward, a blue-tinged hole in the center of his forehead. With his right hand, Smoke made the Indian sign for peaceful journey and then returned to the fight.

He took out one outlaw who made the mistake of exposing too much of his body, knocking the man spinning from behind a tree; a second slug from Smoke's rifle forever stilled the man.

Then there was no time for anything except survival, as the outlaws charged Smoke's position.

Smoke fought savagely, his guns sending several outlaws into that long darkness. Then his position was overrun. Something slammed into the side of his head, and Smoke was dropped into darkness.

CHAPTER FOURTEEN

He was out for no more than a few seconds, never really losing full consciousness. He felt blood dripping down the side of his face. He was still holding onto his guns, and he remembered they were full. Lifting them, as a dozen shapes began materializing around him in the night, Smoke began cocking and pulling the triggers.

Hoarse screams filled the air around him as the slugs from his pistols struck their mark at point-blank range. Unwashed bodies thudded to the ground all around him, the dead and dying flesh unwittingly building a fort around his position, protecting him from the returning fire of the outlaws.

Then, half-naked shapes filtered silently and swiftly out of the timber, firing rifles and pistols. By now, the remaining outlaws were too confused and frightened to understand how a man whom they believed to be dead from a head wound had managed to inflict so hideous a toll on them.

And then the Utes came out of the timber, and in a matter of seconds, what had been twenty outlaws were no more than dying, cooling flesh in the still-warm mountain air slightly above Dead River.

The Utes vanished back into the timber, as swiftly and as silently as they had come.

Smoke reloaded his guns, pistols, and rifles, and slung the rifles across his shoulders. He wrapped his bandana around his head and tied it, after inspecting his head-wound with his fingers and finding it not serious; he knew that a head wound can bleed hard and fast for a few moments, and then, in many cases, stop.

He loaded his pistols, then loaded the sawed-off shotgun. Then he began making his way down the hill, back into the town of Dead River. He was going to take the fight to the outlaws.

He stopped once to tie a white handkerchief around his arm, so not only the Indians would know who he was but so the posse members would not mistakenly shoot him.

He slipped down to the building where the outlaw was still hanging half out of the window and quietly checked out the interior. The building was void of life. Looking up the street, he could see where he, York, and the Utes had taken a terrible toll on the population of the outlaw town. The street, the alleys, and the boardwalks were littered with bodies. Most were not moving.

He did not know how much time had transpired since he and Ranger had opened the dance. But he was sure it was a good half hour or forty-five minutes.

He slipped to the south a few yards and found a good defensible position behind a stone wall that somebody had built around a small garden. Smoke pulled a ripe tomato off the vine, brushed the dust off it, and ate it while his eyes surveyed the street, picking out likely targets.

He unslung the rifles, laid his sack of guns and cartridges by one side, the express guns by his other side, and then picked up and checked out a Henry.

He had found a man stationed on top of a building. Sighting him in, Smoke let the other outlaws know he was still in the game by knocking the man off the roof with one well-placed shot to his belly. The sniper fell screaming to the street below. His howling stopped as he impacted with earth.

Putting his hand to the ground, Smoke thought he could detect a trembling. Bending over, being careful not to expose his butt to the guns of the outlaws, he pressed his ear to the ground and picked up the sound of faint rumblings. The posse was no more than a mile away.

"York!" he yelled.

"Yo, Smoke!" came the call.

"Here they come, Ranger! Shovel the coals to it!"

Smoke began levering and pulling the trigger, laying down a blistering line of fire into the buildings of the town. From his position at the other end, York did the same. The Utes opened up from both sides of the town, and the night rocked with gunfire.

"For the love of God!" Sheriff Larsen cried out, reining up by the lines of tortured men and women on the outskirts of town. His eyes were utterly disbelieving as they touched each tortured man and woman.

"Help us!" came the anguished cry of one of the few still alive. "Have mercy on us, please. We were taken against our will and brought here."

The posse of hardened western men, accustomed to

savage sights, had never seen anything like this. All had seen Indian torture; but that was to be expected from ignorant savages. But fellow white men had done this.

Several of the posse leaned out of their saddles and puked on the ground.

"Three or four men stay here and cut these poor wretches down," Jim Wilde ordered, his voice strong over the sound of gunfire. "Do what you can for them."

"Jim!" Smoke called. "It's Jensen. Hold your fire, I'm coming over."

Smoke zigzagged over to the posse, catching the reins of a horse as the man discounted. "Your horses look in good shape."

"We rested them about a mile back. Let them blow good and gave them half a hatful of water. How's your head?"

"My Sally has hit me harder," Smoke grinned, swinging into the saddle. He patted the roan's neck and rubbed his head, letting the animal know he was friendly.

"You comin' in with us?" the marshal asked.

"I got personal business to tend to. There's an Arizona Ranger named York up yonder." He pointed. "I forgot to tell him to tie something about his arm. He's a damn good man. Good luck to you boys."

Smoke swung the horse's head, and with a screaming yell from the throats of sixty men, the posse hit the main street hard. The reins in their teeth, the posse members had their hands full of .44s and .45s, and they were filling anybody they saw with lead.

Smoke rode behind the buildings of the town and dismounted, ground-reining the horse. He eased the hammers back on the express gun and began walking, deliberately letting his spurs jingle.

"Jensen!" a voice shouted from the forward darkness. "Smoke Jensen!"

Stepping behind a corner of a building, Smoke said, "Yeah, that's me."

"Cat Ventura here. You played hell, Jensen."

"That's what I came here to do, Ventura."

Step out and face an ambush, you mean, Smoke thought. "No, thanks, Ventura. I don't trust you."

As soon as he said it, Smoke dropped to the ground. A half-dozen guns roared and sparked, the lead punching holes in the corner of the building where he'd been standing.

Smoke came up on one knee and let the hammers fall on both barrels of the sawed-off shotgun. He almost lost the weapon as both barrels fired, the gun recoiling in his strong hands.

The screaming of the wounded men was horrible in the night. Smoke thought of those poor people at the end of town and could not dredge up one ounce of sympathy for the outlaws he'd just blasted.

He reloaded the shotgun just as Cat called out, "Goddamn you, Jensen."

Smoke fired at the sound of the voice. A gurbling sound reached his ears. Then silence, except for the heavy pounding of gunfire in the street.

He slipped out of the alley and looked down at what was left of Cat Ventura. The full load of buckshot had taken him in the chest and throat. It was not pretty, but then, Cat hadn't been very pretty when he was alive.

Smoke stepped over the gore and continued his walking

up the back alley. The posse had dismounted and were taking the town building by building. But the outlaws remaining were showing no inclination to give up the fight. The firing was not as intense as a few moments past, but it was steady.

Smoke caught a glimpse of several men slipping up the alley toward him. He eased back the hammers of the express gun and stepped deeper into the shadows, a privy to his left.

Smoke recognized the lead man as an outlaw called Brawley, a man who had been in trouble with the law and society in general since practically the moment of birth. There were so many wanted posters out on Brawley that the man had been forced to drop out of sight a couple of years back. Now Smoke knew where he'd been hiding.

Smoke stepped out of the shadows and pulled both triggers. The sawed-off shotgun spewed its cargo of ball bearings, nails, and assorted bits of metal. Brawley took one load directly in the chest, lifting the murderer off his feet and sending him sprawling. The man to Brawley's right caught part of a load in the face. Smoke recalled that the man had thought himself to be handsome.

That was no longer the case.

The third man had escaped most of the charge and had thrown himself to the ground. He pulled himself up to his knees, his hands full of .44s. Holding the shotgun in his left hand, Smoke palmed his .44 and saved the public the expense of a trial.

"The goddamn Injuns got Cahoon!" a hoarse yell sprang out of the night.

Smoke turned, reloading the sawed-off, trying to determine how close the man was.

"Hell with Cahoon!" another yelled. Very close to Smoke. "It's ever' man for hisself now."

Smoke pulled the triggers and fire shot out of the twin barrels, seeming to push the lethal loads of metal. Horrible screaming was heard for a moment, and then the sounds of bootheels drumming the ground in death.

Smoke reloaded and walked on.

At a gap between buildings, Smoke could see York, still in position, still spitting out lead from his Henry. The bodies in the street paid mute testimony to the ranger's dead aim.

A man wearing a white armband ducked into the gap and spotted Smoke.

"Easy," Smoke called. "Jensen here."

Smoke could see the badge on his chest, marking him as a U.S. Marhsal.

"Windin' down," the man said. "Thought I'd take me a breather. You and that Arizona Ranger played hell, Smoke."

"That was our intention. You got the makin's? I lost my sack."

The man tossed Smoke a bag of tobacco and papers. Squatting down, out of the line of fire, Smoke and the marshal rolled, licked, and lit.

Smoke could see the lawman had been hit a couple of times, neither of the wounds serious enough to take him out of a fight.

"I figure the big boys got loose free," Smoke spoke over a sudden hard burst of gunfire. He jerked his head. "That's Davidson's big house up yonder on the ridge. . . ."

Jim Wilde almost got himself plugged as he darted into the alley and slid to a halt, catching his breath.

"I dearly wish you would announce your intentions,

ol' hoss," the marshal said to him. "You near'bouts got drilled."

"Gimme the makin's, Glen, I lost my pouch. " Jim holstered his guns.

While Jim rolled a cigarette, Smoke elaborated on his theory of the kingpins escaping.

"Well, let us rest for a minute and then we'll take us a hike up yonder to the house. Check it out." He puffed for a moment. "I've arranged for a judge to be here at first light," he said. "The hands from Red Davis's place is gonna act as jury. Red'll be jury foreman. Soon as we clean out the general store, I got some boys ready to start workin' on ropes."

"Hezekiah Jones the judge?" Glen asked.

"Yep."

"Gonna be some short trials."

"Yep."

"And they's gonna be a bunch of newspaper folks and photographers here, too."

"Yep."

An outlaw tried to make a break for it, whipping his horse up the street toward the edge of town. A dozen guns barked, slamming the outlaw out of the saddle. He rolled on the street and was still.

Glen looked at the body of the outlaw. "I'm thinkin' there might not be all that many to be tried."

Jim Wilde ground out the butt of his smoke under his heel and stood up. "Yep," he said.

Jim was known to be a spare man with words.

CHAPTER FIFTEEN

The battle for the outlaw town of Dead River was winding down sharply as Smoke and the marshals made their way up the hill to Rex Davidson's fine home. They passed a half-dozen bodies on the curving path, all outlaws. All three men were conscious of eyes on them as they walked up the stone path. . . . Utes, waiting in the darkness, watching.

Somewhere back in the timber, a man screamed in agony.

"Cahoon," Smoke told the men.

Glen replied, "Whatever he gets, he earned."

That pretty well summed up the feelings of all three men. Jim pulled out his watch and checked the time. Smoke was surprised to learn it was nearly ten o'clock. He stopped and listened for a moment. Something was wrong.

Then it came to him: The gunfire had ceased.

"Yeah," Jim remarked. "I noticed it too. Eerie, ain't it?"

The men walked on, stepping onto the porch of the house. Motioning the lawmen away from the front door in case it was booby-trapped, Smoke stepped to one side and eased it open. The door opened silently on well-oiled hinges.

Smoke was the first in, the express gun ready. Jim and Glen came in behind him, their hands full of pistols. But the caution had been unnecessary; the room was void of human life.

The men split up, each taking a room. They found nothing. The big house was empty. But everywhere there were signs of hurried packing. The door to the big safe was open, the safe empty of cash. Jim began going through the ledgers and other papers, handing a pile to Glen while Smoke prowled the house. At the rear of the house he found the rabbit hole, and he had been correct in his thinking. The home had been built in front of a cave opening. He called for Jim and Glen.

"You was right," Jim acknowledged. "We'll inspect it in the morning. I'll post guards here tonight." He held out the papers taken from the safe. "Interestin' readin' in here, Smoke. All kinds of wanted posters and other information on the men who lived here. What we've done—it was mostly you and York—is clean out a nest of snakes. We've made this part of the country a hell of a lot safer."

On the way back to the town, Smoke spotted the Ute chief, White Wolf. The men stopped, Jim saying, "We're goin' to try them that's still alive, White Wolf. Do that in the mornin'. We should be out of the town by late tomorrow afternoon. When we pull out, the town and everything in it is yours."

"I thank you," the chief said gravely. "My people will not be cold or hungry this winter." He turned to Smoke and smiled. "My brother, Preacher, would be proud of you. I will see that he hears of this fight, young warrior."

"Thank you, Chief. Give him my best."

White Wolf nodded, shook hands with the men, and then was gone.

Cahoon was still screaming.

It was a sullen lot that were rounded up and herded into the compound for safekeeping. A head count showed fifty hardcases had elected to surrender or were taken by force, usually the latter.

But, as Smoke had feared, many of the worst ones had slipped out. Shorty, Red, and Jake were gone. Bill Wilson's body had been found, but Studs Woodenhouse, Tie Medley, Paul Rycroft, and Slim Bothwell were gone. Hart and Ayers were dead, riddled with bullets. But Natick, Nappy, LaHogue, and Brute Pitman had managed to escape. Tustin could not be found among the dead, so all had to assume the so-called minister had made it out alive. Sheriff Danvers had been taken prisoner, and Sheriff Larsen had told him he was going to personally tie the noose for him. Dagget, Glen Moore, Lapeer and, of course, Rex Davidson were gone.

Smoke knew he would have them to deal with—sooner or later, and probably sooner.

Smoke bathed in the creek behind the campsite, and he and York caught a few hours sleep before the judge and his jury showed up. They were to be in Dead River at dawn.

As had been predicted, there were several newspaper men with the judge, as well as several photographers. The bodies of the outlaws still lay in the street at dawn, when the judge, jury, reporters, and photographers showed up. Two of the half-dozen reporters were from New York City and Boston, on a tour of the wild West, and they were appalled at the sight that greeted them.

Old Red Davis, obviously enjoying putting the needle to the Easterners, showed them around the town, pointing out any sight they might have missed.

"See that fellow over yonder?" he pointed. The reporters and a photographer looked. "The man with a gold badge on his chest? That's the most famous gunfighter in all the West. He's kilt two/three hundred men. Not countin' Injuns. That's Smoke Jensen, boys!"

The Easterners gaped, one finally saying, "But why is the man wearing a badge? He's an outlaw!"

"He ain't no such thing," Red corrected. "He's just fast with a gun, that's all. The fastest man alive. Been all sorts of books writ about Smoke. Want to meet him?"

Foolish question.

Luckily for Smoke, Jim Wilde intercepted the group and took them aside. "You boys from back east walk light around the men in this town. This ain't Boston or New York. And while Smoke is a right nice fellow, with a fine ranch up north of here, he can be a mite touchy at times." Then the marshal brought the men up to date on what Smoke had done in Dead River.

The photographer set up his awkward equipment and began taking pictures of Smoke and the Arizona Ranger, York. Both men endured it, Smoke saying to York, "You got any warrants on any of them that cut and run?"

"Shore do. What you got in mind?"

The camera popped and puffed smoke into the air.

"I think Sally told me she was going to give birth about

October. I plan on bein' there when she does. That gives us a few months to prowl. Tell your bosses back in Arizona not to worry about the expenses; it's on me."

The camera snapped and clicked, and smoke went into the air as the chemical dust was ignited.

And Marshal Jim Wilde, unintentionally, gave the newspaper reporters the fuel that would, in time, ignite the biggest gunfight, western-style, in Keene, New Hampshire history.

"Smoke's wife is back in New Hampshire. He'll be going back there when she gives birth to their child. Now come on, I'll introduce you gentlemen to Smoke Jensen."

Judge Hezekiah Jones had set up his bench, so to speak, outside the saloon, with the jury seated to his left, on the boardwalk. Already, a gallows had been knocked together and ropes noosed and knotted. They could hang three at a time.

The trial of the first three took two and a half minutes. A minute and a half later, they were swinging.

"Absolutely the most barbaric proceedings I have ever witnessed," the Boston man sniffed, scribbling in his journal.

"Frontier justice certainly does leave a great deal to be desired," the New York City man agreed.

"I think I'm going to be ill," the photographer said, a tad green around the mouth.

"Hang 'em!" Judge Jones hit the table with his gavel, and three more were led off to meet their maker.

Sheriff Danvers stood before the bench, his hands tied

behind his back. "I have a statement to make, Your Honor," he said.

Hezekiah glared at him. "Oh, all right. Make your goddamn statement and then plead guilty, you heathen!"

"I ain't guilty!" Danvers shouted.

The judge turned to face the men of the jury. "How do you find?"

"Guilty!" Red called.

"Hang the son of a bitch!" Hezekiah ordered.

And so it went.

The hurdy-gurdy ladies and shopkeepers were hauled off in wagons. Smoke didn't ask where they were being taken because he really didn't care. The bodies of the outlaws were tossed into a huge pit and dirt and gravel shoveled over them. "I'd like to keep my federal commission, Jim," Smoke said. "I got a hunch this mess isn't over."

"Keep it as long as you like. You're makin' thirty a month and expenses." He grinned and shook Smoke's hand, then shook the hand of the ranger. "I'll ride any trail with you boys any time."

He wheeled his horse and was gone.

The wind sighed lonely over the deserted town as Smoke and York sat their horses on the hill overlooking the town. White Wolf and his people were moving into the town. The judge had ordered whatever money was left in the town to remain there. Let the Indians have it for their help in bringing justice to the godforsaken place, he had said.

Smoke waved at White Wolf and the chief returned the

gesture. Smoke and York turned their horses and put their backs to Dead River.

"What is this?" York asked. "July, August . . . what? I done flat lost all track of the months."

"I think it's September. I think Sally told me the first month she felt she was with child was March. So if she's going to have the baby the last part of October . . ."

York counted on his fingers, then stopped and looked at Smoke. "Do you want March as one?"

"Damned if I know!"

"We'll say you do." He once more began counting. "Yep. But that'd be eight months. So this might be August."

Smoke looked at him. "York . . . what in the hell are you talking about?"

York confessed that what he knew about the process of babies growing before the birth was rather limited.

"I think I better wire Sally and ask her," Smoke suggested.

"I think that'd be the wise thing to do."

Jim Wilde had told Smoke he would send a wire to Sally, telling her the operation was over and Smoke was all right. And he would do the same for York, advising the Arizona Ranger headquarters that York was in pursuit of those who had escaped.

Smoke and York cut across the Sangre de Cristo range, in search of the cave Davidson and his men had used to escape.

Sally got the wire one day before the Boston and New York newspapers ran the front-page story of the incident, calling it: JUSTICE AT DEAD RIVER. The pictures would follow in later editions.

John read the stories, now carried in nearly all papers in the East, and shook his head in disbelief, saying to his daughter, "Almost fifty men were hanged in one morning. Their trials took an average of three minutes per man. For God's sake, Sally, surely you don't agree with these kangaroo proceedings?"

"Father," the daughter said, knowing that the man would never understand, "it's a hard land. We don't have time for all the niceties you people take for granted back here."

"It doesn't bother you that your husband, Smoke, is credited—if that's the right choice of words—with killing some thirty or forty men?"

Sally shook her head. "No. I don't see why it should. You see, Father, you've taken a defense attorney's position already. And you immediately condemned Smoke and the other lawmen and posse members, without ever saying a word about those poor people who were kidnapped, enslaved, and then hung up on hooks to die by slow torture. You haven't said a word about the people those outlaws abused, robbed, murdered, raped, tortured, and then ran back to Dead River to hide and spend their ill-gotten gain. Even those papers there," she pointed, "admit that every man who was hanged was a confessed murderer, many of them multiple killers. They got whatever they deserved, Father. No more, and no less."

The father sighed and looked at his daughter. "The West has changed you, Sally. I don't know you anymore."

"Yes, I've changed, Father," she admitted. "For the

better." She smiled. "It's going to be interesting when you and Smoke meet."

"Yes," John agreed. "Quite."

It took Smoke and York three days after crossing the high range to find the cave opening and the little valley beneath it.

"Slick," York said. "If they hadn't a knocked down the bushes growin' in front of the mouth of that cave, we'd have had the devil's own hard time findin' it."

The men entered the cave opening, which was barely large enough to accommodate a standing man. And they knew from the smell that greeted them what they would find.

They looked down at the bloated and maggot-covered bodies on the cave floor.

"You know them?" Smoke asked.

"I seen 'em in town. But I never knowed their names. And I don't feel like goin' through their pockets to find out who they was, do you?"

Smoke shook his head. Both men stepped back outside, grateful to once more be out in the cool, fresh air. They breathed deeply, clearing their nostrils of the foul odor of death.

"Let's see if we can pick up a trail," Smoke suggested.

Old Preacher had schooled Smoke well. The man could track a snake across a flat rock. Smoke circled a couple of times, then called for York to join him.

"North." He pointed. "I didn't think they'd risk getting out into the sand dunes. They'll probably follow the timber line until they get close to the San Luis, then they'll ride the river, trying to hide their tracks. I'll make a bet they'll cut through Poncha Pass, then head east to the railroad town. They might stop at the hot springs first. You game?"

"Let's do it."

They picked up and lost the tracks a dozen times, but it soon became apparent that Smoke had pegged their direction accurately. At a village called Poncha Springs, past the San Luis Valley, Smoke and York stopped and re-supplied and bathed in the hot waters.

Yes, about a dozen hard-looking men had been through. Oh, five or six days back. They left here ridin' toward Salida. They weren't real friendly folks, neither. Looked like hard-cases.

Smoke and York pulled out the next morning.

At Salida, they learned that Davidson and his men had stopped, bought supplies and ammunition, and left the same day they'd come.

But one man didn't ride out with the others.

"He still in town?" Smoke asked.

"Shore is. Made his camp up by the Arkansas. 'Bout three miles out of town. But he's over to the saloon now."

Salida was new and raw, a railroad town built by the Denver and Rio Grande railroad. Salida was the division point of the main line and the narrow-gauge lines over what is called Marshall Pass.

"What's this ol' boy look like?" York asked.

The man described him.

"Nappy," Smoke said. "You got papers on him?"

"'Deed I do," York said, slipping the hammer thong off his .44.

"I'll back you up. Let's go."

"You look familiar, partner," the citizen said to Smoke. "What might be your name?"

"Smoke Jensen."

As soon as the lawmen had left, the man hauled his ashes up and down the muddy streets, telling everyone he could find that Smoke was in town.

"I know Nappy is wanted for rape and murder," Smoke said. "What else did he do?"

"Killed my older brother down between the Mogollon Plateau and the Little Colorado. Jimmy was a lawman, workin' out of Tucson. Nappy had killed an old couple just outside of town and Jimmy had tracked him north." York talked as they walked. "Nappy ambushed him. Gutshot my brother and left him to die. But Jimmy wasn't about to die 'fore he told who done him in. He crawled for miles until some punchers found him and he could tell them what happened, then he died. I was fifteen at the time. I joined the Rangers when I was eighteen. That was six years ago."

"I figured you for some younger than that."

"It's all the clean livin' I done," York said with a straight face.

Then they stepped into the saloon.

And Nappy wasn't alone.

The short, barrel-chested, and extremely ugly outlaw stood at the far end of the bar, his hands at his sides. Across the room were two more hardcases, also standing, each wearing two guns tied down low. To Smoke's extreme right, almost in the shadows, was another man, also standing.

"Napoleon Whitman?" York spoke to the stocky outlaw.

"That's me, punk."

"I'm an Arizona Ranger. It is my duty to inform you that you are under arrest for the murder of Tucson deputy sheriff Jimmy York."

"Do tell? Well, Ranger, this is Colorado. You ain't jack-shit up here."

"I have also been appointed a deputy U.S. Marshal, Nappy. Now how is it gonna be?"

"Well," Nappy drawled, as the men at the tables drifted back, out of the line of fire. And since Nappy had men posted all around the room, that meant getting clear out-side, which is what most did. "I think I'm gonna finish my drink, Ranger. That's what I think I'm gonna do. And since both you squirts is about to die, why don't y'all order yourselves a shot?"

Then he arrogantly turned his left side to the man and faced the bar. But both Smoke and York knew he was watching them in the mirror.

"He's all yours," Smoke murmured, just loud enough for York to hear. "Don't worry about the others."

York nodded. "I don't drink with scum," he told the ugly outlaw.

Nappy had lifted the shot glass to his mouth with his left hand. With that slur, he set the glass down on the bar and turned, facing the younger man. "What'd you say to me, punk?" The outlaw was not accustomed to be talked to in such a manner. After all, he was a famous and feared gunfighter, and punk kids respected him. They sure didn't talk smart to him.

"I said you're scum, Nappy. You're what's found at the bottom of an outhouse pit."

All were conscious of many faces peering inside the

dark barroom; many men pressed up against the glass from the boardwalk.

"You can't talk to me lak 'at!" Nappy almost screamed the words, and he could not understand the strange sensation that suddenly filled him.

It was fear.

Fear! The word clutched at Nappy's innards. Fear! Afraid of this snot-nosed pup with a tin star? He tried to shrug it off but found he could not.

"I just did, Nappy," York said. He smiled at the man; he could practically smell the fear-stink of the outlaw.

Nappy stepped away from the bar to stand wide-legged, facing York. "Then fill your hand, you son of a bitch!"

CHAPTER SIXTEEN

Smoke had been standing, half turned away from York, about three feet between them, his arms folded across his lower chest. When Nappy grabbed for iron, Smoke went into a low crouch and cross-drew, cocking and firing with one blindingly fast motion. First he shot the man in the shadows with his right-hand .44, then took out the closest of the two men to Nappy's immediate left.

Nappy had beaten York to the draw, but as so often happens, his first slug tore up the floor in front of York's boots. York had not missed a shot, but the stocky outlaw was soaking up the lead as fast as York could pump it into him and was still standing on his feet, tossing lead in return. He was holding onto the bar with his left hand and firing at York.

Smoke rolled across the floor and came up on his knees, both .44s hammering lead into the one man he faced who was still standing. The .44 slugs drew the life from the man and Smoke turned on one knee, splinters from the rough wood floor digging into his knee with the move. The man in the shadows was leaning against a wall, blood all over his shirt front, trying to level his .45. Smoke shot him in the face, and the man slid down the wall to rest on his butt, dead.

As the roaring left his ears and Smoke could once more see, Nappy was still standing, even though York had emptied his .44 into the man's chest and belly.

But Smoke could see he was not going to be standing much longer. The man's eyes were glazing over, and blood was pouring out of his mouth. His guns were laying on the floor beside his scuffed and dirty boots.

Nappy cut his eyes to Smoke. "That you, Jensen?" he managed to say.

"It's me, Nappy." Smoke stood up and walked toward the dying outlaw.

"Come closer, Jensen. I cain't see you. Dark in here, ain't it?"

Death's hand was slowly closing in on Nappy.

"What do you want, Nappy?"

"They'll get you, Jensen. They're gonna have their way with your uppity wife in front of your eyes, then they're gonna kill you slow. You ain't gonna find them, Jensen. They're dug in deep. But they'll find you. And that's a promise, Jensen. That's . . ."

His knees buckled and his eyes rolled back into his head until only the whites were showing. Nappy crashed to the barroom floor and died.

Both lawmen punched out empties and reloaded. York said, "I'll send a wire to the Tucson office and tell them to recall the dodgers on Nappy. You hit anywhere?"

"'Bout a dozen splinters in my knee is all."

"I'll be back, and then we'll have us a drink."

"Sounds good. I'll have one while I'm waiting. Hurry up, I hate to drink alone."

* * *

Smoke lost the trail. It wasn't the first time it had happened in his life, but it irked him even more this time. Smoke and York had trailed the outlaws to just outside of Crested Butte, and there they seemed to just drop off the face of the earth.

The lawmen backtracked and circled, but it was no use; the trail was lost.

After five more days of fruitless and frustrating looking, they decided to give it up.

They were camped near the banks of Roaring Fork, cooking some fish they'd caught for supper, both their mouths salivating at the good smells, when Drifter's head and ears came up.

"We got company," Smoke said softly.

"So I noticed. Injuns, you reckon?"

"I don't think so. Drifter acts different when it's Indians."

"Hallo, the fire!" a voice called.

"If you're friendly," Smoke returned the shout, "come on in. We caught plenty of fish and the coffee's hot."

"Music to my ears, boys." A man stepped into camp, leading his horses, a saddle mount and a packhorse. "Name's McGraw, but I'm called Chaw."

"That's Buddy York and I'm Smoke Jensen."

Chaw McGraw damn near swallered his chaw when he heard the name Smoke Jensen. He coughed and spat a couple of times, and then dug in his kit for a battered tin cup. He poured a cup of coffee and sat down, looking at Smoke.

"Damned if it ain't you! I figured you for some older.

But there you sit, bigger 'en life. I just read about you in a paper a travelin' drummer gimme. Lemme git it for you; it ain't but a week old. Outta Denver."

The paper told the story of the big shoot-out and the hangings and the final destruction of the outlaw town of Dead River. It told all about Smoke and York and then, with a sinking feeling in the pit of his stomach, Smoke read about Sally being back in Keene, New Hampshire, awaiting the birth of their first child.

"What's wrong, partner?" York asked, looking at the strange expression on Smoke's face.

Not wanting to take any chances on what he said being repeated by Chaw, Smoke minutely shook his head and handed the paper to York. "Nothing."

York read the long article and lifted his eyes to Smoke. The men exchanged knowing glances across the fire and the broiling fish.

"Help yourself, Chaw," Smoke offered. "We have plenty."

"I wanna wash my hands 'fore I partake," Chaw said. "Be right back. Damn, boys, but that do smell good!"

Chaw out of earshot, Smoke said, "You ever been east of the Big Muddy, York?"

"Never had no desire to go." Then he added, "Until now, that is."

"Davidson is crazy, but like a fox. We destroyed his little kingdom, brought his evil down on his head. And now he hates you as much as he does me. And I would just imagine this story is all over the West." He tapped the newspaper. "It would be like King Rex to gather up as many hardcases as he could buy—and he's got the money to buy a trainload of them—and head east. What do you think?"

"I think you've pegged it. Remember what Nappy said back in the bar, just before he died?"

"Yes. But I'm betting he wants the child to be born before he does anything. It would be like him. What do you think?"

"That you're right, all the way down the line. Dagget was one of the men who shot your wife, right?"

"Yes."

"But she wasn't showin' with child then, right?"

"Yes."

"Well, Rex can count. He'll time it so's the baby will be born, I'm thinkin'."

"I think you're right. And I'm thinking none of them would want to get back east too soon. Dagget is wanted back there, remember? You with me, York?"

"All the way, Smoke."

"We'll pull out in the morning. Here comes Chaw. We'd better fix some more fish. He looks like he could eat a skunk, and probably has."

They said their good-byes to Chaw and headed east, taking their time, heading for Leadville, once called Magic City and Cloud City, for it lies just below timberline, almost two miles above sea level. Some have described the climate as ten months winter and two months damn late in the fall. Smoke and York followed old Indian trails, trails that took Smoke back in time, when he and Preacher roamed wild and free across the land, with Preacher teaching first the boy and then the man called Smoke. It brought back memories to Smoke, memories that unashamedly wet his eyes. If York noticed—and Smoke was sure he did—the ranger said nothing about it.

Located in the valley of the Arkansas, Leadville was once the state's second largest city. It was first a roaring gold town, then a fabulous silver boom town, and then once more a gold-rush town. When Smoke and York rode into Leadville late one afternoon, the town was still roaring.

Smoke and York had experienced no trouble on their way into the boom town, unlike so many other not-so-lucky travelers. Roving gangs of thugs and outlaws had erected toll booths on several of the most important roads leading into the town, and those who refused to pay were robbed at gunpoint; many were killed. Robberies, rapes, assaults, and wild shoot-outs were almost an hourly occurrence within the town's limits.

When Smoke and York rode into the busy city, Leadville's population was hovering between fifty thousand and sixty thousand—no one ever really knew for sure. It was the wildest place in the state, for a time. The town's only hospital was guarded by a hundred men, day and night, to keep it from being torn down by thugs. Churches were forced to hire armed guards to work around the clock. The handful of police officers were virtually powerless to keep any semblance of order, so that fell to various vigilante groups. It was a town where you took your life in your hands just by getting out of bed in the morning.

"I ain't too thrilled about no hotel, Smoke," York commented on the way in.

"There wouldn't be a room anyway. We'll stable the

horses, pick up some supplies, and hit the saloons. We might be able to hear something. Let's take off these badges."

The only "hotel" in town that might have had empty beds was the Mammoth Palace, a huge shed with double bunks that could easily sleep five hundred. A guest paid a dollar for an eight-hour sleeping turn.

And in the midst of it all, churches were flourishing. If not spiritually, then financially. One member suggested that he buy a chandelier for the church. Another member asked, "Why? None of us knows how to play it!"

Smoke and York turned their horses onto State Street, where several famous New York chefs operated fancy eating places. Oxtail soup cost five cents a bowl at Smoothey's, and it was famous from the Coast to the Rockies.

Smoke waved at a ragged newsboy and bought a local newspaper, *The Chronicle*. They rode on and found a stable that had stalls to spare.

"We'll sleep with our horses," Smoke told the livery man.

"That'll be a dollar extra, boys. Apiece."

York started to protest, then noted the look on Smoke's face and held his peace.

"Give them a bait of corn and all the hay they can handle," Smoke told the man. "And do it now. If you go into Drifter's stall after I'm gone, he'll kill you."

"Son of a bitch tries to stomp on me," the livery blustered, "I'll take a rifle to him."

"Then I'll kill you," Smoke said softly, but with steel in his voice.

The man looked into those cold, hard eyes. He swallowed hard. "I was jokin', mister."

"I wasn't."

The liveryman gulped, his Adam's apple bobbing up and down. "Yes, sir. I'll take the best of care of your horses. Whatever you say mister . . . ah? . . ."

Smoke smiled and thought, To hell with trying to disguise who we are. "Smoke Jensen."

The liveryman backed up against a stall. "Yes, sir, Mr. Jensen, I mean, whatever you say, sir."

Smoke patted the man on the shoulder. "We'll get along fine, I'm sure."

"Yes, sir. You can bet I'll do my damndest!"

Smoke and York stepped out into the hustle and confusion of the boom town. Both knew that within the hour, every resident of the town would know that Smoke Jensen had arrived.

They stepped into a general store, checked the prices of goods, and decided they'd resupply further on.

"Legal stealin'," York said, looking at the price of a pair of jeans. He put the jeans back on the table.

They walked back outside.

"We can cover more ground if we split up," the Arizona Ranger suggested. "I'll take the other side of the street. What say we meet back at the stable in a couple of hours?"

"Sounds good to me. Watch your back, York."

"I hear you." York checked the busy street, found his chance, and darted across. As it was, he almost got run over by a freighter. The freighter cursed him, and rumbled and rattled on.

Smoke walked on. There was something about the tall

man with the two guns, in cross-draw style, that made most men hurry to step out of his way. If someone had told Smoke that he looked menacing, he would not have believed it. He could never see the savage look that was locked into his eyes.

Smoke turned a corner and found himself on Harrison Avenue, a busy business thoroughfare. He strolled the avenue, left it, and turned several corners, cutting down to hit State and Main.

Then he saw Natick, stepping out of a brothel. Smoke stopped and half turned, blending in better with the crowd. He backed against a building and began reading the paper he'd bought, still keeping a good eye on Natick. He hoped the outlaw might lead him to Davidson and Dagget.

But Natick stepped out into the street and walked toward a saloon. Smoke turned away and walked in the opposite direction, not wanting to stare too long at the man, knowing how that can attract someone's attention.

Smoke lounged around a bit, buying a cup of coffee and a sandwich at prices that would make a Scotsman squall in outrage. The coffee was weak and the sandwich uneatable. Smoke gave both to a ragged man who seemed down on his luck, and then he waited.

Soon he saw York walking up the street and turning into the saloon. Smoke hurriedly crossed the street and stepped into the crowded saloon, elbowing and shouldering his way through the crowd. Several turned to protest, looked into the unforgiving eyes of the tall stranger with the two six-guns, and closed their months much faster than they opened them.

York was facing Natick and two other hard-looking

men that Smoke did not know and did not remember seeing in Dead River.

And the crowd was rapidly moving back and away, out of the line of fire.

It was almost a repeat performance of Nappy and his crew. Except that this time a photographer was there and had his equipment set up, and he was ready to start popping whenever the action began.

The town marshal, a notorious bully and killer, was leaning up against the bar watching it all, a faint smile on his face. He was not going to interfere on behalf of either side.

"Mort!" Smoke called.

The marshal turned and faced Smoke, and his face went a shade paler.

"Jensen," he whispered.

"Either choose a side or get out," Smoke warned him, clear menace in his voice.

It was a warning and a challenge that rankled the town marshal, but not one he wanted to pick up. Quick with his guns and his fists, boasting that he had killed seven men, Mort's reputation was merely a dark smudge on the ground when compared to Smoke's giant shadow.

The marshal nodded and walked outside, turning and going swiftly up the street.

"All right, boys," York said. "You all know Smoke Jensen. Make your play."

The three outlaws drew together. One did not even clear leather before Smoke's guns belched fire and smoke, the slug striking the outlaw in the center of the chest. The second outlaw that Smoke faced managed to get the muzzle free of leather before twin death-blows of lead hammered at his belly and chest.

York's guns had roared and bucked and slammed Natick against a rear wall of the saloon, down but not quite dead.

Smoke walked to him. "Natick?"

"What do you want, Jensen?" the outlaw gasped.

"I know why you broke with Davidson and the others."

"Yeah? Why?"

"Because you may be a lot of bad things, but you're no baby killer."

Natick nodded his bloody head. "Yeah. I couldn't go along with that. I'm glad it was you boys who done me in. Pull my boots off for me, Jensen?"

Smoke tugged off the man's boots. One big toe was sticking through a hole in his sock.

"Ain't that pitiful?" Natick observed. "I've stole thousands and thousands of dollars and cain't even afford to buy a pair of socks." He cut his eyes to Smoke. "Rex and Dagget's got some bad ones with them, Jensen. Lapeer, Moore, The Hog, Tustin, Shorty, Red, and Jake. Studs Woodenhouse, Tie Medley, Paul Rycroft, Slim Bothwell, and Brute Pitman. I don't know where they're hidin', Jensen, and that's the truth. But Davidson plans on rapin' your woman and then killin' your kid."

Natick was whispering low, so only Smoke and York could hear his dying words. The photographer was taking pictures as fast as he could jerk plates and load his dust.

Smoke bent his head to hear Natick's words, but the outlaw would speak no more. He was dead.

Smoke dug in his own pocket and handed some money to a man standing close by. "You'll see that he gets a proper burial?"

"I shore will, Mr. Jensen. And it was a plumb honor to see you in action."

The photographer fired again.

The batwings snapped open and a dirty man charged into the bar, holding twin leather bags. "She's pure, boys. Assayed out high as a cat's back. The drinks is on me! Git them damn stiffs outta the way!"

CHAPTER SEVENTEEN

John and his sons and daughters and their families looked at the pictures John had sent in from New York, looked at them in horror.

Bodies were sprawling in the street, on the boardwalks, hanging half in and half out of broken windows. One was facedown in a horse trough, another was sprawled in stiffened death beside the watering trough.

And John's son-in-law, Smoke Jensen, handsome devil that he was, was standing on the boardwalk, calmly rolling a cigarette.

"That's my Smoke!" Sally said, pointing.

Smoke was wearing his guns cross-draw, and he had another one tucked behind his gunbelt. In another picture, the long-bladed Bowie knife he carried behind one gun could be clearly seen. In still another picture, Smoke was sitting on the edge of the boardwalk, eating an apple. In the left side of the picture, bodies could be seen hanging from the gallows.

John's stomach felt queasy. He laid the pictures aside and stifled a burp when Sally grabbed them up and began glancing at them.

"There's a bandage on Smoke's head," she noted. "But I can't see that he was shot anywhere else."

"Who is that handsome man standing beside him?" Walter's sister-in-law asked. "He's so . . . rugged-looking!"

"Lord, Martha!" her sister exclaimed. "He's savage-looking!"

"He's some sort of law enforcement officer," Walter explained, examining the picture. But his badge is somewhat different from . . . ah . . . Smoke's. Excuse my hesitation, Sister, but I never heard of a man being called Smoke."

"Get used to it, Walt," Sally said, a testy note to her statement. After being in the West, with its mostly honest and open and non-pompous people, the East was beginning to grate on her more and more.

Her father picked up on her testiness. "Sally, dearest, it'll soon be 1882. No one carries a gun around here except the law officers, and many times they don't even carry a gun, only a club. There hasn't been an Indian attack in this area in anyone's memory! We are a quiet community, with plans underway to have a college here; a branch of the state university. We are a community of laws, darling. We don't have gunfights in the streets. Keene was settled almost a hundred and fifty years ago. . . ."

"Yes, Father," Sally said impatiently. "I know. 1736, as a matter of fact. It's a nice, quiet, stable, pleasant little community. But I've grown away from it. Father, Mother, all of you . . . have you ever stood on the Great Divide? Have you ever ridden up in the High Lonesome, where you knew you could look for a hundred miles and there would be no other human being? Have any of you ever watched eagles soar and play in the skies, and knew yours were the only eyes on them? No, no you haven't. None of you. You don't even have a loaded gun in this house. None of you women would know what to do if you were attacked. You haven't any idea how to fire a gun. All you ladies know how to do is sit around looking pretty and attend your goddamn teas!"

John wore a pained expression on his face. Abigail started fanning herself furiously. Sally's brothers wore frowns on their faces. Her sisters and sisters-in-law looked shocked.

Martha laughed out loud. "I have my teacher's certificate, Sally. Do you suppose there might be a position for me out where you live?"

"Martha!" her older sister hissed. "You can't be serious. There are . . . savages out there!"

"Oh . . . piddly-poo!" Martha said. She would have liked to have the nerve to say something stronger, like Sally, but didn't want to be marked as a scarlet woman in this circle.

"We're looking for a schoolteacher right this moment, Martha," Sally told her. "And I think you'd be perfect. When Smoke gets here, we'll ask him. If he says you're the choice, then you can start packing."

Martha began clapping her hands in excitement.

"Smoke is a one-man committee on the hiring of teachers?" Jordan sniffed disdainfully.

"Would you want to buck him on anything, Brother?"

Jordan stroked his beard and remained silent. Unusually so for a lawyer.

* * *

Smoke and York left Leadville the next morning, riding out just at dawn. They rode north, past Fremont Pass, then cut east toward Breckenridge. No sign of Davidson or Dagget or any of the others with them. They rode on, with Bald Mountain to the south of them, following old trails. They kept Mount Evans to their north and gradually began the winding down toward the town of Denver.

"We gonna spend some time in Denver City?" York asked.

"Few days. Maybe a week. We both need to get groomed and curried and bathed, and our clothes are kind of shabby-looking."

"My jeans is so thin my drawers is showin'," York agreed. "If we goin' east, I reckon we're gonna have to get all duded up like dandies, huh?"

"No way," Smoke's reply was grim. "I'm tired of pretending to be something I'm not. We'll just dress like what we are. Westerners."

York sighed. "That's a relief. I just cain't see myself in one of them goofy caps like you wore back in Dead River."

Smoke laughed at just the thought. "And while we're here, I've got to send some wires. Find out how Sally is doing and find out what's happened up on the Sugarloaf."

"Pretty place you got, Smoke?"

"Beautiful. And there's room for more. Lots of room. You ever think about getting out of law work, York?"

"More and more lately. I'd like to have me a little place. Nothin' fancy; nothin' so big me and a couple more people couldn't handle it. I just might drift up that way once this is all over."

"You got a girl?"

"Naw. I ain't had the time. Captain's been sendin' me all over the territory ever since I started with the Rangers. I reckon it's time for me to start thinking about settlin' down."

"You might meet you an eastern gal, York." Smoke was grinning.

"Huh! What would I do with her? Them eastern gals is a different breed of cat. I read about them. All them teas and the like. I got to have me a woman that'll work right alongside me. You know what ranchin' is like. Hard damn work."

"It is that. But my Sally was born back east. Educated all over the world. She's been to Paris!"

"Texas?"

"France."

"No kiddin'! I went to Dallas once. Biggest damn place I ever seen. Too damn many people to suit me. I felt all hemmed in."

"It isn't like that up in the High Lonesome. I think you'd like it up there, York. We need good stable people like you. Give it some thought. I'll help you get started; me and Sally."

"Right neighborly of y'all. Little tradin' post up ahead. Let's stop. I'm out of the makin's."

While York was buying tobacco, Smoke sat outside, reading a fairly recent edition of a Denver paper. The city was growing by leaps and bounds. The population was now figured at more than sixty thousand.

"Imagine that," Smoke muttered. "Just too damn many folks for me."

He read on. A new theatre had been built, the Tabor

Grand Opera House. He read on, suddenly smiling. He checked the date of the paper. It was only four days old.

"You grinnin' like a cat lickin' cream, Smoke," York said, stepping out and rolling a cigarette. "What got your funny bone all quiverin'?"

"And old friend of mine is in town, York. And I just bet you he'd like to ride east with us."

"Yeah? Lawman?"

"Businessman, scholar, gambler, gunfighter."

"Yeah?" Who might that be?"

"Louis Longmont."

"By the Lord Harry!" Louis exclaimed, standing up from his table in the swanky restaurant and waving at Smoke. "Waiter! Two more places here, *s'il vous plait*."

"What the hell did he say?" York whispered.

"Don't ask me," Smoke returned the whisper.

The men all shook hands, Smoke introducing York to Louis. Smoke had not seen Louis since the big shoot-out at Fontana more than a year ago. The man had not changed. Handsome and very sure of himself. The gray just touching his hair at the temples.

Smoke also noted the carefully tailored suit, cut to accommodate a shoulder holster.

Same ol' Louis.

After the men had ordered dinner—Louis had to do it, the menu being in French—drinks were brought around and Longmont toasted them both.

"I've been reading about the exploits of you men," Louis remarked after sipping his Scotch. York noticed that all their liquor glasses had funny-looking square bits of ice in them, which did make the drink a bit easier on the tongue.

"We've been busy," Smoke agreed.

"Still pursuing the thugs?"

"You know we are, Louis. You would not have allowed your name to appear in the paper if you hadn't wanted us to find you in Denver."

York sat silent, a bit uncomfortable with the sparkling white tablecloth and all the heavy silverware—he couldn't figure out what he was supposed to do; after all, he couldn't eat but with one fork and one knife, no how. And he had never seen so many duded-up men and gussied-up women in all his life. Even with new clothes on, it made a common fella feel shabby.

"Let's just say," Louis said, "I'm a bit bored with it all."

"You've been traveling about?"

"Just returned from Paris a month ago. I'd like to get back out in the country. Eat some beans and beef and see the stars above me when I close my eyes."

"Want to throw in with us, Louis?"

Louis lifted his glass. "I thought you were never going to ask."

Smoke and York loafed around Denver for a few days, while Louis wrapped up his business and Smoke sent and received several wires. Sally was fine; the baby was due in two months—approximately.

"What does she mean by that?" York asked, reading over Smoke's shoulder.

"It means, young man," Louis said, "that babies do not

always cooperate with a timetable. The child might be born within several weeks of that date, before it or after it."

Louis was dressed in boots, dark pants, gray shirt, and black leather vest. He wore two guns, both tied down and both well-used and well-taken care of, the wooden butts worn smooth with use.

York knew that Louis Longmont, self-made millionaire and world-famous gambler, was a deadly gunslinger. And a damn good man to have walkin' with you when trouble stuck its head up, especially when that trouble had a six-gun in each hand.

"Do tell," York muttered.

"What's the plan, Smoke?" Louis asked.

"You about ready to pull out?"

"Is tomorrow morning agreeable with you?"

"Fine. The sooner the better. I thought we'd take our time, ride across Kansas; maybe as far as St. Louis if time permits. We can catch a train anywhere along the way. And by riding, we just might pick up some information about Davidson and his crew."

"Sounds good. Damn a man who would even entertain the thought of harming a child!"

"We pull out at dawn."

Sally had not shown her family all the wires she'd received from Smoke. She did not wish to alarm any of them, and above all, she did not wish to alert the local police as to her husband's suspicions about Davidson and his gang traveling east after her and the baby. Her father would have things done the legal way—ponderous and, unknowing to him, very dangerous for all concerned.

John had absolutely no idea of what kind of man this Rex Davidson was.

But Sally did. And Smoke could handle it, his way. And she was glad Louis and York were with him.

York just might be the ticket for Martha out of the East and into the still wild and wide-open West. He was a good-looking young man.

The servant answered the door and Martha entered the sitting room. Sally waved her to a chair with imported antimacassars on the arms and back. The day was warm, and both women fanned themselves to cool a bit.

"I was serious about going west, Sally."

"I thought as much. And now," she guessed accurately, "you want to know all about it."

"That's right."

Where to start? Sally thought. And how to really explain about the vastness and the emptiness and the magnificence of it all?

Before she could start, the door opened again, and this time the room was filled with small children: Sally's nieces and nephews and a few of their friends.

"Aunt Sally," a redheaded, freckle-faced boy said. "Will you tell us about Uncle Smoke?"

"I certainly will." She winked at Martha. "I'll tell you all about the High Lonesome and the strong men who live there."

They pulled out at first light. Three men who wore their guns as a part of their being. Three men who had faced death and beaten it so many times none of them could remember all the battles.

Louis had chosen a big buckskin-colored horse with a mean look to his eyes. The horse looked just about as mean as Smoke knew Drifter really was.

Before leaving Denver, Smoke had wired Jim Wilde and asked for both York and Louis to be formally deputized as U.S. Marshals. The request had been honored within the day.

So they were three men who now wore official badges on their chests. One, a millionaire adventurer. One, a successful rancher. One, a young man who was only weeks away from meeting the love of his life.

They rode east, veering slightly south, these three hard-eyed and heavily armed men. They would continue a southerly line until reaching a trading post on the banks of the Big Sandy; a few more years and the trading post would become the town of Limon.

At the trading post, they would cut due east and hold to that all the way across Kansas. They would stay south of Hell Creek, but on their ride across Colorado, they would ford Sand Creek, an offshoot of the Republican River. They would ride across Spring Creek, Landsman, East Spring, and cross yet another Sand Creek before entering into Kansas.

Kansas was still woolly but nothing like it had been a few years back when the great cattle herds were being driven up from Texas, and outlaws and gunfighters were just about anywhere one wished to look.

But the three men rode with caution. The decade had rolled into the eighties, but there were still bands of Indians who left the reservation from time to time; still bands of outlaws that killed and robbed. And they were riding into an area of the country where men still killed other men over the bitterness of that recent unpleasantness called by some the Civil War and by others the War Between the States.

The days were warm and pleasant or hot and unpleasant as the men rode steadily eastward across the plains. But the plains were now being dotted and marred and scarred with wire. Wire put up by farmers to keep ranchers' cattle out. Wire put up by ranchers to keep nesters out of water holes, creeks, and rivers. Ranchers who wished to breed better cattle put up wire to keep inferior breeds from mixing in and to keep prize bulls at home.

But none of the men really liked wire, even though all could see the reasons—most of the time—behind the erecting of barbed wire fences.

They did not seek out others as they rode toward the east and faraway New Hampshire. Every third or fourth day, late in the afternoon, if a town was handy, they would check into a hotel and seek out a shave and a bath. If not, they would bathe in a handy stream and go unshaven until a town dotted the vast prairie.

"Ever been to this New Hamp-shire, Louis?" York asked the gambler.

"Never have, my friend. But it is an old and very settled state. One of the original thirteen to ratify the Constitution. The first settlement—I can't recall the name—was back in 1623. But I can assure you both, if we ride in like this, armed to the teeth and looking like buccaneers on horseback, we are," he smiled, "going to raise some eyebrows."

"How's that?" York asked. "We don't look no different than anybody else?"

Louis laughed pleasantly and knowingly. "Ah, but my

young friend, we are much different from the folks you are about to meet in a few weeks. Their streets are well-lighted with gas lamps. A few might have telephones— marvelous devices. The towns you will see will be old and settled towns. No one carries a gun of any type; many villages and towns have long banned their public display except for officers of the law. And thank you, Smoke, for commissioning us; this way we can carry firearms openly.

"No, York, the world you are only days away from viewing is one that you have never seen before. Smoke, my suggestion would be that we ride the trains well into Massachusetts and then head north on horseback from our jumping-off place. I would suggest Springfield. And get ready for some very strange looks, gentlemen."

"I'm beginnin' not to like these folks and I ain't even met none of 'em yet," York groused. "Don't tote no gun! What do they do if somebody tries to mess with 'em?"

"They are civilized people," Louis said, with more than a touch of sarcasm in his statement. "They let the law take care of it."

"Do tell," York said. "In other words, they ain't got the sand to fight their own fights?"

"That is one way of putting it, York," the gambler said with a smile. "My, but this is going to be a stimulating and informative journey."

Louis cantered on ahead.

"Smoke?" York asked.

"Huh?"

"What's a telephone?"

CHAPTER EIGHTEEN

"They're in Salina," Sally read from the wire. "Smoke, York and Louis Longmont."

"The millionaire?" John sat straighter in his chair. "Mr. Longmont is coming east by horseback!"

Sally put eyes on her father. She loved him dearly, but sometimes he could be a pompous ass. "Father, Louis is an adventurer. He is also one of the most famous gunfighters in all the West. He's killed a dozen men on the Continent, in duels. With sword and pistol. He's killed— oh, I don't know, twenty or thirty or maybe fifty men out west, with guns. He's such a gentleman, so refined. I'll be glad to see him again."

John wiped his face with a handkerchief. In one breath, his daughter spoke of Louis killing fifty men. In the next breath, she spoke of him being so refined.

Not normally a profane man, John thought: What kind of goddamned people are going to be staying in my house!

Louis lay on his blankets and watched Smoke unroll a warbag from the pack animal. He laughed aloud when he saw what his friend was unpacking: a buckskin jacket, one that had been bleached a gray-white and trimmed ornately by a squaw.

"You have a touch of the theatrical in you, my friend," Louis observed.

"I got to thinking we might as well give the folks a show. I had it stored in Denver."

"Going to be interesting," Louis smiled, pouring another cup of coffee and turning the venison steaks.

York returned from his bath in the creek, his trousers on but shirtless. For the first time, Smoke and Louis noticed the old bullet scars that pocked the young man's hide.

"You've picked up a few here and there," Louis noted.

"Yeah." York slipped into his shirt. "Me and another ranger, name of McCoy, got all tangled up with some bad ones down in the Dos Cabezas mountains; I hadn't been with the Rangers long when it happened. McCoy got hit so bad he had to retire from the business. Started him up a little general store up near Prescott. But we buried them ol' boys where they fell. I was laid up for near'bouts a month. 'Nother time I was trackin' a bank robber up near Carson Mesa. He ambushed me; got lead in me. But I managed to stay in the saddle and rode on up into Utah after him. I nailed him up near Vermillion Cliffs. Picked up a few other scratches here and there."

And Louis knew then what Smoke had already learned: York was a man to ride the river with. There was no backup in the Arizona Ranger.

York looked up from the cooking steaks. "Where you plannin' on us pickin' up the steam cars, Smoke?"

"I'll wire Sally from Kansas City and see how she's

doing. If she's doin' all right and doesn't feel like the baby's due any day, we'll ride on to St. Louis and catch the train there."

The three waited in Kansas City for two days. Sally felt fine and the baby was not due for a month. She urged him to take his time.

Smoke, York, and Louis rode out of Kansas City the next morning, riding into Missouri. It would be days later, when the trio rode into St. Louis and Smoke wired Keene, that he would learn Sally had been taken to the hospital the day after his wire from Kansas City. Sally and babies were doing fine.

"Babies!" Smoke shouted, almost scaring the telegraph operator out of his seat.

"Babies?" Louis exclaimed.

"More 'un one?" York asked.

"Boys," the stationmaster urged, "don't shoot no holes in the ceiling. We just got 'er fixed last month."

They arranged bookings for their horses and themselves, and chugged out of St. Louis the next morning. It was the first time Smoke or York had ever seen a sleeping car, and both were amazed at the luxury of the dining cars and at the quality of the food that was served.

When the finger bowl was brought around, Louis had to leave his seat to keep from laughing when York rolled up his sleeves and washed his elbows in it.

"Ain't you got no soap to go with this thing?" York asked the colored man.

The Negro rolled his eyes and looked heavenward, maintaining his composure despite the situation.

* * *

The train stopped in Ohio and the three got off to change trains. It was an overnighter, so they could exercise their horses, get their ground-legs back, and take a genuine bath in a proper tub. All were getting just a little bit gamey. The three big men, broad-shouldered and lean-hipped, with their boots and spurs and western hats, twin six-shooters tied down low, drew many an anxious look from a lot of men and more than curious looks from a lot of ladies.

"Shore are a lot of fine-lookin' gals around these parts," York observed. "But kinda pale, don't y'all think?"

Smoke and York stood on the shores of Lake Erie and marveled at the sight of it.

"Never seen so damn much water in all my life!" York said, undisguised awe in his voice. "And would you just look at them big boats!"

"Ships," Louis corrected. He pointed to one flying an odd-looking flag. "That one just came down the St. Lawrence. That's a German flag."

"How'd it git here?" York asked.

"Across the Atlantic Ocean."

"Lord have mercy!"

When they stomped and jingled back into the fancy hotel, a platoon of cops were waiting for them.

A captain of the police approached them, caution in his eyes and his step. "Lads, I can see that you're U.S. Marshals, but are ye after someone in our city?"

The cop was Irish through and through. "No," Smoke

said. "But neither have we bothered anyone here." He looked at the mass of cops and smiled. "Kinda reminds me of that time I took on 'bout twenty-five guns at that silver camp."

"You fought twenty-five desperados all by yourself?" the captain asked.

"Yep."

"How did it turn out?"

"I killed them all."

"You . . . killed them all!"

"Yep."

Several news reporters and one photographer had gathered around, for real cowboys and western gunslingers were rare in Cleveland.

"Might I ask your name, sir?" the captain inquired.

"Smoke Jensen."

Pandemonium set in.

Smoke, Louis, and York were given the keys to the city. All three answered an almost endless barrage of questions and endured dozens of cameras popping and clicking at them. A hasty parade was called, and the men rode up and down the city's streets in an open carriage.

"Goddamnedest thing I ever heard of," York muttered. "What the hell have we done to deserve something this grand?"

"You're an Arizona Ranger, York," Louis leaned over and told him. "And a gunfighter, just like Smoke and myself."

"If you say so," York told him. "Seems like a whole bunch to do about nothin' if you ask me."

"Shakespeare felt the same way," the gambler told him, smiling.

"No kiddin'? Seems to me I heard of him. Ain't he from down around El Paso?"

They chugged east the next morning, Smoke and York glad to be out of the hustle and bustle of it all. Louis waved good-bye to a dark-haired young woman who smiled and blushed as the train moved out of the station.

Louis settled back in his seat. "Ah, boys, the freshness and vitality of youth never ceases to amaze me."

Smoke grinned. "I noticed you left the party very early last night, Louis. She certainly is lovely."

But Louis would only smile in reply to questions.

They rolled on through the day and night, across Pennsylvania and into New York. In New York's massive and confusing station, they were met by a large contingent of New York's finest and personally escorted to the train heading to Springfield, with numerous stops along the way.

"It ain't that we don't respect fellow officers, boys," the commander of the police unit said. "It's just that your reputations precede you." He looked at Smoke. "Especially yours, son."

"Yes," a fresh-fashed cop said. "Were it up to me, I would insist you remove those guns."

Smoke stopped, halting the parade. He turned to face the helmeted cop. "And if refused? . . ."

The young cop was not in the least intimidated. "Then I would surely have to use force, laddy."

Louis and York joined Smoke in a knowing smile.

Smoke said, "You have a pencil in your pocket, officer. I can see it. Would you jerk it out as quickly as you can?"

The older and more wiser of the cops—and that was just about all of them—backed up, with many of them holding their hands out from their sides, smiles on their faces. A half-dozen reporters had gathered around and were scribbling furiously. Photographers were taking pictures.

"So we're going to play games, eh, gunfighter?" the young cop asked.

"No. I'm going to show you how easy it is for a loud-mouth to get killed where I come from."

The young officer flushed, and placed his thumb and forefinger on the end of the pencil, and jerked it out.

Smoke swept back his beaded buckskin jacket, exposing his guns. He slipped the hammer-thong of his right hand .44. "Want to try it again?"

The young officer got exactly half of the pencil out of his pocket before he was looking down the muzzle of Smoke's .44.

"Do you get my point, officer?"

"Ah . . . 'deed, I do, sir! As one fellow officer to another, might I say, sir, that you are awfully quick with that weapon."

Smoke holstered. It was unlike him to play games with weapons, but he felt he might have saved the young man's life with an object lesson. He held out his hand, and the cop smiled and shook it.

The rest of the walk to their car was an easy one, with chatter among men who found they all had something in common after all.

* * *

It was growing late when they finally detrained in Springfield. They stabled their horses and found a small hotel for the night.

The weeks on the road had honed away any city fat that might have built up on Louis and had burned his already dark complexion to that of a gypsy. They were big men, all over six feet, with a natural heavy musculature; they were the kind of men that bring out the hostility in a certain type of man, usually the bully.

And with the knowledge that Sally and the babies—twins, Smoke had discovered when he wired during a train refueling stop—were now in danger, none of the men were in any mood for taking any lip from some loudmouth.

They elected to have their supper in the hotel's dining room to further avoid any trouble. As had been their custom, they wore their guns, and to hell with local laws. None of them knew when they might run into Davidson or Dagget or their ilk.

Louis had bought York a couple of suits in St. Louis, and Smoke had brought a suit with him. Longmont was never without a proper change of clothes; if he didn't have one handy, he would buy one.

When the men entered the dining room, conversation ceased and all eyes were on them as they walked to their table, led by a very nervous waiter. With their spurs jingling and their guns tied down low, all three managed to look as out of place as a saddle on a tiger.

The three of them ignored several comments from some so-called "gentlemen"—comments that might have led to a fight anywhere west of the Mississippi—and were seated without incident.

Louis frowned at the rather skimpy selections on the menu, sighed, and decided to order a steak. The others did the same.

"Sorry we don't have no buffalo here for you range-riders," a man blurted from the table next to them. His friend laughed, and the women with them, hennaed and painted up and half drunk, also thought fat boy's comments to be hysterically amusing.

Louis ignored the man, as did Smoke and York. "A drink before ordering, gentlemen?" a waiter magically appeared.

"I'm sure they'll want rye, George," the fat boy blurted. "That's what I read that all cowboys drink. Before they take their semi-yearly bath, that is."

His table erupted with laughter.

"I could move you to another table, gentlemen," the waiter suggested. "That"—he cut his eyes to the man seated with fat boy and the woman—"is Bull Everton."

"Is that supposed to mean something to us?" Smoke asked.

"He's quite the bully," the waiter whispered, leaning close. "He's never been whipped."

"That he's admitted," Louis commented dryly. "If he can't fight any better than he can choose women, he must have never fought a man."

Smoke and York both laughed at that.

"We'll have Scotch," Louis ordered.

"Yes, sir," The waiter was glad to get away from the scene of what he presumed would soon be disaster for the western men.

"You take them damn guns off," the voice rumbled to the men, "and I'll show you what a real man can do."

Smoke lifted his eyes to the source of the voice. Bull Everton. He surveyed the man. Even sitting, Smoke could see that the man was massive, with heavy shoulders and huge wrists and hands. But that old wildness sprang up within Smoke. Smoke had never liked a bully. He smiled at the scowling hulk.

"I'll take them off anytime you're ready, donkey-face," he threw down the challenge and insult.

Bull stood up and he was big. "How about right now, cowboy? Outside."

"Suits me, tub-butt." Smoke stood up and unbuckled and utied, handing his guns to a waiter.

The waiter looked as though he'd just been handed a pair of rattlesnakes.

"Where is this brief contest to take place?" Louis asked Bull.

"Brief, is right," Bull laughed. "Out back of the hotel will do."

"After you," Smoke told him.

When the back door closed and Bull turned around, Smoke hit him flush in the mouth with a hard right and followed that with a vicious left to the wind. Before Bull could gather his senses, Smoke had hit him two more times, once to the nose and another hook to the body.

With blood dripping from his lips and nose, Bull hollered and charged. Smoke tripped him and hit him once on the way down, then kicked him in the stomach while he was down.

Smoke was only dimly aware of the small crowd that

had gathered, several of the spectators dressed in the blue uniform of police officers. He did not hear one of the cops say to Louis, "I've been waiting to see Everton get his due for a long time, boys. Don't worry. There will be no interference from us."

Smoke backed up and allowed Bull to crawl to his feet. There was a light of fury and panic in the man's eyes.

Bull lifted his hands in the classic boxer's stance: left fist held almost straight out, right fist close to his jaw.

Smoke whirled and kicked the bully on his knee. Bull screamed in pain and Smoke hit him a combination of blows, to the belly, the face, the kidneys. Smoke trip-hammered his fists, brutalizing the bigger man, knocking him down, hauling him back up, and knocking him down again.

Bull grabbed Smoke's knees and brought him down to the dirt of the alley. Pulling one leg free, Smoke savagely kicked the bully in the face. Teeth flew, glistening in the night.

Smoke pulled Bull to his feet and leaned him up against the rear wall, then went to work on the man's belly and sides. Only after he had felt and heard several ribs break did he let the man fall unconscious to the ground.

"Drag Bull to the paddy wagon, boys," the cop in charge ordered. "We'll take him to the hospital. I can tell by looking that his jaw is broken, and I'll wager half a dozen ribs are broken as well." He looked at Smoke. "You don't even look angry, young man."

"I'm not," Smoke told him.

"Lord suffer us all!" the officer said. "What would you have done had you been angry?"

"Killed him."

"I'd not like to get on the wrong side of the road with you, young man. But I would like to know your name."

"Smoke Jensen."

The crowd gasped and the cop smiled grimly. "Are you as good with your guns as you are with your dukes, me boy?"

"Better."

Louis handed Smoke a towel and held his coat while his friend wiped his face and hands. York had stood to one side, his coat brushed back, freeing the butts of his .44s.

And the cops had noticed that, too.

The cop looked at all three of the men. "You boys are here for a reason. I'm not asking why, for you're officers of the law, and federal officers at that. But I'd not like to see any trouble in this town."

"There won't be," Smoke said, raising up from a rain barrel where he had washed his face and hands. "We'll be leaving at first light."

"You wouldn't mind if I stopped by the stable to see you off, would you now?"

"Not a bit," Smoke said, smiling.

The waiter stuck his head out the back door. "Gentlemen," he said, "I've freshened your drinks. The management has instructed me to tell you that your dinners are on the house this evening."

"That won't be necessary," Smoke told him. "I assure you, we have ample funds."

The waiter smiled. "Gentlemen, Bull Everton will not be returning to this establishment for quite some time, thanks to you. And," he grinned hugely, "if it isn't worth a free meal to get rid of a big pain in the ass, nothing is!"

CHAPTER NINETEEN

The men were in the saddle and moving out before first light; they would take their breakfast at the first inn they came to once outside of Springfield. It was cold in the darkness before dawn, with more than a hint of fall in the air, and it was going to be a beautiful day for traveling.

The road followed the Connecticut River. The men stayed on the east side of the river, knowing they would have to veer off toward the northeast once inside New Hampshire.

All were taken in by the beauty of the state. Although the leaves were turning as fall approached, the lushness of nature was a beautiful thing to see. As they traveled, the road was bordered by red spruce, red oak, white pine, sugar maple, yellow birch, and white birch.

"It's shore purty," York observed, his eyes taking in the stone fences that surrounded the neat fields and farms. "I can't rightly describe the way I feel about this place. It's, well—" He paused and shook his head.

"Civilized," Louis finished it.

"I reckon that's it, Louis. The only gun I've seen all day is the ones we're totin'. Gives me sort of a funny feelin'."

"Bear in mind," Louis sobered them all, "that all that will change with the arrival of Davidson and his thugs."

By mid-afternoon, the schools out for the day, boys and girls began to appear by the fences and roadways, staring in mute fascination as the cowboys rode slowly by. Smoke and Louis and York all smiled and waved at the young people, and just to give the kids something to talk about and remember, they swept back their jackets, exposing the butts of their guns for the kids' wide eyes.

And the children loved it.

They could have easily made the distance to Keene by nightfall but decided to break it off at the inn on the New Hampshire/Massachusetts line. The innkeeper was a bit startled as the three jingled into his establishment.

"Innkeeper," Louis said, "rooms for three, if you please. And we'll stable our own horses."

"Yes . . . sir," the man said. "Right around back. You'll see the corn bin."

"And warn people to stay away from our horses," Smoke told him. "Anybody gets into Drifter's stall he'll kill them."

"Sir!"

"That's what he did to the last man who owned him."

"Yes, sir! I will so advise any locals."

The man and his wife and the girls who worked in the tavern and dining room were having a hard time keeping their eyes off the twin guns belted around each man's lean waist.

"We'll freshen up a bit and then come down for a drink at the bar," Louis told the man and woman.

Louis, York, and Smoke waited.

The man and woman and hired help contined to stare at the three tall men. No one seemed able to move.

Louis rapped gently on the desk. "The keys, please?"

The man came alive. "Oh! Yes! Here you are, gentlemen."

Smoke smiled at the lady behind the desk. "We don't bite, ma'am. I promise you we don't."

His smile broke the barriers between old, settled, and established codes and those who came from the free-wheeling western part of the nation. She returned his smile and glanced down at the register.

"Enjoy your stay, Mr. Jensen! Smoke Jensen?"

And once more, pandemonium reigned.

The trio crossed into New Hampshire at first light, having paid their bill and slipped out quietly before dawn.

York was dressed in jeans, a red and white checkered shirt, and a leather waist-length jacket. Louis dressed in a dark suit, a white shirt with black string tie, highly polished black boots, and a white duster over his clothing to keep away the dust. Smoke was dressed in dark jeans, a black shirt, a red bandana, and his beaded buckskin jacket. All wore western hats. Only York and Smoke's big bowie knives could be seen; Louis's duster covered his own knife.

About ten miles inside New Hampshire, they picked up the Ashuelot River and followed that toward Keene. Some fifteen miles later, the outskirts of the town came into view.

The men reined up, dismounted, and knocked the dust

from their clothing. Louis, loving every minute of it, removed his linen duster and tied it behind his saddle. A farmer came rattling along in a wagon, stopped, and sat his seat, staring at the heavily armed trio.

"The Reynolds house," Smoke said, walking to the man. "How do we find it?"

The man sat his wagon seat and stared, openmouthed.

"Sir?" Smoke asked. "Are you all right?"

"It's really you," the farmer said, awe in his voice. "I been readin' 'bout you for years. Knew you by your picture."

"Thank you. I'm glad to meet you, too. Could you direct us to the Reynolds house?"

"Oh . . . sure! That's easy. Cross the bridge and go three blocks. Turn right. Two blocks down they's a big white two-story house on the corner. You can't miss it. Wait'll I tell my wife I seen Smoke Jensen!" He clucked to his team and rattled on.

"What day is this?" York asked. "I'm havin' the damndest time keepin' track of things."

"Saturday," Louis told them. "Smoke, do we inform the local authorities as to why we are here?"

"I think not. If we did that, they'd want to handle it the legal way. With trials and lawyers and the such. We'd be tied up here for months. So let's keep it close to the vest and wait until Davidson makes his play. Then we'll handle it our way."

"Sounds good to me," York said. He swung into the saddle.

Smoke and Louis mounted up.

They cantered across the wooden bridge, three big men riding big western horses. They slowed to a walk on the other side of the street. People began coming out of houses to stand and stare at the men as they rode slowly by. Little children stood openmouthed; for all, it was the first time they had ever seen a real western cowboy, much less three real gunslingers like they'd been reading about in the penny dreadfuls and the tabloids.

Louis tipped his hat to a group of ladies, and they simpered and giggled and twirled their parasols and batted their eyes.

A little boy spotted them as they turned the street corner, and he took off like the hounds of hell were nipping at his feet.

"Aunt Sally! Aunt Sally!" he hollered. "They're here, Aunt Sally!"

He ran up the steps of the huge house and darted inside.

The front porch filled with people, all staring at the three horsemen walking their mounts slowly up the street.

"Your relatives, Smoke," Louis said. "Looks like quite a gathering."

"I am not looking forward to this, Louis," Smoke admitted. "I just want to get this over with, see Davidson and his bunch dead in the streets, and take Sally and the babies and get the hell back to the Sugarloaf."

"You'll survive it," the gambler said. "I assure you, my friend. But I feel it will be somewhat trying for the lot of us."

And then Sally stepped out onto the porch to join her family. Smoke felt he had never seen anything so beautiful in all his life. She stood by an older man that Smoke guessed was her father.

The entire neighborhood had left their houses and were standing in their front yards, gawking at the gunslingers.

"Smoke Jensen!" a teenager said, the words reaching Smoke. "He's killed a thousand men with those guns. Bet he took that coat off an Indian after he killed him."

Smoke grimaced and cut his eyes at Louis. The gambler said, "I feel awed to be in the presence of someone so famous." Then he smiled. "A thousand men, eh? My how your reputation has grown in such a short time."

Smoke shook his head and could not help but smile.

John Reynolds said, "That horse he's riding looks like it came straight out of the pits of hell!"

"That's Drifter," Sally told him. "He's a killer horse. Killed the last man who tried to own him."

John looked at his daughter. "Are you serious?"

"Oh, yes. But he's really quite gentle once he gets to know you. I was baking pies one afternoon and he stuck his head into the kitchen and ate a whole pie before I realized it. I picked up a broom and spanked him."

"You . . . spanked him," John managed to say. He muttered under his breath and Sally laughed at his expression.

The riders turned and reined up, dismounting at the hitchrail. Sally stepped off the porch and walked toward the picket fence, a smile on her lips.

Smoke stood by the gate and stared at her, not trusting his voice to speak.

"You've lost weight," Sally said.

"I've been missing your cooking."

He opened the gate.

Her eyes sparkled with mischief. "Is that all you've been missing?" She spoke low, so her words reached only his ears.

Smoke stepped through the open gate, his spurs jingling. He stopped a few feet from her. "Well, let's see. I reckon I might have missed you just a tad."

And then she was in his arms, loving the strong feel of him. Her tears wet his face as she lifted her lips to his.

York lifted his hat and let out a war whoop.

Walter Reynolds swallowed his snuff.

CHAPTER TWENTY

"Should you be out of bed this soon?" Smoke asked his wife.

"Oh, the doctors tried to get me to stay in bed much longer, but since I didn't have the time to get to the city to have the babies, and they came so easily, I left the bed much earlier than most, I imagine."

"I keep forgetting how tough you are." Smoke smiled across the twin cradles at her.

"Have you thought about names, Smoke?"

"Uh . . . no, I really haven't. I figured you'd have them named by now."

"I have thought of a couple."

"Oh?"

"How about Louis Arthur and Denise Nicole?"

Louis for Louis Longmont. Arthur for Old Preacher. And Nicole for Smoke's first wife, who was murdered by outlaws, and their baby son, Arthur, who was also killed. Denise was an old family name on the Reynolds side.

"You don't object to naming the girl after Nicole?"

"No," Sally said with a smile. "You know I don't."

"Louis will be pleased."

"I thought so."

Smoke looked at the sleeping babies. "Are they ever going to wake up?"

She laughed softly. "Don't worry. You'll know when they wake. Come on. Let's go back and join the rest of the family."

Smoke looked around for Louis and York. John caught his eye. "I tried to get them to stay. I insisted, told them we had plenty of room. But Mr. Longmont said he felt it would be best if they stayed at the local hotel. Did we offend them, Son?"

Smoke shook his head as the family gathered around. "No. We're here on some business as well as to get Sally. It would be best if we split up. I'll explain."

John looked relieved. "I was so afraid we had somehow inadvertently offended Mr. Longmont."

John Reynolds stared at Smoke as his son-in-law laughed out loud. "Hell, John. Louis just wanted to find a good poker game, that's all!"

It was after lunch, and the family was sitting on the front porch. Smoke had not removed his guns and had no intention of doing so.

And it was not just the young people who stared at him with a sort of morbid fascination.

"Tell me about Dead River," Sally spoke. She glanced at her nieces and nephews. "You, scoot! There'll be a lot of times to talk to your Uncle Smoke."

The kids reluctantly left the porch.

Smoke shaped and rolled and licked and lit. He leaned back in his chair and propped his boots up on the porch railing. "Got kind of antsy there for the last day or two before we opened the dance."

"You went to a dance?" Betsy asked.

Smoke cut his eyes. "Opening the dance means I started the lead flying, Betsy."

"Oh!" Her eyes were wide.

"You mean as soon as you told the hooligans to surrender, they opened fire?" Jordan inquired.

Smoke cut his eyes to him. "No," he drawled. "It means that me and York come in the back way of the saloon, hauled iron, and put about half a dozen of them on the floor before the others knew what was happening." It wasn't really accurate, but big deal.

"We don't operate that way in the East," Walter said, a note of disdain in his voice.

"I reckon not. But the only thing Dead River was east of was Hell. And anybody who thinks they can put out the fires of Hell with kindness and conversation is a damn fool. And fools don't last long in the wilderness."

John verbally stepped in before his son found himself slapped on his butt out in the front yard. "A young lady named Martha will be along presently. She had some foolish notion of traveling back west with you and Sally. She wants to teach school out there."

"Fine with me." He looked at Sally. "Has she got the sand and the grit to make it out there?"

"Yes. I believe she does."

"Tell her to start packing."

"But don't you first have to get the permission of the school board?" Jordan asked.

"Ain't got none," Smoke slipped back into the loose

speech of the western man. "Don't know what that is, anyways."

Sally laughed, knowing he was deliberately using bad grammar.

And cutting her eyes to her mother, she knew that Abigal did, too.

But her father appeared lost as a goose.

And so did her brothers.

"Well, sir," Jordan began to explain. "A school board is a body of officials who—"

"—sit around and cackle like a bunch of layin' hens and don't accomplish a damn thing that's for the good of the kids," Smoke finished it.

Abigal smiled and minutely nodded her head in agreement.

With a sigh, Jordan shut his mouth.

Smoke looked at him. "Are you a lawyer?"

"Why, yes, I am."

"Thought so."

"Do I detect a note of disapproval in your voice, Son?" John asked.

"Might be some in there. I never found much use for lawyers. The ones I knowed, for the most part, just wasn't real nice people."

"Would you care to elaborate on that?" Walter stuck out his chin. What there was of it to stick out.

Smoke took a sip of coffee poured from the freshly made pot. Made by Sally and drinkable only by Smoke. Jordan said it was so strong it made his stomach hurt. Walter poured half a pitcher of cream in his, and John took one look at the dark brew and refused altogether.

"I reckon I might," Smoke replied. But first he rolled

another cigarette. "Man chooses a life of crime, he does that deliberate. It's his choice. Hell with him. You ladies pardon my language. On the other side of the coin, a man breaks into another house and starts stealing things, the homeowner shoots him dead, and they'll be those in your profession who'll want to put the property-owner in jail. It don't make any sense. And now, so I read and hear, you folks are beginning to say that some criminals was drove to it, and the courts ought to take into consideration about how poor they was. Poor!" he laughed. "I was a man grown at thirteen; doing a man's work and going to school and looking after my sick mother, all at once. My daddy was off fighting in the war—for the gray," he added proudly. "Not that he believed in slaves, because he didn't. War wasn't fought over slaves nohow.

"We didn't have any money. Tied the soles of our shoes on with rawhide. Ate rabbit stew with wild onions for flavor. Shot them when we had the ammunition; trapped them and chunked rocks at them when we didn't.

"Or didn't eat at all," he added grimly. "But I never stole a thing in my life. Some of our neighbors had more than they needed; but I didn't envy them for it, and if I caught myself covetin' what they had, I felt ashamed.

"Y'all got a big fine house here, and I 'spect you all got lots of money. But how many times have you turned a begger-man away from your back door without givin' him a bite to eat? That don't happen often out where me and Sally live. If that man is able, we hand him an axe and tell him to chop some wood, then we'll feed him. If he ain't able, we'll feed him and see to his needs. There ain't no need to talk on it a whole lot more. Y'all know what I'm talkin' about. But if I find somebody tryin' to steal from me, I'm gonna shoot him dead."

Smoke stood up. "I'm gonna take me a ride around your pretty town." He looked down at John. "We'll talk after supper."

He stepped off the porch and around the stables, his spurs jingling.

John smiled, then he laughed. "I like your man Smoke, Sally. I didn't think I would, but I do. Even though, or perhaps because, he is a man of conviction."

"And is more than willing, just anytime at all, to back up those convictions, Father."

"Yes," John's words were dryly given. "I just bet he is."

"That's the way it shapes up, John Reynolds," Smoke finished telling his father-in-law.

The men were in the study, the door closed. Sally was the only woman present. Her brothers had not been included in the discussion. It was after dinner, and the men had smoked their cigars and had their brandy.

John looked at York; the young Arizona Ranger met his gaze without flinching. He looked at Louis Longmont; the man was handling a rare book from John's library, obviously enjoying and appreciating the feel of the fine leather. There was no doubt in John's mind that the gambler had read it.

He cut his eyes to his son-in-law. "Of course you are going to inform our local police department of this?"

"No."

"But you must!"

"No, I must not. I don't want these men tried in some damn eastern court of law and have them serve five to ten years and then walk scot-free. And you know far better than I that is exactly what would happen, John."

"Then what do you propose to do, Son?"

"I propose to notify your local police when we see them ride into town. Louis has alerted people along the way, people who work both sides of the law. Davidson is not going to ride all the way here from Colorado. Neither is Bothwell or Rycroft or Brute or any of the others. They'll be coming in on trains, one by one, and pick up horses as close to here as possible. I got a hunch they're going to try to tree this town."

"Tree?"

"Hold it hostage. You can't do that to a western town; folks there would shoot you so full of holes your mother wouldn't recognize you. But an eastern town is different. You don't have a loaded gun in this house and damn few others do, either. But I am about to correct that little problem."

"How?" John asked, seemingly stunned by the news.

"I gave York some money this afternoon. He rode over to Brattleboro and picked up some weapons."

"You are going to arm the boys and me?"

"No." Smoked dashed that. "I'm going to arm Sally." Her father looked crestfallen.

"John," Louis asked, "have you ever killed a man?"

"What? Why . . . no."

"Any of your sons ever used a gun in anger?"

"Ah . . . no."

"That's why we're not arming you, John," Smoke told him. "It isn't that we don't believe you're one hundred percent man. It's just that you'd be out of your element. You, and ninety percent of the people in this town. Oh, a lot of men in this town fought in the War Between the States and were heroes, I'm sure. But that was war, John. I'd be very surprised if one of them could ambush a man and shoot him in cold blood."

"Yes," the lawyer agreed. "So would I."

"There you have it, Mr. Reynolds," York said. "You'd be thinkin' about them bein' human bein's and all that. Well, these people ain't worth a cup of puke."

"How quaintly put," John muttered. "And you have other officers coming in to assist you, right?

"What for?" Smoke asked.

"Well, how many outlaws will there be?"

"Oh . . . probably twenty or so. We'll handle it."

John jumped up. "Are you serious?" he shouted.

"Hell, Mr. Reynolds," York said, "that ain't but six or seven apiece. I recall the time down near the Painted Rock me and two other guys fought off a hundred or more 'paches. Kilt about forty of 'em."

He turned his head and winked at Louis.

"But those were savages!" John protested, not sure whether he believed the ranger's story or not.

Louis said, "Believe you me, John, Davidson and his bunch are just as savage as any Apache that ever lived."

Then Smoke told the man about some of the methods of torture Rex and Dagget enjoyed at Dead River.

The lawyer left the room. A few seconds later, they could hear him retching in the water closet.

"I believe you finally convinced him," Sally said.

John returned to the study, his face pale. "Son," he said to Smoke, "I'll start cleaning my shotguns and my rifle."

CHAPTER TWENTY-ONE

The nights were cool and the days were pleasantly warm as autumn slipped into the northeast. Smoke, for the most part, stayed close to the Reynolds house; York and Louis spent their days riding around the countryside, ranging from the Vermont line to the west, up to Claremont to the north, over to Manchester to the east, and down to the state line to the south.

There was no sign of Davidson or any of his men, and Smoke began to wonder if he had figured wrong. But there was still that nagging suspicion in his gut that the outlaws were on their way and that they would make their move before the first snow. And the first possible snow, John had said, would probably come around the middle of November.

The twins were growing fast. They were fat and healthy babies, who laughed and gurgled and hollered and bawled and messed their diapers.

It was fascinating to John to watch the gunslinger with the big rough hands handle the babies with such gentleness. And the twins responded to the firm gentleness, apparently loving the touch of the big, rough-looking man who, or so it seemed to John Reynolds, never took off his guns.

The sheriff of the county and the chief of police of the town came to see Smoke, demanding to know what was going on: Why had the three come to town? What were they still doing in town?

Smoke answered that he had come to town to see his wife's family, and that he was still in town waiting for the babies to get big enough to travel.

Neither the sheriff nor the chief believed Smoke's explanation. But neither the sheriff nor the chief wanted to be the one to call him a liar.

For exercise, Smoke took a wagon out into the timber and spent the better part of several days chopping wood. He chopped enough wood to last the Reynolds family most of the winter, and he stacked it neatly.

On one cool and crisp afternoon in November, Louis rode over and chatted with Smoke, who was currying Drifter. York lounged nearby, the thongs off the hammers of his .44s. Only Smoke and Sally noticed that.

"Four of them left St. Louis a week ago," Louis said, leaning up against a stall wall. "My man was certain that one of them was Davidson. They bought tickets for Boston. Six hard-looking western men pulled out of New York City day before yesterday, after buying some fine horse-flesh. Some others pulled into Pittsburgh on the river more than a month ago, bought supplies and horses, and left within a week. Still another group rode the cars from Nebraska to St. Louis, bought horses, and left weeks ago. It's taken my people some time to put all this together."

Louis's people, Smoke had learned, included not

only foot-padders and whores, but paid members of the Pinkertons.

"So we can look for them by the end of the week," Smoke said, continuing to curry Drifter. "But Davidson is too smart to come riding into town in a gang, shooting the place up. From what you've said, I gather we'll be looking at twenty to twenty-five men."

"At least," the gambler agreed. "I'd guess close to thirty." Smoke was silent for a moment, trying to recall a news article he'd read several weeks back. Then it came to him.

"There was an Army depot robbed down in Maryland several weeks back. Did either of you read that article?"

Louis snapped his fingers. "Yes! I did. Uniforms and military equipment taken. Smoke, do you think—?"

"Yes. Yes, I do. That would probably be the group who left St. Louis weeks ago." He was thoughtful. "Let's play it that way. I sure wish we had Jim Wilde and a few of the boys up here with us."

"Yes. That would be nice," Louis concurred. "But it's too late to get them here. Do we still play it close to the vest?"

Smoke sighed. "Louis, I've been thinking about that. I can't put these peoples' lives in danger. They've got a right to know what and who is about to enter this area. As bad as I hate to do it, when the so-called Army patrol is sighted, I'm going to level with the sheriff and the chief of police."

"And Mr. Reynolds?" York asked.

"I'll do that as soon as he comes in from the office."

* * *

John Reynolds listened, his face impassive. When Smoke concluded, he leaned back in his chair and sighed. "I'm glad you decided to confide in me, Son. I felt that you would, after further thought, take the lives of the people of this community under deeper consideration."

"John, listen to me," Smoke urged. "Where is the nearest military unit based?"

"Why . . . New York State, I'm sure. But we have a fine militia here in New Hampshire. I'll get right on it the first thing in the morning. I'll wire the governor and he'll see to it immediately."

John did not see the look that passed between the three gunfighters.

"How long is this going to take, sir?" York was the one who asked.

"Oh, several days, I'm sure. The governor has to sign the orders mobilizing the unit, then the men have to be notified and moved into place . . ." He fell silent with a curt wave of Smoke's hand. "What is it, Son?"

"We don't have time, John. Not for all that. Can you contact the governor tonight and have him notify the Army?"

"I'm . . . why, certainly. And tell the Army what?"

"Of our suspicions."

"I'll get a wire off immediately." He shrugged into his coat and called for his buggy. He looked at Smoke. "I'll handle this part of it, Son. Be back in half an hour."

When he returned, his face was long. "The governor is taking an early Thanksgiving vacation." He grimaced. "A very early Thanksgiving vacation. I sent a wire to the commanding officer of the Army post over in New York State. He's in Washington, D.C., for some sort of hearings.

Son, we appear to be hitting a stone wall every way we turn in this matter."

"I got a bad feelin' about this thing," York said. "I got a feelin' it's gonna break loose on us tomorrow."

"And those are my sentiments, as well," Louis agreed. "What is your opinion of the sheriff and the chief of police, John?"

"Oh, they're good men. But with only a small force between them."

Smoke and Louis and York had already checked on the cops in the town and county. A very small force. Five men, to be exact. But they all agreed the cops and deputies checked out to be good, stable men. But not gunfighters.

The hall clock chimed. It was growing late. "We see them first thing in the morning," Smoke said.

"I've packed my things," Louis said. "I'll stay here, with your permission, John."

"Of course, of course. I insist that the both of you stay." He glanced at York, received a nod, then looked at Smoke. "We'll see the sheriff and the chief first thing in the morning."

The sheriff was very indignant. "I don't see why you couldn't have leveled with us first thing, Marshal," he said to Smoke.

"Because by doing that, you would have alerted the militia and the Army and deputized every man in the county. And that would have scared them off."

"So? That would have been a bad thing?"

"In a way, yes. They would have just laid back and hit

you when you stood the men down and sent them home. How many men can you muster? Good men, Sheriff."

"Jensen, we don't have gunfighters in this town. We have shopkeepers and schoolteachers and farmers and small businessmen. And a nice fat bank," he added grimly.

"How fat?" Louis inquired.

The sheriff hesitated. But Louis Longmont was known worldwide, not only for his talents with a gun and with cards, but also as a very rich man. "Very fat, Mr. Longmont. And need I remind you all that today is the last day of the month?"

Payday for most working people. The bank would have pulled in more money to meet the demand.

"They planned it well," Smoke said, as much to himself as to the others. "How well do the people listen to you, Sheriff?"

The question caught the lawman off guard. "Why . . . I don't know what you mean. They elected me."

"What I mean is, if you told them to stay off the streets today, would they heed your words?"

"I feel certain they would."

The door to the office burst open and a flustered-looking stationmaster stepped in.

"What's the matter, Bob?" Chief of Police Harrison asked.

"I can't get a wire out in any direction, Harrison. My unit is dead as a hammer."

Louis snapped his fingers. "They're planning on using the train to get away. Remember all the horses I was told they'd bought, Smoke? They've stashed them along the railway, and they'll ride the train north to their horses."

"Huh? Huh?" the stationmaster asked, his eyes darting from man to man.

"And the uniforms they stole were not meant to be used here," Smoke added. "They'll be used as a getaway after they've ridden the train north. And it will be north. When they get close to the Canadian line, they'll peel out of those uniforms and ride across as civilians, after splitting up."

The mayor of Keene had stepped in while Louis was talking. "What's all this?" George Mahaffery asked. "I'm trying to get a wire out to my sister in Hanover, Bob. Old Sully tells me the wires are down. What's going on here?"

Nobody paid any attention to Hizzonor.

Sheriff Poley pointed at his lone deputy on duty that day. "Peter, get the women and the kids off the streets. Arm the men."

"Oh, crap!" York muttered.

"I demand to know what is going on around here?" the mayor hollered.

Nobody paid any attention to him.

Smoke stopped the deputy. "Just hold on, partner." To Sheriff Poley: "You're gonna get a bunch of good men hurt or killed, Sheriff."

Poley stuck out his chest. "What the hell do you mean by that, Marshal?"

"This is New Hampshire, Sheriff, not Northfield, Minnesota. Parts of Minnesota is still wild and woolly. When is the last time any man in this town fired a gun in anger?"

That brought the sheriff up short.

"Goddamn!" Mayor Mahaffery hollered. "Will somebody tell me what the hell is going on around here?"

"Shut up," York said to him.

Hizzonor's mouth dropped open in shock. Nobody ever talked to him in such a manner.

"And keep it shut," York added.

"I'd guess the Civil War, Marshal," Poley finally answered Smoke's question.

"That's what I mean, Sheriff. Ten men, Sheriff. That's all I want. Ten good solid men. Outdoorsmen if possible."

The deputy named a few and the sheriff added a few more. The stationmaster named several.

"That'll do," Smoke halted the countdown. "Get them, and tell them to arm themselves as heavily as possible and be down here in one hour." He glanced at the clock. Eight-thirty. "When's the next train come in?"

"Two passengers today, Marshal," Bob told him. "Northbound's due in at eleven o'clock."

"They'll hit the bank about ten-forty-five then," Louis ventured a guess.

"That's the way I see it," Smoke's words were soft. "But when will they hit the Reynolds house? Before, or after?"

Farmer Jennings Miller and his wife had left the day before to visit their oldest daughter over in Milford. That move saved their lives, for the Miller farm was the one that had been chosen by Dagget for a hideout until it was time to strike.

The outlaws had moved in during the last two nights, riding in by ones and twos, stabling their horses in the Millers' huge barn.

The outlaws had been hitting banks on their way east and had amassed a goodly sum of money. This was to be their last bank job before moving into Canada to lay low for as long as need be.

And Davidson was paying them all extra for this job, and paying them well. The bank was only secondary; the primary target was Sally Jensen and the babies.

Studs Woodenhouse had three men with him. Tie Medley had four from his original gang left. Paul Rycroft had brought two men with him. Slim Bothwell had three. Shorty, Jake, and Red. Brute Pitman. Tustin. LaHogue. Glen Moore. Lapeer. Dagget. Rex Davidson.

Twenty-six men in all. Over one hundred thousand dollars in reward money lay on their heads.

All were wanted for multiple murders, at least. The outlaws had nothing at all to lose.

"Let's start gettin' the saddles on the horses," Davidson ordered. He laughed. "One damn mile from the center of town, and nobody ever thought to look here. It was a good plan, Dagget."

"All I want is a shot at that damned John Reynolds," Dagget growled. "I want to gut-shoot that fancy-talkin' lawyer so's it'll take him a long time to die."

"They any kids in the Reynolds house?" Brute asked. "Say ten or eleven years old?"

No one answered the man. He was along solely because of his ability to use a gun and his nerves of steel. Other than that, no one had any use at all for Brute Pitman.

Not even his horse liked him.

The outlaws began a final check of their guns. They were going in heavily armed, and Rex Davidson had said he wanted the streets to run red with Yankee bluenose blood: Men, women, and kids; didn't make a damn to him.

And it didn't make a damn to the outlaws. Just as long as Davidson paid in cash or gold.

They had gotten a third of the money. The other two-thirds they'd receive in Canada.

Two men eased out of the cold house and slipped to the barn to curry and then saddle their mounts.

"I sure will be glad to have me a hot cup of coffee," Tie bitched.

"You want to take a chance on smoke being seen from the chimney?" Dagget asked him.

"I ain't complainin'," Tie replied. "I just wish I had a cup of coffee, that's all."

"Coffee on the train," Rex told them all. "And probably some pretty women."

"Yeah!" several of the outlaws perked up.

"And maybe some children," Brute grinned.

The outlaw seated next to Brute got up and moved away, shaking his head.

CHAPTER TWENTY-TWO

Good men, Smoke thought, after looking at the men that had been chosen. Not gunfighters, but good, solid, dependable men. Their weapons were not what Smoke would have chosen for his own use, but they seemed right in the hands of local citizens. Their pistols were worn high, in flap holsters; but they wouldn't be called upon to do any fast-draw work.

Smoke looked outside. The streets of the town were empty. The storeowners had locked their doors but left the shades up, to give the impression that all was well.

"You men are going to protect the bank and other buildings along Main Street," Smoke told the locals. "When you get the bastards in gunsights, pull the damn trigger! We don't have time to be nice about it. You're all veterans of the Army. You've all seen combat. This is war, and the outlaws are the enemy. The sheriff has deputized you, and I've given you federal commissions. You're protected both ways. Now get into the positions the sheriff has assigned you and stay put. Good luck."

The men filed out and began taking up positions. Some were hidden behind barrels and packing crates in alley openings. Others were on the second floor of the buildings on both sides of the street.

The sheriff and his deputy, the chief of police and his one man on duty, armed themselves and took their positions.

Smoke, Louis, and York swung in their saddles and began a slow sweep of the town.

At the Reynolds home, the twins had been taken down into the basement, where a warm fire had been built, and they were being looked after by Abigal and her daughter-in-law.

"I say, Father," Walter asked, his hair disheveled and his face flushed with excitement, "whatever can Jordan and I do?"

"Stand aside and don't get in the way," the father ordered, picking up a double-barreled shotgun and breaking it down, loading it with buckshot. He did the same to two more shotguns and then loaded a lever-action rifle. He checked the loads in the pistols Smoke had given him and poured another cup of coffee. Cowboy coffee. John was beginning to like the stuff. Really pepped a man up!

He shoved two six-shooters in his belt, one on each side. Then he took up another notch in his belt to keep his pants from falling down.

"Who is that man running across the street?" Walter asked, peering out the window.

John looked. "This isn't a man, Son. That's Martha, in men's jeans."

"Good Lord, Father!" Jordan blurted. "That's indecent!"

John looked at the shapely figure bounding up onto the

front porch. He smiled. "That's . . . not exactly the way I'd describe the lass, boy." He opened the door and let her in.

Martha carried a Smith & Wesson pocket .32 in her right hand. She grinned at John. "You know me, Mr. Reynolds. I've always been somewhat of a tomboy."

"Sally is guarding the back door, Martha. She is . . . ah . . . also in men's britches."

"Yes." Martha grinned. "We bought them at the same time." She walked back to the rear of the house.

Sally was sitting by the rear window, a rifle in her hand. She had a shotgun leaning up against the wall and wore a six-gun belt around her waist.

"Can you really shoot all those guns?" Martha asked.

"Can and have, many times. And if you're moving west, you'd better learn how."

"I think today is going to be a good day for that."

"The Indians have a saying, Martha: It's a good day to die."

"I say, Father," Jordan asked, "wherever do you want us to be posted?"

John looked at his two sons. He loved them both but knew that they were rather on the namby-pamby side. Excellent attorneys, both of them. But in a situation like the one about to face them all, about as useless as balls on a bedpost.

John laughed at his own vulgarity. "I think it would please your mother very much, boys, if you would consent to guard them in the basement."

They consented and moved out. Smartly.

Sally came in and checked on her father. She grinned at him and patted him on the shoulder. "You look tough as a gunslinger, Father."

"I feel like an idiot!" He grinned at her. "But I do think I am capable of defending this house and all in it against thugs and hooligans."

"There isn't a doubt in my mind about that, Father. Don't leave your post. I'll handle the back."

Probably with much more proficiency and deadliness than I will handle the front, he thought.

He leaned down and kissed her cheek and winked at her.

"Don't let them get on the porch, Father," she cautioned the man. "When you get them in gunsights, let 'er bang."

He laughed. "I shall surely endeavor to do that, darling!"

Smoke rode alone to the edge of town, and the huge barn to the southeast caught his eyes. There was no smoke coming from the chimney of the house, and the day was cool enough for a fire. He wondered about that, then put it out of his mind. He turned Drifter's head and rode slowly back to town.

The town appeared deserted.

But he knew that behind the closed doors and shuttered windows of the homes, men and women and kids were waiting and watching. And the people of the town were taking the news of the outlaws' arrival calmly, obeying the sheriff's orders without question.

Smoke, York, and Louis, all in the saddle, met in the center of town.

"What's the time, Louis?" Smoke asked.

The gambler checked his gold watch. "Ten-fifteen, and not a creature is stirring," he said with a small smile.

"Unless they're hidin' awful close," York said, rolling

a tight cigarette, "they're gonna have to make their first move damn quick."

Smoke looked around him at the quiet town. "They're close. Maybe no more than a mile or two outside of town. I've been thinking, boys. Jim Wilde told me that those ledger books of Davidson's showed him to be a very rich man; money in all sorts of banks . . . in different banks, under different names, Jim guessed. The assumed names weren't shown. So why would he be interested in knocking off a bank? It doesn't make any sense to me."

"You think the primary target is Sally and the babies?" Louis asked.

"Yes. And something else. John Reynolds told me that Dagget has hated the Reynolds family for years, even before he got into trouble and had to leave."

"So John and Abigal might also be targets."

"Yes."

"This Dagget, he have any family still livin' in town?" York asked.

Smoke shook his head. "I don't know. But I'd bet he does."

"But Dagget would still know the town," Louis mused aloud.

"Yes. And he would know where the best hiding places were."

"And he just might have supporters still livin' here," York interjected.

"There is that, too."

The men sat their horses for a moment, quiet, just listening to the near silence.

"Me and Louis been talkin'. Smoke, we'll take the

main street. You best head on over toward the Reynolds place."

Smoke nodded and tightened the reins. "See you boys." He rode slowly toward the Reynolds house.

York and Louis turned the other way, heading for the main street of town.

Smoke put Drifter in the stable behind the house but left the saddle on him. Pulling his rifle from the boot, he walked around the big house on the corner. The house directly across the street, on the adjacent corner, was empty. The home facing the front porch was occupied. John had said the family had taken to the basement. To the rear and the left of the Reynolds house, looking from the street, the lots were owned by John; in the summers, neat patches of flowers were grown by Abigal.

Smoke stood on the front porch, the leather hammer thongs off his .44s, the Henry repeating rifle, loaded full with one in the chamber, held in his left hand. Without turning around, he called, "What's the time, John?"

"Ten-thirty, Son," John called through the closed front door.

"They'll hit us in about ten minutes. Relax, John. Have another cup of coffee. If you don't mind, pour me one while you're at it. I'll keep an eye on the front."

The man is utterly, totally calm, John thought, walking through the house to the kitchen. Not a nerve in his entire body. He looked at his daughter. Sally was sitting in a straight-back chair by a kitchen window, her rifle lying across her lap. She looked as though she just might decide to take a nap.

"Coffee, girls?"

"Thanks, Father. Yes, if you don't mind."

Calm, John thought. But then, he suddenly realized, so am I!

Amazing.

"Why hasn't the Army been notified?" Mayor Mahaffery demanded an answer from the sheriff.

Sheriff Poley puffed on his pipe before replying. "Wire is down, George. 'Sides, Mr. Reynolds tried to get in touch with the governor last night. He's on a vacation. Tried to get in touch with the commander of that Army base over in New York State. He's in Washington, D.C. Relax, George, we'll handle it."

George pulled a Dragoon out of his belt, the barrel about as long as his arm.

Sheriff Poley looked at the weapon dubiously. "Is that thing loaded, George?"

"Certainly, it's loaded!" Hizzoner replied indignantly. "I carried it in the war!"

"What war?" Poley asked. "The French and Indian? Git away from me before you try to fire that thing, George. That thing blow up it'd tear down half the building."

Muttering under his breath, George moved to another spot in the office.

"Look at those guys," Deputy Peter Newburg said, awe in his voice.

"What guys?" Poley asked.

"Mr. Longmont and that Arizona Ranger, York. They're just standing out on the sidewalk, big as brass. Got their coats pulled back so's they can get at their guns. That York is just calm as can be rolling a cigarette."

"Hell, the gambler is reading a damn newspaper!"

George spoke up. "They behave as though they're just waiting for a train!"

"In a way," Poley said, "they are."

"What time is it?" George asked.

Sheriff Poley looked at him. "About a minute later than the last time you asked."

Before George could tell the sheriff what he could do with his smart remarks, the deputy said, "The gambler just jerked up his head and tossed the paper to the street. He's lookin' up Main."

"Here they come!" a lookout shouted from atop a building. "And there's a mob of them!"

Louis and York separated, with York ducking behind a horse trough and Louis stepping back into the shallow protection of a store well. Both had drawn their guns.

Tie Medley and his bunch were leading the charge, followed by Studs Woodenhouse and his gang, then Paul Rycroft and Slim Bothwell and their followers. Bringing up the rear were Tustin, LaHogue, Shorty, Red, and Jake. Davidson, Dagget, Lapeer, Moore, and Brute were not in the bunch.

Louis yelled out, "You men on the roof, fire, goddamnit, fire your rifles!"

But they held their fire, and both Louis and York knew why: They had not been fired upon. It was the age-old myth of the fair fight; but any realist knows there is no such thing as a fair fight. There is just a winner and a loser.

Louis stepped out of the store well and took aim. His first shot knocked a rider from the saddle. York triggered off a round and a splash of crimson appeared on an outlaw's shirtfront, but he stayed in the saddle. A hard burst of returning fire from the outlaws sent Louis back into the store well and York dropping back behind the horse trough.

The outlaws took that time to ride up to the bank and toss a giant powder bomb inside; then they charged their horses into an alley. When the bomb went off, the blast blew all the windows out of the bank front and sent the doors sailing out into the street.

Smoke and dust clouded the street. The outlaws tossed another bomb at the rear of the bank building and the concussions could be felt all over the town. The outlaws rode their horses into the back of the bombed-out bank building, and while a handful worked at the safe, the others began blasting away from the shattered front of the building.

The suddenness and viciousness of the attack seemed to stun the sheriff, the chief, and the local volunteers. From the positions chosen by the lawmen, there was nothing for them to shoot at; everything was happening on their side of the street.

Pinned down and fighting alone, Louis lost his composure and shouted, "Will you yellow-bellied sons of bitches, goddamnit, fire your weapons!"

Of course the locals were not cowardly; not at all. They just were not accustomed to this type of thing. Things like this just didn't happen in their town.

But Louis's call did get their attention, which was all he wanted.

"Call me a yellow-bellied son of a bitch, will you?" Mayor George muttered, his ears still ringing from the bomb blasts. Before anyone could stop him, George charged out of the building and onto the sidewalk. Kneeling down, he cocked the Dragoon and squeezed the trigger.

The force of the weapon discharging knocked Hizzoner to the sidewalk. His round missed any outlaw in the bank, the slug traveling clear through the wall and into the hardware store, where it hit the ammunition case and set off several boxes of shotgun shells.

The outlaws in the bank thought they were coming under attack and began shooting in all directions.

George raised to his knees and let bang another round from the Dragoon.

The slug struck an outlaw in the chest and knocked him halfway across the room.

"Clear out!" Tie hollered. "We're blowin' the vault!"

Fifteen seconds later, it seemed the gates to Hell opened up in the little town in New Hampshire.

CHAPTER TWENTY-THREE

The force of the giant powder exploding sent half the roof flying off and blew one wall completely down. George Mahaffery ended up in Sheriff Poley's lap and the chief of police found himself sitting on a spittoon, with no one really knowing how they got in their present positions.

"I got money in that bank!" a volunteer suddenly realized.

"Hell, so do I!" another called from a rooftop.

"Get 'em boys!" another called.

Then they all, finally, opened up.

"They just blew the bank building," Smoke called.

"Place needed renovating anyway," John returned the call.

Smoke laughed. "You'll do, John. You'll do!"

And John realized his son-in-law had just paid him one of the highest compliments a western man could give.

Smoke heard the pounding of hooves on the street and jerked up his Henry, easing back the hammer. He recognized

Glen Moore. Bringing up the butt to his shoulder, Smoke shot the killer through the belly. Moore screamed as the pain struck him, but he managed to stay in the saddle. He galloped on down the street, turning into a side street.

Out of the corner of his eye, Smoke saw Brute Pitman cut in behind the house, galloping across the neatly tended lawn.

"Coming up your way, Sally!" Smoke called, then had no more time to wonder, for the lawn was filled with human scum.

Smoke began pulling and levering at almost point-blank range. Lapeer taking a half-dozen round in his chest. Behind him, Smoke could vaguely hear the sounds of breaking glass and then the booming of a shotgun. An outlaw Smoke did not know was knocked off the porch to his left, half his face blown away.

"Goddamned heathen!" Smoke heard John say. "Come on, you sorry scum!"

Smoke dropped the Henry and jerked out his six-guns just as he heard gunfire from the rear of the house. He heard Brute's roar of pain and the sounds of a horse running hard.

Splinters flew out of a porch post and dug into Smoke's cheek from a bullet. He dropped to one knee and leveled his .44s at Tustin, pulling the triggers. One slug struck the so-called minister in the throat and the other took him in the mouth.

Tustin's preaching days were over. He rolled from his saddle and hit the ground.

"We've beaten them off!" John yelled, excitement in his voice.

"You stay in the house and keep a sharp lookout, John," Smoke called. "Sally! You all right?"

"I'm fine, honey. But Martha and I got lead in that big ugly man."

Brute Pitman.

And Smoke knew his plan to ride into town must wait; he could not leave this house until Brute was dead and Rex and the others were accounted for.

Reloading his guns, Smoke stepped off the porch and began a careful circling of the house and grounds.

Louis took careful aim and ended the outlaw career of Studs Woodenhouse, the slug from Longmont's gun striking the outlaw leader dead center between the eyes. A bit of fine shooting from that distance.

A rifleman from a second-floor window brought down two of Davidson's gang. Another volunteer ended the career of yet another. Several of the men had left their positions, at the calling of Sheriff Poley, and now the townspeople had the outlaws trapped inside the ruined bank.

One tried to make a break for it at the exact time Mayor George stepped out of the office, his Dragoon at the ready. The Dragoon spat fire and smoke and about a half pound of lead, the slug knocking the outlaw from his horse and dropping him dead on the cobblestones.

"Bastard!" George muttered.

Four rounds bouncing off cobblestones sent the mayor scrambling back into the office.

Tie Medley exposed his head once too often and Sheriff Poley shot him between the eyes. The Hog, along with Shorty, Jake, and Red, slipped out through a hole blown in the wall and crept into the hardware store. There, they stuffed their pockets full of cartridges and began chopping a hole in the wall, breaking into a dress shop and then into an apothecary shop. They were far enough away from the bank building then to slip out, locate their horses, and get the hell out of that locale.

"Let's find this Reynolds place!" Shorty said. "I want Jensen."

"Let's go!"

Smoke came face to face with Brute Pitman at the rear of the corner of the house. The man's face was streaked with blood and there was a tiny bullet hole in his left shoulder, put there by Martha's pocket .32.

Smoke started pulling and cocking, each round striking Brute in the chest and belly. The big man sat down on his butt in the grass and stared at Smoke. While Smoke was punching out empty brass and reloading, Brute Pitman toppled over and died with his eyes and mouth open, taking with him and forever sealing the secret to his cache of gold.

Smoke holstered his own .44s and grabbed at Brute's six-guns, checking the loads. He filled both of them up with six and continued his prowling.

Sally and Martha watched as he passed by a rear window, blood staining one side of his face. Then they heard his .44s roar into action, and each listened to the ugly sounds of bullets striking into and tearing flesh.

Glen Moore lay on his back near the wood shed, his chest riddled with .44 slugs.

Smoke tossed Bruce's guns onto the back porch and stepped inside the house.

"You hurt bad?" Sally asked.

"Scratched, that's all." He poured a cup of coffee and carried it with him through the house, stopping by John Reynolds's position in the foyer.

"It didn't go as King Rex planned." Smoke sipped his coffee. "I got a hunch he and Dagget have turned tail and run."

"Then it's over?"

"For now. But I think I know where the outlaws holed up before they hit us."

The gunfire had intensified from the town proper.

"Where?"

"That big house with the huge barn just outside of town."

"That's Jennings Miller's place. Yes. Come to think of it, I believe he went to visit one of his children the other day."

"When this is over, I'll get the sheriff and we'll take a ride over there. Does Dagget still have kin in this town?"

John grimaced. "Unfortunately, yes. The Mansfords. A very disagreeable bunch. They live just north of town. Why do you ask?"

"Probably never be able to prove it, but I'll bet they helped Dagget out in casing the town and telling them the best place to hide."

"I certainly wouldn't put it past them."

The firing had lessened considerably from the town.

"I'll wire the marshal's office first thing after the wires are fixed."

A train whistle cut the waning gunfire.

"I'll ask them to give any reward money to the town. I reckon that bank's gonna be pretty well tore up."

The train whistle tooted shrilly.

John laughed.

Smoke cut his eyes. "What's so funny, John?"

The gunfire had stopped completely; an almost eerie silence lay over the town. The train tooted its whistle several more times.

"I wouldn't worry about the bank building, Son. Like I said, it needed a lot of work done on it anyway."

"Bank president and owners might not see it that way, John."

"I can assure you, Son, the major stockholder in that bank will see it my way."

"Are you the major stockholder, John?"

"No. My father gave his shares to his favorite grand-daughter when she turned twenty-one."

"And who is that?"

"Your wife, Sally."

Chapter Twenty-four

Only two outlaws were hauled out of the bank building unscathed. Several more were wounded, and one of those would die in the local clinic.

Paul Rycroft and Slim Bothwell had managed to weasel out and could not be found.

Almost miraculously, no townspeople had even been seriously hurt in the wild shooting.

Rex Davidson and Dagget, so it appeared, were long gone from the town. The sheriff and his deputy went to the Mansford home and gave it a thorough search, talking with the family members at length. The family was sullen and uncooperative, but the sheriff could not charge anyone. After all, there was no law on the books against being a jackass.

The bodies of the dead were hauled off and the street swept and cleaned up in front of the ruined bank building. The townspeople began gathering around, oohing and aahing and pointing at this and that.

The sheriff had deputized two dozen extra men and sent them off to guard all roads and paths leading out of the town. People could come in, but you had damn well better be known if you wanted to get out.

The telegraph wires had been repaired—they had been deliberately cut by Davidson's men, so the prisoners had confessed—and they were once more humming. A special train had been ordered from Manchester and Concord, and the small town was rapidly filling up with reporters and photographers.

Pictures were taken of Mayor George Mahaffery, holding his Dragoon, and the sheriff and his deputy and of the chief of police and his men. Smoke, Louis, and York tried to stay out of the spotlight as much as possible.

That ended abruptly when a small boy tugged at Smoke's jacket.

"Yes, son?" Smoke looked down at him.

"Four men at the end of the street, Mr. Smoke," the little boy said, his eyes wide with fear and excitement. "They said they'll meet you and your men in the street in fifteen minutes."

Smoke thanked him, gave him a dollar, and sent him off running. He motioned for the sheriff and for Louis and York.

"Clear the street, Sheriff. We've been challenged, Louis, York." Then he briefed his friends.

"Why, I'll just take a posse and clean them out!" Sheriff Poley said.

Smoke shook his head. "You'll walk into an ambush if you try that, Sheriff. None of us knows where the men are holed up. Just clear the street."

"Yeah," York said. "A showdown ain't agin the law where we come from."

Since they had first met, Martha and York had been

keeping close company. Martha stepped out of the crowd and walked to York. She kissed him right on the mouth, right in front of God and everybody—and she was still dressed in men's britches!

"I'll be waiting," she whispered to him.

York blushed furiously and his grin couldn't have been dislodged with an axe.

Louis and Smoke stood back, smiling at the young woman and the young ranger. Then they checked their guns, Louis saying, "One more time, friend."

"I wish I could say it would be the last time."

"It won't be." Louis spun the cylinder of first his right-hand gun, then the left-hand .44, dropping them into leather. Smoke and York did the same, all conscious of hundreds of eyes on them.

The hundreds of people had moved into stores and ducked into alleyways. Reporters were scribbling as fast as they could and the photographers were ready behind their bulky equipment.

"There they stand," Louis said quietly, cutting his eyes up the street.

"Shorty, Red, Jake, The Hog," Smoke verbally checked them off. He glanced up and down the wide street. It was free of people.

"You boys ready?" York asked.

"Let's do it!" Louis replied grimly.

The citizens of the town and the visiting reporters and photographers had all read about the western-style shoot-outs. But not one among them had ever before witnessed one. The people watched as the outlaws lined up at the far end of the wide street and the lawmen lined up at the other. They began walking slowly toward each other.

"I should have killed you the first day I seen you, Jensen!" Jake called.

Smoke offered no reply.

"I ain't got but one regret about this thing," Jake wouldn't give it up. "I'd have loved to see you eat a pile of horse shit!"

This time Smoke responded. "I'll just give you some lead, Jake. See how you like that."

"I'll take the Hog," York said.

"Shorty's mine," Louis never took his eyes off his intended target.

"Red and Jake belong to me," Smoke tallied it up. "They're all fast, boys. Some of us just might take some lead this go-around."

"It's not our time yet, Smoke," Louis spoke quietly. "We all have many more trails to ride before we cross that dark river."

"How do you know them things, Louis?" York asked.

Louis smiled in that strange and mysterious manner that was uniquely his. "My mother was a gypsy queen, York."

Smoke glanced quickly at him. "Louis, you tell the biggest whackers this side of Preacher."

The gambler laughed and so did Smoke and York. Those watching and listening did so with open mouths, not understanding the laughter.

The reporters also noted the seemingly high humor as the three men walked toward hot lead and gunsmoke.

"It's a game to them," a reporter murmured. "Nothing more than a game."

"They're savages!" another said. "All of them. The

so-called marshals included. They should all be put in cages and publicly displayed."

Martha tapped him on the shoulder. "Mister?"

The reporter turned around.

The young woman slugged him on the side of the jaw, knocking the man sprawling, on his butt, to the floor of the store.

Jordan Reynolds stood with his mouth open, staring in disbelief.

"Good girl," John said.

A man who looked to be near a hundred years old, dressed in an ill-fitting suit, smiled at Martha. He had gotten off the train that morning, accompanied by two other old men also dressed in clothing that did not seem right for them.

Sally looked at the old men and smiled, starting toward them. The old man who had smiled at Martha shook his head minutely.

The three old mountain men stepped back into the crowd and vanished, walking out the rear of the store.

The reporter was struggling to get to his feet.

"Who was that old man, Sally?" Martha asked.

"I don't know," Sally lied. Then she turned to once more watch her man face what many believed he was born to face.

There was fifty feet between them when the outlaws dragged iron. The street erupted in fire and smoke and fast guns and death.

The Hog went down with three of York's .44 slugs in his chest and belly. He struggled to rise and York ended it with a carefully aimed slug between the Hog's piggy eyes.

Shorty managed to clear leather and that was just about

all he managed to do before Louis's guns roared and belched lead. Shorty fell forward on his face, his unfired guns shining in the crisp fall air.

Smoke took out Red first, drawing and firing so fast the man was unable to drag his .45 out of leather. Then Smoke felt the sting of a bullet graze his left shoulder as he cocked and fired, the slug taking Jake directly in the center of his chest. Smoke kept walking and firing as Jake refused to go down. Finally, with five slugs in him, the outlaw dropped to the street, closed his eyes, and died.

"What an ugly sight!" Smoke heard a man say.

He turned to the man, blood running down his arm from the wound in his shoulder. "No uglier than when he was alive," Smoke told him.

And the old man called Preacher chuckled and turned to his friends. "Let's git gone, boys. It was worth the train ride just to see it!"

The reporter that Martha had busted on the jaw was leaning against another reporter, moral and physical support in his time of great stress. "I'll sue you!" he hollered at the young woman.

Martha held up her fists. "You wanna fight instead?"

"Savage bitch!" the man yelled at her.

Lawyer John Reynolds stepped up and belted the reporter on the snoot with a hard straight right. The reporter landed on his butt, a sprawl of arms and legs, blood running down his face from his busted beak.

John smiled and said, "Damn, but that felt good!"

CHAPTER TWENTY-FIVE

BANK ROBBERY ATTEMPT FOILED BY WESTERN GUNSLINGERS screamed one headline.

SAVAGES MEET SAVAGE END IN PEACEFUL NEW HAMPSHIRE TOWN howled another front-page headline.

Smoke glanced at the headlines and then ignored the rest of the stories about him. He was getting antsy, restless; he was ready to get gone, back to the High Lonesome, back to the Sugarloaf.

"Is that reporter really going to sue you, Father?" Sally asked John.

The lawyer laughed. "He says he is."

"You want me to take care of it, John?" Smoke asked with a straight face.

"Oh, no, Son!" John quickly spoke up. "No, I think it will all work out."

Then Smoke smiled, and John realized his son-in-law was only having fun with him. John threw back his head and laughed.

"Son, you have made me realize what a stuffed shirt I had become. And I thank you for it."

Smoke opened his mouth and John waved him silent. "No, let me finish this. I've had to reassess my original opinion of you, Son. I've had to reevaluate many of the beliefs I thought were set in stone. Oh, I still believe very strongly in law and order. And lawyers," he added with a smile. "But I can understand you and men like you much better now."

York was out sparking Miss Martha, and Louis was arranging a private railroad car to transport them all back to Colorado. His way of saying thank you for his namesake.

"I'd like nothing better than to see the day when I can hang up my guns, John," Smoke said after a sip of strong cowboy coffee. "But out where I live, that's still many years down the road, I'm thinking."

"I'd like to visit your ranch someday."

"You'll be welcome anytime, sir."

John leaned forward. "You're leaving soon?"

"Probably day after tomorrow. Louis says he thinks he can have the car here then. About noon."

"And this Rex Davidson and Dagget; the others who got away?"

"We'll meet them down the road, I'm sure. But me and Sally, we're used to watching our backtrail. Used to keeping a gun handy. Don't worry, John, Abigal. If they try to take us on the Sugarloaf, that's where we'll bury them."

"I say," Jordan piped up. "Do you think your town could support another attorney? I've been thinking about it, and I think the West is in need of more good attorneys, don't you, Father?"

His father probably saved his son's life when he said, "Jordan, I need you here."

"Oh! Very well, Father. Perhaps someday."

"When pigs fly," John muttered.

"Beg pardon, sir?" Jordan asked.

"Nothing, Son. Nothing at all."

They pulled out right on schedule, but to Smoke's surprise, the town's band turned up at the depot and were blaring away as the train pulled out.

Louis had not arranged for one private car but for two, so the ladies could have some privacy and the babies could be tended to properly and have some quiet moments to sleep.

"Really, Louis," Sally told him. "I am perfectly capable of paying for these amenities myself."

"Nonsense. I won't hear of it." He looked around to make sure that Smoke and York were not watching or listening, then reached down and tickled his namesake under his chin.

"Goochy, goochy!" the gambler said.

Louis Arthur promptly grabbed hold of the gambler's finger and refused to let go.

They changed engines and crews many times before reaching St. Louis. There, all were tired and Louis insisted upon treating them to the finest hotel in town. A proper nanny was hired to take care of the twins, and Louis contacted the local Pinkerton agency and got several hard-looking and very capable-appearing men to guard the babies and their nanny.

Then they all went out on the town.

They spent two days in the city, the ladies shopping and the men tagging along, appearing to be quite bored with it all. It got very un-boring when York accidentally got lost in the largest and most expensive department store in town and wound up in one of the ladies' dressing rooms . . . with a rather matronly lady dressed only in her drawers.

Smoke and Louis thought the Indians were attacking from all the screaming that reverberated throughout the many-storied building.

After order was restored, York commented. "Gawd-damndest sight I ever did see. I thought I was in a room with a buffalo!"

The train chugged and rumbled across Missouri and into and onto the flat plains of Kansas. It had turned much colder, and snow was common now.

"I worry about taking the babies up into the high country, Smoke," Sally expressed her concern as the train rolled on into Colorado.

"Not to worry," Louis calmed her. "I can arrange for a special coach with a charcoal stove. Everything is going to be all right."

But Louis knew, as did Smoke and York, that the final leg of their journey was when they would be the most vulnerable.

But their worry was needless. Smoke had wired home, telling his friends when they would arrive in Denver. When they stepped out of the private cars, he knew that not even such a hate-filled man as Rex Davidson would dare attack them now.

Monte Carson and two of his men were there, as were

Johnny North and Pearlie and a half dozen others from the High Lonesome; all of them men who at one time or another in their lives had been known as gunslingers.

York was going to head south to Arizona and officially turn in his badge and draw his time, then come spring he'd drift back up toward the Sugarloaf. And toward Martha.

This was the end of the line for Louis. He had many business appointments and decisions to make, and then he would head out, probably to France.

"Oh, I'll be back," he assured them all. "I have to check on my namesake every now and then, you know."

Smoke stuck out his hand and the gambler/gunfighter shook it. "Thanks, Louis."

"Anytime, Smoke. Just anytime at all. It isn't over, friend. So watch your back and look after Sally and the kids."

"I figure they'll come after me come spring, Louis."

"So do I. See you, Smoke."

And as he had done before, Louis Longmont turned without another word and walked out of their lives.

Christmas in the high country and it was shut-down-tight time, with snow piled up to the eaves. For the next several months, taking care of the cattle would be back-breakingly hard work for every man able to sit a saddle.

Water holes would have to be chopped out daily so the cattle could drink. Hay would have to be hauled to them so they would not starve. Line cabins would have to be checked and restocked with food so the hands could stay alive. Firewood had to be stacked high, with a lot of it stacked close to the house, for the temperature could drop to thirty below in a matter of a few hours.

This was not a country for the fainthearted or for those who did not thrive on hard brutal work. It was a hard land, and it took hard men to mold it and make it liveable.

It was a brutal time for the men and women in the high country, but it was also a peaceful time for them. It was a time when, after a day's back-breaking and exhausting work, a man could come home to a warm fire and a table laden with hot food. And after supper, a man and woman could sit snug in their home while the wind howled and sang outside, talking of spring while their kids did homework, read or, as in Smoke and Sally's case, laid on the floor, on a bearskin rug in front of the fire, playing with toys their father had carved and shaped and fitted and pegged together with his own strong hands. They could play with dolls their mother had patiently sewn during the long, cold, seemingly endless days of winter.

But as is foretold in the Bible, there is a time for everything, and along about the middle of March, the icy fingers of winter began to loosen their chilly grip on the high country of Colorado.

Smoke and Sally awakened to the steady drip-drop of water.

Martha, who had spent the winter with them and had been a godsend in helping take care of the babies, stuck her head inside their bedroom, her eyes round with wonder.

"Raining?" she asked.

Smoke grinned at her. He and Sally had both tossed off the heavy comforter some time during the night, when the temperature began its steady climb upward.

"Chinooks, Martha," he told her. "Sometimes it means

spring is just around the corner. But as often as not, it's a false spring."

"I'll start breakfast," she said.

Smoke pulled on his clothes and belted his guns around him. He stepped outside and smiled at the warm winds. Oh, it was still mighty cool, the temperature in the forties, but it beat the devil out of temperatures forty below.

"Tell Sally I'll milk the cows, Martha. Breakfast ought to be ready when I'm—"

His eyes found the horse standing with head down near the barn. And he knew that horse. It belonged to York.

And York was lying in the muddy snow beside the animal.

Smoke jerked out his .44 and triggered two fast shots into the air. The bunkhouse emptied in fifteen seconds, with cowboys in various stages of undress, mostly in their longhandles, boots, and hats—with guns in their hands.

Sally jerked the front door open. "It's York, and I think he's hard hit . . ."

"Shot in the chest, boss!" a cowboy yelled. "He's bad, too!"

"You, Johnny!" Smoke yelled to a hand. "Get dressed and get Dr. Spalding out here. We can't risk moving York over these bumpy roads." The cowboy darted back inside the bunkhouse. Smoke turned to Sally. "Get some water on to boil and gather up some clean white cloths for bandages." He ran over to where York was sprawled.

Pearlie had placed a jacket under York's head. He met Smoke's eyes. "It don't look good. The only chance he's got is if it missed the lung."

"Get him into the house, boys."

As they moved him as gently as possible, York opened

his eyes and looked at Smoke. "Dagget and Davidson and 'bout a dozen others, Smoke. They're here. Ambushed me 'bout fifteen miles down the way. Down near where them beaver got that big dam."

Then he passed out.

Johnny was just swinging into the saddle. "Johnny! Tell the sheriff to get a posse together. Meet me at Little Crick."

The cowboy left, foggy headed.

York was moved into the house, into the new room that had been added while Smoke and Sally were gone east.

Smoke turned to Pearlie. "This weather will probably hold for several days at least. The cattle can make it now. Leave the hands at the lineshacks. You'll come with me. Everybody else stays here, close to the house. And I mean nothing pulls them away. Pass the word."

Smoke walked back into the house and looked in on York. Sally and Martha had pulled off his boots, loosened his belt, and stripped his bloody shirt from him. They had cut off the upper part of his longhandles, exposing the ugly savage wound in his chest.

Sally met her husband's eyes. "It's bad, Smoke, but not as bad as I first thought. The bullet went all the way through. There is no evidence of a lung being nicked; no pink froth. And his breathing is strong and so is his heart."

Smoke nodded, grabbing up a piece of bread and wrapping it around several thick slices of salt meat he picked from the skillet. "I'll get in gear and then Pearlie and me will pull out; join the posse at Little Crick. All the hands have been ordered to stay right here. It would take an army to bust through them."

Sally rose and kissed his lips. "I'll fix you a packet of food."

Smoke roped and saddled a tough mountain horse, a bigger-than-usual Appaloosa, sired by his old Appaloosa, Seven. He lashed down his bedroll behind the saddle and stuffed his saddlebags full of ammo and food and a couple of pairs of clean socks. He swung into the saddle just as Pearlie was swinging into his saddle. Smoke rode over to the front door of the house, where Sally was waiting.

Her eyes were dark with fury. "Finish it, Smoke," she said.

He nodded and swung his horse's head—the horse was named Horse. He waited for Pearlie and the two of them rode slowly down the valley, out of the high country and down toward Little Crick.

By eight o'clock that morning, Smoke and Pearlie had both shucked off their heavy coats and tied them behind their saddles, riding with only light jackets to protect them from the still-cool winds.

They had met Dr. Spalding on the road and told him what they knew about York's wound. The doctor had nodded his head and driven on.

An hour later they were at the beaver dam on Little Crick. Sheriff Monte Carson was waiting with the posse. Smoke swung down from the saddle and walked to where the sheriff was pointing.

"Easy trackin', Smoke. Two men have already gone on ahead. I told them not to get more'un a couple miles ahead of us."

"That's good advice, Monte. These are bad ones. How many you figure?"

"Ground's pretty chewed up, but I'd figure at least a dozen; maybe fifteen of them."

Smoke looked at the men of the posse. He knew them all and was friends with them all. There was Johnny North, at one time one of the most feared and respected of all gunslingers. There was the minister, a man of God but a crack shot with a rifle. Better hit the ground if he ever pulled out a six-shooter, for he couldn't hit the side of a mountain with a short gun. The editor of the paper was there, along with the town's lawyer, both of them heavily armed. There were ranchers and farmers and shopkeepers, and while not all were born men of the West, they had blended in and were solid western men.

Which meant that if you messed with them, they would shoot your butt off.

Smoke shared a few words with all of the men of the posse, making sure they all had ample food and bedrolls and plenty of ammo. It was a needless effort, for all had arrived fully prepared.

Then Smoke briefed them all about the nature of the men they were going to track.

When he had finished, all the men wore looks of pure disgust on their faces. Beaconfield and Garrett, both big ranchers in the area, had quietly noosed ropes while Smoke was talking.

Monte noticed, of course, but said nothing. This was the rough-edged west, where horse thieves were still hanged on the spot, and there was a reason for that: Leave a man without a horse in this country, and that might mean the thief had condemned that man to death.

Tit for tat.

"Judge Proctor out of town?" Smoke asked.

"Gone to a big conference down in Denver," Monte told him.

Beaconfield and Garrett finished noosing the ropes and secured them behind their saddles. They were not uncaring men. No one had ever been turned away from their doors hungry or without proper clothing. Many times, these same men had given a riderless puncher a horse, telling him to pay whenever he could; if he couldn't, that was all right, too.

But western men simply could not abide men like Davidson or Dagget or them that chose to ride with them. The men of the posse lived in a hard land that demanded practicality, short conversations, and swift justice, oftentimes as not, at the point of a gun.

It would change as the years rolled on. But a lot of people would wonder if the change had been for the better.

A lot of people would be wondering the same thing a hundred hears later.

Smoke swung into the saddle. "Let's go stomp on some snakes."

CHAPTER TWENTY-SIX

The posse caught up with the men who had ranged out front, tracking the outlaws.

"I can't figure them, Sheriff," one of the scouts said. "It's like they don't know they're headin' into a box canyon."

"Maybe they don't," Pearlie suggested.

One of the outriders shook his head. "If they keep on the way they're goin', we're gonna have 'em hemmed in proper in about an hour."

Garrett walked his horse on ahead. "Let's do it, boys. It's a right nice day for a hangin'."

The posse cautiously made their way. In half an hour, they knew that King Rex and Dagget were trapped inside Puma Canyon. They was just absolutely no other way out.

"Two men on foot," Monte ordered. "Rifles. And take it slow and easy up the canyon. Don't move until you've checked all around you and above you. We might have them trapped, but this is one hell of a good place for an ambush. You—"

"Hellooo, the posse!" the call came echoing down the

long, narrow canyon. It was clearly audible, so Davidson and his men were not that far away.

Monte waved the two men back and shouted, "We hear you. Give yourselves up. You haven't got a chance."

"Oh, I think not, Sheriff. I think it's going to be a very interesting confrontation."

"Rex Davidson," Smoke said. "I will never forget that voice."

Monte turned to one of his deputies. "Harry, you and Bob ride down yonder about half a mile. There's a way up to the skyline. You'll be able to shoot right down on top of them. Take off."

"This is tricky country," Beaconfield said. "Man can get hisself into a box here 'fore he knows. Took me several years to learn this country and damned if I still don't end up in a blind canyon ever now and then."

They all knew what he meant, for they all had, at one time or the other, done the same them.

"Hellooo, the posse!" the call came again.

"We hear you! What do you want?" Monte yelled, his voice bouncing around the steep canyon walls.

"We seem to have boxed ourselves in. Perhaps we could behave as gentlemen and negotiate some sort of settlement. What do you say about that?"

"Bastard's crazy!" Monte said.

"You noticed," Smoke replied.

Raising his voice, Monte called, "Toss your guns to the ground and ride on out. One hand on the reins, the other hand in the air."

"That offer is totally unacceptable!"

"Then you're going to get lead or a rope. Take your choice!"

"Come on and get us then!" Dagget yelled, laying down the challenge.

"We got three choices," Garrett said, a grimness to his voice. "We can starve them out; but that'd take days. We could try to set this place on fire and burn them out; but I don't want no harm to come to their horses. Or we can go in and dig them out."

Smoke dismounted and led Horse back to a safe pocket at the mouth of the canyon. He stuffed his pockets with .44s and pulled his rifle from the boot.

The others followed suit, taking their horses out of the line of fire and any possible ricocheting bullet. Monte waved the men to his side.

"The only way any of us is gonna take lead this day is if we're stupid or downright unlucky. What we're gonna do is wait until Bob and Harry get into position and start layin' down some lead. Then we can start movin' in. So lets have us a smoke and a drink of water and relax. Relaxin' is something them ol' boys in that box canyon ain't liable to be doin'."

The men squatted down and rolled and licked and shaped and lit. Beaconfield brought out a coffee pot, and Smoke made a small circle of rocks and started a hat-sized fire. The men waited for the coffee to boil.

With a smile on his lips, Smoke walked to the curve of the canyon and shouted, "We're gonna have us some coffee and food, Davidson. We'll be thinking about you boys all hunkered up there in the rocks doing without."

A rifle slug whined wickedly off the rock wall, tearing through the air to thud against the ground.

"This is the Jester, King Rex, Your Majesty!" Smoke shouted. "How about just you and me, your royal pain in the ass?"

"Swine!" Davidson screamed. "You traitor! You turned your back to me after all I'd done for you. I made you welcome in my town and you turned on me like a rattlesnake."

He is insane, Smoke thought. But crazy like that much-talked-about fox.

"That doesn't answer my question, Davidson. How about it? You and me in a face-off?"

"You trust that crud, Smoke?" Johnny North asked, edging close to Smoke.

"No, I just want to see what he'll do."

They all got that answer quickly. All the hemmed-in outlaws began pumping lead in Smoke's direction. But all they managed to do was waste a lot of lead and powder and hit a lot of air.

"So much for that," Smoke said, after the hard gunfire had ceased.

He had no sooner gotten the words out of his mouth when Harry and Bob opened up from the west side of the canyon wall. Several screams and howls of pain told the posse members the marksmanship of the men on the rim was true.

"That got their attention," Monte said with a grim smile.

They heard the clatter of a falling rifle and knew that at least one of the outlaws had been hard hit and probably killed.

"You have no honor, Jester!" Davidson screamed. "You're a foul person. You're trash, Jester."

"And you're a coward, Davidson!" Smoke called.

"How dare you call me a coward!"

"You hide behind the guns of a child rapist. You're afraid to fight your own battles."

"You talkin' about Dagget?" Johnny asked.

"Yeah."

Johnny grimaced and spat on the ground, as if trying to clear his mouth of a bad taste. "Them kind of people is pure filth. I want him, Smoke."

"He's all mine, Johnny. Personal reasons."

"You got him."

"Dagget!" Smoke yelled. "Do you have any bigger bolas than your cowardly boss?"

There was a long moment of silence. Dagget called out, "Name your poison, Jensen!"

"Face me, Dagget. One on one. I don't think you've got the guts to do it."

Another moment of silence. "How do we work it out, Jensen?"

"You call it, Dagget."

Another period of silence. Longer than the others. Smoke felt that Dagget was talking with Davidson and he soon found that his guess was correct.

"I reckon you boys got ropes already noosed and knotted for us, right, Jensen?" another voice called.

"I reckon."

"Who's that?" Monte asked.

"I think it's Paul Rycroft."

"I ain't lookin' to get hung!" Rycroft yelled.

Smoke said nothing.

"Jensen? Slim Bothwell here. Your snipers got us pegged out and pinned down. Cain't none of us move more'un two/three inches either way without gettin' drilled. It ain't no fittin' way for a man to go out. I got me an idea. You interested?"

"Keep talking, Slim."

"I step out down to the canyon floor. One of your men steps out. One of us, one of you. We do that until we're all facin' each other. Anybody tries anything funny, your men on the ridge can drop them already out. And since I'll be the first one out . . . well, you get the pitcher, don't you?"

Smoke looked back at the posse members. "They're asking for a showdown. But a lot of you men aren't gunslicks. I can't ask you to put your life on the line."

"A lot of them ol' boys in there ain't gunslicks, neither," Beaconfield said. "They're just trash. Let's go for it."

Every member of the posse concurred without hesitation. The minister, Ralph Morrow, was the second to agree.

"All right, Bothwell. You and Rycroft step out with me and Pearlie."

"That's a deal. Let's do 'er."

Each taking a deep breath, Smoke and Pearlie stepped out to face the two outlaws. Several hundred feet separated the men. The others on both sides quickly followed, the outlaws fully aware that if just one of them screwed up, the riflemen on the skyline of the canyon would take a terrible toll.

Davidson and Dagget were the last two down from the rocks. Davidson was giggling as he minced down to the canyon floor.

And Davidson and Dagget positioned themselves so they both were facing Smoke.

"And now we find out something I have always known," Davidson called to Smoke.

"What's that, stupid?" Smoke deliberately needled the man.

"Who's the better man, of course!" Davidson called.

"Hell, Davidson. I've known that since the first time I laid eyes on you. You couldn't shine my boots."

Davidson flushed and waved his hand. "Forward, troops!" he shouted. "Advance and wipe out the mongrels!"

"Loony as a monkey!" Garrett muttered.

"But dangerous as a rattlesnake." Smoke advised. "Let's go, boys."

The lines of men began to walk slowly toward each other, their boots making their progress in the muddy, snowy canyon floor.

The men behind their rifles on the canyon skyline kept the muzzles of their guns trained on the outlaws.

No one called out any signals. No one spoke a word. All knew that when they were about sixty feet apart, it was time to open the dance. Rycroft's hands jerked at the pistol butts and Beaconfield drilled him dead center just as Bothwell grabbed for his guns. Minister Morrow lifted the muzzle of his Henry and shot the outlaw through the belly, levered in another round, and finished the job.

The canyon floor roared and boomed and filled with gunsmoke as the two sides hammered at each other.

Smoke pulled both .44s, his speed enabling him to get off the first and accurate shots.

One slug turned Dagget sideways and the other slug hit Davidson in the hip, striking the big bone and knocking the man to the ground.

Smoke felt the lash of a bullet impact with his left leg. He steadied himself and continued letting the hot lead fly. He saw Dagget go down just as Davidson leveled his six-gun and fired. The bullet clipped Smoke's right arm, stinging and drawing the blood. Smoke leveled his lefthand .44 and shot Davidson in the head, the bullet striking him just about his right eye.

Dagget was down on his knees, still fighting. Smoke walked toward the man, cocking and firing. He was close enough to see the slugs pop dirt from the man's shirt and jacket as they struck.

Dagget suddenly rose up to one knee and his fingers loosened their hold on his guns. He fell forward on his face just as Smoke slumped against a huge boulder, his left leg suddenly aching, unable to hold his weight.

Smoke punched out empties and reloaded as the firing wound down. He watched as Pearlie emptied both Colts into the chests of two men; Minister Morrow knocked yet another outlaw to the ground with fire and lead from his Henry.

And then the canyon floor fell silent.

Somewhere a man coughed and spat. Another man groaned in deep pain. Yet another man tried to get up from the line of fallen outlaws. He tried then gave it up, falling back into the boot-churned mud.

The outlaw line lay bloody and still.

"My wife told me to finish it this morning," Smoke said, his voice seeming unnaturally loud in the sudden stillness.

"Anything my wife tells me to do, I do it," Garrett spoke.

"Looks like we done it," Johnny summed it up.

CHAPTER TWENTY-SEVEN

Beaconfield and Garrett called in some of their hands and the outlaws were buried in a mass grave. Reverend Ralph Morrow spoke a few words over the gravesite.

Damn few words.

Smoke tied off the wound in his leg and the men swung into the saddles. This part of Colorado was peaceful again, for a time.

The men turned their horses and headed for home. No one looked back at the now-quiet-but-once-roaring-and-bloody canyon floor. No one would return to mark the massive grave. The men of the posse had left the outlaws' guns on top of the mound of fresh earth.

Marker enough.

York would make it, but it would be a long, slow healing time. But as Dr. Spalding pointed out, Martha would make a fine nurse.

York had been ambushed in the late afternoon, but he'd somehow managed to stay in the saddle and finally made the ranch. He had crawled into some hay by the barn and that had probably saved his life.

"We'll call our ranch the Circle BM," York told her.

Martha thought about that. "No," she said with a smile. "Let's call it the Circle YM. It . . . sounds a little bit better."

Spring came to the High Lonesome, and with the coming of the renewal of the cycle, a peaceful warm breeze blew across the meadows and the canyons and the homes of those who chose to brave the high country, to carve out their destiny, working the land, moving the cattle, raising their families, and trying their best to live their lives as decently and as kindly as the circumstances would permit them.

Martha would be hired as the new schoolmarm, and in the summer, she and York would wed. Her teaching would be interrupted every now and then, for they would have six children.

Six to add to Smoke and Sally's five.

Five?

Yes, but that's another story . . . along the trail of the last mountain man.

VENGEANCE OF THE MOUNTAIN MAN

CHAPTER ONE

Smoke Jensen swung the big double-bladed ax in a high arc, muscles bulging in his arms as the ax split a log neatly in two. The pieces fell onto a pile of wood that reached to Smoke's knees. Shirtless, his skin bronzed by the bright sunlight of the High Lonesome, he was sweating freely though the air was cool and dry.

"Smoke, you think you oughta leave the heavy cuttin' to us young'uns?" a boyish voice called from behind him.

He stood up straight, stretching back muscles knotted from the unaccustomed chopping, and looked over his shoulder. Cal and Pearlie were standing next to a buckboard they had been loading with wood.

Smoke shook his head and grinned, thinking of the different ways they had come to work for him. Calvin Woods, going on sixteen years old now, had been just fourteen two years ago when Smoke and Sally had taken him in as a hired hand. It was during the spring branding, and Sally was on her way back from Big Rock to the Sugarloaf. The buckboard was piled high with supplies, because branding hundreds of calves makes for hungry punchers.

As Sally slowed the team to make a bend in the trail, a rail-thin young man stepped from the bushes at the side of the road with a pistol in his hand.

"Hold it right there, Miss."

Applying the brake with her right foot, Sally slipped her hand under a pile of gingham cloth on the seat. She grasped the handle of her short-barrelled Colt .44 and eared back the hammer, letting the sound of the horses' hooves and the squealing of the brake pad on the wheel mask the sound. "What can I do for you, young man?" she asked, her voice firm and without fear. She knew she could draw and drill the young highwayman before he could raise his pistol to fire.

"Well, uh, you can throw some of those beans and a cut of that fatback over here, and maybe a portion of that Arbuckles' coffee, too."

Sally's eyebrows raised. "Don't you want my money?"

The boy frowned and shook his head. "Why, no ma'am. I ain't no thief. I'm just hungry."

"And if I don't give you my food, are you going to shoot me with that big Navy Colt?"

He hesitated a moment, then grinned ruefully. "No ma'am, I guess not." He twirled the pistol around his finger and slipped it into his belt, turned, and began to walk down the road toward Big Rock.

Sally watched the youngster amble off, noting his tattered shirt, dirty pants with holes in the knees and torn pockets, and boots that looked as if they had been salvaged from a garbage dump. "Young man," she called, "come back here, please."

He turned, a smirk on his face, spreading his hands, "Look, lady, you don't have to worry. I don't even have any bullets." With a lightning-fast move he drew the gun from his pants, aimed away from Sally, and pulled the trigger. There was a click but no explosion as the hammer fell on an empty chamber.

Sally smiled. "Oh, I'm not worried." In a movement every bit as fast as his, she whipped her .44 out and fired, clipping a pinecone from a branch, causing it to fall and bounce off his head.

The boy's knees buckled and he ducked, saying, "Jiminy Christmas!"

Mimicking him, Sally twirled her Colt and stuck it in the waistband of her britches. "What's your name, boy?"

The boy blushed and looked down at his feet, "Calvin, ma'am, Calvin Woods."

She leaned forward, elbows on knees, and stared into the boy's eyes. "Calvin, no one has to go hungry in this country—not if they're willing to work."

He looked up at her through narrowed eyes, as if he found life a little different than she described it.

"If you're willing to put in an honest day's work, I'll see that you get an honest day's pay, and all the food you can eat."

Calvin stood a little straighter, shoulders back and head held high. "Ma'am, I've got to be straight with you. I ain't no experienced cowhand. I come from a hardscrabble farm and we only had us one milk cow and a couple of goats and chickens, and lots of dirt that weren't worth nothing for growin' things. Ma and Pa and me never had nothin', but we never begged and we never stooped to takin' handouts."

Sally thought, *I like this boy. Proud, and not willing to take charity if he can help it.* "Calvin, if you're willing to work, and don't mind getting your hands dirty and your muscles sore, I've got some hands that'll have you punching beeves like you were born to it in no time at all."

A smile lit up his face, making him seem even younger than his years. "Even if I don't have no saddle, nor a horse to put it on?"

She laughed out loud. "Yes. We've got plenty of ponies and saddles." She glanced down at his raggedy boots. "We can probably even round up some boots and spurs that'll fit you."

He walked over and jumped in the back of the buckboard. "Ma'am, I don't know who you are, but you just hired you the hardest workin' hand you've ever seen."

Back at the Sugarloaf, she sent him in to Cookie and told him to eat his fill. When Smoke and the other punchers rode into the cabin yard at the end of the day, she introduced Calvin around. As Cal was shaking hands with the men, Smoke looked over at her and winked. He knew she could never resist a stray dog or cat, and her heart was as large as the Big Lonesome itself.

Smoke walked up to Cal and cleared his throat. "Son, I hear you drew down on my wife."

Cal gulped, "Yessir, Mr. Jensen. I did." He squared his shoulders and looked Smoke in the eye, not flinching though he was obviously frightened of the tall man with the incredibly wide shoulders standing before him.

Smoke smiled and clapped the boy on the back. "Just wanted you to know you stared death in the eye, boy. Not many men are still walking upright who ever pulled a gun on Sally. She's a better shot than any man I've ever seen except me, and sometimes I wonder about me."

The boy laughed with relief as Smoke turned and called out, "Pearlie, get your lazy butt over here."

A tall, lanky cowboy ambled over to Smoke and Cal, munching on a biscuit stuffed with roast beef. His face was lined with wrinkles and tanned a dark brown from hours under the sun, but his eyes were sky-blue and twinkled with good-natured humor.

"Yessir, boss," he mumbled around a mouthful of food.

Smoke put his hand on Pearlie's shoulder. "Cal, this here chowhound is Pearlie. He eats more'n any two hands, and he's never been known to do a lick of work he could get out of, but he knows beeves and horses as well as any puncher I have. I want you to follow him around and let him teach you what you need to know."

Cal nodded, "Yes sir, Mr. Smoke."

"Now let me see that iron you have in your pants."

Cal pulled out the ancient Navy Colt and handed it to Smoke. When Smoke opened the loading gate, the rusted cylinder fell to the ground, causing Pearlie and Smoke to laugh and Cal's face to flame red. "This is the piece you pulled on Sally?"

The boy nodded, looking at the ground.

Pearlie shook his head. "Cal, you're one lucky pup. Hell, if'n you'd tried to fire that thing, it'd have blown your hand clean off."

Smoke inclined his head toward the bunk house. "Pearlie, take Cal over to the tack house and get him fixed up with what he needs, including a gun belt and a Colt that won't fall apart the first time he pulls it. You might also help pick him out a shavetail to ride. I'll expect him to start earning his keep tomorrow."

"Yes sir, Smoke." Pearlie put his arm around Cal's shoulders and led him off toward the bunkhouse. "Now the first thing you gotta learn, Cal, is how to get on Cookie's good side. A puncher rides on his belly, and it 'pears to me that you need some fattenin' up 'fore you can begin to punch cows."

Pearlie had come to work for Smoke in as roundabout a way as Cal had. He was hiring his gun out to Tilden Franklin in Fontana when Franklin went crazy and tried to take over Sugarloaf, Smoke and Sally's spread. After Franklin's men raped and killed a young girl in the fracas, Pearlie sided with Smoke and the aging gunfighters he had called in to help put an end to Franklin's reign of terror.

Pearlie was now honorary foreman of Smoke's ranch.

Smoke stopped with his ax in mid-swing and narrowed his dark eyes at Pearlie, who was grinning from ear to ear. "Pearlie, I suspect you've been neglecting your teaching chores with young Calvin here," he drawled.

Pearlie's grin faded a bit. "How's that, Smoke? The boy can ride like an Injun, herd beeves like he was born to it, and can damn near shoot as good as me."

Smoke used a beefy forearm to sleeve sweat off his forehead. "Well, 'pears the boy's a mite short on respect for his elders." Dropping the ax and moving almost faster than the eye could follow, Smoke took two steps and grabbed Cal by the pants, lifting him and throwing him over his shoulder like a sack of potatoes.

As Cal kicked and fought, and Pearlie laughed, Smoke loped down the side of the hill toward a mountain stream twisting through the valley. Since it was the second week in September, and snow was already falling on mountain peaks surrounding Sugarloaf, the water was only a few degrees above freezing.

When he stood on the creek bank, Smoke took a deep breath through his nose. "Whew, this boy is ripe, Pearlie. How long since he's had a bath?"

"No-o-o-o," wailed Cal, kicking all the more to get free. "I'm sorry, Smoke. I's jest teasing 'bout you bein' old and all."

"Why Smoke," laughed Pearlie, "I'm almost sure it hadn't been hardly two weeks since Cal bathed last. He's not due for at least another week."

"Wrong," snorted Smoke. He bent over quickly, straightened, and flipped Cal ass-over-heels into the frigid water. As Cal came up gulping and yelling and flapping his arms, Smoke said, "Preacher always said a man shouldn't bathe more'n twice a year, otherwise he'd get sick and die." Smoke put his hands on his hips and smiled at the dripping boy as he scrambled out of the stream, shivering and shaking. "Course, that only applies to mountain men, not whelps like Cal here." He cocked his head at Pearlie and pointed a finger at Cal. "In the future, I expect him to have a bath at least every week."

Pearlie looked aghast. "Even in the winter?"

"Especially in the winter. Maybe it'll teach him to respect his elders. Right, Cal?"

"Ye-ye-ye-yes sir!" Cal answered through chattering teeth. Smoke ambled back uphill where he picked up his shirt and slipped it on. "Now, this old man is tired from all this hard work, so I'm gonna take me a little nap under that pine tree over yonder while you young bucks cut up the rest of those logs." He looked at storm clouds hanging like dark cotton over the mountain peaks around them. "It's gonna be an early winter, and that means we're gonna need lots of wood."

He handed the ax to Cal. "Here, young un'. Maybe chopping those logs'll warm you up a bit." He winked at Pearlie as he walked over to where his horse was ground-hitched. He dipped into his saddlebags and withdrew a handful of donuts, or bearsign as mountain men called them, and chewed as he lay back against the tree. "If you hurry, maybe there'll be a few of these bearsign left when you get done." He took a huge mouthful and mumbled loud enough for the two men to hear, "and, then again, maybe there won't be none left after all."

Pearlie looked at Cal. "Come on boy, I've been waiting all mornin' for a taste of Sally's bearsign. Start swingin' that ax like you mean it."

The sound of a gunshot brought Smoke instantly awake and alert. Years in the mountains with the first mountain man, Preacher, had taught Smoke many things. Two of the most important were how to sleep with one ear open, and never to be without one of his big Colt .44s nearby. The gun was in his hand with the hammer drawn back before echoes from the shot had died.

"Sh-h-h Horse," he whispered, not wanting the big Appaloosa to nicker and give away his position. He buckled his gun belt on, holstered his .44, and slipped a sawed-off ten-gauge American Arms shotgun out of his saddle scabbard. Glancing at the sun, he figured he had been asleep about two hours. Cal and Pearlie were nowhere in sight.

Raising his nose, Smoke sniffed the breeze. The faint smell of gunpowder came from upwind. He turned and began to trot through the dense undergrowth of the mountain woods, making not a sound.

Smoke peered around a pine tree and saw Cal bending over Pearlie, trying to stanch the blood running down his left arm. Four men on horseback were arrayed in front of them, one still holding a smoking pistol in his right hand. "Okay, now I'm not gonna ask you boys again. Where is Smoke Jensen's spread? We know it's up in these hills somewheres."

Cal looked up, and if looks could kill, the men would have been blown out of their saddles. "You didn't have to shoot him. We're not even armed."

"You going to talk, boy? Or do you want the same as your friend there?" The man pointed the gun at Cal, scowling in anger.

Cal squared his shoulders and faced the man full on, fists balled at his sides. "Get off that horse, mister, and I'll show you who's a boy!"

The man's scowl turned to a grin. His lips pulled back from crooked teeth as he cocked the hammer on his weapon. "Say good-bye, banty rooster."

Smoke stepped into the clearing and fired one barrel of the shotgun, blowing the man's hand and forearm off up to his elbow, to the accompaniment of a deafening roar.

The men's horses reared and shied as the big gun boomed, while the riders clawed at their guns. Smoke flipped Cal one of his Colts with his left hand as he drew the other with his right.

Cal cocked, aimed, and fired the .44 almost simultaneously with Smoke. Smoke's bullet hit one rider in the middle of his chest, blowing a fist-sized hole clear through to his back. Cal's shot took the top of another man's head off down to the ears. The remaining gunman dropped his weapon and held his hands high, sweating and cursing as his horse whirled and stomped and crow-hopped in fear.

Smoke nodded at Cal, indicating he should keep the man covered, then he walked over to Pearlie. He bent down and examined the wound, which had stopped bleeding. "You okay, cowboy?"

Pearlie smiled a lopsided grin. "Yeah, boss. No problem." He reached in his back pocket and pulled out a plug of Bull Durham, biting off a large chunk. "I'll just wet me some of this here tabaccy and stuff it in the hole. That'll take care of it until I can get Doc Spalding to look at it."

Smoke nodded. He remembered Preacher had used tobacco in one form or another to treat almost all of the many injuries he endured living in the mountains. And Preacher had to be in his eighties, if he was still alive, that is.

With Pearlie's wound seen to, Smoke turned his attention to the man Cal held at bay. He walked over to stand before him. "Get off that horse, scum."

The man dismounted, casting an eye toward his friend writhing on the ground trying to stop the bleeding from his stump. "Ain't ya gonna hep Larry? He's might near bled to death over there."

Smoke walked over to the moaning man, stood over him, and casually spat in his face as he took his last breath and died, open eyes staring at eternity. With eyes that had turned ice-gray, Smoke turned to look at the only one of the men still alive. "What's your name, skunk-breath?"

"George. George Hampton."

"Who are you, and what're you doin' here looking for me?"

"Why, uh, we was lookin' fer Smoke Jensen."

Smoke sighed, shaking his head. "I *am* Smoke Jensen, you fool. Now you found me, what do you want?"

Hampton's eyes shifted rapidly back and forth from Cal to Smoke. "You can't hardly be Smoke Jensen. You're too danged young. Jensen's been out here in the mountains killing people for nigh on ten, fifteen years."

"I started young." He drew his .44 and eared the hammer back, the sear notches making a loud click. "And I'm not used to asking questions more than once."

Hampton held up his hands. "Uh, look Mr. Jensen, it was all Larry's idea. He said some gunhawk gave him two hundred dollars to come up here and kill you." He started speaking faster at the look on Smoke's face. "He said he'd share it with we'uns if we'd back his play."

Smoke raised his pistol. "What was this gunhawk's name?"

Hampton shook his head. "I don't know. Larry never told us."

Smoke looked at Hampton over the sights of his .44. "You sold your life cheap, mister."

Cal cried out, "Smoke! No!"

Smoke lowered his gun, sighing. "Cal's right. I've gone this long without ever killing an unarmed man. No need to change now, even you sorely need it." He stopped talking, a funny expression on his face. He sniffed a couple of times, then looked at Hampton through narrowed eyes. "That smell coming from you, mister?"

Hampton's face flared red and he looked down. "Uh, yessir. My bowels kinda let loose when you cocked that big pistol of yours."

Pearlie let out a guffaw. "Hell, Smoke. You don't want to kill this 'un. Let him go and if he's any kind of man he'll die of shame 'fore the day's over."

Smoke holstered his gun and turned to walk away. Cal nodded at Hampton. "Drop your gun belt and rifle and get out of here while the gettin's good."

As Hampton stepped in his saddle and took off looking for a hole, Pearlie called out, "And you can tell your kids you once looked over the barrel of a gun at Smoke Jensen and lived to tell about it. Damn few men can say that!"

Smoke flipped open the loading gate of his .44 and began to punch out his empties as he spoke to Pearlie. "I'll bet you think that scratch on your arm is going to keep you from loading up all this wood Cal cut, don't you?"

Pearlie looked back through wide eyes, then grabbed his arm and moaned, loud and long.

Smoke continued reloading his gun without looking at Pearlie. "Course, if you're hurtin' that bad, I don't guess you'd want any of those bearsign I've got left."

The moaning stopped and Pearlie jumped to his feet and started back toward Smoke's horse. "I'll just go and get some java started while you and Cal finish loading up. I'll wait for you at camp."

"Leave a few for me, you polecat!" Cal yelled to the rapidly disappearing man.

Chapter Two

On their way back to his cabin, with Cal driving the buckboard and Pearlie in the back cussing every rock and bump in the trail, Smoke reflected on how many men he had carried home with enemies' lead in them. Quite a few, he thought. Horse, Smoke's Palouse, had been sired by old Seven, a gift to Smoke from the Nez Perce who started the breed. He knew the way home without prompting, leaving Smoke to his thoughts about his early days in the mountains.

Young Kirby Jensen had come to the mountains with his father while barely in his teens. The pair teamed up with a mountain man, who some call the first mountain man, named Preacher. For some reason, unknown even to Preacher, the loner took to the boy and began to teach him the ways of the mountains: how to live when others would die, how to be a man of your word, and how to fear no other living creature. On the first day they met, Preacher gave the boy a name that would become legend in the West over the years, Smoke.

Preacher was with Smoke when he killed his first man

during an Indian attack, and he took the boy in when his dying father left him in Preacher's care.

While still a teenager, Smoke left Preacher's tutelage and set out on his own to marry and raise a family in the wilderness he learned to call home. Marauders raped and killed his wife and baby son while Smoke was away. He tracked them down and killed them to a man, then he rode into an Idaho town owned by the men who had sent the killers and wiped it and those that lived there off the face of the earth.

Smoke had been married to Sally, a former schoolteacher, for years and was happier than he thought any man had a right to be. Their ranch in the valley called Sugarloaf was just beginning to become famous as a source of fine-bred Palouse horses and beef that grew fat and juicy on the sweet grass of mountain meadows.

As Horse neared the cabin, he nickered, glad to be home. Sally came running out of the door, an anxious expression on her face at the sight of Pearlie lying in the wagon, a blood-soaked bandage around his left arm.

Her face softened as she reached into the wagon and brushed the bearsign crumbs off his face. "Well, I can see your wound hasn't hurt your appetite any. Are you okay, Pearlie?"

"Yes, ma'am. It's just a scratch. I'll be back at work in no time."

Smoke swung his leg over the saddle horn and slid to the ground, giving Sally a hug that lifted her off her feet. "Pearlie's lucky, Sally. That bushwhacker was using one of those new .44/.40 pistols, otherwise that slug would've taken his arm off clean."

Cal looked up, eyebrows raised. "What's a .44/.40, Smoke?"

"It's a .40 caliber barrel and works on a .44 caliber frame. Gives less of a kick and is more accurate for amateurs, but has lots less stopping power." He nodded his head toward the valley where the other hands were with the beeves. "Cal, would you ride down to the herd and send one of the boys to Big Rock to see if Doc Spalding can come up here and take a look at Pearlie's arm?"

Before Cal could answer, Pearlie said, "Oh boss, you don't have to do that. I'll heal just fine without any old doctor messing with it."

Cal chuckled. "He's just afraid the doc'll give him some stitches, Smoke. I'll get someone to go fetch him right now."

Sally put her hand on Pearlie's shoulder. "It'll heal a lot faster if Doctor Spalding closes the wound."

Pearlie shook his head. "Well, I'm not in any real hurry, Miss Sally, and I'm not real partial to needles."

"Well," she said with a wink at her husband, "I've got some fresh hot apple pie cooling in the kitchen. If you're not in too much pain, perhaps you can have a piece while we're waiting for the doctor to get here."

"Yes ma'am, I mean, no ma'am . . . oh, you know what I mean."

As tough as mountain folks needed to be to survive, Sally thought, the men were like little kids when it came to sweets from the oven. Miners and farmers had been known to endure a day's ride for bearsign, and pies cooling on the window sill would make cowboys forget their branding and spur their mounts home.

That night, after Doc Spalding had tended to Pearlie's

arm and been treated to Sally's home cooking and an after-dinner whiskey and cigar for his trouble, Smoke and Sally strolled through the moonlight, arm in arm.

"Smoke, who do you think that man meant when he said a gunhawk had paid them to kill you?"

He shrugged. "I don't know. I've been in this country for a lot of years and made a lot of enemies." He looked out over their valley shimmering in the moonlight and sighed. "It could be anyone of a dozen or more, I suppose."

Sally took his face in her hands and pulled it close for a gentle kiss. "You ride with your guns loose, Smoke Jensen. Sugarloaf wouldn't be the same without you."

He grinned. "You mean you'd miss me?"

She took him by the sleeve and pulled him toward their cabin. "Follow me and I'll show you."

The next morning, over scrambled eggs, bacon, and coffee, Smoke told Sally he was going in to Big Rock to discuss the disposition of the bushwhackers' bodies with Sheriff Monte Carson.

She arched her eyebrows. "You mean you left those men lying on the ground up in the north woods?"

He blew on his coffee, then sipped cautiously. "Yep."

"Smoke, those men deserve a Christian burial."

"Well, Sally, they weren't acting like Christians when they came up on our mountain to kill me."

"But—"

He placed his hand over hers on the table. "But nothing, dear. I know you're a forgiving lady, one not taken with revenge and such, but in this country, a man deserves only what he can carve out of the mountain, nothing else.

Those men up there made the decision to ride the owlhoot trail, to live or die by their guns. Well, they died. That's the long and the short of it. I don't owe those men nothing but what I gave them, an ounce of lead in a .44 caliber."

Smoke knew Sally was no fool. She realized when Smoke put his foot down it was time to keep her opinions to herself. In the way of women since time immemorial, she would bide her time, come at him from a different direction, and, more often than not, get her way in the end without him even realizing it. Such was marriage, even in the High Lonesome and even among the singular breed called the mountain men.

As he sauntered outside and climbed on Horse, she handed him a package of jerked beef, biscuits, and a couple of apples. He laughed, "You never forget my trail food, do you?"

She smiled, a mischievous smile. "Got to keep your strength up." She walked up to his horse and put her hand on Smoke's thigh. "I don't want you too tired when you get home. There's lots of work to be done around the cabin."

He laughed out loud, making her blush a fiery red. "I was about to say I'd stay the night in Big Rock, but now I think I'll come home if I have to ride the entire way after dark."

He whirled the big Palouse around and took off down the trail toward town, waving his hat at Sally as he rounded the curve in the road.

CHAPTER THREE

Smoke was halfway to Big Rock when Horse began to act up. First the horse snorted, pricked his ears, and looked back toward Smoke with eyes wide. Smoke had been lost in thought about who might be gunning for him, letting Horse find his own way to town. He came fully awake and alert when the animal began to nicker softly.

Leaning forward in the saddle, he patted Horse's neck and whispered, "Thanks, old friend. I hear you." Mountain-bred ponies were better than guard dogs when it came to sensing danger. Smoke shook his head, thinking Preacher would be disgusted with him. If there was one thing the old mountain man stressed, it was the mountains were a dangerous world, not to be taken lightly. Riding around with your head in the clouds, especially when you knew someone was trying to nail your hide to the wall, was downright stupid, if not suicidal.

Smoke slipped the hammer thongs from his Colts, then put his hand on the butt of the Henry rifle in the scabbard next to his saddle and shook it a little to make sure it was loose and ready to be pulled.

He tugged gently on the reins to slow Horse from a trot

to a walk and settled back in the saddle, hands hanging next to his pistols.

Even with his precautions, he was surprised when a man jumped out of the brush into the middle of the trail in front of him. It was George Hampton, and he was pointing a Colt Navy pistol at Smoke.

"Get down off that horse, you bastard."

Smoke spread his hands wide and swung his leg over the cantle and dropped, cat-like, to the ground. "Hampton, I thought you'd be halfway home by now."

"I ain't gonna go home 'til I've put a bullet between the eyes of the famous Smoke Jensen."

Smoke glanced at the revolver Hampton was holding, smiled, and shook his head. "Hampton, I really don't want to kill you. Why don't you just put that gun down and head on home?" He spread his hands wider, stepping closer to him. "And just where is your home anyway? You never got around to telling me yesterday."

Hampton licked his lips, the gun trembling a little in his hand. "Just keep your distance, Jensen. I'll admit I ain't no expert with this six-gun like you are, but I can't hardly miss at this distance."

Smoke kept his hands in front of him. "Okay, okay, don't get nervous. I'll stay back, but it seems to me a man oughta know just why he's bein' killed."

Hampton nodded. "Well, you're right. I can see the justice in that, 'cept I don't rightly know. Larry, the man you kilt yesterday, he made me and the other boys the offer down on the Rio Bravo in Texas. Seems that gunhawk met him in a saloon in Laredo and told him he wanted you dead in the worst way . . . somethin' about how you had humiliated him a while back and he wanted you in the ground because of it."

Smoke's eyes narrowed and turned slate gray. "So you and the other boys decided to pick up some easy money on the owlhoot trail, huh?"

Sweat was beading on Hampton's forehead in spite of the cool mountain air. "Naw, it wasn't like that. We're just cowboys, not gunslicks. There's an outbreak of Mexican fever in the cattle down Texas way and there ain't much work for wranglers, leastways not unless you've hooked up with one of the big spreads." He shook his head, gun barrel dropping a little. "Hell, it was this or learn to eat dirt."

Smoke relaxed, his muscles loosening. "I'll tell you what, Hampton. There's always work for an honest cowboy in the high country. If you're willing to give an honest day's labor, you'll get an honest day's pay."

The pistol came back up and Hampton scowled. "You're just sayin' that cause I got the drop on you."

Smoke smiled, then quick as a rattlesnake's strike, reached out and grabbed Hampton's gun while drawing his own Colt .44 and sticking the barrel under Hampton's nose. "No George, you're wrong. You never had the drop on me." He nodded at Hampton's pistol. "That there is a Colt Navy model, a single-action revolver. You have to cock the hammer 'fore it'll shoot, and I can draw and fire twice before you can cock that pistol."

Hampton's shoulders slumped and he let go of his gun and raised his hands. "Okay Jensen, it's your play."

Smoke holstered his Colt and handed the other one back to Hampton. "I told you, George, you got two choices. You can get on that pony there and head on back to Texas, or I can give you a note and send you up to one of the spreads hereabouts and you can start working and feeling like a man again. It's all up to you."

Hampton looked down at his worn and shabby boots and britches, then back to Smoke. "That's no choice, Mr. Jensen. You give me that note and I promise I'll not make you sorry you trusted me."

Smoke walked to Horse and took a scrap of paper and pencil stub out of his saddlebags. After a moment, he handed the paper to Hampton. "Take this note to the next place you see up to the north of mine. It belongs to the Norths. They can always use an extra hand, and Johnny pays fair wages."

Hampton held out his hand. "I don't know how to thank you, Mr. Jensen, but . . . thanks."

Smoke grinned, knowing Hampton was a friend for life. In the rough-hewn country of the West, favors, or slights, were not soon forgotten. Help a man who's down on his luck, and he's honor-bound to repay you, even at the cost of his life, if it comes to that.

Smoke rode into Big Rock, Colorado, the town he had helped build, and began to relax again. If there was any place he felt safe, other than the Sugarloaf, it was here. Though it was growing faster than he liked, Smoke knew just about everyone in town and counted all of them as friends. In spite of his reputation as one of the most feared shootists in the country, the citizens of Big Rock knew Smoke personally for what he was, a good neighbor who would never let a friend down and a man any would be proud to ride the river with.

As Smoke nodded to the men and tipped his hat to the ladies he passed, he saw Sheriff Monte Carson in front of the jail. He was sitting in a chair tilted back on its hind legs with his back against the wall and his hat down over his face, snoring loudly.

Smoke smiled at the sight of the sheriff sleeping peacefully. He and Monte Carson had become very good friends over the past few years. Carson had once been a well-known gunfighter, though he had never rode the owlhoot trail.

A local rancher with plans to take over the county had hired Carson to be the sheriff of Fontana, a town just down the road from Smoke's Sugarloaf spread. Carson went along with the man's plans for a while, 'til he couldn't stomach the rapings and killings any longer. He put his foot down and let it be known that Fontana was going to be run in a law-abiding manner from then on.

The rancher, Tilden Franklin, sent a bunch of riders in to teach the upstart sheriff a lesson. The men killed Carson's two deputies and seriously wounded him, taking over the town. In retaliation, Smoke founded the town of Big Rock, and he and his band of aging gunfighters cleaned house in Fontana.

When the fracas was over, Smoke offered the job of sheriff of Big Rock to Monte Carson. He married a grass widow and settled into the job like he was born to it. Neither Smoke nor the citizens of Big Rock ever had cause to regret his taking the job.

Being careful not to make a sound, Smoke eased down off Horse and took one of the apples Sally had given him from his saddlebag. He walked over to stand in front of Carson and pitched the apple into his lap.

Carson snorted, flipped his chair forward, and drew his pistol with his right hand while pushing his hat back with his left, all in one quick movement.

As his pistol cleared leather, Smoke reached out and grabbed the barrel in his left hand, saying, "Hold on there, Hoss."

A sheepish Monte Carson grinned. "Oh, it's you, Smoke."

Smoke released the weapon and hooked another chair over with the toe of his boot. He straddled the chair backward, leaning his arms on the back of the chair and his chin on arms. "Pretty fast draw for an old fart like you, Monte. Been practicing?"

"An old fart, am I?" Carson glared at Smoke through narrowed eyes. "Best I remember, I'm only a couple of years older than you, and you're—"

"Too old to remember all my birthdays, that's for sure." Smoke interrupted. "Matter of fact, I'm old enough to remember when a fella used to be offered some coffee or a drink when he came to visit the big city, but I guess times have changed."

Carson shook his head. "Smoke Jensen acting like company, now that's a laugh. The coffeepot's in the same place it's always been, and this here jail ain't no restaurant and this here sheriff ain't no waiter. You want some, you're welcome to it."

With that statement, Carson leaned his chair back and pulled his hat down over his eyes.

Smoke laughed and got up to pour himself a cup of coffee. As he was pouring the evil-looking brew, he heard Carson say, "And pour me a cup while you're at it. These legs are so old I don't know if they'll carry me in there to get my own."

Smoke carried both cups out on the boardwalk and handed one to Carson. "Monte, I know cowboys like their coffee strong and all, but," he looked down at the liquid in his cup that had the color and consistency of axle grease in winter, "don't you think this bellywash is just a touch past due for thinning?"

Carson smiled as he blew on the coffee to cool it and drank a mouthful. He smacked his lips and said, "Ahhh. That's good. It's like an old trail cook once told me. The secret to makin' good coffee is that it don't take near as much water as you think it do."

Laughing, Smoke set his cup down and pulled his tobacco pouch out. As was the Western way, he offered it first to Carson, who declined and began to fix his pipe. Smoke sprinkled tobacco on the paper, tamped both ends with his fingers, and rolled the cigarette into a tube. As he licked the paper, he glanced up at Carson. "Heard anything interesting lately, Monte?"

They had been friends long enough for Carson to catch the change in Smoke's tone and he looked up from his pipe with raised eyebrows. "No, why? Something going on I ought to know about?"

Smoke scratched a match into flame with his thumbnail, lit his cigarette, and handed the match to Carson. "Well, something strange happened the other day up on the Sugarloaf. Four men came gunning for me and shot up Pearlie a little bit."

Carson narrowed his eyes. "Oh? Well, men gunning for Smoke Jensen, now there's a novel thought. Did you bother to bury 'em or do I have to send someone from town to go and cart the carcasses back down here to Boot Hill?"

Smoke shook his head, "Now, there's no need to be sarcastic, Monte. These men were different from the usual type that are just after making a name for themselves. Cal and I let the hammer down on three of them, but I let one of the men live. He said a gunhawk down Texas way, on the Rio Grande, hired them to kill me to pay me back for something I did to him a while back."

"Oh, well then. That narrows the field of men who want to kill you down from a thousand to maybe only a hundred or so."

"Yeah, those were my thoughts, too." Smoke flipped his butt out into the dusty street and drank the last of his coffee. "Well, guess I'll amble on over to the saloon and see if there's been any newcomers to town who might have heard something."

Carson looked up from under his hat-brim. "You want some company?"

Smoke put on an innocent expression. "Naw, you know me. I'm a peaceable rancher, not looking for any trouble, just going to have a sociable drink at the neighborhood dog hole."

"Yeah, and I'm my aunt Bertha. Smoke, you know if things get out of hand, you've always got help right here." He patted his pistol. "I may be old and half civilized, but I haven't forgotten how to use this peashooter if the need ever arises."

Smoke put his hand on Carson's shoulder. "Thanks, Monte, but you know out here a man saddles his own horse and kills his own snakes."

Just then a small boy of about seven years old ran up

to Smoke and Carson. "Sheriff Carson, there's a feller down at the saloon who's plumb alkalied. He's dressed up like a sore toe and tellin' everyone he's gonna kill Smoke Jensen."

"Oh shit. Thanks, Jerome. You run along home now and get off the street, and get your friends off the street, too." He turned to Smoke. "I don't guess you'd ride on out of town and let me handle this, would you?"

Smoke gave a smile that didn't go to his eyes. "Monte, that sounds like one of those snakes we were just talking about."

Carson drew his pistol and opened the loading gate to check his loads. "Well, if you've only got five beans in the wheel, you'd better load up six and six; no telling if he's got friends to back his play or if he's alone."

Smoke loaded his Colt, spun the cylinder for luck, then holstered the big gun. "You got my back, Monte?"

Carson grinned like a schoolboy about to bust some noses out in the yard. "Don't I always?"

They walked down the center of the street, womenfolk and children scattering at the serious expressions on their faces and at their purposeful strides. In the mysterious way of Western towns, faster than any telegraph, word spread that there was going to be trouble, meaning gunplay, and that Smoke Jensen was involved. The streets and boardwalks emptied, and the townspeople gathered behind windows and doors to watch some other poor fool try his hand against Smoke Jensen.

Smoke pushed through the batwings of the saloon and immediately stepped to the side, giving his eyes a moment to adjust to the dusky light of the place. Through the cigar smoke and beer smell, he could see a young tough leaning on the bar, waving his hands in drunken hyperbole, talking loud and being whiskey-brave.

"Yeah, tha's right. I'm gonna kill me a Smoke Jensen, tha's for sure. Soon's that yellow sonofabuck gits here, he's a dead man."

Smoke took in the stranger's garb with a glance. Shiny black leather vest over a boiled-white shirt, string tie, and a double-rig holster of fancy tooled leather with rawhide strings hanging from the belt. Two brand-new Colt Peacemaker .45s were in the holsters, conspicuous notches cut in both handles so new that fresh wood showed at the bottom of the cuts.

Smoke and Carson looked at each other and laughed. Smoke whispered, "He's so booze-blind he couldn't hit the ground with his hat in three tries."

Carson grinned and sat down at a table while Smoke walked to the bar and stood next to the man doing all the talking. When the man looked up at him, Smoke grinned a huge grin and said, "Hi there, Pilgrim. Can I buy you a drink?"

The man swayed as if he might fall, before nodding and saying, "Sure, then someday you kin tell your kids you bought a drink for the man that kilt Smoke Jensen."

Smoke's eyes opened wide and he let his mouth drop open. "You mean you're going to go up against the famous shootist Smoke Jensen?"

"Yep. Gonna kill him, too."

"Well let me shake your hand, pardner." After they shook hands, Smoke opened his shirt and showed the man an old bullet wound scar. "See this here scar? That's where Smoke Jensen shot me through the arm."

The man narrowed his eyes. "You mean you faced Jensen in a gunfight and he didn't kill ya?"

Smoke shook his head. "Wasn't no need. Hell, I didn't even clear leather 'fore he shot me and my partner both."

"Ya mean there was two of you and he got you both?"

"Yep. The bastard gut-shot my partner and winged me without even breaking a sweat. Left us both on the trail to die. Took my partner three days to die, and he died hard, let me tell you."

The man leaned his head back and tried to focus on Smoke. "You a gunfighter?"

"Naw, I'm just a rancher and cowhand. I'm much too slow on the draw to be a gunfighter. Hell, half the men in town can outdraw me. Here, I'll show you." Smoke stepped away from the man and in the blink of an eye his Colt was drawn, cocked, and pointing at the man's face. "See, I couldn't touch Smoke Jensen. The only reason we tried was his back was turned and we thought we had the drop on him."

Frowning, the man asked. "You mean his back was to you and he still beat you to the draw?"

"Sure." Smoke leaned close to the man and whispered, "Jensen said he heard our guns leaving our holsters and knew he had to draw."

"Jesus!" the man whispered back. "That's mighty fast."

"Yeah, my partner and I thought so, too. But I've been practicing since then. I think maybe I can surprise him if I use my left hand." No sooner had Smoke finished his sentence than his lefthand gun appeared in the man's face, the draw so quick it was just a blur. "Course," Smoke continued as he holstered his pistol, "since you're obviously a gunman, you're probably not too impressed with my draw."

Smoke put an anxious expression on his face. "Say, do you think maybe you could show me how fast a real gunslinger is? Maybe even give me some pointers?"

Sweat beaded the man's forehead and he turned back to his whiskey, drinking it down in one quick draught. "No, I think you'd better leave gunfighting to us experts." He pulled his hat down and threw two bits on the bar. "Well, it don't look like Smoke Jensen is gonna come to town today, so I guess I'll just mosey on down the road a ways."

Smoke put a hand on the man's shoulder. "Hey, I could get one of the guys here in town to ride out to his ranch and bring him in, if you want."

"No, no, not today. I think I'll just let him live another day and come back some other time." With that, the sweating man bolted from the saloon to the raucous laughter of the other patrons, got on his horse, and got out of town in a hurry.

Carson walked to the bar and clapped Smoke on the back. "Smoke, it's a shame old Erastus Beadle wasn't here to see that show you put on. He'd have you in one of his dime novels going up against Deadwood Dick, sure as shootin'."

Smoke grinned. "Yeah, and maybe I'd win the fair hand of Hurricane Nell, if'n she didn't shoot me first."

From a dark corner of the saloon came the sound of someone clapping their hands very slowly, then a gravelly voice growled, "Yeah, that was some show, Jensen. You sure impressed that tinhorn. Too bad he didn't have the sand to go against you anyway, since I think you're all blow and no do."

Smoke looked at Carson and sighed, before turning and facing the man in the corner. He narrowed his eyes as he recognized Joe Bob Dunkirk, a man who had made his name in the Lincoln County wars a few years back. He hired his gun to the highest bidder and wasn't above back-shooting to earn his money.

"Well, Monte, look who's here. Old Joe Bob himself." Smoke took a sip of his whiskey with his left hand, unhooking the hammer-thong of his Colt with the right. "Guess I'm lucky you were sitting there next to the door or I'd probably have been back-shot, like the others he's killed."

Dunkirk jumped to his feet, knocking his chair over and pointing his finger at Smoke. "Shut up, you bastard! I don't need to back-shoot you, I can kill you face-to-face."

Smoke smiled a slow, contemptuous smile. "That's not the way I hear it, Joe Bob. I hear unless a man's blind in one eye and can't see out of the other, you tend to wait until he's facing the other way 'fore you gun him down."

Dunkirk's hand quivered as he held it out from his side, while Smoke continued to sip his whiskey, seemingly unconcerned.

Carson held out his left hand and the bartender placed a Greener sawed-off double-barrelled 12 gauge shotgun in it. Carson pulled both hammers back with a loud click and said, "Okay, Joe Bob, you want to commit suicide, it's okay with me. But you're gonna do it outside so the bartender don't have to spend all day cleaning your guts off the floor."

Dunkirk flicked his eyes over at Carson. "What do you

mean, commit suicide? I'm gonna kill Mr. Smoke Jensen here."

Carson sighed loudly. "Like I said, Joe Bob, it's your funeral." He waved the barrel of the shotgun and both Joe Bob and Smoke walked out onto the street. As they faced off, Carson called, "Speaking of funerals, Joe Bob, what do you want carved on your cross after Smoke curls you up—other than *here lies a man who died of a case of the slow*?"

"Shut up Carson, or you'll be next!"

"Say, Joe Bob," Smoke said, "before I send you to meet Jesus, tell me how much he paid you."

Dunkirk's forehead wrinkled and he cocked his head to the side. "Huh? What did you say?"

Smoke spread his hands. "I just wanted to know what you thought your life was worth. I know you don't never do nothing without being paid for it, so . . . how much did you get paid to die today?"

"Uh . . . a hundred dollars, in advance, and another five hundred after you're in the ground."

"Want to tell me who it was who bought you so cheap?"

"Naw, let's just get it on."

"Okay, back-shooter. Fill your hand."

Dunkirk grabbed at his pistol and actually had it halfway out of his holster when a piece of molten lead in a .44 caliber slammed into his chest and knocked him off his boots. He lay there in the dirt, eyes blinking, legs quivering, still trying to clear leather.

Smoke walked over and squatted next to him, casting his shadow over the dying man's face to shield it from the sun. "Tell me Joe Bob, did that gunhawk pay you enough for this?"

"Jensen," he croaked, his voice filled with pain.

"Yeah."

"You know he's comin' for you . . ."

"Yeah, Joe Bob, I know." But he was talking to a man staring the long stare into nothing.

"Monte," Smoke said softly, "give whatever money he's got left of the hundred to the preacher's wife for her fund for widows and orphans. She can always use a donation."

"Sure, Smoke, and I'll keep my eyes open for any more trash like this that blows into town. What are you gonna do?"

Smoke shrugged as he punched out his casings and reloaded. "Guess I'll go back up to Sugarloaf and wait. Not much else I can do."

As Smoke stepped in his saddle, a man came running up to him waving a piece of paper in the air. "Mr. Jensen, this telegram just came over the wire for your wife, Miss Sally. The telegraph operator asked me to give it to you."

Smoke reached down and took the paper from his hand. "Thanks, Mr. Hanson. I'll see that she gets it."

Hanson's brow furrowed. "Sure hope it's not bad news."

Smoke smirked. "You ever know anybody to telegraph *good* news?"

CHAPTER FOUR

The Silver Spur Saloon in Laredo, Texas, was over half full even though it was only ten o'clock in the morning. Since the outbreak of Mexican Fever in local cattle herds two months before, a great many area cowhands had been out of work. Those who hadn't left town were spending what little money they had getting and staying drunk.

The border punchers, rowdy and wild to begin with, were now surly, quarrelsome, and downright mean. Fights were a daily occurrence in town, and the doctor was kept busy sewing up knife wounds and trying to plug bullet holes as best he could.

In a dim corner of the Silver Spur, a poker game was in progress that had been going on for three days straight. One man, sitting with his back to the wall, had a bandanna over his head, draping down to cover his ears and tied in the back, over which he wore his hat. If any of the other players thought this strange attire for a cowhand, they took one look at his eyes and didn't mention it.

The man was lean to the point of emaciation, with a scraggly moustache, yellowing, tobacco-stained teeth, and haunted eyes that continually swept the room as if for danger. Every time the batwings would swing open, his hand would slip under the table to wrap around the handle of a belly-gun he kept in his waistband.

The man won a hand with two pair, beating a pair of aces and a king-high hand. As he raked in his winnings, one of the two Mexican *vaqueros* sitting at the table said, "Tha's pretty good playin', Mr. Morgan. You winnin' most of our moneys."

Lester Morgan's eyes flicked from his winnings to the man across the table who spoke. He growled, "I win because you don't play poker any better than you speak English."

When the Mexican's eyes narrowed, his friend put a hand on his shoulder, "Easy, *amigo,* we got plenty of time to win it back."

As Morgan leaned back and put a cigar in his mouth, the batwings swung open and a dust-covered cowboy ambled in. He stood just inside the door, letting his eyes adjust to the light, sleeving sweat off his forehead with his arm. When Morgan lit his cigar, the flaming of the match illuminated his face, drawing the man's attention to it.

The stranger took off his hat and dusted some of the trail dirt off his clothes with it, and set it back on his head. He slipped the hammer thong off his pistol, worn low and tied down, then walked over to stand in front of the table in the corner.

At his approach, Morgan's hand slipped out of sight. The newcomer nodded at him, "How'r ya doin', Sundance?"

Morgan's eyes slitted and shifted quickly around the room to see if anyone else was listening. He took the cigar out of his mouth with his left hand and blew smoke at the ceiling. "You must be mistaken, mister. My name's Lester Morgan."

"No, I'm not mistaken. I followed you here from Del Rio. You was calling yourself Sundance there—at least you was when you gunned down my kid brother by shootin' him in the back."

"I never—"

Before Morgan could finish, the stranger reached across the table and jerked the hat and bandanna off his head, revealing a missing left ear. He grinned. "Maybe you should change your name to the One Ear Kid instead of Sundance."

Other men at the table began to pull their chairs back. One of them said, "Sundance? Isn't that the name of the man who shot that old gunfighter, Luke Nations, just before Smoke Jensen shot his ear off?"

The gunman standing at the table laughed. "Yeah, it is, only the bastard shot Nations in the back, too. Seems the only way this snake can make a reputation is to back-shoot someone." He squared his shoulders and flexed the fingers of his right hand. "Well, Mr. One-Ear, I ain't gonna turn my back on you, so if you ain't completely yeller clear through, let's get it on."

Morgan smiled, just before he fired his short-barreled .44 Smith and Wesson belly-gun up through the table. The shot blew a hole in the tabletop, then traveled upward and hit the gunman under his chin, shattering it and taking the top of his skull off. He was dead before he hit the ground. Money, cards, and pieces of brain were scattered all over the floor.

Morgan took a deep drag on his cigar, and with smoke

trailing out of his nostrils, yelled, "Bartender, clean this mess up and bring us another table. This one seems to have a hole in it."

While two cowboys were dragging the dead man's body out and the bartender was spreading sawdust on the pool of blood on the floor, the other men in the poker game quietly gathered up their money and began to leave.

Morgan spread his hands. "Hey, boys, what's the matter? My money not good enough for you?"

One of the players stopped and said, "If we'd known you was Sundance, we'd never have sat at the table with you to begin with." He pulled a pocketwatch out of his vest and snapped it open. He glanced at the time before looking up at Morgan, "The sheriff's due back from the county seat at sundown. I'd make myself scarce 'fore then if I was you." He snapped the watch closed and walked over to the bar with the other players, turning his back on Morgan and ignoring him.

Goddammit, thought Morgan, run out of another town, thanks to that bastard Smoke Jensen and the way he marked me for life.

He scrapped his winnings into his hat and left the saloon with as much dignity as he could muster.

Not having anywhere else to go, he mounted and walked his horse over the wooden bridge across the Rio Grande into Mexico and pulled up at the first saloon he could find, El Caballero Cantina, where he swung down.

The clientele here was a mixed bag of Mexican *vaqueros,* professional and semi-professional outlaws, both Mexican and American, and cowboys so down on their luck they couldn't afford to drink on the American side.

Sundance sat alone in a corner, his back to the wall as usual, and began to observe his fellow drinkers. He was formulating a plan to get even with Smoke Jensen, but he needed just the right sort of men: men who were born with the bark on; men who were as hard as the sun-baked chalice of the Sonoran desert; men who would kill for a dollar and give you change. Evidently, the others he had sent to kill Jensen had not been up to the task. Time to get some men who were used to earning their keep with their guns. The Mexicans had a word for them: *buscaderos*. Tough, pistol-toting gunslicks who lived only to kill. If it was the last thing he ever did, he would make Jensen pay for ruining his life.

By midnight he had made his selection. First, he picked a Mexican who went by the name El Gato, the cat. To a Mexican, the only cat worth mentioning is the puma, or mountain lion. El Gato lived up to his name. He was big for a Mexican, over six feet tall. With wide shoulders and massive arms, and a belly to match, he looked like he weighed over three hundred pounds. He had a drooping moustache and smelled like he didn't believe in bathwater. He drank his tequila straight, laughing at the *gringos* who had to cut it with salt and lime juice. In the last hour alone he had knocked two men out cold who didn't laugh with him at one of his jokes. His English was tolerable, and he wore two pistols and acted like he knew how to use them.

The next man Sundance picked was an American who answered to the name Toothpick. He was thin and wiry, all gristle and muscle without an ounce of fat on his body. He wore a thick, hand-tooled belt with a pistol on the left side with the butt forward, and a knife scabbard on the right. At first Sundance thought he got his name either because he was never without a toothpick between his lips, even when he smoked or drank, or on account of his thinness. Then, about an hour before midnight, one of the Mexican peons in the bar spilled his beer on Toothpick's boots. In the blink of an eye, Toothpick pulled a long, narrow-bladed knife out of the scabbard on his belt and sliced the man's moustache off. When El Gato complimented him on the knife, Toothpick said, "Yeah, this is my Arkansas Toothpick. I never go anywhere without it." As he looked at the knife, his hands unconsciously caressed it, as if it were a woman, and his eyes glittered with madness. He was just the sort of man Sundance was looking for.

The third man Sundance chose that night was quieter. He stood at the bar without drawing attention to himself, just watching the other patrons through narrow, suspicious eyes. He was stockily built, more square than long, and had hugely muscled arms more suited to a blacksmith than a cowboy. Sundance recognized him from a Wanted poster he had seen in Laredo. His name was Lightning Jack Warner. He rode at one time with Quantrill's Raiders, until his savagery and ruthlessness made him unwelcome even among that bloodthirsty crowd. He was called Lightning not because he was fast with a gun, but because he was originally from Alabama, and had an inordinate fondness and need for moonshine whiskey, or white lightning. He was mean as a snake when sober, and even worse when drunk. Sundance remembered hearing that he was nearsighted and therefore used a Greener ten-gauge shotgun as his weapon of choice. It was never out of his reach, and could be seen leaning against the bar next to him.

When the Regulator clock on the saloon wall struck

midnight, Sundance made his move. He sauntered over to the bar and invited El Gato, Toothpick, and Lightning Jack to have a drink with him at his table. They were suspicious at first, until he said, "Give me five minutes of your time and you get a free drink. What have you got to lose?"

When the men were seated around his table in the rear corner of the saloon, Sundance got a bottle of tequila and a handful of limes from the bartender. While Toothpick sliced the limes with his slender knife, Sundance filled everyone's glass. Lightning Jack took a deep draught, coughed once, then whispered, "Smooth. Bitter, but smooth," in a rasping voice.

El Gato laughed and clapped the Southerner on the back. "I like this *gringo.* He knows how to drink the fruit of the cactus . . . quick and deep, like a man should take a woman."

Toothpick sipped his drink, made a face, and quickly sucked on a lime. He blew through his mouth once to cool it, then looked at Sundance with a furrowed brow. "Okay, Sundance, or whatever you call yourself. We're here, and we've had our drinks. Now what?"

Sundance took a cigar from his pocket and struck a match on his spur. As he held it under the end of the stogie, puffing it to life, he peered over the flame at the men who sat around the table looking at him expectantly.

"First, let me tell you about me." He drew deeply on the cigar and let the smoke trail out of his nostrils as he spoke, eyes unfocused and almost dreamy as he recalled his past. "A few years ago, I was just a kid, dreaming of becoming a famous gunfighter. I bought me some fancy clothes and a couple of pearl-handled Peacemaker Colts, and went on the prod to make my reputation. I hired out my gun to a rancher named Tilden Franklin, who planned to take over his town. Things were goin' pretty good until this bastard named Smoke Jensen got a bunch of old broken-down gunslicks to back his play against Franklin."

At the mention of Smoke's name, Toothpick's eyes narrowed and Lightning Jack snorted, a half-smile on his face. El Gato just sat there, staring into his tequila.

Sundance continued, as if talking to himself, his mind in the past. "During the final shoot-out, I happened to get the drop on one of Jensen's old friends, a man named Luke Nations . . ."

They all heard the shot and whirled around. Luke Nations lay crumpled on the boardwalk, a large hole in the center of his back.

Sundance stepped out of a building, a pistol in his hand. He looked up and grinned.

"I did it!" he hollered. "Me. Sundance. I kilt Luke Nations!"

"You goddamned back-shootin' asshole!" Charlie Starr said, lifting his pistol.

"No!" Smoke's voice stopped him. "Don't, Charlie." Smoke walked over to Sundance, one hand holding his bleeding side. He backhanded the dandy, knocking him sprawling. Sundance landed on his butt in the street. His mouth was busted, blood leaking from one corner. He looked up at Smoke, raw fear in his wide eyes.

"You gonna kill me, ain't you?" he hissed.

The smile on Smoke's face was not pleasant. "What's your name, lowlife?"

"Les . . . Sundance. That's me, Sundance!"

"Well, Sundance!" Smoke put enough dirt on the name to make it very ugly. "You wanna live, do you?"

"Yeah!"

"And you wanna be known as a top gunhand, right, Sundance?"

"Yeah!"

Smoke kicked Sundance in the mouth. The young man rolled on the ground, moaning.

"What's your last name, craphead?"

"M . . . Morgan!"

"All right, Les Sundance Morgan. I'll let you live. And Les, I'm going to have your name spread all over the West. Les Sundance Morgan. The man with one ear. He's the man who killed the famed gunfighter Luke Nations."

"But," his face wrinkled in puzzlement. "I got both ears!"

Before his words could fade from sound, Smoke had drawn and fired, the bullet clipping off Sundance's left ear. The action forever branded him.

Sundance rolled in the dirt, crying and hollering.

"Top gun, huh, bushwhacker?" Smoke said. "Right, that's you, Sundance." He looked toward Johnny North. "Get some whiskey and fix his ear, will you, Johnny?"

Sundance really started hollering when the raw booze hit where his ear had been. He passed out from the pain. Johnny took that time to bandage the ugly wound.

Then Smoke kicked him awake. Sundance lay on the blood- and whiskey-soaked ground, looking up at Smoke.

"What you do this to me for?" he croaked.

"So everybody, no matter where you go, can know who you are, punk. The man who killed Luke Nations. Now, you listen to me, you son of a bitch! You want to know how it feels to be a top gun? Well, just look around you, ask anybody."

Sundance's eyes found Charlie Starr. "You're Charlie Starr. You're more famous than Luke Nations. But I'm gonna be famous too, ain't I?"

Charlie slowly rolled a cigarette and stuck it between Sundance's lips. He held the match while Sundance puffed. Charlie straightened up and smiled sadly.

"How is it, you ask? Oh, well, it's a real grand time being a well-known gunfighter. You can't sit with your back to no empty space, always to a wall. Lots of back-shooters out there. You don't never make your fire, cook, and then sleep in the same spot. You always move before you bed down, 'cause somebody is always lookin' to gun you down . . . for a reputation.

"You ain't never gonna marry, kid. 'Cause if you do, it won't last. You got to stay on the move, all the time. 'Cause you're the man who kilt Luke Nations, dogscrap. And there's gonna be a thousand other piles of dogscrap just like you lookin' for you.

"You drift, boy. You drift all the time, and you might near always ride alone, lessen you can find a pard that you know you can trust not to shoot you when you're in your blankets.

"And a lot of towns won't want you, back-shooter. The marshal and the townspeople will meet you with rifles and shotguns and point you the way out. 'Cause they don't want no gunfighter in their town.

"And after a time, if you live, you'll do damn near anything so's people won't know who you are. But they always seem to find out. Then you'll change your name agin. And agin. Just lookin' for a little peace and quiet.

"But you ain't never gonna find it.

"You might git good enough to live for a long time, mister Sundance Morgan. I hope you do. I hope you ride ten thousand lonely miles, you back-shootin' bastard. Ten thousand miles of lookin' over your back. Ten thousand towns that you'll ride in and out of in the dead of night. Eatin' your meals just at closin' time . . . if you can find a eatin' place that'll serve you.

"A million hours that you'll wish you could somehow change your life . . . but you cain't. You cain't change, 'cause *they* won't let you.

"Only job you'll be able to find is one with the gun, if you're good enough. 'Cause you're the man who kilt Luke Nations. You got your rep, boy. You wanted it so damned bad, you got 'er." He glanced at Johnny North.

Johnny said, "I had me a good woman one time. We married and I hung up my guns, sonny. Some goddamned bounty hunters shot into my cabin one night. Killed my wife. I'd never broke no law until then. But I tracked them so-called lawmen down and hung 'em, one by one. I was on the owlhoot trail for years after that. I had both the law and the reputation hunters after me. Sounds like a real fine life, don't it? I hope you enjoy it."

Smoke kicked Sundance to his feet. "Get your horse and ride, you pile of crap! 'Fore one of us here takes a notion to brace the man who killed Luke Nations."

Crying, Sundance stumbled from the street and found his horse in back of the building that once housed a gun shop.

"It ain't like that!" the gunfighters, the gambler, the ranchers, and the minister heard Sundance yell as he rode off. "It ain't none at all like what you say it was. I'll have women a-throwin' themselves at me. I'll have money and I'll have . . ."

His horse's hooves drummed out the rest.

"What a story this will make," Haywood Arden, the newspaperman said, his eyes wide as he looked at the bullet-pocked buildings and empty shell casings on the ground.

"Yeah," Smoke said wearily. "You be sure and write it, Haywood. And be sure you spell one name right."

"Who is that?" the newspaperman asked.

"Lester Morgan, known as Sundance."

"What'd he do?" Haywood was writing on a tablet as fast as he could write.

Smoke described Sundance, ending with, "And he ain't got but one ear. That'll make him easy to spot."

"But what did this Lester Sundance Morgan *do*?"

"Why . . . he's the gunfighter who killed Luke Nations."

Lightning Jack interrupted Sundance's reverie. "Luke Nations? I heard that old man was a mean sonofabitch about as fast on the draw as anybody."

Sundance studied the glowing end of his cigar. "Well, he weren't fast enough. Anyway, after I dusted him, Smoke Jensen stuck his nose in and drew down on me when I wasn't ready. He wounded me, then shot off my ear."

El Gato looked up from his tequila and stared at the lump of scar tissue on Sundance's head. "He shot off your ear, man? *Santa Maria!* Why he do such a thing?"

"He said it was to teach me a lesson. He wanted to mark me so that all the other young guns who were on the prod to make a reputation would come after me, hoping to make their name by killing the man who shot Luke Nations."

El Gato's lips curled in an evil smile. "Ah. I see."

Sundance paused to refill their glasses with tequila, then went on. "Well, it happened just like he said. For the last few years I haven't been able to take a breath without some gun-happy *hombre* trying to kill me. I've been on the owlhoot trail ridin' low, and haven't been able to spend more'n two nights in a row in any town since then."

Lightning Jack chugged his drink down without a blink. "This is all real interestin', Sundance, but what the hell does it have to do with us?"

Sundance stabbed his cigar out on the table, face turning red. "Just this. Since I have to live as an outlaw anyway, I decided to make it pay. I've robbed lots of banks, stages, and pilgrims in the years I've been on the trail. I can't go into town and live it up, so I still have most of the money I've stolen. I plan to use every cent of that money to get even with Smoke Jensen."

Toothpick's eyebrows raised. "Just how much money are we talkin' about, Sundance?"

"Twenty thousand and change."

"So just what is your proposal?"

Sundance took a swallow of tequila and leaned his head back and squeezed a lime into his mouth. After a deep breath, he croaked, "I want to put together a gang of men to go up into the Colorado mountains and put Jensen in the ground. I figure it'll take between thirty and forty men to get the job done."

Toothpick shook his head. "Twenty thousand isn't a lot of money to go around among that many hands."

Sundance grinned "The twenty's just seed money to get us started. With all the cattle around here sick with Mexican Tick Fever, most of the big spreads haven't been buying any beef. They're fat with cash and have let most of their punchers go since there's not any work to be done. I figure with a gang of the right sort of men, we could hit a few spreads here and there and anything else that interested us between Texas and Colorado. By the time we get to Jensen's ranch, we'd probably have twenty thousand for every member of our group."

Lightning Jack whistled. "That's a mighty ambitious plan, but that much activity would bring down a lot of heat on us. Every lawman in Texas would be after us."

Sundance shrugged. "So what? If we keep on the move, hit and run, they'll never catch up to us. By the time they know where we are, we won't be there anymore."

Just as he finished speaking, the batwings flew open and a group of ten men walked in, laughing and talking. Their leader was a short Mexican with a huge potbelly. He was unshaven, had a large black moustache, and was wearing crossed cartridge belts on his chest and a double-holster rig around his ample waist. He had a long purple scar running down his face from his left eyebrow to the corner of his mouth. The men with him were covered with trail dust and looked as tough as horseshoe nails.

El Gato cursed under his breath and pulled his hat down to shadow his face. Sundance leaned over and asked him, "What's the matter? Who's that?"

He whispered, "That's Benito Valdez, the meanest *hombre* in Mexico, and he swore to kill me the next time he saw me."

Sundance shrugged and leaned back in his chair.

"Don't worry, El Gato, you're with me now." He reached under the table and loosened his pistol in its holster, leaving his hand wrapped around the butt.

Valdez took the drink the bartender poured him and turned, leaning back with his elbows on the bar. After a moment, he saw El Gato and called, "Hey, *amigos,* look who's here. It is El Gato." As his men turned and stared, Valdez growled, "How're you doin', pussy cat? You remember what I said I was going to do if I saw you again?" He let his hand drop to his pistol.

Before he could do anything, Sundance gave a big yawn. He flipped a handful of change on the floor at Valdez's feet. "Hey lardbutt. How about bringing my friends and me another bottle of tequila? We've about finished this one off."

Valdez's eyes slitted and he glared hate. "What means lardbutt?"

Sundance grinned. "It means your ass is so fat that I bet you have to tie two horses together to ride anywhere. Now are you going to bring me my drink or am I going to have to kick your fat ass outta here?"

Valdez screamed, "Filthy *gringo*," and grabbed for his gun.

Sundance kicked his chair over sideways and rolled once on the floor, coming up in a crouch, both hands filled with iron. Before Valdez's pistol cleared his holster, Sundance opened fire.

Twin holes blossomed in Valdez's chest, the bullets punching through his body and out his back to star the mirror over the bar. Valdez was knocked off his heels, bounced once against the bar, and fell to the floor.

His men drew and began to fire just as El Gato, Toothpick, and Lightning Jack opened up on them. The big Greener in Lightning Jack's hands boomed twice, spitting death and cutting two of the Mexicans almost in half and showering the others with blood and guts.

One of the Mexicans' bullets gouged a shallow furrow along Toothpick's cheek before the thin man's Navy model Colt blew his face into a bloody pulp.

El Gato screamed, *"Chinga tu madre!"* as he fired with both hands, pumping the pistols as if that would make the bullets go faster. Two more of the *bandidos* whirled and fell to the floor, to die among the bloody entrails and bodies there.

Sundance fired at the last of Valdez's men left standing, blowing a hole in his heart at the same time Toothpick's knife twirled through the air and entered the man's open, screaming mouth, to pierce his neck and embed itself in his spine. He dropped like a stone, dead from two mortal wounds.

The survivors walked through the fog of heavy smoke and cordite to the pile of bodies next to the bar. Sundance used his boot to roll Valdez over onto his back, where he lay convulsing and kicking, his big Mexican spurs gouging tracks in the wooden floor that soon filled with blood.

Toothpick bent over and jerked his knife free from his victim's mouth and wiped it on the man's bloody shirt. Eyes dreamy and unfocused, he brought his beloved Arkansas Toothpick up and kissed the blade, licking the last drops of blood off, murmuring something to the instrument the others couldn't hear.

El Gato stood over the bodies, smoking pistols still in his hands, greasy hair hanging down, and sweat making rivulets in the dirt on his face. "Well, *compañeros,* we fixed those men's wagons pretty damn *bueno,* eh?"

Sundance holstered his Colt. He looked around the room, which was now empty except for his men. "Well, we'd better burn the breeze outta here." He looked into each of their faces. "We did good tonight. We make a pretty good team, *compadres.* Gather all the men you think are tough enough for what I outlined earlier, and we'll meet on the American side of the Rio tomorrow at noon. There's a grove of cottonwood trees about ten miles north of Laredo. I'll make camp there and wait for you and your men."

They shook hands and swaggered out of the saloon to their mounts without looking back.

CHAPTER FIVE

Sunset comes early in the high lonesome, and the sun was disappearing over the edge of the western peaks when Smoke spurred his mount toward home. Though he wondered what was in the telegram that came for Sally, he didn't look. He figured he would find out soon enough.

Smoke could almost taste the crispness and tang of early fall on the night air, and the sky was cloudless and clear, making the stars as brilliant as diamonds scattered on black velvet. He leaned back against the cantle, letting Horse have his rein, as he watched the stars and dreamed dreams of wilderness lands unsullied by people. His reverie led him to think of Preacher, and he wondered momentarily if the old grizzly was still alive and sitting around a small fire in the up-high enjoying the feel and smell of the mountain air as he was.

He thought the first shot he heard was thunder, until it was repeated several times in quick succession. He leaned forward in the saddle and used his spurs. "Come on, Horse," he cried, "that's coming from home!"

The deep booming of an express shotgun was answered

by the higher pitch of some .44's and the slightly deeper cough of a Henry rifle. As he came closer to the conflagration, Smoke first slowed Horse to a trot, then a walk.

Just before he came within sight of his cabin, Smoke slipped off Horse and tied him in some brush beside the path. He shucked his Winchester from its saddle boot and eared back the hammer. He ducked and weaved through the forest of high-mountain pines and underbrush, until he came to a small brook, gurgling in the darkness.

Kneeling, he reached down and spooned a handful of mud into his palm, smearing it over his face and neck and the brass of his rifle to minimize the glare in the starlight. With his dirt-covered face and dun-colored buckskins, he was all but invisible in the night. His mountain man training kept him from making the slightest sound as he scurried up the ridge overlooking his compound.

From this vantage point, he watched as gunfire exploded in several windows of the cabin, to be answered by at least four other guns in the woods surrounding it. He could make out two bodies lying motionless in the yard by the hitching post in front of the bunkhouse, and another sprawled spread-eagled partway up the ridge to the south of the cabin. So, he thought, at least two of ours and one of theirs down.

He grinned a death grin. Time to even up the odds and bring religion to the scum attacking his home. Leaning his head back, he opened his mouth and let out a great, screaming cry of a mountain lion on the hunt. While the yell echoed and reverberated throughout the small valley, the shooting stopped for a moment. From inside the cabin, the wailing, undulating cry of a she-wolf calling her mate emanated, lifting a great weight from Smoke's shoulders.

His beloved Sally was alive and now she knew he was nearby.

Smoke crouched and began to move through the forest as silently as a wraith. He seemed to know instinctively where to place his feet so as not to make a sound. Even without being able to see where his target was, he found his way to the spot by following the ripe smell of unwashed flesh, mingled with beer and tobacco odor and the sharp scent of the turnips the man had eaten for supper.

Within less than five minutes, Smoke was standing directly behind a figure kneeling beside a fallen tree. The man was firing a Henry rifle at flashes of gunfire from the cabin windows. The gunman never knew what struck him until seconds after Smoke's huge bowie knife sliced through his trachea and carotid arteries.

The bushwhacker turned, blood spurting from the gaping hole in his neck, and Smoke reversed the knife and swung backhanded with all his strength, severing the head from its neck. The body stood there for a moment, as though uncertain what to do next, then crumpled as if boneless. Smoke picked up the head by its hair and trotted toward his next appointment.

Jesus Garza, called Borrachón by friends and enemies alike because he was seldom seen completely sober, pulled back from his position on the hillock overlooking the rear of the cabin. Both his pistols were empty and he needed to reload. He also needed another swallow of the tequila he always kept handy.

Squatting, with his back to a tree to prevent being hit by a lucky shot, he tilted his bottle up toward the stars and gulped until there was nothing left but air. He belched loudly and returned to his position, when something hit him in the back. Whirling, both pistols cocked and ready to fire, he looked down at his feet. Lying there among the pinecones and needles, staring up at him with unblinking, dead eyes, was the head of his *compadre,* Jorge Busta- monte.

"Aiyee-e-e! *Madre de Dios,* aiyee-e-e," he screamed, firing both pistols into the darkness while backing up as fast as he could.

As he backed into the clearing, still firing, the angry grunt and growl of a grizzly bear came at him out of the night. He turned and ran as fast as his boots would carry him toward the cabin, forgetting in his terror what waited for him there. The last thing Garza saw was the flame blossoming out of a Greener ten-gauge shotgun as it blew him into hell.

A voice from the woods on the other side of the cabin called out, "Jorge. Are you there, boy?"

Smoke picked up Jorge's head and spent a few mo- ments preparing his next surprise as he trotted toward the sound of the voice. He found the man's horse reined to a tree and placed his surprise on the saddle horn, then stole quietly over behind a nearby bush.

Jerry Mason was worried. He had just seen Jesus Garza blown almost in two by that big shotgun in the cabin, and now Jorge Bustamonte wasn't answering his yells. That meant there was only himself and old Pig-eye Petersen against God-only-knew how many in the cabin. It had seemed like easy money when that gunslick down in Texas offered the four out-of-work cowhands three months' wages to come up here and kill some old mountain man, but it sure as hell wasn't working out like they thought.

"Damnation," he whispered to himself. "I think I'll just

head on over to Petersen and see if he's ready to skedaddle on outta here." With that, Mason holstered his pistols and walked to his horse. He untied the reins from the tree branch, put his left foot in the stirrup, and reached for the saddle horn.

"What the . . . ?" he murmured as he felt something hairy and sticky under his hands. He pulled the object off his saddle horn and held it up where he could see it. The air left his lungs in a loud whoosh and he bent over and vomited all over his boots.

Gulping and swallowing bile, he threw the severed head of his friend Jorge back into the woods. He leaped up on his horse and spurred the animal into a run.

Smoke stepped out of the bushes he was hiding in as Mason galloped past and swung his Winchester rifle in a horizontal arc, catching Mason full in the face and catapulting him backwards off his mount. Smoke stood over the moaning man and kicked him once in the side of the head, turning out his lights temporarily.

He wiped blood and pieces of teeth off the stock of the Winchester and went after the lone remaining gunman. No stealth this time, he walked directly toward the man, not bothering to mask his noise.

Petersen stepped back from the tree he had been firing around and began to reload his Colt Peacemaker .45. He looked up when he heard someone coming through the underbrush toward him from where Mason had been stationed.

"Hey Jerry," he whispered loudly, "you gettin' tired of shootin' those fish in that barrel down there?"

His eyes narrowed when there was no answer. He

cocked the Peacemaker and pointed it toward the sounds. "Jerry, that you, boy?"

Light blossomed and exploded in the darkness and the bullet from Smoke's rifle smashed against Petersen's gun-hand, knocking his pistol spinning away. He screamed and bent over, holding his broken hand and moaning. When he looked up, one of the biggest men he had ever seen was standing before him, grinning a grin with no mirth in it.

Smoke backhanded him across the face with his fist, smashing his nose and loosening his teeth. As the man spun away from him, Smoke propped his rifle against a tree and pulled his big bowie knife from its scabbard. "You wanted to fight, skunk-breath. Well, here's your chance. Pull that frog-sticker I see there in your belt and let's dance."

Petersen straightened up, squared his shoulders, and said, "No, I don't want to fight. I give up."

Smoke's grin widened. "No, I don't think you understand. You weren't given a choice, just like those two boys lying dead down there in front of my cabin weren't given a choice. You are going to die, mister. The only question is, are you going to die like the coward you are, gutless and unarmed, or are you at least going to die like a man, with a weapon in your hand?" Smoke shrugged. "It's up to you."

Petersen's lips tightened into a thin line and he drew his knife lefthanded. "I can't hardly use my good hand."

"Not to worry. I never take advantage of a coward." Smoke shifted his weapon to his left hand. As they circled each other in the darkness, weaving their knives before them, Smoke asked, "Where you from, fatso?"

Petersen sucked in his gut, trying to hide his substantial paunch. "I'm from Texas, and that's where I'm goin' back to soon's I gut your ass." He feinted left, then moved quickly to his right, swinging his left arm in a roundhouse swing at Smoke's stomach.

Smoke didn't even move back. As Petersen's knife sliced through his buckskins, barely scraping the skin, Smoke flicked his arm straight out and sliced off Petersen's right ear. The fat man gave a high-pitched yell and put his ruined right hand up to stanch the flow of blood, staring at Smoke with fear-brightened eyes.

Smoke continued to move in a slow circle, talking as if in a normal conversation. "You know what I hate, fat-butt? I mean, what really makes me want to throw up?"

Petersen narrowed his eyes, but didn't answer as he shuffled sideways, looking for an opening. "I hate back-shooters, ambushers, and bushwhackers almost more than anything," Smoke continued, flicking his left hand out again so fast that Petersen didn't even see it, just felt the sting as his left ear was left hanging by a thread. With an agonized growl, he reached up and tore the ear loose, looking at it for a moment before he threw it to the ground. Blood was streaming down both sides of his face, giving him an unearthly look in the starlight. "I'm not gonna stand here and let you cut me up, mister."

Smoke smiled, a little. "Oh? Well just what are you gonna do about it, snake-scum?"

"I'm gonna kill you right now." With a terrible, insane yell, Petersen rushed straight at Smoke, his arm extended in what he hoped was a killing thrust.

Smoke brushed the attack aside with his forearm, and as Petersen came up against him, he calmly buried his knife to the hilt in his opponent's right eye. Petersen uttered a strangled scream which quickly turned into a gurgle, then a death rattle as he collapsed to the ground.

Smoke left him where he fell and retraced his steps to where Mason lay unconscious. He took the rope off his saddle, looped it under the sleeping man's arms and back to the saddle horn, and led his horse down toward the camp.

"To the cabin," he yelled.

"Smoke, is that you?"

"Yeah, Sally, it's me. Hold your fire, I'm coming in with a prisoner."

Sally, Cookie, Pearlie, Cal, and the remaining men from the bunkhouse gathered in the cabin yard to meet him. When he walked up, Sally was bending over the two hands lying on the ground. One was dead, the other seriously wounded. She straightened and waved over one of the men standing in front of the bunkhouse.

She put her hand on the cowboy's shoulder, "Sam, would you take one of the horses and ride into Big Rock and see if you can get Doctor Spalding out here? Tell him we have one dead and Woodrow has a bullet in the shoulder and one through his chest." She looked over at the man Smoke had dragged into the camp yard, noticing his ruined face. "Also tell him Smoke has worked a little on one of the attackers in his usual manner, so he may need to do some reconstruction of a face." Hesitating for a moment, she smiled and shook her head. "I know it's no use, but I'd better ask. Smoke," she called, "did you happen to leave any up in the woods who might need Doctor Spalding's attention?"

He pursed his lips, "Not unless he's considerably more

skilled than I remember. You might send word to the undertaker to get busy cuttin' some wood, cause he's gonna have some business shortly."

While Smoke was talking to Sally, Cal and Pearlie untied his prisoner and dragged him over to the front porch, propping him up against the hitching post. The men gathered around him with angry, sullen faces. Hank Collier, Woodrow's saddlemate and best friend, eared back the hammer on his pistol and aimed it at Mason's face.

Smoke put his hand on the gun, gently pushing it toward the ground. "Not just yet, if you don't mind, Hank." He looked over his shoulder at the man lying there. "I've got some questions for this pile of cowcrap, then you men can take care of business."

Hank's eyes never left Mason. "Yes sir, Mr. Smoke. But if Woodrow dies 'cause of this man, don't try to stop what's gonna happen next."

Smoke slowly shook his head. "Wouldn't think of it, Hank."

Pearlie walked out of the cabin with a pitcher of water and threw it on Mason's face and smiled as the man coughed, strangled, and sat up gasping for breath.

Smoke squatted directly in front of Mason, elbows on knees, and asked in a kind, quiet tone. "What's your name, mister?"

Mason looked over Smoke's shoulder at the crowd of men gathered with angry, set faces and eyes that looked at him as if he were already dead. "Uh . . . Mason, Jerry Mason."

"Where you from, cowboy?"

Mason's eyes narrowed suspiciously. "I'm . . . that is, we . . . my friends and I are all from Texas."

Smoke smiled. "That wouldn't be down Laredo way, would it?"

Mason shook his head. "No. We worked near there, on a little shirttail spread down to Del Rio."

"Well Jerry, I'm kind'a wondering why a bunch of sorry-assed dumb ole' boys from Texas come all the way up here and decide to shoot up my home in the middle of the night."

Mason's gaze lowered and he mumbled. "I don't know either, mister. I just rode with them others and took orders from the big guy, Petersen. Maybe you could ask him?"

Smoke shook his head. He pulled his knife and reached down and wiped some of the blood and tissue off the blade onto Mason's pants. "I'm afraid Petersen ain't gonna be talkin' again real soon, not without no tongue anyway."

Mason's face twisted in terror as Smoke said this, then he screamed in fright when Smoke dropped Bustamonte's severed head into his lap. "I believe this belonged to one of your other friends, and I don't think he's in the mood to talk, either."

Mason sat there, staring into the glazed, lifeless eyes of his friend.

Smoke said, "Tell us what happened. Who hired y'all to come up here and attack us?"

Mason sleeved snot and tears off his face with the back of an arm. "Will ya let me go if'n I tell ya?"

"I'm afraid not, Jerry. You've killed at least one of our friends, and maybe another if the doc can't fix him up. In this country, murder is a hangin' offense." He reached out and flipped the head off Mason's lap with the point of his knife. "But, hangin' is preferable to some other ways of dyin', if you get my meanin'."

Mason moaned, closed his eyes, and hung his head. "Okay, okay. Some man came up to us in a saloon and asked if we was lookin' for work. We said sure, so he said he'd give us three months' pay to come up here to the high country and put a bullet in Smoke Jensen. Said there was dirt between 'em."

"What was this man's name?"

He looked up into Smoke's eyes. "I don't know, and that's the honest truth, 'cept there's one thing funny 'bout him."

"What's that?"

"He ain't got but one ear. Said his right'un had been shot off."

Smoke's brow furrowed. "Was he a shootist?"

"I dunno." Mason shook his head. "Wore a fancy double-rig though, and looked like he knew how to use it."

Smoke patted him on the shoulder. "Okay, boy, thanks for bein' honest with me."

"You gonna hang me now?" His eyes were streaming tears.

"I don't know. That's up to the boys here. After all, it was them that you ambushed and one of them that you killed." Smoke stood and dusted his hands on his pants, as if to rid them of the stain of having touched the killer.

"Smoke," Sally said, "I think we ought to wait for Sheriff Carson and let him take this boy into town for a trial."

Smoke looked at her a moment. "How's Woodrow?" he asked quietly.

She lowered her eyelids. "He's pretty bad. He was hit hard, but he's young and strong and fightin' back. If he lives until Doc Spalding gets here, I think he'll make it."

Smoke cut his eyes over to Hank Collier. "Sally, I'm

gonna leave it up to the men what to do. If they want to be merciful and let Monte have him, okay. If they want to form a string party and decorate a cottonwood tree with his carcass, that's okay, too."

"But . . ."

He put his arm around her shoulder and began to lead her into the cabin. "I know it's hard, dear, but this is a hard country, and those men made their choice to come up here and kill people for money." He opened the door for her and followed her in.

Hank went over to stand before Mason. "Men, we have a choice here. Do we take this bandit into town to hang, or do we do it here and save the town the trouble?"

"Let 'im stretch hemp!"

"Make 'im do a midair dance!"

"Let him do a Texas cakewalk!"

Hank shook his head, sympathy in his eyes. "Sorry, Hoss. Looks like you go to meet Jesus tonight."

Mason wiped his eyes and nose again and got to his feet. "Okay. I'm not gonna cry about it. Let's do it."

The men put him on a horse and rode into the woods. Pearlie and Cal went into the cabin to sit with Woodrow until the doc came.

CHAPTER SIX

Doctor Cotton Spalding had Pearlie hold a cloth with chloroform on it while he put some deep stitches in the wounds to Woodrow's chest and arm. It wasn't long before Pearlie's face was the color of chalk and he was swallowing rapidly to keep from fainting at the sight of the doctor's needles at work.

Sally was helping by handing Spalding his instruments as he needed them. She looked up when Pearlie started to sway, with sweat beading his forehead. "Pearlie, hand me that cloth and go sit in the other room until you feel better."

"Yes ma'am." He wasted no time doing just as she suggested, pausing in the kitchen to grab a couple of biscuits and a cut of beef left over from supper. He walked out the door onto the porch to find Smoke sitting there, cigar in hand, looking over the Sugarloaf range.

Smoke glanced up to see Pearlie standing in the doorway. "Light and set, Pearlie. Is the doc through in there?"

"No sir, but might near. He says Woody's gonna be okay if'n he don't get suppuration."

Smoke nodded, blowing cigar smoke toward the stars.

"Pearlie, what did you make of Mason's description of the man who paid them to come up here?"

Pearlie thought on it for a moment, then shrugged. "Could be most anybody, I reckon." He stuffed the biscuit-surrounded beef into his mouth. "'Cept somethin' about that one-ear business is kinda familiar."

Smoke offered him a cigar. "No thanks, I'll just roll me a blanket of my own." He pulled a cloth bag of tobacco out of his pocket and began to build a cigarette. "What do you make of it, Smoke?"

"I only remember one *hombre* who fits that description who has cause to hate me enough to pay someone to kill me, and who's coward enough to be afraid to do it himself."

"Who's that?"

"Lester Morgan."

Pearlie thought for a moment, then snapped his fingers. "You mean that dandy who went around acting like some big gunhawk? The one that shot Luke Nations in the back?"

Smoke shrugged. "You recollect any other man with one ear who's crossed our paths in the last few years?"

"Naw, I don't. But I heard old Lester Morgan had gone to Mexico, tryin' to outrun his reputation."

"So had I, Pearlie. But when you think on it, Texas isn't that far from Mexico, is it?"

Just then, Doctor Spalding and Sally walked out onto the porch. Smoke jumped up. "How's Woody, Doc?"

"I think he's going to be all right, Smoke. I've asked Sally to let him rest in the cabin tonight, then send him in to Big Rock on a buckboard tomorrow. I'll have to probe for the bullet in his chest, and I want him to get a little stronger before I put him through that."

Sally asked, "Can we fix you some supper, Cotton, or would you like coffee or a drink?"

He shook his head. "No thanks, one of the town ladies is in labor and I need to get back down there." He smiled. "Can't have these women learning they can have those babies without me; wouldn't be good for business."

"I'll bring old Woody to town first thang in the mornin', Doc," said Pearlie.

"Okay, thanks Pearlie. Good night, all." He tipped his hat, climbed into his buggy, and settled back to grab a quick nap as his horse found its way back to Big Rock.

Pearlie waved good night to Smoke and Sally and sauntered toward the bunkhouse, cigarette dangling from his lips.

Smoke put his arm around Sally and she laid her head on his shoulder. "Tired?"

"Yes. We'd just finished feeding the hands supper when those men opened fire on us." She sighed. "It's been pretty much going on since then."

"Is Woody taken care of?"

"Yes, he's sleeping soundly. Doctor Spalding gave him some laudanum."

He gently steered her through the door and toward their bedroom. "You get in bed, I'll get us a glass of wine, and we'll relax a little before trying to go to sleep."

She caressed his cheek with her palm, then walked tiredly toward their room as he turned to look for the wineglasses.

When he entered the bedroom, Sally was propped up in bed wearing one of her silk nightshirts. He could see the outline of her breasts through the thin material and had to concentrate to keep from spilling their wine.

They touched glasses and he said, "To us." She answered with a smile and repeated the toast, "To us, dear."

After taking a sip of the dark-red burgundy, Smoke handed her the telegram he had been given in town. She pursed her lips, looked at him once, then drank the rest of her wine in one swallow as if to fortify herself against whatever news was in the message.

Tears formed in her eyes as she read, and Smoke put his hand on her thigh, squeezing lightly to let her know he was there for her. "My father's had a stroke," she whispered, voice cracking.

Smoke refilled her glass and said, "Is it bad?"

She shook her head. "My brother says not, but he has some weakness in his right arm and leg, and the left side of his face droops a little." Her eyes found his. "They ask if I can come and be there with him while he heals."

Smoke nodded without speaking. Sally clenched her jaw and blinked away her tears. "I'll send an answer with Pearlie in the morning, telling them to give my love to Dad, but I won't be able to join them."

Surprised, Smoke asked, "Why not? I could take you over to the railhead and you'd be there in less than a week."

She looked at him with a defiant expression. "Why? Because someone is after my man, trying to kill him. I'm damned if I'm going to let anyone hurt you, Smoke. We've worked too long and too hard to build a good life here in the mountains, and nobody is going to take that away from us. Not without a hell of a fight, they're not."

Smoke took her in his arms and hugged her tight, loving her more at that moment than he ever had. "You're right, darling. Someone is trying to kill me, or have me killed. I think it's that young gunfighter, Lester Sundance Morgan, that I treed and marked a few years back."

She leaned back and looked him in the eye. "All the more reason for me to stay where I belong, right here by your side."

He shook his head. "No, dear. I think it'd be better if you were somewhere else for a while."

Sally opened her mouth to speak, an angry expression on her face. He put a finger to her lips. "Hang on and listen to me for a minute. With you here, I'm not free to move around and do what I need to do to prepare for when this skunk gets tired of sending second-raters up here to be killed. Sooner or later he's going to come and try to do the job himself, and since I know he's a devout coward, he won't be coming alone."

"But Smoke, I want to help you when that time comes."

"No, sweetheart, I don't want a war here in our valley. Too many of our friends might get hurt. I plan to set up some hands as guards to keep any sizable force away from our home here, and I'm going to go to the high lonesome, where they'll have to come and get me on my terms and in my country."

She searched his face, trying to decide if he was just saying this to give her a way out so she could go to her family. After a moment, she shrugged. "Okay, Smoke Jensen. I'll go and take care of my dad, and leave you here to take care of whoever is behind tonight's attack." She took his face in her hands, "But you hear me and hear me well. You ride with your guns loose and your temper short and you stay off the ridgeline, because if you let anybody kill you, I'll never forgive you."

He laughed and kissed her softly on the lips. "You hear

me, Sally Jensen. You get your father well in a hurry, 'cause every minute without you is like a month to me."

Sally smiled a familiar smile. She pulled the nightshirt over her head and sat there, looking at Smoke with heavy eyelids and chest heaving. "How come you're not undressed yet? Don't you know it's time for bed?"

Smoke blew the lamp out and began to rip off his bloody, torn shirt. "Yes, ma'am, I do. Do you want some more wine?"

From the darkness came her answer. "No. Just you."

The next morning, as Pearlie loaded Woodrow on the buckboard, Smoke gave him a telegram to send to Sally's family in New Hampshire telling them she would be there within two weeks or so, depending on the weather and the state of the railroad tracks.

After Pearlie left, with Hank riding in the back with the wounded man, Smoke called the hands together. "Men, Sally's in the cabin packing now, and in a little while, I'm going to take her over to where she can catch a train back East to see her folks. After I leave, I want you all to keep a skeleton crew on the horse and cattle herds—just enough men to keep them safe and protected. I want the rest of you scattered along the various trails that anyone could use to get to Sugarloaf."

One of the men asked, "You expectin' more trouble, Mr. Smoke?"

"Yeah. Some lowlife gunslick I took down a few years back is out to pay me back. I figure he'll have to have plenty of help before he gets the courage to come up here and face me, so I want you men to cover all the places on the trails where one or two men can keep a large party from passing. Most of you know this country about as well as I do, and there are plenty of passes and tight spots where you can bottle up those flatlanders so they can't get up here to do any mischief."

Another asked, "What are you gonna be doin', boss?"

"I'm gonna let it be known around the territory that I've gone up into the high country for a while to visit some of my ole mountain man friends. That way, hopefully, all the action will be away from here and you all will be safe."

"To hell with bein' safe," the man who had spoken said, "you need any help, boss, all you gotta do is ask."

"I know, Billy, but if I can get those scum to come after me in the up-high, they're the ones who'll be needin' help. Thanks for your loyalty and your help. Now, I'd better get in the cabin and help Sally pack or I won't have to worry about it, she'll kill me."

The men laughed as they broke into small groups to decide who was going to which pass and who would be minding the herd.

Smoke went into the cabin and found Sally filling a steamer trunk, tears running down her face. "Sweetheart, what's the matter?"

She looked at him with red-rimmed eyes. "I don't like to be away from you. You always seem to get into trouble when I'm gone."

He smiled and put his arms around her as she continued, "Of course, you also always seem to get into mischief when I'm here." She leaned her head back and kissed him on the lips. "It's a good thing I love you so much, Smoke, 'cause you sure need a lot of taking care of."

"But worth it, right?"

"Oh yes," she said, remembering the night before.

When she was finished packing, and Smoke had loaded her trunk and small valise onto the buckboard, she motioned him into their bedroom. As he entered, she began unbuttoning her shirt. "Smoke, there's one thing you forgot."

He raised his eyebrows. "Oh?"

She stripped her shirt off and began to undo her britches. "Yes. You haven't told me good-bye yet."

Smoke was astounded. Surely she couldn't intend for them to do it in the daytime, with all the hands roaming around. Naked, she pulled the curtains and looked back over her shoulder at Smoke as she slid under the covers and into their bed. "Am I going to have to start without you?" she asked, smiling a lazy half-smile.

"Oh no, not on your life." he answered huskily, shucking boots and pants as fast as he could.

As they approached Big Rock in the buckboard, Smoke asked Sally, "Have you got your short-barrelled .44 handy?"

Before he could turn his eyes back to the road, she had it in her hand, grinning at him. "Why, are you expecting more trouble this morning?"

He shook his head, proud of her readiness. "Well, like I told you, one of the first and strongest lessons Preacher taught me was that if you always expect trouble, it never surprises you when it comes, as it usually does sooner or later in this country."

Sally smiled as she put the .44 away in her handbag. "You think about Preacher often, don't you?"

"Every day." He shook his head as he spoke. "You

know, it's funny, but even as civilized as we've become here, with towns and railroads and people all over the place, not a day goes by that I don't use one of the lessons that Preacher taught me about survival in a wilderness."

Sally snorted. "Hmph, perhaps we're not as civilized as you think we are, Smoke. Most of the people out here are just one generation away from the frontier folks like Preacher who settled this country in the first place."

He smiled. "Yeah, and some are less than one generation up from the animals that preceded the mountain men."

"Oh, so now you're insulting the grizzlies and wolves, huh?"

They laughed together as the buckboard pulled into the main street of Big Rock. Townspeople of all ages waved and shouted hello. Smoke pulled the wagon up in front of the Emporium, so Sally could stock up on some female essentials she said she needed for the train trip.

He left her to her shopping and ambled down the street to the saloon owned by Louis Longmont, his gambler friend of many years. There Louis plied his trade, which he called teaching amateurs the laws of chance.

Louis was a lean, hawk-faced man, with strong, slender, clean hands and long fingers, nails carefully manicured. He had jet-black hair and a black pencil-thin moustache. He was, as usual, dressed in a black suit, with white shirt and dark ascot—something he'd picked up on a trip to England some years back. He wore low-heeled boots, and a pistol hung in tied-down leather on his right side. It was not for show, for Louis was snake-quick with a short gun and was a feared, deadly gunhand when pushed.

Louis was not an evil man. He had never hired his gun out for money. And while he could make a deck of cards do almost anything, he did not cheat at poker. He did not have to cheat. He was possessed of a phenomenal memory, could tell you the odds of filling any type of poker hand, and was one of the first to use the new method of card counting.

He was just past forty years of age. He had come to the West with his parents as a very small boy, arriving from Louisiana. His parents had died in a shantytown fire, leaving the boy to cope as best he could.

He had coped quite well, plying his innate intelligence and willingness to take a chance into a fortune. He owned a large ranch up in Wyoming Territory, several businesses in San Francisco, and a hefty chunk of a railroad.

Though it was a mystery to many why Longmont stayed with the hard life he had chosen, Smoke thought he understood. Once Louis had said to him, "Smoke, I would miss my life every bit as much as you would miss the dry-mouthed moment before the draw, the challenge of facing and besting those miscreants who would kill you or others, and the so-called loneliness of the owlhoot trail."

Sometimes Louis joked that he would like to draw against Smoke someday, just to see who was faster. Smoke allowed as how it would be close, but that he would win. "You see, Louis, you're just too civilized," he had told him on many occasions. "Your mind is distracted by visions of operas, fine foods and wines, and the odds of your winning the match. Also, your fatal flaw is that you can almost always see the good in the lowest creatures God ever made, and you refuse to believe that anyone is pure evil and without hope of redemption."

When Louis laughed at this description of himself, Smoke would continue. "On the other hand, when some snake-scum draws down on *me* and wants to dance, the only thing I have on my mind is teaching him that when you dance, someone has to pay the band. My mind is clear and focused on only one problem, how to put that stump-sucker across his horse toes down."

Louis looked up from his breakfast table and smiled as Smoke entered his saloon. "Smoke, my old friend, have a seat and let André fix you something to chase the pangs of hunger away."

Smoke flipped his hat onto a rack next to the door and sat at Louis's table, narrowing his eyes at what was before him on his plate. "Good morning, Louis." He pointed at the eggs covered with what appeared to be curdled buttermilk. "Just what is that you are fixing to eat?"

"It is called eggs Benedict, and it is truly *magnifique*," said Louis, kissing his fingertips in the French fashion.

Smoke pursed his lips, then shook his head. "I don't think so, Louis. If your fancy French chef, André, can remember how to make some bacon and plain old hen eggs and fried taters, I'd 'preciate it."

"Oh Smoke," Louis looked disappointed. "At least try these eggs Benedict. They are to die for!"

"I'd just as soon live, if you don't mind. Just have him pour a little sweet cream in with the eggs and scramble 'em up. That'll do me just fine."

"Okay then, how about some *café au lait*?"

"If that's coffee, I'll have about a gallon."

Louis's eyebrows raised. "Late night last night?"

André appeared with a large silver service coffeepot and a china cup and saucer, which he placed in front of Smoke. "Good morning, Mr. Smoke, sir. May I serve you some eggs Benedict?"

Louis relayed Smoke's order, and André went away with a pained look on his face.

Smoke took a drink of his coffee, making sure his little finger was out and that Louis saw it. Then he pulled his makin's out and said, "You mind?"

Louis waved a dismissive hand, "No, of course not. What is morning coffee without tobacco?"

After Smoke had his cigarette going and had taken another sip of coffee, he said, "Had a little excitement up at Sugarloaf last night."

"Oh?"

"Yeah. Seems four bushwhackers thought they was good enough to take on Sally and the hands. Had 'em pinned down for a while until I showed up."

Around a mouthful of food, Louis said, "All dead, I presume?"

Smoke looked startled. "Of course, what'd you expect?"

"Nothing less, my friend. Are you aware of the reasoning behind the cowardly attack?"

Smoke filled him in on what he had heard and who he suspected was behind the various attacks on him recently, and of his plan to send Sally to New Hampshire to see her folks.

"And I'd like you to spread the word to the patrons of your establishment that I've gone to the high country for a visit with some old mountain man friends up there."

"Certainly, Smoke, but wouldn't you like another pair of Colts to help you when Sundance finally comes for you? Knowing his character, or complete lack thereof, as we both do, I'm certain he's going to come with lots of company."

Smoke shook his head and put out the cigarette as

André served his breakfast. "No thanks, Louis. I 'preciate the offer, but the more men he brings up into my country, the worse off he'll be. Easier to sow confusion and doubt when there's a crowd."

Louis put down his knife and fork and pulled a huge, black cigar out of his vest pocket. He lit it and blew a large, blue cloud of cigar smoke at the ceiling. "Yes, I understand your strategy. Still, someone to watch your back might not be inappropriate."

Smoke grinned. "Things must be awfully slow around here. You sound bored to me, Louis."

"Well, now that you mention it, there has been a notable lack of excitement in Big Rock lately. I'm afraid that word has gotten out that this is Smoke Jensen's town and the rowdier element bypasses us for more suitable entertainment." He took another pull on the stogie, "Hell, I may have to move to a livelier town before dry rot sets in. I haven't drawn my gun in anger in several months. I'm afraid I'm getting out of practice."

Before Smoke could answer, there came the sound of a gunshot from the direction of the Emporium, and Smoke and Louis bolted for the door together.

Sally was standing in front of the store, holding her short-barrelled .44 in front of her. One sleeve of her shirt was torn, a man lay doubled over the hitching post, blood dripping from a hole between his eyes and out of the enormous gap in the back of his head, and four other men were standing arrayed around her, hands near their guns.

Smoke, Louis, and Sheriff Monte Carson, carrying a sawed-off shotgun, arrived at the same time. Smoke went to stand beside Sally, fire in his eyes. "What happened, Sally?"

She inclined her head toward the dead man. "This . . . fellow," she spat with distaste, "saw me carrying some packages out of the Emporium and thought if he offered to help, that gave him other rights, too."

One of the saddlebums pointed his finger at Sally and shouted, "She kilt our friend. He wasn't doin' nothin', jest bein' friendly, that's all."

The man next to him joined in. "Yeah, now she's gonna get a whuppin'."

Smoke's smile didn't include his eyes. "Oh? And just which one of you thinks he's man enough to do it?"

The biggest one of the four, a man well over six and a half feet tall and weighing two hundred and fifty pounds, hitched his thumb in his belt and stepped forward. "I figure I'm man enough. I see you're wearing a mighty fancy shootin' rig, but I'm wondering how good you are with your fists?"

Smoke looked at Sally. "Did any of these men bother you?"

She shook her head. "No, but the tall one there was encouraging the other one to show me what a real man is like. As if he knew!" She looked at the big man and spat in his face.

He sleeved the saliva off and backhanded Sally, almost knocking her down. He raised his hands when suddenly he was looking down the barrels of Smoke's and Louis's Colts and Monte's shotgun with both hammers eared back. "Hey wait a minute," he cried. "She started it."

Smoke holstered his pistol and put his hand on top of Louis's gun, pushing it down. "Hold on, Louis, Monte.

Killing this big, brave man who hits women is too fast and too painless for him. Let me show him what happens to men who abuse women in this country."

He took his gun belt off and handed it to Louis, first removing his padded, black gloves and putting them on. He stepped into the street and waved the man toward him.

The big fellow spit in his hands and rubbed them together. "What rules you want to fight by?" he asked.

Smoke raised his eyebrows. "Rules? I promise to quit hitting you after you're dead. That's the only rule I fight by."

The man grinned, showing yellow, rotten teeth. "Good. My kinda fight." He showed no finesse, just put his hands up and walked toward Smoke, evidently counting on his size to overpower the shorter man. He hadn't noted the size of Smoke's biceps, as big around as most men's necks, or his forearms, steel-hard from years of labor in the mountain woods.

When he was within arm's reach, he took a big round-house swing that would have taken Smoke's head off if it had connected. Instead, Smoke ducked under the blow and swung a straight punch with all of his weight behind it into the cowboy's exposed right kidney.

Everyone present could hear the snap of the lower two ribs on that side, even over the man's grunt of pain. As he doubled over, Smoke stepped in close and clipped him behind the right ear with a left cross, spinning the giant around with his back to Smoke.

When he straightened up and turned around, he was holding a knife he had pulled from his boot. Blood was running down the right side of his face from his ear, and he was canted over to the side, cradling his broken ribs with his arm. He extended his knife hand and rushed at Smoke, screaming incoherently.

Smoke leaned to the side as he rushed past and planted the toe of his boot in the man's ample paunch, burying it all the way to the spurs. The man bent over, heaving his breakfast onto the street. Smoke grabbed a handful of hair in one hand and his chin in the other, and twisted. The bully's neck broke with a loud snap like dry wood and he fell dead on his face in the dirt.

Smoke looked at the cowboy's friends. "Only a man with a death wish brings a knife to a fight. Now you gents have two choices. You can apologize to the lady and ride out of town, or I can put my guns on and you can spend eternity eating dirt in Boot Hill over there."

With downcast eyes, the cowboys all told Sally they were sorry before they mounted their horses and began to ride down the street. Smoke went over to the horse trough and splashed water on his face. He turned to get his pistols from Louis and was startled to see Louis draw his Colt in a blur and fire right over Smoke's head.

He whirled. One of cowboys had turned his horse around and was riding back toward Smoke with a pistol in his hand. He was blown out of the saddle by Louis's shot. The snap shot had taken the man in the throat and almost decapitated him. The other two wasted no time hightailing it out of town.

Smoke turned to Louis with upraised eyebrows. "I thought you were out of practice, old friend."

Louis frowned. "I am. I was aiming between his eyes."

Smoke put his arm around his shoulders. "No problem, he was just taller than you remembered, that's all."

Smoke helped Sally up into the buckboard and they rode out of Big Rock with a wave.

Louis said to Monte Carson, "Monte, would you care to join me for a drink?"

Monte sleeved the sweat off his forehead and shouldered his shotgun. "Sure would, Louis. All this excitement has given me a powerful dry I need to wet."

Louis looked after the couple leaving town. "Sheriff, you ever seen anyone with hands as fast as Smoke's?"

Monte winked. "Nope. He's faster than a hound dog goin' after a bone, all right. Main difference is, though, that ole mountain dog is all bite and no bark!"

CHAPTER SEVEN

Sundance stood on a small knoll near the grove of cottonwoods he had designated as a meeting place for his lieutenants and their men. They arrived an hour before and were now drinking coffee by the gallon, most of them trying without much success to sober up and get rid of their hangovers.

El Gato brought twelve men with him, all *pistoleros,* with no Anglos among them. He was most proud of Carlito Suarez, a man he called *perro muerte,* the hound of death. Suarez, according to El Gato, had killed so many men he could not keep track of them on his fingers and toes. He carried two pistols, each facing butt forward, and the usual crossed bandoliers holding spare cartridges, and had an ancient '73 Winchester slung over his shoulder that looked as if it had seen better days. He was said to be able to knock the eye out of an eagle in flight with the rifle. We'll see, thought Sundance, with some skepticism. The remainder of El Gato's men were the usual assortment of scruffy looking Mexican *bandido* types. Heavy moustaches that drooped low, uncut, scraggly hair and beards, and a smell of onions and unwashed flesh that made Sundance's nose curl when they came upwind of him.

Toothpick brought ten men with him. They were a mixed bunch, mostly Anglos with a few Mexicans thrown in. They were all hardcases, and Sundance recognized several faces from Wanted posters he had seen around towns in south Texas. One-Eye Jordan, wearing a patch over his left eye, was wanted for robbery, rape, and murder in at least four towns that Sundance knew of. He wore only one gun, but was reputed to be as quick as a rattlesnake with it, and just as likely as the dreaded serpent to strike without provocation. It was said he lost his eye in a fight, gouged out by his opponent's thumb. Jordan, according to local legend, had bitten the man's thumb off and swallowed it before killing him.

Another of Toothpick's gang was Curly Bill Cartwright. This angelic-faced kid was no more than eighteen years old, and looked only fourteen. He was, however, a stone-cold killer whose pretty face was inhabited by eyes as dead as dirt, and the same color. He was reputed to kill without mercy and could use a knife as well as a pistol.

One of his Mexicans was called Chiva, which Sundance didn't understand. The word *chiva* was like *cabrón,* one of the worst insults you could give a Mexican. He later learned it meant not only cuckold, but also scurrilous outlaw, or thoroughly bad *hombre.* Chiva was all of that. He had a scar from ear to ear, and was said to have choked to death with his bare hands the man who gave it to him, after the gent had cut his throat. He never smiled and rarely talked, just sat constantly worrying his knife blade on an old whetstone. Sundance could see why he and Toothpick had teamed up together.

Lightning Jack Warner brought fourteen men, all Anglos and all sporting distinctly Southern accents. Several still wore parts of Confederate Army uniforms and smelled as if they hadn't bathed or washed their clothes since the end of the war. These men eyed the Mexicans nervously and acted as if they would rather fight them than make some money. One of his men, simply called Bull, was one of the biggest, widest men Sundance had ever seen. He made even El Gato seem small. He rode a horse that must have been seventeen hands and it looked like a pony between his legs. In spite of his size, he had a high, almost girlish voice with a bit of a lisp. God help the man, or men, who mentioned it, however. His hands were so big it was hard for him to handle a six-gun; fingers wouldn't fit in the trigger guard. He carried a pair of twelve-gauge shotguns cut down to fourteen inches long. He wore a homemade rig for his converted shotguns with two holsters fitted to a belt like scabbards for pistols. It was said that he was as fast with his scatterguns as most men with Colts. He made his own loads for the shells out of wire, glass, and cut-off heads of horseshoe nails. His effective range was only about twenty yards, but it was a rare man who could hit the side of a barn with a Colt at a greater distance. His friends bragged that anything Bull shot at he hit, and anything Bull hit, he killed. He was known to have been wounded eleven times, three in one battle, and had never gone down from his injuries. Either too mean, or too stupid to die, thought Sundance.

Sundance stood on his knoll and whistled to get the gunmen's attention. Several, those with hangovers of larger than average proportions, winced and held their heads, or just lay on the ground with their eyes shut. *"Compadres* and partners. I don't know what the men who brought you here told you, but if you ride with me, you'll either become rich, or you'll die."

A few of the men stopped cleaning their guns or drinking their coffee and looked up with puzzled expressions.

Sundance paced as he spoke, waving his arms with excitement. "Together, we can form the most feared gang the West has ever seen. We can rob and pillage and steal anything we want. We can go wherever we want, and no town, no marshal, no sheriff can stand against us. For every man we lose in battle, we'll have two more who want to join the Sundance Morgan gang. We'll move fast and strike hard. No one will be safe and nobody will know where we're going to hit next."

One of the Southerners stood and shouted, "Okay, now we know how we'll die. Just how will we get rich?"

Sundance laughed. "A man after my own heart. We'll split the proceeds of every job equally among us. Even though I will plan the jobs and our raids. I will take no more than anyone else. We are all equals where money is concerned." He paused, and walked a few steps in silence before turning back to the group. "On this there can be no disagreement, however. I'll be boss and I'll call the shots—where we go, who we hit, and when we leave camp. Are there any questions about that?"

One of the *pistoleros* who had come into camp with El Gato came to his feet. He had an Army Colt in his hand and was idly spinning the cylinder. "I got a question. Why should we, *los pistoleros,* take orders from *un gabacho*?"

Sundance smiled and cocked his head. "Excuse me," he said with sarcasm, "but what does *gabacho* mean?"

The Mexican grinned insolently. "Is not so nice word for *gringo,* my friend."

Without hesitation, Sundance drew and fired in an instant, his bullet taking the man in the forehead and blowing brains and blood all over his friends behind him. The gunman stood there for a moment with a surprised look on what was left of his face, before he toppled into the dust.

Sundance aimed his Colt in the air. "What do you call a dead Mexican?" he shouted. When no one moved, he yelled, "The same thing you call a dead American. A corpse!" He shook his head and spread his arms to include all of the men gathered under the cottonwood trees. "We are all *compadres* here, we are all *compañeros,* we are all partners. There is no race or religion in this gang. We will fight together, whore together, and live or die together." His expression turned fierce. "Anyone who can't live with that can leave now, or be killed later. It's your choice."

Most of the group cheered and waved their bandannas in the air or fired off their pistols. A few of Lightning Jack's Southerners got on their mounts and rode off silently, and a couple of Mexicans took their horses and went toward the Rio Bravo just beyond the trees. Overall, Sundance thought, he now had a gang of better than thirty of the meanest, lowest, and most deadly men in the state of Texas riding with him.

He aimed his pistol at a grove of trees nearby. "Over there, I've two cases of tequila and two cases of whiskey. What say we have a few drinks to settle our partnership and help cut the trail dust?"

A great shout of joy erupted and the men all scrambled to get a bottle, get some shade, and get alkalied.

* * *

It was almost sundown by the time Smoke and Sally made it to a small station on the Rocky Mountain Line railroad tracks that served as the closest point to Sugarloaf where they could board an eastbound train. The station consisted of a small, one-room cabin and loading platform, with a pole to hang a lantern on to signal the engineer to stop.

Smoke lit the lantern, hung it on the pole, and settled back to await the train's arrival. He built a cigarette and poured himself and Sally a small dollop of whiskey to cut the ever-present dust.

Sally took his cigarette between her fingers and pulled a drag, then took a small sip of liquor. As she exhaled, she looked at him. "I'm going to miss you, Smoke," she said huskily.

He took her hand. "I'm going to miss you, too, honey." He smiled, "but I'll tell you this, the boys are going to miss you almost as much. Cookie just doesn't know his way around a kitchen nearly as well as you do. They'll all probably lose weight while you're gone."

She leaned away from him and gave a mock frown. "Oh, so it's just my cooking you're going to miss, huh?"

He placed a huge callused palm against her cheek and gently pulled her face to his. Kissing her lightly, he said, "Now, you know that's not true. I value your cleaning and washing just as much as your cooking. I won't hardly have any clean clothes by the time you get back."

Without warning, her eyes flashed and she punched him in the stomach. "You keep talking like that, and I may just decide not to return to my old mountain man at all, Smoke Jensen!"

They both laughed and hugged each other tightly. The remaining time until the train arrived was spent saying those things that a man and woman who are deeply in love say to one another when they are about to be separated for a lengthy time.

Finally, as the sun was sinking below the mountains to the west, a locomotive chugged toward the tiny station and pulled to a stop amid squealing wheels, belching clouds of steam. Smoke loaded Sally's luggage into the baggage car, then helped her up the steps and to a seat in the passenger section. A final kiss, a quick caress of her face, and he was gone.

In typical mountain man fashion, Smoke didn't watch the train as it took his beloved far away. He put her and that tender part of his life out of his mind and concentrated on the task before him: luring Sundance into the mountains and dealing with him in his usual manner—as harshly as he knew how.

He drove the buckboard toward peaks to the north. After driving roughly ten miles, he unhitched and ground-reined the two horses, made a small cold camp, and ate his supper of jerked beef, cold biscuits, and a small sip of whiskey to wash it down. He rolled one cigarette while he was lying on his back gazing at the stars, then he dropped off to sleep. He wanted to get an early start at dawn.

Smoke figured he was at seven thousand feet when he decided the buckboard had carried him far enough. He unharnessed his team and pulled the buckboard off the trail into the brush. He donned his buckskins, moccasins, and leggings, fixed his pack of supplies on one of the horses, and put his saddle on the other. Now he was ready for the final portion of his journey, to get to the up-high where the old cougars, his mountain man friends, camped and lived most of their lives.

As the sun peaked over the mountains and began to burn off the early-morning fog, Pearlie yawned, stretched, and scratched. Padding over to the stove in the center of the bunkhouse, he started a fire to get some coffee heating.

He stropped his razor and began to scrape at the stubble on his face, gasping as he splashed the near-freezing water over his cheeks. Holy Jesus, he thought, the summers are short in this high country.

While combing his unruly hair, he noticed in the mirror that Cal's bed was empty. "Hmmm, ain't like that boy to be first outta his bunk," he mumbled. It was no secret among the hands that Cal liked to sleep almost as much as Pearlie liked to eat. He pulled on his boots and jeans and shirt and hurried out into the chilly fall air.

Cal was just putting his boot in his stirrup when Pearlie came out of the bunkhouse.

"Whoa there, Cal. Just back on outta that saddle and tell me what you figger you're doin'."

Cal blushed a dark crimson. "Well, uh, I'm goin' for a ride."

"I can see that, boy, I ain't blind. Where are ya' aimin' on ridin' to, and why are ya' takin' off a'fore breakfast?"

"I'm just going to go up into the hills around the ranch, to, uh, look around a bit."

Pearlie walked to Cal's horse, a small buckskin Palouse with bloodred spots on its rump. He ran his hand over the .22 rifle in the saddle boot and over a bedroll and full saddlebags behind the cantle. "Uh-huh. And I'm gonna go on a diet, too!" Pearlie shook his head. "What's goin' on, young'un?" He put his finger in front of Cal's face and wiggled it. "And don't you try and feed your uncle Pearlie any bull-splat, neither."

Cal's face got a determined look on it and he hitched his pants up and pulled his hat down. "I'm plannin' on ridin' up in the mountains and helpin' Smoke out when those *bandidos* come up after him."

"You figger that peashooter," Pearlie said, pointing to Cal's .22 rifle, "and that little .36 caliber Navy Colt you're sportin' is gonna help the big man?"

Smoke's first pistol had been a Navy Model Colt .36 caliber, and when Cal came to work for him, Smoke unpacked his old gun and gave it to Cal, figuring a smaller caliber would be easier on the young boy's arm.

Smoke had been right, for Cal became a dead shot with the handgun, though Pearlie and some of the other hands teased him that it was so small it would only irritate and anger whoever he shot. Cal had replied that any gun good enough for Smoke was good enough for him—and besides, the folks Smoke had shot with it surely died as dead as those he shot with his .44's.

Cal's blush deepened and spread to include his ears. "You're damn right, Pearlie. Maybe I don't carry the biggest artillery in the territory, but I can damn sure hit what I aim at, and that's what counts in a gunfight."

Pearlie grinned, raising his eyebrows. "Oh, and how do you know what counts in a gunfight?"

Cal raised his chin and assumed a haughty look. "'Cause that's what Smoke tole me counts."

"Well, it don't matter none no-how, 'cause I can't let you go. Smoke said we was to hang here at the ranch and make sure the beeves and horses are all right."

"Well, it does matter, and I'm damn sure goin'."

Pearlie glared at the boy. "No you're not, not as long as you work for this spread, and not as long as I'm ramrod."

"Then I quit, 'cause I don't intend for Smoke to fight a gang of hardcases all by hisself."

Pearlie rolled his eyes and gritted his teeth until his jaws ached. What was he going to do, he thought. Smoke would flay him alive if he let Cal go up into those mountains alone, especially with a madman like Sundance Morgan on the prowl. "Okay, okay, just wait a minute and let me think."

He went into the bunkhouse and poured himself a cup of coffee to get his juices going, and built himself a cigarette. He sat on the small bunkhouse porch and smoked and drank his coffee while trying to figure out what Smoke would want him to do, short of hog-tying the kid to keep him out of trouble.

Finally, he thought of a way to handle the situation that just might let him keep his job and his hide. "Okay, Cal. Here's the deal. I'm gonna get you a rifle that'll do more than just piss those polecats off, then we're gonna get supplied up plenty good, an' we're both gonna go up in the high country and look for Smoke." He held up his palm to halt Cal's ear-to-ear grin. "Hold on there. Unless I miss my guess, when we find Smoke, he's gonna kick your butt all over them mountains and send us right back down here, but I'm gonna give you a chance to talk him into lettin' us lend him a hand."

"Great, then let's shag the trail. We're burnin' daylight."

"Whoa there, bronco. First, I gotta eat, then I gotta get my horse saddled and get Cookie to fix us up with some vittles for the trail, then we gotta get you a man's gun for that saddle boot."

He rubbed his chin in thought. "I figure we got an old Winchester '73 around here. It shoots .44's so you'll have to carry double ammunition since you cain't use those .36's your little peashooter needs."

"That's okay. You go get Cookie to get your breakfast, an' I'll pack your horse and get the rifle and extra ammunition outta the tack room, and we'll be ready to get gone as soon as you finish stuffin' your face."

Pearlie shook his head and mumbled something about angels rushing in as he walked over toward the main cabin to get Cookie started on breakfast and their provisions.

CHAPTER EIGHT

Sundance lay on his belly in the moonlight on a small bluff overlooking a Mexican *hacienda*. He and his lieutenants. Toothpick, El Gato, and Lightning Jack, had decided to strike one of the rich Mexican ranches near the border for their first target. Sundance explained this was important for two reasons. First, the American authorities were notoriously lax in prosecuting crimes that occurred in Mexico. And, second, he wanted to test his gang in an area where there was likely to be only token resistance.

El Gato told Sundance that he knew of just such a place. A distant cousin of his, Enrique Hernandez, owned a fine spread a few miles from Laredo. Since the outbreak of fever in the cattle of the region, Hernandez had let most of his *vaqueros* go in order to conserve his cash until such time as healthy beeves could be bought to replenish his herd.

Sundance asked, "Why would you want us to hit one of your relatives, El Gato?"

El Gato's eyes burned with hatred. "The filthy *bastardo*." He spit on the ground at Sundance's feet. "He turned his back when El Gato asked for help. *Federales* wanted to hang El Gato, so I asked Señor Hernandez to hide me. He refused. Called me, how you say in English, garbage!"

"Is he wealthy?"

"That *cabrón* has more money than *El Presidente de Mexico.*" El Gato frowned. "And he does not even give moneys to church."

Toothpick grinned around a *cigarillo* dangling from his mouth. "And you, my friend. Do you give to the church?"

El Gato's lips curled in an evil smirk. "Me? I am but a poor peon. God made church to help peons." He shrugged. "When I come to *El casa de Dios,* is to take moneys from poor box. Is what is for."

Sundance interrupted. "But what about Hernandez? I don't want to rob his place and end up with a handful of paper *pesos.*"

"*No, el Patrón* does not deal in paper moneys. He keeps *oro* at his *hacienda* because that is what is required by *Americano* cattle buyers and sellers."

Lightning Jack grunted. "Gold? Well, like I always said, it's easier to liberate gold from a man's poke than it is to dig it outta the ground. Let's go for it."

It was almost midnight as the moon reached its zenith over the northern Mexican desert. The sky was clear and the moonlight reflecting off the sand made the night as bright as day. Sundance lay on the parched caliche of the bluff, which was still warm from the scorching daylight sun even though the air was chilly. He was peering through his binoculars at Hernandez's ranch below. "I don't see no lights nor any activity. He doesn't 'pear to have any guards out."

El Gato snarled. "The old man thinks he safe because is far from town."

Sundance got to his feet, brushing dirt off his pants and elbows. "Okay, this is it, then. El Gato, take your men to the bunkhouse and have them ready to bust in on my signal. Lightning Jack and the rest of the men will surround the house in case any of the family wants to make a stand there."

"What are you gonna be doin', boss?" asked Lightning Jack.

Sundance's teeth glowed in the moonlight. "Me? Why, Toothpick and me're goin' into the house and see if Señor Hernandez won't agree to make a donation to the Sundance Morgan gang."

"And if'n he don't?"

Toothpick pulled his knife from its scabbard and licked the blade, causing it to shine and reflect the moon. "Then me and Baby here will have a talk with him."

After his men were positioned, Sundance and Toothpick walked their horses up to the front of the *hacienda* and dismounted, Sundance draping a coil of rope over his shoulders. They tried the door, but it wouldn't open. Toothpick inserted his blade into the doorjamb and gently lifted, raising a wooden bar blocking their way.

Easing into the house, they began to search it room by room, aided by the moonlight streaming through windows. They found three young males, looking like they ranged in age from twelve to eighteen, and two females of about thirteen and sixteen sleeping soundly in their beds. Taking several pistols from the bedrooms, they continued their search until they came to the master bedroom.

Hernandez and his wife were asleep, covered only by a light sheet, curtains billowing in the gentle night breeze. Hernandez appeared to be in his early fifties, while his wife looked to be no more than forty. Toothpick used the point of his knife to gently pull the sheet down, revealing a full-figured woman clad only in a sheer nightshirt. He licked his lips and grinned at Sundance, raising his eyebrows.

Sundance put the barrel of his Colt against Hernandez's temple and thumbed back the hammer. The loud click brought the man instantly awake, his hand reaching under his pillow. Sundance drew back and rapped him sharply in the face with the gun, breaking his nose with a cracking noise and awakening his wife.

She opened her mouth, but gasped and swallowed her scream when Toothpick stuck the point of his blade against her throat, drawing a small drop of blood that rolled slowly down her neck. The crimson liquid appeared black against her pale skin in the moonlight.

Hernandez's eyes rolled frantically, as Sundance removed a large-bore *pistola* from underneath his pillow, his shattered nose streaming blood all over his chest. "What do you *gringos* want?" he asked urgently in English.

"First of all, we're not *gringos,* we're outlaws, and we want your gold."

He shook his head, wincing at the pain it caused. "I have no gold. You must be mistaken."

"Oh?" Sundance asked politely. "Then, I guess we'll just be on our way."

Toothpick glanced across the bed at him, a puzzled expression on his face.

"Of course," Sundance continued in the same quiet tone, "if there's no gold for my *compadres*, they're probably gonna be very angry." He let the terrified rancher see his eyes shift to his wife. "I may have to let them amuse themselves some other way, just to keep them in line."

"Bastardos! My *vaqueros* will cut you to pieces if you harm anyone in this house!"

"Oh yes, I almost forgot about your men." Sundance, keeping his pistol trained at Hernandez, walked to the window and pulled back the curtains. He whistled shrilly, his signal to Lightning Jack and his men.

From the direction of the bunkhouse came the sound of a door splintering, followed immediately by twin booming explosions of Lightning Jack's big scattergun and the staccato popping of pistols in the night. There were several screams and shouts at first, then only moaning and crying and pleas for mercy could be heard. After a few isolated shots, even the moaning stopped, replaced by an ominous silence.

The bedroom door burst open and the Hernandez children rushed into the room, brought to a halt by the sight of their parents lying on the bed under the gun and knife of the intruders.

Sundance pulled Hernandez out of bed by his hair, and ushered the entire family into a large room in the center of the *hacienda*. He tied Hernandez and his three sons with the rope he brought with him, and sat them on the floor in front of a huge fireplace dominating one wall. His wife and daughters were left huddled in a group in the middle of the room, crying and weeping and clinging together in fear.

El Gato and Lightning Jack sauntered in, Jack reloading his shotgun as he walked. "The men're all taken care of, boss. How're ya'll doin' in here?"

"We got a small problem here, Lightning. Señor Hernandez says he don't have no gold."

El Gato's eyes narrowed and he walked rapidly over to stand before the bleeding man. "No gold?" he asked, his voice thick with sarcasm.

Hernandez glared hate at Gato. *"Bastardo!"* he whispered under his breath.

El Gato kicked him in the stomach, causing him to double over and vomit on the tile floor. His wife and daughters screamed and began to wail even louder. His sons' faces contorted with hate and anger at the big Mexican standing over their father.

"Viejo! Donde esta el oro?" El Gato snarled.

"Chingale, animale!" Hernandez gasped from his position lying on his side in his vomit.

"Toothpick!" Sundance inclined his head at Hernandez's wife and daughters. Toothpick grinned and drew his blade. He walked to the woman and girls and one by one, slit their nightshirts. Their clothing fell to the floor, leaving them naked and cowering under the lustful gazes of the *desperados*.

Toothpick holstered his knife, put his left arm around Mrs. Hernandez's shoulders, and fondled her breasts with his right hand, whispering filth in her ear about what he was going to do to her.

Tears filled Hernandez's eyes and he hung his head,

defeated. *"Sí,* you win. If I tell you where the gold is, will you let my family live?"

Sundance squatted in front of the man. "No, I gotta be honest with you, Señor Hernandez. But I will give them a quick and painless death." He shrugged and cocked his head, as if bestowing a favor to a friend. "That's about all you can hope for at this point after lying to us about the gold and all."

Mrs. Hernandez, in a strangled voice, whispered, "The gold is in a chest in the bedroom, under some blankets."

Señor Hernandez sobbed and closed his eyes and began to pray softly.

"El Gato, check it out," Sundance ordered, without moving from his position in front of Hernandez.

After a moment, El Gato returned, dragging behind him a chest that was heavy enough to leave gouge marks in the tile floor.

"Señor Sundance, I think we very, very rich now!"

Sundance smiled a kind smile, then drew his pistol and put the barrel against Hernandez's forehead. "You through with all that preacher-talk, old man?"

Hernandez opened his eyes and looked up at Sundance, then he grinned defiantly and spit in his face. Enraged, Sundance cocked and fired, the sound magnified by the room's walls, blowing parts of Hernandez's head into the fireplace, splattering blood and bits of hair and brains all over the wall.

As his sons' eyes spread wide in terror, El Gato pulled both his Colts and emptied them into the boys, the banging of his guns filling the house, making them jump and contort as the hot lead tore through their flesh. The bodies quivered and spasmed for a moment, then became still as death claimed them one at a time.

Sundance sighed and punched out his empty shell, reloading the cylinder as he walked toward the women. "I said we share the money equally, but not necessarily the . . . spoils." He grasped the thirteen-year-old daughter by the back of her neck and pushed her ahead of him toward one of the bedrooms. He called over his shoulder, "You and the rest of the men can take turns with the other two, but I plan to be with this one until dawn. If I finish early, I'll let you know."

As the women continued to cry and moan, Lightning Jack dragged Mrs. Hernandez into a side room, while El Gato grabbed the sixteen-year-old by her hair and pulled her outside to a spot in the yard of the *hacienda* where the rest of the gang waited.

Soon the night was filled with terrified screams from the women and grunts and howls of animalistic passion from the men.

CHAPTER NINE

The sun was kissing the tops of the western peaks of the Rockies when Pearlie held his hand up and said to Cal, "Well, it's 'bout time to fix us a camp and let the horses blow. The air's pretty thin up here and there's no need to overdo it on our first day."

Cal shook his head. "Pearlie, we got another hour 'fore full dark yet. We can get another few miles, if'n we keep on goin'."

Pearlie narrowed his eyes at the youngster. "Cal, you don't know squat about travelin' in the high country." He walked his horse up to the bank of a small mountain stream gurgling in the twilight, leaned back as the horse dipped his head to drink, and crossed his leg over his saddle horn. He tilted his hat back and began to build himself a cigarette as he talked. "First of all, night comes quick in the up-high, a lot faster'n you think. Second, it takes time to get a camp ready and that's no fun in the dark."

He scratched a match to flame on his pants leg and lit his cigarette, sighing as he exhaled. "There's wood for the fire to gather, water to get to boilin' fer coffee, and since we neglected to take a proper nooning, I've got a powerful hunger on."

"But—"

"No buts, boy. This time of year it's gonna get might near freezin' up here, and I don't intend to turn into no icicle just so's we kin get to Smoke a little sooner." He took his hat off and sleeved the trail dust off his forehead. "Now, you wanted to come up here, so you'll listen to someone who knows just a mite more than you do about travelin' and campin' in the mountains."

He slid off his horse and tied the reins to a small bush near good grass so the horse could graze a while. "You go gather up some wood—dry, not too green—and I'll arrange a few rocks and build us a campfire that'll work to cook us some dinner and keep us from freezing tonight." He scowled and looked around at the heavy woods surrounding their camp area. "Hell, maybe it'll even keep the grizzlies and wolves from eatin' us while we sleep."

After they got the fire burning, and Pearlie sliced and fried some pork fatback and beans and made a pot of coffee and a batch of pan bread, the pair hobbled the horses to stay near camp and settled into their bedrolls in front of the fire.

Pearlie rolled himself a cigarette, then pitched the makings to Cal. "Go ahead and fill you a blanket, after-supper coffee's a lot better with a cigarette." He smiled, "Course, a dollop or two of whiskey in it don't hurt none neither, but I guess we'll do without that tonight."

It took Cal a couple of tries, but finally he put together a makeshift cigarette and lit it off a burning twig from the fire. A deep cough, a gasp, and he was into his first cigarette.

"Pearlie . . ."

"Yeah, kid?"

"How much do you know about Smoke's past?"

Pearlie raised his eyebrows and glanced over at Cal. "Why? You figgerin' to write one of those penny dreadfuls like those tenderfeet back East are always doin'?"

Cal took another drag on his smoke and coughed and hacked for a while before he could answer. "Naw, nothin' like that. It's just that ever since Smoke and Miss Sally took me on as a hand, I've been hearin' stories that's hard to believe. Things like he's kilt over two hundred men and all. I's just wonderin' how much of that's true, is all."

Pearlie chuckled. "Boy, you kin take anythin' ya' hear 'bout Smoke Jensen and double it, and you might be close to the truth. That *hombre* is a full sixteen hands high and that's no exaggeration."

"Well, I'm not near sleepy yet. How 'bout you tellin' me what you know about him?"

Pearlie sighed. "Okay, move that Arbuckles' off the fire so it don't git bitter and let me get another butt goin' and I'll tell ya what I know."

Cal grinned. "So it don't git bitter? Hell, I almost had to cut it outta the cup with my knife to drink it."

"Boy, that's real mountain man coffee. If you're gonna run with the big dogs, ya gotta be prepared to eat 'n drink the way they do." He held out his cup. "Now pour me another swig or two and settle back in your covers for the damndest tale you ever heared."

Pearlie lay back against his saddle, lit another cigarette,

and blew smoke at the stars as he thought about how to begin. "A few years back, I was in the employ of a man who made the biggest mistake of his life. He decided to go up against Smoke Jensen. After a while, I found I couldn't stomach the things that man was askin' me to do, so I switched sides and joined up with Smoke and his friends."

"You mean Smoke let you come over to his side after you'd been against him?"

"Yep. Matter of fact, t'was Smoke's idea in the first place. He asked me if'n I was happy workin' fer a scumbag like Franklin. When I said I wasn't, he said he always had room on his payroll for a good worker. So I packed my war bag an' left the same day."

"What happened then? Was your previous boss mad about you leavin' and all?"

Pearlie snorted as he refilled his tin cup with coffee. He took another puff off his cigarette and as the smoke trailed from his nostrils he continued his story. "You bet your boots he was plenty pissed at me. He sent a group of the men riding for his brand after me and they shot me up a little bit, then dragged me to hell and back through cactus and rocks and such."

His eyes narrowed as he recalled how he had to walk almost ten miles with two bullets in him to get to Smoke's place and help. "Well, Smoke had Doc Spalding yank those lead peas outta my hide, and then put me up in a boardinghouse in Big Rock to give me time to heal."

The memory of the pain he went through made his voice husky and he took a long drink of the steaming coffee to clear it. "That's when I first met Louis Longmont, a longtime *compadre* of Smoke's."

"You mean that dandy gamblin' feller that owns the saloon in Big Rock?"

Pearlie grinned. "One and the same, though he's no dandy. He's might near the fastest man with a short-gun I ever seen, 'cept for Smoke, o'course. Anyway, he admired the way I stood up to Franklin and took to visitin' me every day and we'd kinda get to talkin', mostly 'bout Smoke." He took a last drag and flipped the butt into the fire. "Seems he was pretty close friends with Preacher and knew Smoke when he came out West, when he was just a young'un. These stories I'm 'bout to relate to you are the same ones he tole me."

He shook his head. "Hell, sittin' here jawin' has got me so jiggered on all that *cafecito* that I'm never gonna git to sleep." He rolled to the side and took a pint of whiskey from his saddlebag, hesitated a moment, then poured a small measure in Cal's cup and a much larger one in his.

Cal's eyes got big and he sucked air in his mouth after his drink. "Whew-eee! That's mighty stout stuff," he rasped.

Pearlie chuckled. "If'n it ain't hairy, it's not worth drinkin'. Now here's what Longmont tole me about Smoke's first years here in the high lonesome, and some of the adventures he and that ole' mountain man, Preacher, had.

"Smoke's dad, Emmett, came back from the War Between the States in the summer of 1865, when Smoke, who was known as Kirby then, was only about fourteen or fifteen years old. Emmett sold their scratch-dirt farm in Missouri, packed up their belongin's, and they headed north by northwest."

"Why'd they do that?"

"That'll become clear later in the story, but Smoke's

dad didn't even tell why they were goin' west at that time. Anyway, long about Wichita, they met up with an old mountain man who called hisself Preacher. Fer some reason, unknown even to the old-timer, he took them under his wing when he saw they was as green as new apples, and they traveled together for a spell.

"Soon, they was set upon by a band of Pawnee Injuns, an' Smoke kilt his first couple of men. Longmont says that Preacher tole him he couldn't hardly believe it when he saw Smoke draw that old Colt. Says he knew right off Smoke was destined to become a legend, if'n he lived long enough, that is. That's when Preacher gave young Kirby Jensen his nickname, Smoke, from the smoke that came outta that Navy Colt.

"Right after that, Emmett tole Preacher that he had set out lookin' fer three men who kilt Smoke's brother and stole some Confederate gold. Their names was Wiley Potter, Josh Richards, and Stratton, I don't 'member his first name. Emmett went on to tell Preacher that he was goin' gunnin' fer those polecats, and if'n he didn't come back, he wanted Preacher to take care o' Smoke 'til he was growed up enough to do it fer hisself. Preacher tole Emmett he'd be proud to do that very thing.

"The next day, Emmett took off and left the old cougar to watch after his young'un. They didn't hear nothin' fer a couple of years, time Preacher spent teaching the young buck the ways of the West and how to survive where most men wouldn't. Longmont says Preacher tole him that during that time, though Smoke was about as natural a fast draw and shot as he'd ever seen, the boy spent at least an hour ever day drawing and dry-firin' those Navy Colts he wore."

"Wait a minute," interrupted Cal. "I thought Smoke only had the one Colt. Where'd he get the other one?"

"Oh, I forgot. That first Pawnee brave he kilt was carryin' one, and, naturally, Smoke claimed it fer his own. That's when he started wearin' two guns in that special way he has, with the left 'un butt-forward and the right 'un, butt-backwards. That's also where he got that big ole sticker he carries in his belt scabbard."

Pearlie leaned over and refilled Cal's cup, then his own. "And quit interruptin' me if'n you want to hear this story." He drank half the cup down in one draught, fashioned another cigarette, and lay back to continue his tale.

"'Bout two years later, at Brown's Hole in Idaho, an old mountain man found Smoke and Preacher and tole Smoke his daddy was dead, that those men he went after kilt him. Smoke packed up an' he and Preacher went on the prod.

"They got to Pagosa Springs, that's Injun fer healin' waters, just west of the Needle Mountains, and stopped to replenish their supplies. They rode into Rico, a rough 'n tumble mining camp that was an outlaw hangout."

Pearlie took a deep drag of his cigarette, and paused as the smoke rose toward the stars, imagining how it must have been for the young boy and his old friend in those rough and rowdy days . . .

Smoke and Preacher dismounted in front of the combination trading post and saloon. As was his custom, Smoke slipped the thongs from the hammers of his Colts as soon as his boots hit dirt.

They bought their supplies and turned to leave when

the hum of conversation suddenly died. Two rough-dressed and unshaven men, both wearing guns, blocked the door.

"Who owns that horse out there?" one demanded, a snarl in his voice, trouble in his manner. "The one with the SJ brand?"

Smoke laid his purchases on the counter. "I do," he said quietly.

"Which way'd you ride in from?"

Preacher had slipped to his right, his left hand covering the hammer of his Henry, concealing the click as he thumbed it back.

Smoke faced the men, his right hand hanging loose by his side. His left hand was just inches from his lefthand gun. "Who wants to know—and why?"

No one in the building moved or spoke.

"Pike's my name," the bigger and uglier of the pair said. "And I say you came through my diggin's yesterday and stole my dust."

"And I say you're a liar," Smoke told him.

Pike grinned nastily, his right hand hovering near the butt of his pistol. "Why . . . you little pup. I think I'll shoot your ears off."

"Why don't you try? I'm tired of hearing you shoot your mouth off."

Pike looked puzzled for a few seconds. No one had ever talked to him in this manner. Pike was big, strong, and a bully. "I think I'll just kill you for that."

Pike and his partner reached for their guns.

Four shots boomed in the low-ceilinged room, four shots so closely spaced they seemed as one thunderous roar. Dust and bird droppings fell from the ceiling. Pike and his friend were slammed out the open doorway. One fell off the rough porch, dying in the dirt street. Pike, with two holes in his chest, died with his back against a support pole, his eyes still open, unbelieving. Neither had managed to pull a gun more than halfway out of leather.

All eyes in the black powder-filled and dusty, smoky room moved to the young man standing by the bar, a Colt in each hand. "Good God!" a man whispered in awe. "I never even seen him draw.'

Preacher moved the muzzle of his Henry to cover the men at the tables. The bartender put his hands slowly on the bar, indicating he wanted no trouble.

"We'll be leaving now," Smoke said, holstering his Colts and picking up his purchases from the counter. He walked out the door slowly.

Smoke stepped over the sprawled, dead legs of Pike and walked past his dead partner.

"What are we 'sposed to do with the bodies?" a man asked Preacher.

"Bury 'em."

"What's the kid's name?"

"Smoke."

A few days later, in a nearby town, a friend of Preacher's told Smoke that two men, Haywood and Thompson, who claimed to be Pike's brother, had tracked him and Preacher and were in town waiting for Smoke.

Smoke walked down the rutted street an hour before sunset, the sun at his back—the way he had planned it. Thompson and Haywood were in a big tent at the end of the street, which served as saloon and café. Preacher had pointed them out earlier and asked if Smoke needed his help. Smoke said no. The refusal came as no surprise.

As he walked down the street a man glanced up, spotted him, then hurried quickly inside.

Smoke felt no animosity toward the men in the tent saloon: no anger, no hatred. But they came here after him, so let the dance begin, he thought.

Smoke stopped fifty feet from the tent. "Haywood! Thompson! You want to see me?"

The two men pushed back the tent flap and stepped out, both angling to get a better look at the man they had tracked. "You the kid called Smoke?" one said.

"I am."

"Pike was my brother," the heavier of the pair said. "And Shorty was my pal."

"You should choose your friends more carefully," Smoke told him.

"They was just a-funnin' with you," Thompson said.

"You weren't there. You don't know what happened."

"You callin' me a liar?"

"If that's the way you want to take it."

Thompson's face colored with anger, his hand moving closer to the .44 in his belt. "You take that back or make your play."

"There is no need for this," Smoke said.

The second man began cursing Smoke as he stood tensely, legs spread wide, body bent at the waist. "You're a damned thief. You stolt their gold and then kilt 'em."

"I don't want to have to kill you," Smoke said.

"The kid's yellow!" Haywood yelled. Then he grabbed for his gun.

Haywood touched the butt of his gun just as two loud gunshots blasted in the dusty street. The .36 caliber balls struck Haywood in the chest, one nicking his heart. He dropped to the dirt, dying. Before he closed his eyes and death relieved him of the shocking pain by pulling him into a long sleep, two more shots thundered. He had a dark vision of Thompson spinning in the street. Then Haywood died.

Thompson was on one knee, left hand holding his shattered right elbow. His leg was bloody. Smoke had knocked his gun from his hand, then shot him in the leg.

"Pike was your brother," Smoke told the man. "So I can understand why you came after me. But you were wrong. I'll let you live. But stay with mining. If I ever see you again, I'll kill you."

The young man turned, putting his back to the dead and bloody pair. He walked slowly up the street, his high-heeled Spanish riding boots pocking the air with dusty puddles.

Cal's eyebrows went up when Pearlie paused in his story to take another sip of whiskey. "How old was he when this happened?"

"I dunno. 'Bout eighteen or so, I guess."

"Jiminy Christmas! That's a couple 'a years older'n me!"

Pearlie grinned in the darkness. "Yeah, only Smoke was eighteen goin' on thirty, while you're sixteen goin' on ten."

"Aw, Pearlie. That's not fair. I'm pretty good with my irons—you said so yourself."

"No offense meant, kid. Just be glad you ain't never had to kill nobody, it ain't hardly never nothin' to be proud of. You heard how Smoke tried to get men to back down?

He never goes out lookin' fer blood, it just seems to find him more'n most people."

Pearlie turned over, pulled his blanket up over his head, and said, "Now that's enough stories for one night. Get some shuteye. Dawn's gonna come earlier than you think, and we got to get on the trail early if'n we're ever gonna ketch up with Smoke."

Cal stifled huge yawn. "Okay, but if'n we don't catch him by tomorrow night, will ya tell me some more 'bout Smoke when he was first startin' out?"

"Yeah, yeah. Now go to sleep."

CHAPTER TEN

Smoke smelled a fire long before he could see evidence of it. He figured it was coming from about a mile or so upwind. His horse snorted and shook his head, telling Smoke there was water thereabouts. He stepped out of the saddle and tied his horse and packhorse to a bush where they could graze. Time to get down and dirty, he thought.

He pulled his Henry rifle out of the saddle boot and loosened rawhide hammer thongs on his Colts, then began to creep up the mountain through thick underbrush, toward the fire.

He knew it was much too soon to worry about Sundance and his gang, but in the high lonesome your enemies weren't necessarily known to you. As Preacher had told him on more than one occasion, strangers are always hostile, unless you know both their first and last names.

Moving through the forest so silently most of its wildlife was unaware of his passage, he inched ever closer to the source of a column of woodsmoke above him.

Slowly, so as not to make a sound, he came close to a small clearing and peered from behind a ponderosa pine at the camp. A rough-hewn log cabin of one room sat in the trees. A paint pony grazed nearby, enjoying lush green mountain meadow grass. There was a fire going in front of the shack, with coffee heating on a trestle and a deer haunch roasting on a spit.

Smoke relaxed when he saw the horse, straightened up and walked into the clearing. "Yo, the cabin. Can I join you?" he called, holding his rifle pointed down, his hands in plain sight.

He felt the barrel of a rifle touch his neck seconds after a sixth sense warned of someone's approach from behind, then a high-pitched chuckle followed. "Heh-heh, thought you's gonna sneak up on old Puma, huh, boy?"

Smoke laughed and raised his arms in the air. "Please don't shoot, Mr. Mountain Man, I'm just a poor pilgrim who's lost his way in the woods."

He turned and the two men embraced, pounding each other on the back, Smoke's pats raising dust and dirt from the old man's buckskins.

"Puma Buck, you old cougar, you get uglier every time I see you," Smoke said around a grin. "And that cayuse has got to be twenty years old if it's a day."

"Smoke Jensen, I thought old Preacher taught you better trail-smarts than that. Hell, I heared you comin' nearly an hour ago, an' that's why I put that there deer on to cook."

Smoke shook his head. "Mighty hard to keep in practice trackin' when you live 'round civilization, Puma. Matter of fact, a body can forget plenty of important lessons if he stays away from the up-high too long."

Puma nodded and threw his arm around Smoke's

shoulder, leading him over to the fire. "That's true, boy, that's surely true. Bein' 'round people just purely sucks the smarts right outta a man. Come on, light and set and let me pour you some coffee."

Smoke squatted and held out a tin cup he found near the fire. After Puma filled it, he took a drink. "Yeah, I've missed your cookin', Puma. Been a long time since I had coffee that'd float a horseshoe."

"Takes a long time to cook it just right. Guess you civilized folks don't never take the time to do it right. I been workin' on that pot fer might' near three days now, and it's just about ripe. Maybe another day or two . . ."

Smoke took his knife from its scabbard and sawed a hunk of meat off the deer haunch, handing the first piece to Puma, who took it and nodded his thanks.

There was little more in the way of conversation until both had eaten their fill. Puma grunted once and pitched Smoke some wild onions. They were strong and sweet and went well with wild venison and boiled coffee.

After supper, Smoke trotted back to retrieve his horses and returned to the cabin. The mountain man had his makings out and was about to fashion a cigarette. Smoke said, "Uh-huh, just a minute Puma." He reached in a pouch on his packhorse and pulled out a package wrapped in wax paper. He pitched it to Puma and stooped to pour himself another cup of coffee.

Puma unwrapped the package and grinned widely, exposing yellow stubs of teeth. "Hoss, it seems like years since I had any store-bought ceegars." He licked one, bit the end off, and lit it with a flaming stick from the fire's edge. "Young'un," he sighed, "this is one of the few things I miss about civilization, ready-made stogies."

He flipped one to Smoke, and they lay back against a log, smoking and drinking coffee and swapping tales until the sun went down and the temperature began to drop.

Puma glanced at clouds covering the peaks turned orange-red by a setting sun. He raised his nose like an old wolf sniffing for his mate. "Smells like snow's on the way. Seems to come earlier and colder every year."

Smoke grunted and grinned in the twilight. "That's just 'cause you're older'n dirt, Puma. You're gettin' a mite long in the tooth to winter up here. Maybe it's time for you to winter in the desert, where the cold don't make your bones as brittle as dead wood."

Puma snorted and ambled into his cabin, returning after a moment with three half-cured bearskin blankets. He threw one over his paint pony and handed the other one to Smoke.

Smoke's nose wrinkled as he wrapped the green hide around his shoulders. "Whew! Puma, you done forgot how to cure skins? This bear's 'bout as ripe as you are."

"That's what's wrong with you city folk. You bathe too much. That's how I knowed you was a'comin', I smelt soap on you from three miles off, an me bein' upwind!"

"I brought some extra if'n you'd care to try it."

Puma got a horrified expression on his face. "Hell no. I bathed in the spring. Don't wanna overdo it, might git sick'n die, then who'd be here to teach you the thangs you done forgot 'bout wilderness livin'?"

"Preacher always washed two, maybe three times a year," Smoke answered.

"Yeah, Preacher did git a mite too civilized in his old age. I heared in his later years he kilt a couple'a old boys and didn't even take their hair." He shook his head. "Don't do to git too soft up here or folks'll take 'vantage of ya."

Smoke sobered at the thought of his old mentor. "Puma, do you think Preacher is still alive?"

Puma's gaze shifted to the distant mountains, their snow-covered peaks still burnished pink by the fading sun. "I 'spect so, boy. There's still beaver in them ponds, an' grizzlies still look over their shoulders fer him in fear when they hunt. Ole Preacher ain't about to cross over while there's still game to be had or grizzlies to wrassle." He studied the glowing end of his stogie, blue smoke curling toward stars just becoming visible at dusk. "By the by, speakin' of ole warriors, I heared you was comin' up here to put the war paint on."

Smoke shook his head in wonderment. It amazed him how these old cougars, who thought the up-high was getting too crowded if they saw another white man more than every two or three months, could know what was happening in flat country so soon.

He pitched his cigar into the fire and settled deeper into his bearskin. "Yeah, that's so. A feller back-shot a friend of mine a few years back. I took his ear and sent him on his way with a couple'a ounces of lead in his hide. Now he thinks it's time I paid the fiddler for that little dance."

Puma grimaced. "Shoulda taken his hair, Hoss, then you wouldn't have to be watchin' your back-trail." He took a final drag on his cigar, pinched the ash off, and began to chew the butt. "Man makes hisself enough enemies just livin', without havin' to go out and try to make more."

"I guess so. Preacher told me don't never leave a man alive with your lead in'im. Just makes 'em wanna heal up and give it back to you when you're least 'spectin' it."

Puma chuckled. "Preacher knew which way the stick floats, all right. Took his share o' scalps, too—both white and red." He cut his eyes over at Smoke. "You figger on needin' any hep, or some'un to watch your back in this war your' gettin' ready fer?"

"Well, Preacher also said don't never turn down help when it's offered, though I hope these ole boys are like most flatlanders and don't know nothin' 'bout the high lonesome. I got some surprises planned for 'em that may make 'em think twice 'bout comin' after me."

Puma spit tobacco juice into the fire, making it hiss and crackle. "Don't underestimate the strength of vengeance, Hoss, it be a powerful motivator fer most folks." He spit again. "Gold, women, and blood-feuds kilt more men than all the wars put together. I wouldn't count on those ole boys turning tail and runnin' just cause you tweak their noses a little. You listen to an expert, boy, and don't go halfway. You git a chance, you lift some hair and count some coup, 'cause as sure as beavers build dams, they'll do it to you if'n they can."

"I'll do it, Puma. Now, you think we can get under that shack you call home before my eyeballs freeze, or you gonna stay out here 'til the spring thaw?"

"Heh-heh. You sure be gittin' soft, Smoke. Good thang you come up here to relearn what Preacher and us other ole mountain beavers taught you, afore it's too late. Come on, we'll git covered and git some shuteye and talk more on this war of yours at sunrise." Puma got up slowly and led the way into his cabin.

As snowflakes began to drift down to cover the mountainside in winter's white coat, Smoke snuggled deeper under his bearskins in the unheated room and hoped the coffee he drank wouldn't cause him to have to venture forth into the frigid night air to relieve his bladder.

Lying there, watching his breath frost and disappear in the moonlight coming through a crack in the roof, he began to question what he was doing. "Do I have the right to come up here and endanger my old friends in one of my fights?" he murmured to himself, on the edge of sleep. After all, he thought, he knew when he made his plans to make his final stand in the up-high, mountain men holing up in the area wouldn't permit one of their own to fight against heavy odds alone. Some of the old cougars were likely to get dusted in the upcoming fracas. He considered, for a moment, spreading the word among them that he wanted to kill his own snakes without their help. Of course, he realized almost immediately, that would do no good at all. Asking mountain men, the most independent breed in the world, not to interfere in a fight would almost certainly make them all the more determined to buy chips in his game.

Most of these old-timers were only a few years shy of going forked end up anyway, he thought. They'd like nothing more than to go out with rifles and cap and ball pistols in their hands, facing death and spitting in its face.

Sighing, he turned to the side, pulled the skins up over his face, and slid into sleep, still undecided if he was doing the right thing.

* * *

After a fitful night of tossing and turning, Smoke awoke before dawn and went out into the snow-covered clearing in front of the cabin. He stoked the campfire embers to life and added more wood, warming his hands in the heat from the flames. He opened his supply pack and took out breakfast makings and began to cook.

A short while later a yawning Puma Buck limped out of the cabin door, cursing his aching bones. "Smoke, I don't know what you're cookin' up over there, but it smells right good enough to eat."

"Light and set, Puma. I made us some *pan dulce,* Mexican sweet bread, fried some bacon and 'taters, and opened a can of sliced peaches for dessert."

Puma glanced over at his paint pony and shook his head. "Good thang you're not up here very often, Smoke, otherwise old Spot there wouldn't be able to carry me around no more. I'd be so damn overfed I'd break his back."

Smoke poured some steaming coffee into Puma's cup, saying, "Sorry about the bellywash. I had to add a little water 'cause it was so thick it wouldn't come outta the pot."

Puma arched an eyebrow and frowned. "I hope you ain't plumb ruined it, boy. Took a lotta cookin' to git it just right."

To ease his feelings, Smoke cut a chunk of sweet bread out of the skillet and handed the sugary cake to the old man.

Puma tasted it, then smiled and began to chew in earnest.

The pair ate in amiable silence, enjoying the majestic views of mountain peaks, snow-covered valleys and meadows, and white-capped ponderosa pines.

After they finished breakfast, Smoke rolled a cigarette and Puma started on another stogie, both men drinking a final cup of coffee.

Smoke sighed. "You know, Puma, every time I come up here to God's country, I wonder why I ever bother to leave and head back to the flatlands."

Puma grinned, dislodging crumbs of bread from his scraggly beard. "Might be that sweet woman who warms your blankets has more'n a little to do with it."

"She's a big part of it, all right," Smoke agreed. "But I think when this little dustup is over, I'll bring Sally up here to show her why I can't never get this country outta my heart."

Puma said, "Leave it to Smoke Jensen to call a war with thirty or forty men against him a little dustup. Well, Hoss, if this child is still kickin' when that happens, I'd be honored if you and the missus would make camp with me for a spell." His lips curled in a sardonic smile. "I promise not to tell her too many tales about you in the old days, when your juices were jest startin' to flow."

Smoke clapped him on the back, stood up, and began to put together his pack. "Yours will be the first stop on our journey, Puma. Now, I've gotta get busy if I'm gonna get my surprises ready for that polecat and his gang afore they get up here." He looked over his shoulder as he tied his packs on his packhorse. "You might spread word among the others up here to walk carefully on the trails. I wouldn't want any of my friends to get hurt by my traps."

Puma shook his head. "Boy, if'n a mountain man don't know enough to watch where he's steppin', he don't hardly deserve to be in the high lonesome no-how."

Smoke stepped into the saddle and reined away with only a wave over his shoulder as a farewell.

CHAPTER ELEVEN

Sundance Morgan sat on his mount, a cigarette stuck in a face full of stubble, and looked out at his gang gathered before him. They had crossed the border just before dawn, in small groups of five men to avoid being noticed, and gathered at the same grove of cottonwoods on the Rio Bravo where they first met.

The *desperados* were bleary-eyed and surly from a night without sleep. The Hernandez women lasted for hours, until finally Sundance ordered his men to put them out of their misery and ride north.

Two of the Mexicans argued over the scalps, and the loser of the fight now sat with his arm bandaged from a knife wound while the winner proudly displayed bloody hanks of hair on his saddle horn.

Sundance tipped a pint bottle of whiskey at the sky and sleeved the excess off his lips with his forearm before speaking. *"Hombres,* we are like *los corrientes,* the wild longhorns who live in the *brasada,* obeying no man's laws and answering to no one for our actions." He waved his bottle in the air. "From now on, we ride hard and we ride fast. We will take what we want, and send those to the devil who oppose us."

The group nodded and laughed among themselves, too sleepy to work up much enthusiasm at such an early hour. Sundance continued. "We'll ride 'til midday to put some trail between us and Mexico, then find a shady place for a *siesta* and for our nooning."

He pitched the empty whiskey bottle in the air and blew it to pieces with his Colt, the booming echo of the gunshot continuing long after the fragments of glass fell to the ground. "Now, *ándale, compadres,* shag your mounts! *Vámonos!*"

The gang rode north on the trail toward San Antonio for several hours. When the sun reached mid-sky and heat waves danced over the desolate land of the Texas bush country, they pulled off the road into a stand of live oak trees and dismounted. Some men cooked bacon and beans, while others lay in the shade, drinking whiskey and eating jerked meat. A few slumped on the dirt snoring, hats pulled down over their eyes.

Sundance took this time to call a meeting of his lieutenants to plan their next move. Lightning Jack, swigging out of a bottle with no label on it, said, "Sundance, there be a small settlement on the coast just north o' here called Corpus Christi. Not much there, but it might be worth a look or two."

El Gato shook his head. "No, I don't think so. I there last year. It is full o' *campesinos* and fishermen. There no gold in that town."

Toothpick looked up from spooning beans into his mouth, juice running down his chin into his whiskers. "I heared there's a big spread hearabouts." His brow furrowed in thought for a moment. "King Ranch, I think it's called."

Sundance smirked. "You heard right, Toothpick. Trouble is, they's a bunch o' hairy ole boys ridin' fer that brand. Mainly Mexicans, but they all carry sidearms and they all know how to use 'em. Old man King hired him a bunch o' buff'lo soldiers from the Union Army after the war, and them boys ain't afraid of nuthin' nor nobody."

He rolled a cigarette and placed it between his lips. "A bunch o' *pistoleros* from down the border tried to tree that particular spread a few months back." He grinned as he lit his smoke. "What was left of 'em, 'bout a third I reckon, came straggling back through Del Rio with their tails 'tween their legs, lookin' mighty shot up."

Toothpick shrugged and went back to eating beans. Lightning Jack asked, "You got a better plan then?"

Sundance tilted his head toward the road, just over a small ridge from their camp. "Yeah. The noon stage from San Antone is due to come down that trail in a couple o' hours. The station where they change horses for the final leg into Laredo is 'bout three miles north o' here." He flipped his butt in the fire. "After the boys are finished eatin', I figger we'll just mosey on over the hill and be waitin' on that stage when it pulls in."

Lightning Jack nodded, grinning. "Yeah, that's a good idee. I'm in need of a fresh mount anyhow."

Gato threw his empty bottle against a nearby tree. "And *más* tequila, eh, *compadres*?"

Sundance spent a few more minutes outlining his plan for taking the stage station, then the men were rounded up and they rode north.

* * *

Catherine Johanson looked up from her cooking as she heard the door to the way station slam shut. She peered out the small serving window and saw four disreputable-looking men enter. Something about their manner, swaggering and loud, alarmed her. Frowning, she turned to her teenaged daughter, Missy, and whispered for her to remain hidden in the closet and not to come out until she called her. Without haste, she slipped a derringer .44 over-and-under into her apron pocket.

Her husband, the station manager Olaf Johanson, was wiping down the bar when Carlito Suarez, One-Eye Jordan, Curly Bill Cartwright, and Bull burst through the door.

He slipped his hand around a Greener shotgun out of sight beneath the bar and said, "Howdy, gents. Mighty windy out there today, huh?"

Suarez grinned widely, exposing a greenish-yellow front tooth. A dentist in Monterey had told him it was gold, but it turned out to be brass. It was a costly lie. The dentist lived to regret it, and died cursing the day he met Perro Muerte. *"Sí, señor."* He took his *sombrero* off and dusted his arms and pants with it. "The dust, she is flying pretty damn *mucho* today."

One-Eye Jordan turned his head and surveyed the clapboard shack. Along one wall were homemade shelves lined with canned goods, a few bolts of cloth, and barrels of dried beans and flour. "This here a store or a dog hole?"

Johanson grinned. "Well, boys, I 'spect it's a bit of both. If you're short of supplies, we can fix you up, at fair prices, and if'n you're thirsty or hungry, we can do something about that, too."

The men sauntered up to the bar and leaned against it. Suarez ordered a tequila and Curly Bill smiled with his lips, but his eyes never changed. "I'd like a whiskey, with a beer chaser if'n it's not flat."

"Make that two," joined in Bull, in his high voice.

Johanson's lips started to curl in a smile, but the look on Bull's face stopped him cold. He shivered, as if someone had walked over his grave, and reluctantly let go of his shotgun to fix the men their drinks.

Jordan walked to a window and glanced toward a corral behind the building. There were eight horses grazing on hay piled on the ground. "Them the horses for the stage?" he asked.

Johanson looked back over his shoulder. "Yeah. Should be here any time now, 'less they broke a wheel or something."

He put the drinks on the bar in front of Bull and Cartwright. "You boys up from Laredo?"

Cartwright threw back his whiskey and followed it with a draught of beer. "Yeah, why?"

Johanson shrugged. "Oh, no reason. A couple of punchers came through from there earlier today and said a Mexican rancher south of there was burned out. All of his hands and family was killed and his wife and daughter was scalped."

Cartwright smiled and held out his glass for a refill. "Yeah, awful what them greasers do to one another, ain't it?"

Suarez glanced at the kid, death on his face, then grinned, exposing his tooth again. *"Sí,* is terrible."

Johanson looked from one of the men to another, sweat beginning to bead on his forehead.

Bull sipped his whiskey slowly, almost delicately. "You say that stage is due here soon?"

Johanson nodded, his hand searching under the bar for his shotgun.

Bull took another drink. "You work this place all by yourself?"

Johanson glanced quickly over his shoulder and said in a loud voice. "Yes, I'm here alone."

"Lotta work fer one man." Bull sniffed. "Smells like ya left somethin' cookin' in the back room there."

Johanson started to bring the shotgun up, but, faster than the eye could follow, a knife appeared in Cartwright's hand and he swung backhanded across the bar.

Johanson stepped back, looking startled, and reached for his throat. He found a hole he could stick his fist in, before he fell to the floor, gurgling and drowning in his own blood.

One-Eye Jordan stepped quickly into the kitchen and came out a moment later dragging a struggling Catherine Johanson into the room by her hair.

"Hey boys, look what I found me. A wildcat of a woman."

He spun her around and grabbed her head and pulled it toward his face, trying to kiss her. A loud boom sounded in the small room, rattling the walls and filling the area with smoke. Catherine backed out of the gunpowder cloud, holding the derringer in front of her. Jordan rolled on the floor, cradling his left hand against his stomach. "Jesus, the bitch shot my fingers off!" he cried, adding to the confusion.

When Catherine saw her husband writhing on the floor, his blood spurting in the air, she gasped and put her hands to her mouth.

Bull took two quick steps and slapped her backhanded, knocking her against the wall, unconscious, the derringer falling beside her.

Suarez bent over Jordan and pulled his hand out where he could see it. It was missing the index and middle finger and was tattooed black from the gunpowder blast. He poured tequila over the hand, causing Jordan to begin wailing again, and wrapped his filthy bandanna around the mutilated stumps. "Git up, Señor One-Eye. You cryin' like a woman is makin' my head hurt."

"I'm gonna kill that bitch fer what she did to me," he groaned.

Bull stepped in front of Catherine's limp body. He began to undo his belt. "Not just yet, you ain't," he growled. "I got me some business with her first."

Suarez looked over his shoulder at Cartwright. "Curly, go signal Sundance. We must clean floor before stage come."

Cartwright stepped out the door and fired his pistol in the air three times, then returned to the room. He walked to Johanson's body and squatted before it, careful not to step in the blood that pooled the boards around him. Without haste, he pulled the dead man's shiny black boots off and took them across the room to the table. He sat and removed his threadbare boots and put on the station-master's newer ones. He stood and shined them on his pants, one at a time, admiring their sheen for a moment. Then, with a jaunty step, he pitched his old boots onto

Johanson's body and dragged it out the rear door and covered it with some firewood he found there.

Sundance entered the room to find Suarez throwing dirt over the bloodstains and Jordan sitting propped against a wall, rocking back and forth with his wounded hand against his stomach, swigging whiskey with the other, tears streaming down his face.

Cartwright was in the kitchen, eating some of the food that Catherine had been preparing. Sundance glanced around the small enclosure. "Where's Bull?"

Suarez shrugged. "He in other room. Say he have business with lady there."

Sundance grimaced and shook his head. "Lord save me from galoots who think with their balls 'stead o' their brains."

He pointed to Jordan. "Git off your ass and pull the mounts around back and outta sight. The stage'll be here any minute an' we don't have much time."

Once the blood was covered and the horses were hidden, he stationed Suarez and Cartwright behind the door to the building and told Jordan to stay in the kitchen. Bull strolled in from the Johansons' living quarters, fixing his pants, sweat running down his face and making rivulets in the dirt.

"Where're the rest of the boys, boss?"

"I left them outta sight over that ridge yonder. I figger we got enough to do what we need right here."

"What you want me to do?"

Sundance inclined his head toward the back door. "You station yourself behind the corner of the building. The stage driver will send the passengers in while he and the man riding shotgun change horses. They's your responsibility."

Bull tipped his hat and drew his shotguns, breaking them open to check the loads as he ambled out the door.

A few minutes later, the stage pulled up outside amid a squealing of wheel-brakes and a cloud of dust. There was much excited talking and laughing as four passengers unloaded and headed for the station, anxious to get out of the stifling Texas heat and to stretch muscles cramped from the jolting ride.

Sundance was behind the bar, wearing an apron he had liberated from the kitchen. The first person through the door was a middle-aged white man, dressed in black, carrying a brown case worn yellow in spots. He looked like a drummer to Sundance. He was followed by three women, all appearing past forty years of age and wearing heavy makeup and brightly colored dresses with hats and carrying small parasols to ward off the sun. Saloon girls, unless I miss my guess, thought Sundance as they approached the bar.

Sundance inclined his head. "Mister, ladies. How can I help you?"

The man put his case down and leaned his elbows on the bar-rail. "Whiskey, if you please, my good man."

Two of the women asked for beer, and one ordered whiskey. Sundance grinned as he fixed the drinks, thinking he was the most expensive bartender these folks would ever meet.

As he set the glasses down, there came a loud double explosion from behind the building, shaking dust out of the ceiling, to fall and settle like snow on the bar top. The women screamed and the man reached inside his coat, stopping when he felt the barrel of Cartwright's Colt against his ear.

Sundance raised his hands, palms out. "Settle down, now, folks. Finish your drinks and nobody'll get hurt."

Suarez put his arms around two of the women. "Especially you ladies," he murmured, dropping his hands to caress their breasts.

From outside came a single scream, followed by a sound like a watermelon falling off a table onto the floor. A moment later, Bull walked in, wiping blood and hair off the butt of his shotgun with a dusty bandanna. He raised his eyebrows at Sundance's look. "The driver didn't wanna die, so I helped him along a little. Weren't no need to waste a shell on 'im, so I jist tapped him on the head." He frowned, looking down at his gun. "Damn near broke my stock."

One of the women moaned softly and sunk to the ground in a faint. The other two shut their eyes and began to pray to themselves, evidently hoping for more mercy than they typically gave their clients.

Sundance glanced at the drummer. "What's in the case?"

He sleeved sweat off his forehead before answering, then placed the case on the bar. "Airtights." He opened the case to reveal several tin cans bearing the names Beef Biscuit, Meat Biscuit, and Condensed Milk. "I work for the Gail Borden company. She's trying to expand her market to the southwest."

He continued, sweat pouring off his face. "It's really quite popular up north."

Cartwright picked up one of the cans, sniffing it to see if it had a smell. "Mister, that's 'bout the dumbest thang I ever heared." He waved his hand at the window. "Look around, pardner. There ain't nothin' out there 'ceptin' beeves. We got pretty near all the meat and milk we want, jest fer the takin'. What fer we need beef in a can?"

Suarez laughed. *"Si,* is said, only fool eats his own meat in this country."

The drummer stammered, "But this is different. You can carry these tins with you in your saddlebags and not have to eat bacon and beans with every meal. We even have tinned peaches and tomatoes so you can have them in the winter."

Bull pushed his way into the group. "Hey, I like peaches. You got any of those in there?"

Sundance jerked his Colt and shot the drummer in the face, the booming of his gun causing the others to curse and cover their ears, and the drummer to be thrown backwards, landing spread-eagled on his back on top of a small rough-hewn table in the middle of the room.

"Enough of this chatter. Bull, put that tin down and go out to the stage and see what's in the strongbox. We need to git outta here 'fore anybody else decides to come visitin'."

The women began crying and begging Suarez and Cartwright to let them live. "We won't tell anyone anything," one said, rubbing her hand up and down Cartwright's arm, pleading for her life. "I can make you happy, just give me a chance," she purred, tears on her cheeks and terror in her eyes.

"Well darlin'," he drawled, no life at all in his eyes, "I intend to give you that chance."

Bull walked into the room, a metal strongbox looking small on his shoulder. He dropped it to the ground with a loud thump. "H'yar it is, boss."

Sundance inclined his head at Suarez. "Carlito," he said.

Suarez walked to the box and drew his pistol, then shot the lock off. His bullet ricocheted off the metal and buried itself in the wall next to Bull's head, causing him to curse and duck. "Goddamn, Suarez, watch what you're doin'!"

Suarez grinned. "Sorry, *amigo.* I aim a little better next time."

Bull nodded, then frowned and glowered at Suarez through narrowed eyes, wondering just what he meant by that remark.

Sundance toed the box open with his boot, revealing a pile of letters and two canvas bank bags. He reached down and picked out the bags, holding them up in front of Cartwright. The kid drew his knife and slit them without a word, letting handfuls of greenbacks and double-eagle gold coins fall to the floor.

Sundance's face broke into a toothy grin. "Okay, boys, fun's over. Pack that *dinero,* saddle up some of those broncs out back, set fire to this place, and let's git outta here."

Cartwright said, "Hey, wait a minute. What about the women?" He rubbed his crotch in an obscene gesture. "I'm not finished here jest yet."

Sundance said, "Hell, bring 'em along." He waved his hands at the corral behind the building. "We got plenty of horseflesh to carry 'em on."

One of the women groaned and said, "Oh no."

Cartwright put his palm against her cheek. "It's your choice, darlin'." He glanced at the cooling body of the drummer, still leaking blood and gore out of his skull. "We kin leave ya here, if'n ya want."

Sundance started to leave, hesitated, and pointed over

his shoulder at the shelves against the far wall. "Bull, before you torch this place, pack up any supplies we might need and bring 'em along. It might be a while 'fore we git to town again."

Cartwright, his arm around the woman's shoulder, asked, "Where we headed, boss?"

Sundance raised his eyebrows. "Why, north, of course. We're heading for Smoke country. I got me a score to settle, boys, and I'm tired of waitin'."

As the group mounted and rode off, no one noticed a small figure scramble out the back door of the burning building, her dress on fire.

CHAPTER TWELVE

Cal hollered, "Gosh darn it, Pearlie. Why for do we have to do this?"

He and Pearlie were standing waist deep in a small brook three quarters of the way up the mountain they'd been climbing. Pearlie had ordered Cal into the water with him, and was now standing behind him, picking ticks and fleas off his hide. Cal was shivering and shaking and had turned a light blue color in the near-freezing stream.

"Listen up, pup," Pearlie answered, as though talking to a small child. "If'n we don't git these critters off'n our skin now, they'll fester up and cause itchin' like you never had before in your born days."

"Aw, Pearlie. I had ticks afore. They didn't bother me none. Hell, anybody who herds beeves gits used to ticks 'n fleas and such."

Pearlie shook his head. "Yeah, boy. You've had ticks before, but these'r high mountain ticks. They's a difference. Kinda like the difference 'tween a tame shorthorn you're always dealin' with, an' a rangy ole longhorn out in the bush. These here critters'll eat you fer lunch, and carry off your horse fer dessert."

The two men had ridden through very thick underbrush for the last half day, switching back and forth and trying to find a trail through the dense undergrowth. The ride left them covered from head to toe with hundreds of thick, voracious mountain ticks, and not just a few fleas.

When it came time to pitch camp, with still no sign of Smoke Jensen, Pearlie stripped down to his longjohns and told Cal to do the same. With much protesting, Cal followed him into the frigid water.

After picking each other as clean of the pests as they could, Pearlie made Cal take a currycomb to both mounts to try and rid them of some of the ticks, while he made a fire and prepared their supper.

Cal, with a blanket thrown over his shoulders, walked to the campfire, still grumbling about never having taken so many baths in his life until he met up with Smoke and joined his crew.

Pearlie grinned and tossed him a steaming biscuit. "Here, young'un, eat this sinker and maybe it'll take your mind off'n your troubles fer a spell."

Cal juggled the hot biscuit from hand to hand, trying to keep it from burning him. Finally, with a deep sigh, he shoved the entire thing in his mouth and began to chew as if he hadn't eaten for days. "Hmmm, I swear Pearlie, you're damn near as good a cook as Miss Sally is."

Shaking his head, Pearlie poured them both cups of coffee as black as Mississippi mud. "You only think that 'cause you're 'bout starvin' to death, being as how it's been mite near six hours since we last ate."

Cal squatted before the fire, took his tin plate and heaped it full of beans and fried fatback, and piled three more biscuits on top of that. After a giant draught of coffee, he began to shovel food into his mouth as fast as he could, making Pearlie grin in disbelief.

"I don't know how you do it, boy. If'n you ate any faster, you wouldn't need teeth a'tall. You could jest git an ole kerosene funnel and put it in your mouth and pour the food down your gullet."

Cal tried to smile, but his bulging cheeks wouldn't allow it, so he continued to eat, ignoring Pearlie's remarks. Finally, satiated, he put his plate and empty coffee cup down and leaned back against his saddle. He raised his eyebrows and inclined his head toward Pearlie's saddle-bags. "How about throwin' me your fixin's and gittin' that there bottle of Kaintuck whiskey out'n your bag and let's have us a little smoke and a drink or two?"

Pearlie put his head in his hands and mumbled, "Oh God, Smoke is gonna kill me. I've done gone and corrupted this poor young'un and taught him evil ways."

With a sigh, he handed Cal his pouch of Bull Durham and a packet of papers. "You'll have to git your own fire," he mumbled sarcastically to the boy.

While Cal fumbled and cursed, spilling more tobacco than he managed to roll in the paper, Pearlie poured small amounts of whiskey into their cups and passed one over to Cal.

They smoked and sipped the harsh alcohol in amiable silence, enjoying the sight of the sun easing down behind mountain peaks to the west.

"You know, Pearlie?" Cal drawled, sprawled back against his saddle, snuggled in his blanket. "I wish I could draw pitchers like I seen in Mr. Smoke's cabin. That sunset sure produces some pretty colors in the clouds when it's settin'."

Pearlie leaned back, hands behind his head, and stared at the orange and yellow snow-clouds playing around the peaks. "Yeah, that'd make a right pretty picture all right. I seen some drawin's once in a magazine from back East. Drawn by a feller name of Remington, if I recollect correctly. Showed some punchers ridin' hard, bein' chased by Injuns, firing their Colts over they shoulders, dodgin' arrows."

He grinned, his teeth glittering in the flickering fire-light. "I swear, he made it look almost like fun, the way they was ridin', mounts sweatin', guns shootin', and the Injuns yellin' and waving they hands in the air."

Cal frowned. "Bein' chased by Injuns don't sound like fun to me, Pearlie."

Pearlie nodded. "It ain't, boy, it ain't and that's a fact."

Cal flipped his cigarette butt into the fire. "How 'bout you tellin' me more 'bout Smoke's 'ventures when he was first come out West?"

Pearlie expertly rolled another cigarette and lit it off the butt of his first. He lay back, watching his smoke trail toward the stars and thought about how to begin.

"After Smoke shot and killed Pike, his friend, and Haywood, and wounded Pike's brother, Thompson, he and Preacher went after the other men who kilt Smoke's brother and stole the Confederates' gold. They rode on over to La Plaza de los Leones, the plaza of the lions. T'was there that they trapped a man named Casey in a line shack with some of his *compadres*. Smoke and Preacher burnt 'em out and captured Casey. Smoke took him to the outskirts of the town and hung him."

Cal's eyebrows shot up. "Just hung 'em? No trial nor nuthin'?"

Pearlie flicked ash off his cigarette without taking it out of his mouth. "Yep, that's the way it was done in those days, boy. That town would never have hanged one of their own on the word of Smoke Jensen." He snorted, "Like as not they'd of hanged Smoke and Preacher instead. Anyway, after that, the sheriff of that town put out a flyer on Smoke, accusin' him of murder. Had a ten-thousand-dollar reward on it, too."

"Did Smoke and Preacher go into hidin'?"

"Nope. Seems Preacher advised it, but Smoke said he had one more call to make. They rode on over to Oreodelphia, lookin' fer a man named Ackerman. They didn't go after him right at first. Smoke and Preacher sat around doin' a whole lot o' nothin' fer two or three days. Smoke wanted Ackerman to git plenty nervous. He did, and finally came gunnin' fer Smoke with a bunch of men who rode fer his brand . . ."

At the edge of town, Ackerman, a bull of a man, with small, mean eyes and a cruel slit for a mouth, slowed his horse to a walk. Ackerman and his hands rode down the street, six abreast.

Preacher and Smoke were on their feet. Preacher stuffed his mouth full of chewing tobacco. Both men had slipped the thongs from the hammers of their Colts, Preacher wore two Colts, .44's. One in a holster, the other stuck behind his belt. Mountain man and young gunfighter stood six feet apart on the boardwalk.

The sheriff closed his office door and walked into the empty cell area. He sat down and began a game of checkers with his deputy.

Ackerman and his men wheeled their horses to face the men on the boardwalk. "I hear tell you boys is lookin' for me. If so, here I am."

"News to me," Smoke said. "What's your name?"

"You know who I am, kid. Ackerman."

"Oh yeah!" Smoke grinned. "You're the man who helped kill my brother by shooting him in the back. Then you stole the gold he was guarding."

Inside the hotel, pressed against the wall, the desk clerk listened intently, his mouth open in anticipation of gunfire.

"You're a liar. I didn't shoot our brother; that was Potter and his bunch."

"You stood and watched it. Then you stole the gold."

"It was war, kid."

"But you were on the same side," Smoke said. "So that not only makes you a killer, it makes you a traitor and a coward."

"I'll kill you for sayin' that!"

"You'll burn in hell a long time before I'm dead," Smoke told him.

Ackerman grabbed for his pistol. The street exploded in gunfire and black powder fumes. Horses screamed and bucked in fear. One rider was thrown to the dust by his lunging mustang. Smoke took the men on the left, Preacher the men on the right. The battle lasted no more than ten to twelve seconds. When the noise and the gunsmoke cleared, five men lay in the street, two of them dead. Two more would die from their wounds. One was shot in the side—he would live. Ackerman had been shot three times: once in the belly, once in the chest, and one ball had taken him in the side of the face as the muzzle of the .36 had lifted with each blast. Still Ackerman sat in his saddle, dead. The big man finally leaned to one side and toppled from his horse, one boot hung in the stirrup. The horse shied, then began walking down the dusty street, dragging Ackerman, leaving a bloody trail.

Preacher spit into the street. "Damn near swallowed my chaw."

"I never seen a draw that fast," a man spoke from his storefront. "It was a blur."

The editor of the paper walked up to stand by the sheriff. He watched the old man and the young gunfighter walk down the street. He truly had seen it all. The old man had killed one man, wounded another. The young man had killed four men, as calmly as picking his teeth.

"What's that young man's name?"

"Smoke Jensen. But he's a devil."

Cal whistled through his teeth. "Wow! That was somethin'! What did they do next, Pearlie?"

"Well, they both had some minor wounds, and there was a price on Smoke's head, so they took off to the mountains to lay up fer a while and lick their wounds and let the heat die down."

Pearlie cut his eyes over at Cal. "'Cept it didn't work out exactly that way. They chanced upon the remains of a wagon train that'd been burned out by Injuns, and rescued a young woman. Nicole was her name. She was the lone survivor of the attack. There wasn't nothin' else they could do, so they took her up into the mountains with them where they planned to winter."

Cal's eyes were big. "You mean Smoke and Preacher took a woman with 'em up into the mountains?"

Pearlie frowned. "What'd ya expect 'em to do, leave her out there fer the Injuns to come back and take? Course they took her with them."

"Where'd they live?"

"Way I heared it, Smoke built 'em a cabin outta 'dobe and logs, and they spent two winters and a summer in that place, up in the high lonesome. After the first year, Smoke and Nicole had a kinda unofficial marrying, and by the second winter she had Smoke a son."

"I didn't know Smoke had no son."

Pearlie sighed. "That there's the sad part of the story. When the boy was about a year old, Smoke had to go lookin' fer their milk cow that wandered off. When he came back, he found some bounty hunters had tracked him to the cabin and were in there with Nicole and the baby."

"Jiminy! What'd he do?"

"Same thing any man'd do . . ."

Some primitive sense of warning caused Smoke to pull up short of his home. He made a wide circle, staying in the timber back of the creek, and slipped up to the cabin.

Nicole was dead. The acts of the men had grown perverted and in their haste, her throat had been crushed.

Felter sat by the lean-to and watched the valley in front of him. He wondered where Smoke had hidden the gold.

Inside, Canning drew his skinning knife and scalped Nicole, tying her bloody hair to his belt. He then skinned a part of her, thinking he would tan the hide and make himself a nice tobacco pouch.

Kid Austin got sick at his stomach watching Canning's callousness, and went out the back door to puke on the ground. That moment of sickness saved his life—for the time being.

Grissom walked out the front door of the cabin. Smoke's tracks had indicated he had ridden off south, so he would probably return from that direction. But Grissom felt something was wrong. He sensed something, his years on the owlhoot back trails surfacing.

"Felter?" he called.

"Yeah?" He stepped from the lean-to.

"Something's wrong."

"I feel it. But what?"

"I don't know." Grissom spun as he sensed movement behind him. His right hand dipped for his pistol. Felter had stepped back into the lean-to. Grissom's palm touched the smooth wooden butt of his gun as his eyes saw the tall young man standing by the corner of the cabin, a Colt .36 in each hand. Lead from the .36s hit in the center of the chest with numbing force. Just before his heart exploded, the outlaw said, "Smoke!" Then he fell to the ground.

Smoke jerked the gun belt and pistols from the dead man. Remington Army .44's.

A bounty hunter ran from the cabin, firing at the corner of the building. But Smoke was gone.

"Behind the house!" Felter yelled, running from the

lean-to, his fists full of Colts. He slid to a halt and raced back to the water trough, diving behind it for protection.

A bounty hunter who had been dumping his bowels in the outhouse struggled to pull up his pants, at the same time pushing open the door with his shoulder. Smoke shot him twice in the belly and left him to scream on the outhouse floor.

Kid Austin, caught in the open behind the cabin, ran for the banks of the creek, panic driving his legs. He leaped for the protection of a sandy embankment, twisting in the air, just as Smoke took aim and fired. The ball hit Austin's right buttock and traveled through the left cheek of his butt, tearing out a sizable hunk of flesh. Kid Austin, the dreaming gun hand, screamed and fainted from the pain in his ass.

Smoke ran for the protection of the woodpile and crouched there, recharging his Colts and checking the .44's. He listened to the sounds of men in panic, firing in all directions and hitting nothing.

Moments ticked past, the sound of silence finally overpowering gunfire. Smoke flicked away sweat from his face. He waited.

Something came sailing out the back door to bounce on the grass. Smoke felt hot bile build in his stomach. Someone had thrown his dead son outside. The boy had been dead for some time. Smoke fought back sickness.

"You wanna see what's left of your woman?" a taunting voice called from near the back door. "I got her hair on my belt and a piece of her hide to tan. We all took a time or two with her. I think she liked it."

Smoke felt rage charge through him, but he remained still, crouched behind the thick pile of wood until his anger cooled to controlled, venom-filled fury. He unslung the big Sharps buffalo rifle Preacher had carried for years. The rifle could drop a two-thousand-pound buffalo at six hundred yards. It could also punch through a small log.

The voice from the cabin continued to mock and taunt Smoke. But Preacher's training kept him cautious. To his rear lay a meadow, void of cover. To his left was a shed, but he knew that was empty, for it was still barred from the outside. The man he'd plugged in the butt was to his right, but several fallen logs would protect him from that direction. The man in the outhouse was either dead or passed out; his screaming had ceased.

Through a chink in the logs, Smoke shoved the muzzle of the Sharps and lined up where he thought he had seen a man move, just to the left of the rear window. He gently squeezed the trigger, taking up slack. The weapon boomed, the planking shattered, and a man began screaming in pain.

Canning ran out the front of the cabin to the lean-to, sliding down hard beside Felter behind the water trough. "This ain't workin' out," he panted. "Grissom, Austin, Poker, and now Evans is either dead or dying. The slug from that buffalo gun blowed his arm off. Let's get the hell outta here!"

Felter had been thinking the same thing. "What about Clark and Sam?"

"They're growed men. They can join us or they can go to hell."

"Let's ride. There's always another day. We'll hide up in them mountains, see which way he rides out, then bushwhack him. Let's go." They raced for their horses, hidden in a bend of the creek, behind the bank. They kept the cabin between themselves and Smoke as much as possible, then bellied down in the meadow the rest of the way.

In the creek, in water red from the wounds in his butt, Kid Austin crawled upstream, crying in pain and humiliation. His Colts were forgotten—useless anyway; the powder was wet. All he wanted was to get away.

The bounty hunters left in the house, Clark and Sam, looked at each other. "I'm gettin' out!" Sam said. "That ain't no pilgrim out there."

"To hell with that," Clark said. "I humped his woman, I'll kill him and take the ten thousand."

"Your option." Sam slipped out the front and caught up with the others.

Kid Austin reached his horse first. Yelping as he hit the saddle, he galloped off toward the timber in the foothills.

"Your wife don't look so good now," Clark called out to Smoke. "Not since she got a haircut and one titty skinned."

Deep silence had replaced the gunfire. The air stank of black powder, blood, and relaxed bladders and bowels. Smoke had seen the men ride off into the foothills. He wondered how many were left in the cabin.

Smoke remained still, his eyes burning with fury. Smoke's eyes touched the stiffening form of his son. If Clark could have read the man's thoughts, he would have stuck the muzzle of his .44 into his mouth and pulled the trigger, ensuring himself a quick death, instead of what waited for him later on.

"Yes, sir," Clark taunted him. He went into profane detail of the rape of Nicole and the perverted acts that followed.

Smoke eased slowly backward, keeping the woodpile in front of him. He slipped down the side of the knoll and ran around to one wall of the cabin. He grinned. The bounty hunter was still talking to the woodpile, to the muzzle of the Sharps stuck through the logs.

Smoke eased around to the front of the cabin and looked in. He saw Nicole, saw the torture marks on her, saw the hideousness of the scalping and the skinning knife. He lifted his eyes to the back door, where Clark was crouching just to the right of the closed door.

Smoke raised his .36 and shot the pistol out of Clark's hand. The outlaw howled and grabbed his numbed and bloodied hand.

Smoke stepped over Grissom's body, then glanced at the body of the armless bounty hunter who had bled to death.

Clark looked up at the tall young man with the burning eyes. Cold, slimy fear put a bony hand on his shoulder. For the first time in his evil life, Clark knew what death looked like.

"You gonna make it quick, ain't you?"

"Not likely," Smoke said, then kicked him on the side of the head, dropping Clark unconscious to the floor.

When Clark came to his senses, he began screaming. He was naked, staked out a mile from the cabin, on the plain. Rawhide held his wrists and ankles to thick stakes driven into the ground. A huge ant mound was just inches from him. And Smoke had poured honey all over him.

"I'm a white man," Clark screamed. "You can't do this to me." Slobber sprayed from his mouth. "What are you, half Apache?"

Smoke looked at him, contempt in his eyes. "You will not die well, I believe."

He didn't.

Cal's face glowed red in the light of the campfire. "That's a tough way to die, but those bastards deserved it for what they did to Nicole and his son."

Pearlie raised his eyebrows. "Cal, deserve don't hardly have nothin' to do with how you die out here in the wild country. Those men died that way 'cause they crossed Smoke Jensen, and he was twice as mean and tough as they was. That's the long and the short of it. Don't never bite off more'n you can chew, and you'll never choke on it."

He rolled over, his back to the fire. "Now it's time to sleep. We got to catch up with Smoke tomorrow some-time."

Cal slid down against his saddle and pulled his hat over his eyes. "Night, Pearlie."

"Night, Cal."

CHAPTER THIRTEEN

Monte Carson was in his usual position in front of the jail, leaning back in a chair with his hat down over his eyes and his feet crossed on the hitchrail. A barefoot boy of nine or ten ran up to him and tugged on his shirtsleeve. "Mr. Carson, Bob over at the post office said fer me to give you this." He stuck a wrinkled envelope in Monte's hand.

Monte pushed his hat back and scowled at the boy in mock anger for a moment. "Didn't your momma ever teach you not to wake a man when he's sleepin'?"

The kid frowned, then his eyes started to tear. "But, Mr. Bob said to give it to you right away, an' not to go messin' 'round 'til I done it."

Monte grinned and winked, "I'm just funnin' with you, Jeremy. Here, this is for doin' such a good job of deliverin' messages." He reached in his pocket and handed Jeremy a coin.

The boy's face lit up with happiness. "Wow! A whole dime! That'll git me ten peppermint sticks over at the store."

Monte waggled his finger in Jeremy's face. "Now, don't

you go eating all of 'em at one time and gittin' a bellyache. Your momma will have my hide if you do."

"Yessir, Mr. Carson, I mean, no sir!" He said it over his shoulder as he hightailed it toward a group of boys playing in a mud hole down the street.

Monte sighed, trying to remember when he had been that young and life had been simple. He slit the envelope with a thumbnail and pulled the letter out. As he read it, his face wrinkled in a frown over its contents. After a moment he rested the piece of paper in his lap and sat there, eyes unfocused, thinking about what he should do.

Finally, he got up and stretched, groaning like an old dog forced to move from in front of a fireplace. "I'll be over at Longmont's if you need me," he called through the door to Jim, his deputy.

"Okay, boss. I'll holler if'n anyone tries to rob the bank," he replied, grinning around his plug of tobacco.

Monte walked down the street toward Louis Longmont's saloon, his gunfighter's eyes scanning buildings and the citizens of Big Rock he was sworn to protect. He was about to put them in more danger than they had ever been in before.

Walking slowly through batwing doors, he paused for a moment out of habit, to let his eyes adjust to the semi-darkness.

A deep voice called from the gloom. "You may enter, Monte. There isn't anyone here waiting to bushwhack you."

Monte grinned. Louis, an expert gunman himself, had recognized and appreciated his caution when entering a room without knowing who might be waiting inside.

"That's mighty easy for you to say, Louis. You ain't walkin' around town with a tin target pinned to your chest."

Louis shook Monte's hand without rising from his corner table, one reserved for the owner of the saloon and gambling house. "Can I have André fix you something to eat, or are your taste buds permanently ruined by eating that fire-food down at Maria's *cantina* on the edge of town?"

Monte raised his eyebrows. "Sure, I'd love some grub, long as it ain't frogs or snails or any of those other French delicacies your man is always trying to push on me."

Louis chuckled and called over his shoulder. "André, how about fixing the sheriff some real Western cuisine? Something like a beefsteak, burnt black and charred, fried potatoes, and some of those vine-ripened tomatoes we were saving for someone special."

Monte added, "And a pot of coffee. Hot, black, and strong. We're gonna need it."

Louis cocked his head, staring into his friend's eyes. "Bad news? Not about Smoke, I hope."

Monte handed him the letter. "Here, read this and then we'll talk."

Louis took the paper and read out loud. "To Sheriff Monte Carson, Big Rock, Colorado. From Texas Ranger's branch office in San Antonio. Dear Sheriff Carson, In answer to your inquiry of last week, there has been some news of the gunfighter Sundance Morgan. He and a gang of about twenty or thirty men are alleged to have robbed a stage line office in South Texas and killed the stationmaster, his wife, the stage driver and shotgun guard, and a passenger. Apparently, three female passengers were taken with the men when they fled. The stationmaster's daughter, a girl of thirteen, managed to hide and escape serious injury when the station and stage were set on fire. She didn't see much, but remembers the name Sundance being mentioned several times by the bandits. When they left, she said they rode off to the north. She says she also heard the name Smoke Jensen mentioned. Regards, Ranger Captain Ted Longley."

Louis looked up from the paper just as André placed a plate with a large steak, potatoes, tomatoes, and a hunk of fresh-made bread in front of Monte. A young man brought out a silver coffee server and placed it along with two china cups and saucers in front of them.

Louis folded the letter neatly and laid it on the table. "Looks like Smoke was right. This Sundance character is on the prod for him, and has an abundance of help."

Monte nodded around a mouthful of steak. "Yep," he mumbled, "my guess is that they'll be here within a week. That letter is dated ten days ago, so the gang could be over halfway here by now. I don't figger Sundance is gonna let any grass grow under his feet lookin' for Smoke. Vengeance is a powerful motivator."

Louis poured them both coffee, adding a dollop of fresh cream and two spoonfuls of sugar to his cup. He took a sip, then pulled a long black cigar out of his vest pocket and lit it with a lucifer. When he had it going to his satisfaction, he pointed it at Monte and said, "And, unless I miss my guess, you have a plan for when the gang arrives in Big Rock."

Monte grunted and held up his hand. "Just let me finish this steak and I'll tell you all about it."

While the sheriff ate, Louis leaned back and smoked his cigar, thinking about all the times he and Smoke had pulled iron together. He wished Smoke had dealt him into this hand, but he supposed he respected the man's desire not to get any of his friends hurt because of his actions.

Finally, Monte was through with his meal. "Jesus, Louis, but that André can cook a mean steak. If you ever want to get rid of him, he can come live with me and the missus."

Louis grinned. "Not likely, Monte, not while I still have teeth an' can chew. Now, tell me what you have planned for Sundance if he and his men ride into Big Rock."

Monte shook his head, frowning. "Not if, Louis, but when. I know that snake will come here lookin' for Smoke first. He don't know the area, and I doubt if he's smart enough to find out where Smoke's ranch is without trying here first."

Louis smoothed some ash into a pewter ashtray on the table. "You aren't planning to try to handle twenty to thirty men with just you and your three deputies, are you?"

"No, not exactly. I intend for the good citizens of Big Rock to take care of Sundance Morgan and his gang. With your help, if you're willin'."

Louis smiled and puffed his cigar until the end glowed red, sending blue clouds of smoke spiraling toward the ceiling. "Monte, I think I know what you have in mind, and I like it."

"Meet me on the field where we had the Fourth of July picnic, at five o'clock. I'm callin' a town meeting."

He reached in his pocket for money, but Louis waved a dismissive hand. "No, Monte, the meal's on me. I'll close the saloon and have all my employees come with me. We'll need every gun we can get."

* * *

The fall sun was inching toward the horizon, casting long, cool shadows by the time the town's inhabitants had all gathered at a large field just beyond the city limits. Every store and commercial establishment was closed, with handwritten notes in most windows, "Gone to the meeting."

Monte stood on a small wooden bandstand and addressed the crowd. "Good citizens of Big Rock, we've got trouble headed our way, and unless we stand together, we're gonna be in for a tough time."

Al Jamison, owner of the livery stable, was standing in the front row. He held up his hand like a kid in school. Monte nodded at him. "Al?"

"What kinda trouble, sheriff?"

"You all remember that little fracas we had here a few years back, when Tilden Franklin attacked the town? Well, one of the gunmen he hired at the time, man name of Sundance Morgan, is on the prod and wants some revenge for what happened that day."

A lady in the middle of the crowd cried, "Is he comin' for you, Sheriff Carson?"

Monte shook his head. "No. Matter of fact, he's not coming for anyone in this town. He's got him a gang of thirty or so men and he aims to kill Smoke Jensen."

Al Jamison spoke again. "But Smoke ain't here. He headed on up into the mountains. Left several days ago with Miss Sally. He tole me he was taking her to the train to go back East and he was goin' huntin' up in the high lonesome."

Monte spoke louder, to make himself heard over the murmur of the crowd. "That's true. Trouble is, Sundance Morgan don't know that. I figger he and his men will head here to find out where Smoke's ranch is, and to see if he happens to be in town."

A man near the front of the crowd shouted, "If that's so, why do you think the town's in for trouble? Seems to me, the onliest one in trouble is Smoke Jensen."

Monte scowled. "Cyrus, just what do you think thirty of the toughest desperados this side of Texas are going to do when they get to town and find out Smoke Jensen ain't here? Go to church, maybe?"

Monte gave the crowd time to stop laughing at the blushing Cyrus, then he continued. "Hell no, they're not. They'll try to ride roughshod over this town and all its citizens. At the very least, they'll shoot up the place to send Smoke a message about how tough they are."

He paused a moment, then pointed at a young lady carrying a parasol. "Mary, you want bullets around town while Jeremy and his friends are playin' in the street? Or do we just lock ourselves in our houses and let this Texas trash come up here and scare us into being cowardly moles, hidin' in the dark until they go on their way?"

"Hell no," a couple of men shouted, to be joined after only a few moments by most of the others. Soon everyone quieted and one asked, "Monte, sounds like you have some idea about what we oughta do 'bout these skunks that're on their way up here."

Monte held his hands over his head to quiet the townspeople. "I do. I've been thinkin' on it and I've come to the conclusion that the best way for us to survive this invasion by gunfighters, is to be ready for them when they hit the outskirts of town."

A voice shouted from the crowd. "Whatta you mean, ready for 'em?"

"From this day on, I want every person in town, 'cepting the children, to go armed at all times. I want volunteers to station themselves on top of some of the buildings where they can command a good line of fire into the street."

A woman with a soft, almost timid voice said, "What about those of us who don't know how, or don't want to use a gun, Mr. Carson? What can we do to help the town?"

Monte smiled. "You're right, Miss Kathy, lots of folks don't know nothin' 'bout shooting other folks. After all," he spread his arms, "this is a civilized town."

At that comment, most of the citizens laughed, realizing that Colorado in the late 1880s was anything but civilized.

"Anyway," Monte went on, "those of you who don't want to use firearms can help the men on lookout by bringing them water and food and such so they don't have to leave their posts every time they get the urge. A few of you, and the children, can help out by staying a couple of miles out of town on that ridge down there to the south, and rushing back here to give the rest of us some warning when they see the others comin'. Thirty men on horseback will kick up quite a dust cloud and they should be visible long before they get here."

"What about those of us who want to help, but don't no money nor job so's we can buy a gun?" asked a grizzled, poorly dressed old-timer known to spend most of his time hanging around the saloon, cadging drinks.

Louis Longmont climbed on the bandstand next to

Monte. "I will provide every man in this town with a pistol, rifle, or shotgun who will agree to use it to protect his fellow citizens." He pointed to Gus McRae, owner and operator of the shop with the largest selection of firearms in town. "Gus, you have my pledge, in front of the entire town. I will stand good for any guns you sell for this purpose. Just keep a list and I'll settle with you after all this is over. That includes ammunition, too."

"Wait just a minute." A sour-faced woman stepped forward, pushing and shoving her way through the crowd. When she arrived in front of the platform on which Monte and Louis stood, she pointed at them with a bony finger. "Why should the good, law-abiding citizens of Big Rock go out of their way to help a known gunfighter and killer like Smoke Jensen?" She faced the crowd. "I'm asking you women out there, especially those of you in the Sunday school class that I teach, to go home to your husbands and tell them you won't abide their taking part in this violence." After she spoke, her face turning red and beading with sweat although the early evening air was cool, she stood there, hands on hips, looking righteous in her anger.

Monte looked down on her with a pitying expression. "Oh, I can see your point, Miz Jones, I surely can." He looked out over the gathering of his friends and neighbors. "Why should we go out of our way to help Smoke and Sally Jensen? What have they done for us that should make us stand behind them in their need?"

He searched the faces for a moment, then pointed to Reverend Jackson. "Reverend, tell the good folks here about the fund for widows and orphans."

The man's naturally deep and sonorous voice boomed

when he spoke. "Well, right after Smoke founded Big Rock, and Miss Sally had her folks get a bank set up that has, over the years, given most of you loans to set up your businesses or buy crop seed and horses in bad times, Smoke came to me and gave me ten thousand dollars." There was a murmur from the group, most of whom would never see that amount of money in their entire lives. "He said it was cash he'd been paid for going after a few outlaws a while back, reward money. He said he wanted it to do some good, so he gave it to me and told me to parcel it out to anyone I thought needed a helping hand. No restrictions other than they needed it." He paused for a moment and rubbed his cheek as he thought. "Oh, one more thing. He asked me to keep quiet about it, said he didn't want anyone to know where it came from, other than the church and good folks of Big Rock."

Monte said, "Thank you, Reverend. Now, how about you saying a few words, Miss Goodlaw."

Priscilla Goodlaw, the schoolmarm, raised her face and took off her bonnet so she could be heard. "Miss Sally Jensen came to me right after I arrived from New York. It seems she and Smoke had paid my way out here and guaranteed my salary for five years, plus they built the schoolhouse out of their own funds and provided most of the books and other teaching materials that I use to teach your children how to spell and cipher. Miss Sally also takes over the class when I'm sick and can't teach, as most of you know, and she gives me money each and every month to give to those kids I see who don't have enough to eat, or who don't have proper clothes or shoes to come to school in. She made me promise to give the money to the children in private so they wouldn't have to be embarrassed about taking charity, and to never tell them where it came from."

Monte grinned and said, "Thank you, Miss Goodlaw." Turning his eyes back to the group, he said, "I could go on for hours about all the things Smoke and Sally Jensen have done for Big Rock—all the drunks and down-and-outers he's taken out of my cells and put to work on his ranch so's they could feed their families, all the children that've gotten ponies to ride to school and back on, all the businesses he's bailed out of trouble when times were lean. But I won't. If there's anybody in this town," he inclined his head downward toward Miz Jones, "other than Miss Fiona there, who don't know who this town's best citizen and best friend is, then they ought to move on down the line, 'cause they've been livin' here with their heads buried in the sand. I say we do this not so much for Smoke Jensen, though God knows he deserves it, but for Big Rock and ourselves. If it ever gets known that our town can be treed by a bunch of sorry gunslicks who ride the owlhoot trail, then we might as well burn down the buildings ourselves and settle somewhere else, 'cause it'll happen again."

The crowd let out a cheer and some of the men threw their hats in the air. Fiona Jones whirled and hurried off toward her house, where she lived alone. It was rumored only her cats could put up with her sour disposition.

Monte said, "See my deputy, Jim, for your assignments and stations. He'll also keep track of who's gonna be on lookout for the gang's arrival."

Louis shouted, "After you talk to Jim, come on over to my place for a free round of beer."

This caused a louder cheer than before and a general movement back toward town, especially of the men.

Monte put his hand on Louis's shoulder. "Thanks for your help, Louis."

"Don't mention it, Monte. I owe Smoke my life, on several occasions." He grinned. "And even more important than that, he's my friend."

The two men walked back toward town, where, together, they would plan how best to defend their small community and make it a fortress against Sundance Morgan and his gang.

CHAPTER FOURTEEN

Smoke Jensen was enjoying his time alone in the up-high. The sight of wild game, the explosion of color in the late-blooming fall wildflowers, and the extreme wildness of the high country recharged his soul and brought him inner peace.

"Horse," he said to his mount as they traversed the mountainside, packhorses trailing behind, "this is surely the most beautiful country God ever made."

Horse snorted and waggled his ears, as if in agreement with his master.

Smoke rode with his Henry rifle slung across his saddle horn, eyes scanning the mountain above him for just the right place to make his stand. The air was crisp and cold, but not bitterly so, and smelled of pine needles and fresh snow on the way. Patches of ice-covered snow had gathered in shady areas, but most of the trail was still clear, with occasional small boggy mud holes from previous ice-melts.

Smoke had removed his buckskin shirt and hat, taking advantage of the bright afternoon sun to tan his hide even darker than it already was. He didn't want any pale skin to reflect moonlight and give his position away in the nighttime fighting he knew was coming.

On the second day after he left Puma Buck's camp, he found what he was looking for. A natural fortress only a few hundred yards below the top of the mountain. Backed on three sides by sheer rock walls extending skyward, the place had a level meadow dotted with large ponderosa pines and a ridge in front. From there, the ground fell off at a steep angle downward to end along a single trail up the mountain.

There were few trees or boulders large enough to provide cover for his enemies between his fort and the path the men would have to take to get to him. He had a clear line of fire, and the grade was too steep for the outlaws' horses to climb with riders on their backs. They would have to approach him on foot, if they dared.

Leaving Horse down below on the trail, he pulled and tugged his packhorses up the hill, one at a time. Once there, he unloaded some of his supplies. He whistled as he unpacked his gear. After he had it all laid out on the ground, he planned how he wanted it distributed and set various rifles and guns and bundles of dynamite in different spots. He knew he was likely to take some lead in the upcoming fight and he feared he might not be as mobile as he wanted to be. It was essential that he have weapons in several locations because he didn't know where he might be if he got hit.

He made a mark, a blaze with his knife, down low on each of the trees behind which he hid weapons. His bright mark on the wood would show up well in either moon or starlight. With each bundle of dynamite he secreted some lucifers wrapped in wax paper to keep them dry in the event of snow.

After a while, when he was certain he had done all he could to prepare his battleground, he took the pack animals back down the hill to where he had left Horse. He removed his saddle and bridle from Horse and gave him an apple while he spent a moment rubbing his mount's neck. He knew his gelding would find its way back to Sugarloaf and that there was plenty of sweet grass in the meadows along the way, and sooner or later one of the mountain men or miners who knew Smoke would find him and take him back to the ranch.

He slapped Horse on the rump and watched as he trotted off down the slope. Smoke saddled one of the pack-horses and began to make his way back down the mountain. He had a few surprises to construct, and he didn't know how much time he had before the gang would arrive.

It was full dark when he reached the lower regions of the mountain, where it first began its steep climb toward the summit. He built a small fire and cooked some of the venison Puma had smoked for him, made some pan bread, and fixed a pot of strong coffee. The air would get very cold, even at this lower elevation, and he wanted something warm in his stomach to get him through the night.

When he was finished eating, he rolled two cigarettes and smoked them both with the last of his coffee. He put out the fire and moved his camp a mile over to the south, not wanting to sleep where there had been any light from his cooking fire.

He picketed the packhorses and snuggled down in his

bedroll, covered with an additional layer of pine boughs and leaves. His breath sent frost-smoke from his nostrils and small beads of ice formed on his eyebrows as large, fluffy flakes of snow began to drift down from the clouds overhead.

At dawn, he began working without taking the time to cook breakfast. He shared some apples and sugar and some cold mountain water from his canteen with the horses and then got busy. Finding a muddy, boggy area, he squatted and got large handfuls of mud and smeared it over rolls of lariat rope and rawhide he brought from the ranch. Once covered with the black mud, the rope blended in perfectly when laid on the ground or wound around a tree. It couldn't be seen from more than a foot or two away. He left one roll of the rope uncovered. This particular rope he wanted to be noticed.

He cut down a bunch of young saplings, five to six inches in diameter, and ranging from five to ten feet in length. Using a small hatchet, since he didn't want to dull his tomahawk on the tough trees, he sharpened each end of the spear-like lengths of wood, then tied them to a pack-horse. They would be needed later.

As he moved along the trail, he stopped and gathered all the wild pumpkins and gourds he could find, storing them in a gunnysack tied to the side of his packhorse. Whenever he came to a rockfall, he picked up as many small, fist-sized rocks as he could find, throwing them in the sack with the gourds and pumpkins.

Several times, he stopped at narrow places on the trail and got his shovel out and dug holes, about twice the diameter of a horse's hoof and two feet deep. In the bottom of these, he would place a sharpened wooden stake, then fill the hole with pine needles, making it look as though it was part of the trail. If stepping in the hole didn't break a horse's leg, the stake would impale its hoof and make it unable to carry any weight. Smoke hated the idea of injuring innocent animals, but in this case, it was them or him. He needed any advantage he could create, and putting flat-landers afoot in these altitudes would quickly sap them of their strength and will to fight.

In some places, next to drop-offs and cliffs, he dug parts of the side of the trail away, then made a frame of small branches covered with more dirt and pine needles to hide the defect. Any bronc stepping on these would stumble to the side, carrying its rider over the edge with it.

Some heavy limbs were pulled back, with the help of the horses, and tied so that anyone passing would release them and be smacked in the chest, breaking ribs and arms and sowing more confusion.

Fear was to be Smoke's strongest ally. These men were completely unused to being afraid of anything. Most were certainly not afraid of dying, at least not in ways familiar to them. But, give them a situation in which they felt they were not in control, a situation where they didn't know what was going to happen to them next, where they were continually seeing their comrades-in-arms dying or being injured without warning, and even the strongest of them was liable to break and head back home.

As Smoke made his rounds, laying traps and setting deadfalls and other surprises for his pursuers, he occasionally came upon lone mining camps and small enclaves of miners and trappers. He felt it was his obligation to warn them of the impending battle. Most of the occupants just shrugged and said they'd take their chances, not having much that would interest the outlaws. Some immediately packed their meager belongings and headed down the mountain, figuring on a short vacation before the snow made their mining impossible anyway.

The following morning, as Smoke was riding through pine forest, familiarizing himself with the layout of the area, he saw smoke rising from just over the next ridge. He loosened the rawhide thongs on his Colts and shucked a shell into his Henry.

With eyes even more alert, scanning the woods and underbrush to either side as he rode, he walked his mount to the top of the hill to take a look. He saw an old, weathered miner's cabin in flames, with two bodies lying nearby in a small clearing in front of a makeshift tunnel in the side of a mountain.

He spurred his horse and loped down toward the burning building. Before dismounting, he took another look around, but saw no one in the area. Swinging down from his saddle, he approached the bodies, the Henry cocked and ready.

There were two corpses, an older, bearded man who looked to be sixty years old or so, and a younger, clean-shaven boy who had some facial resemblance to the first. "Father and son, probably," thought Smoke, as he bent and checked for signs of life. There were none. Both men had been shot through the head and were dead as yesterday's news.

Smoke examined the area. Tracks and boot prints indicated four to six men and their mounts. The majority of the prints led to and from the mine entrance in the side of the cliff. He laid his rifle down, filled his hands with Colts, and walked slowly toward the black hole in the mountain.

His boots kicked up small puffs of dirt, and smoke from the cabin swirled around him, ruffling the fringe on his buckskin shirt and stinging his eyes and nose.

Turning sideways to present less of a target when he was backlighted in the entrance, he slipped into the cool darkness of the tunnel. He could hear a soft sound a short distance down the shaft, like rats scrabbling for food or prey.

He parted his lips and breathed through his mouth to lessen the sound, crouched, and inched his way along, feeling his way in the darkness.

Sensing a movement in the still air, he dove to the ground just as a shadowy figure appeared before him and swung a two-by-four at his head. He heard the board whistle past his ear, and tackled his attacker, the two of them rolling in the dirt and rocks of the tunnel floor.

A woman's scream pierced the gloom, yelling that she was going to kill him and all his damned friends. After a brief struggle, Smoke managed to subdue the woman, sitting on her with her arms pinned to the ground.

She flung her head from side to side and tried to bite his hands where he held her. When she realized he had her under complete control, she relaxed and went limp, mumbling the Lord's Prayer to herself.

Astonished and surprised, Smoke helped her to her feet and managed to convince her that he meant her no harm. She began to cry hysterically and told him to help her mother-in-law, pointing farther down the tunnel.

Smoke holstered his pistols and went in search of the other lady. He found her fifteen yards deeper in, and picked up her limp and unresponsive body and carried her to the mine's entrance.

After finding she was unconscious from a severe beating, but had no life-threatening injuries, he got his bedroll and bundled her in it, just inside the mine shaft. When he had the sleeping lady wrapped and protected from the chilly air, he asked the younger woman what had happened.

She sleeved tears and dried blood off her face, patted her ratted and disheveled hair into some semblance of order, then held out her hand. "I'm Jessica Aldritch, and she is my husband's mother, Aileen Aldritch."

Smoke took her hand and said softly, "I'm sorry about your husband and his father. There was nothing I could do for them."

Jessica nodded, straightening her shoulders and standing straight. "I know. The outlaws killed them before they took us and . . ." She began to cry again, unable to finish her sentence.

She didn't have to. Smoke could tell what had happened by the ladies' torn dresses and the bruises and streaks of blood on their thighs.

He found his teeth clenching so hard his jaws ached. "How many were there, and when did this happen?" he asked, his mild voice betraying none of the emotion he felt.

Jessica looked out the tunnel entrance and watched their cabin burn for a moment before she answered. Finally, in a hoarse whisper, she said, "They came to the cabin yesterday, six of them, and asked for food and water. While my husband and his father gathered up some supplies, two of the men grabbed them and two others shot them." She paused to take a deep breath, "Then they took Aileen and me down into the mine." Her eyes looked haunted. "They kept at us 'til this morning, then took off, leaving us for dead."

"I was wondering why they didn't kill you."

"Aileen passed out hours ago, and I pretended to faint, hoping that would stop them." She wiped at her eyes. "It didn't."

Smoke walked to his horse and took two extra pistols out of his saddlebag. He gave them to Jessica. "You know how to use these?"

She opened the loading gate of the Colt, spun the cylinder to check the loads, then snapped it shut with a flick of her wrist. "Yes, sir, I do."

Smoke smiled, thinking, this one would do to ride the river with, all right. He didn't feel that about many other women other than his Sally.

"I'm going to go after them, then I'll come back here and see that you two get down to town. Okay?"

"What's your name, mister?"

"Smoke Jensen."

"Mr. Jensen, if the chance avails itself, I'd appreciate it if you could manage to bring the red-haired one back with you, alive."

Smoke raised his eyebrows. "Any particular reason why you want that one?"

Her eyes bored into his. "He's the one who shot my husband." Her eyes flashed, reflecting the shimmering flames of her burning home. "I would like to discuss that act with him, and watch his face while I kill him."

Smoke nodded. "You got every right, I guess. If it's possible, I'll be back before sundown."

As he turned to go, she touched his arm. "Mr. Jensen,

do you have a shovel with you? I'm afraid they burned ours."

Smoke left the ladies with his shovel and rode off, bending low over the saddle to follow tracks the killers left.

It was almost noon when he found their camp. The sleepless night must have made them exceedingly tired, as they were all sprawled around their campfire snoring. No one was standing watch.

Smoke slipped off his mount and walked on cat feet up to the camp, slipping his knife out on the way and filling his other hand with iron.

At the edge of their campsite, next to a saddle, he found a leather bag with the name Aldritch stamped into the leather. That settled it as far as Smoke was concerned; these were the men he was hunting.

He squatted between two of the sleeping men, and quick as a rattler striking, he slit their throats with his big knife. One of the men only moaned, and lay there bleeding his life out into the dirt. The other squealed like a gut-shot pig and sat up, his hands at his throat, blood pumping and squirting from his neck, glistening scarlet in the bright afternoon sunlight.

Two of the desperados came instantly awake, clawing at their sidearms. Smoke cocked and fired, hitting one in the chest and the other in the abdomen, his second bullet punching through flesh, blowing out part of the gunman's spine. The gunshots were so close together they sounded like one noise. As his big Colts exploded, shots booming and echoing off the mountains, two of the others shook their heads and stared groggily around them, trying to make sense of what was happening.

Smoke stepped over and kicked one in the side of the face, snapping his head around and shattering his jaw. The other, the red-haired one Jessica had told him about, Smoke grabbed by the throat and jerked to his feet.

The dazed man looked around him, a puzzled expression in his eyes. "Why . . . why did you do this mister? We ain't done nothin' to you."

Smoke pulled the killer's face close to his. "Did you enjoy what you did to those women last night?"

The outlaw's eyes widened, then narrowed to slits as he glared at Smoke. "Why . . . what the hell do you mean?"

Smoke's lips curled in a sardonic grin, but his eyes were dark with hate. "I want you to reflect on it. I want you to remember how much *fun* you and your friends had, killing two men who were trying to help you; how *good* it felt to rape and beat their defenseless wives all night."

The killer's expression became defiant. "Why should I do that . . . and what business is it of yours anyway?"

The mountain man picked the two-hundred-pound man up effortlessly and threw him facedown over one of the horses. As he tied his feet to his hands beneath the nervous animal's belly, Smoke leaned down and spoke quietly in his ear. "I just hope it was worth it for you. That little episode of fun is going to have to last you an eternity."

"What do you mean?" the man stammered, fear-sweat dripping off his face.

"You got about an hour left to live. I'm taking you to meet the grim reaper, and she can't wait to say hello."

When he started blubbering and pleading for his life, Smoke left him and put the gent with the broken jaw across his horse the same way. After he was certain they were both securely tied, he began to move around their camp, searching carefully for anything that might belong to the Aldritch women.

The leather satchel contained a quantity of gold dust and nuggets, and in addition, he found almost ten thousand dollars, some in old bills and some in new ones. Figuring it was probably stolen from other folks like the Aldritches, Smoke gathered up the gold and money and put it all in the satchel.

The ammunition and guns that he could use, he strung on one of their horses.

Finally, when he had taken everything of use, he strung the rest of their horses together and dallied them to his saddle horn. As he pulled out, headed back to the Aldritch mine, the two killers continued to beg and plead with him to let them go. They promised him untold wealth if he'd only relent and let them live.

Smoke spoke to them one last time over his shoulder. "Your rotten lives aren't mine to give. I'll let you ask the women you raped, whose husbands you shot, what should be done with you."

His final comment sentenced the outlaws to spend their last hours on earth thinking about their miserable lives, and wondering just how they were going to die.

It was almost dusk by the time Smoke and his prisoners arrived back at the Aldritch place. Aileen Aldritch was awake, and was eating soup that Jessica had heated over a small campfire in the clearing. The cabin fire was almost out, though several logs were still smoldering and smoking, and likely would be for days.

Jessica glanced over her shoulder at the procession, and paled when she saw who was on the horses. She handed the soup bowl to Aileen, stood and smoothed her dress, and waited for Smoke with crossed arms.

Smoke dismounted and inclined his head at the red-haired prisoner. "Now what? It's your call," he asked Jessica.

She grabbed the man by his hair and bent his head up where she could look him in the eyes. She smiled, and the sight of it sent chills down Smoke's spine. He knew then the man was going to die very painfully.

"Mr. Jensen, if you would be so kind as to tie this coward to that tree over there, I'd be much obliged."

"Oh Jesus, oh Jesus, don't let her do nothin' to me mister! Just shoot me right now! Please!"

Without changing expression, Jessica slapped the gunman across the face, the sound like a gunshot in the quiet afternoon air. "You miserable coward! You never had the decency to live like a man your entire life, at least try to have the courage to die like one."

Smoke bent and cut the rope beneath the horse's belly, leaving the killer's hands and feet tied together. He flipped the end of the rope attached to his wrists over a low-hanging branch and pulled the man upright.

The gunman's eyes were wide with fright, and tears were running down his face while he was crying and shouting and yelling for mercy.

Before Smoke could move, Jessica slipped his knife out of his scabbard and stepped in front of the red-haired cowboy. "Aileen, you can watch or not, it's up to you," she called over her shoulder.

After a moment, mother-in-law and daughter-in-law were standing side by side in front of the hysterical outlaw. Aileen took the knife and stepped up to him. "Forty-three years. We were together longer than you've lived, young man. You might as well have shot me when you killed my man. One thing is certain, you'll never make another woman a widow." She held the knife out and with a flick of her wrist slashed his belt and waistband. His pants fell to the ground. He wasn't wearing any underwear or longjohns.

Aileen handed the knife to Jessica and stepped aside. Jessica said, "When I was a young girl, my father told me that when a stallion, a bull, or a male dog gets vicious or bad, there's only one cure. Do you know what that is, mister?"

"No . . . no . . . no!" he screamed, twisting his body back and forth, trying to protect his private parts from the women. "You're plumb crazy . . . you can't do this to me!" He turned his head toward Smoke. "Mister, for God's sake! Stop her!"

Smoke shrugged and grinned. "I told you, she couldn't wait to say hello."

Jessica laid the razor-sharp edge of Smoke's knife underneath the outlaw's testicles, and it was over in one quick upward motion.

The killer looked down at his parts on the ground and screamed. Jessica moved to the side to avoid the stream of blood, and wiped the blade on his shirt. She handed the knife to Smoke and pulled one of the Colts he had given her out of her dress pocket.

Without hesitating, she placed the barrel against the head of the man still tied to his horse. "I don't recall your name, mister, but I do recall that you weren't as brutal as the others." She smiled down at him. "That deserves some leniency."

As he smiled hopefully up at her, she pulled the trigger, blowing most of his skull out over the ground.

As the horse bucked and danced in fear, she handed the Colt to Smoke and put her arm around Aileen. "Let's go finish that soup before it gets cold, dear."

Smoke looked at the bodies of the two men and thought, "God, protect me from the wrath of a woman!"

CHAPTER FIFTEEN

Sundance Morgan removed his hat and sleeved sweat off his forehead. Though the air was cooler the farther north they rode, a mid-afternoon sun in a cloudless sky was brutally hot. In the last few days on the trail they hadn't come near a town of any size and his men were getting testy and short-tempered. Three days with no whiskey or females was beginning to cause problems.

The saloon women they had taken from the stage line station lasted only a few days. Two were killed trying to escape, the other, two days later, had taken her own life. While one of the outlaws was having his way with her, she pulled his Colt from its holster, shot him, and then put the barrel in her mouth and pulled the trigger, ending her torture. They left their companion to die in the dirt beside the bullet-torn body of the prostitute.

Sundance knew if they didn't come to a town soon, there would be trouble—blood trouble. Lightning Jack had taken to taunting some of the Mexican riders, calling them greasers and chili-eaters. It was only a matter of time before one of them, or Perro Muerte himself, stuck a knife between someone's ribs, and that would be the end of the uneasy alliance of the desperados.

Just when he was about to call the gang to a halt for their nooning, Sundance topped a ridge and saw a small group of buildings in the distance. He twisted in his saddle and waved his hat at his followers. *"Mi compadres,* a town!"

The killers perked up and spurred their horses to a trot, anxious to sit on something that didn't move and drink something stronger than water.

On the outskirts of the village was a hand-lettered sign nailed to a pole: Hell's Hole, Colorado Territory.

The place was little better than a mining camp, with more tents than buildings. The good news was a large tent with a board front attached that had the word Saloon printed in large block letters at the top.

Sundance held up his hand. "Okay, men, I know you're ready for some whiskey and women, but we got to get the horses cared for first. Take 'em to the livery stable and get 'em fed and brushed down before headin' for the dog hole."

His pronouncement was greeted with several hoots and groans, but he scowled them into silence. "Don't forget who's in charge here! We got us a ways to go yet 'fore we get to Smoke's grounds, and I want no broncs pullin' up lame." He whirled his mount around and headed toward the far end of town where corral stables were visible from high ground. "We've got plenty of time to get alkalied, and to get laid if that's what you're hankerin' for," he added.

They rode off the ridge at a short lope.

After leaving their horses in the care of an elderly man at the livery, the entire group of paid gunmen walked down a dusty street to the saloon.

The townspeople didn't pay them much attention, since the town was full of characters not much different from Sundance's gang. Typical of many of the small mining camps in the Colorado mountain regions, it was full of rowdy, rough miners, few ladies other than camp-town whores, and not a few outlaws and men riding the owl-hoot trail looking for a place to hide until their reputations died down.

Sundance paused before pushing through the batwings and looked at a sign, painted in bloodred paint that had dripped down the wall next to the entrance. "The Hole," he read out loud, with a chuckle. "Then I guess it'll be 'bout right for this group, huh, El Gato?"

The big Mexican grunted and pushed past him into the darkness of the saloon. "Only if it has *tequila.*"

Even though it was early afternoon, the place was full of hard-looking men. Sundance let his eyes adjust to the gloom, then walked to the far rear corner of the room and stood before two large tables, occupied by six men wearing denim jeans and the thick shoes common to miners. They appeared to be well on their way to being drunk.

Sundance smiled, looked over his shoulder at his men, then back to the seated miners. "Sorry, gents, it appears we're gonna need these tables."

One of the men looked up, too deep in his whiskey to see the menace in Sundance's eyes. "That's too bad, mister. These here seats're taken," he slurred, and reached for a liquor bottle in front of him.

Sundance spoke softly, "Carlito."

Suarez pushed through the crowd to stand next to his boss and slowly slipped his knife out of its scabbard and stood there, caressing the blade. His brass tooth gleamed in the meager light from a kerosene lantern overhead.

Sundance leaned down, placing his hands on the table with his face near the miner's nose. "Do you speak Mexican, mister?"

Red-rimmed, bloodshot eyes looked up at Suarez. "Yeah, a little. Why?"

"Do you know what they call my friend here?"

"No, what?"

"Perro Muerte."

The man thought for a moment, then his eyebrows raised. "Dead dog? What kind of name is that?"

In spite of himself, Sundance had to laugh, causing Suarez to take a step toward the drunk. Sundance held him back with a gesture. "No, no. It means 'Hound of Death.' Now, how do you suppose he got that name?"

The man snorted, a sarcastic expression on his face. "By killin' dogs?"

Before the miner could laugh at his own joke, Suarez stepped forward and buried his blade in soft flesh, slitting the drunk's throat so deeply that his neck was almost severed.

As his head flopped back and blood spurted, the other men at the table jumped back. Sundance planted a boot in the dead man's chest and kicked him over backwards. He called to the bartender, "Get this trash outta here and bring us some drinks."

By the time the gang was seated at the recently vacated tables, the barman had dragged the body out the door and brought several bottles of liquor to set before them.

"Will there be any thin' else?" he stammered.

El Gato took a swig of the whiskey, then leaned over

to spit it on the floor, where it mixed with the pool of coagulating blood. He looked up, eyebrows knitted together in anger. *"Sí!* Tequila and womens."

"We only got two whores, and they's busy in the rooms out back."

El Gato shrugged. "Make them less busy, *pronto,* or El Gato do it."

"Uh . . . yes sir. I'll go git 'em myself. And I don't have no tequila, but I got some *mescal.* That do?"

Lightning Jack asked, "You got any limes?"

"Limes?"

"Never mind," interrupted Sundance, "just get the girls and get the *mescal* and come back real soon."

"Yes sir!"

As the barkeep scurried back to the bar, a tall, rangy man walked into the saloon, a Greener cradled in his arms and a Colt slung low on his hip. "All right, everybody just stay calm! Now," he said, pushing back his hat, "I want to know who's been killin' people and leavin' 'em layin' on my street, bleedin' all over the place."

Sundance stood, and his men, all thirty-two of them, swung in their chairs, clearing their gun sides for action and letting their hands rest on wooden butts worn smooth by use. Even in the semi-darkness, the cowboy with the shotgun could be seen to pale. He glanced at the men, then down at his two-shot Greener, apparently realizing it would bring him nothing but a short ride to Boot Hill if he tried to use it.

"Are you the sheriff of this town?" asked Sundance.

"Name's Jake," he said uneasily.

"Well, Jake, I guess I'm the one you got to blame for

that body out there. Seems he insulted my man here," he inclined his head at Suarez. "Called him a dirty name."

"Well, I—"

Sundance spread his arms. "We don't want no more trouble, Sheriff. If there's a fine for littering, or anything like that, I'd be glad to pay it."

Sweat beaded the lawman's forehead. "Yeah . . . okay. Fine for litterin's two dollars."

"Two dollars?" Sundance frowned.

"Uh, yeah, but since you're new to town, I'll overlook it this time. How's that?"

Sundance stepped up to the cowboy and slapped him on the back. "Jake, I knew when you walked in you was a reasonable man. How about havin' a drink with us?"

"Sure, why not?" he replied, his voice thin, a bit shaky.

El Gato moved his chair to make room for Jake to sit, and Lightning Jack poured him a tumbler full of whiskey.

"Just what do you folks do in this town for fun, Sheriff?" asked Bull.

Jake raised an eyebrow at Bull's high voice and slight lisp, but wisely decided not to mention it. "There's only two things to do around here after dark. You're already doin' one of 'em, an' that's drinkin'."

As the sheriff spoke, two women, dressed in well-worn, once brightly colored but now faded and shabby dresses, emerged from the back of the tent.

Jake nodded in their direction. "And there's the other." He leaned forward and whispered, "'Ceptin' drinkin's more fun than those two. They're mighty well used, if you git my drift."

Lightning Jack laughed and slapped the man on the shoulder, Jack's big arm almost knocking the man off his chair. "After a week on the back of a bronc with nothin' better to look at than the butt of the horse in front of ya', I don't 'spect we'll be too choosy, my friend."

The women walked toward Sundance's men, stopping when they got within range of the smell of the group. One turned to the other and wrinkled her nose, rolling her eyes. Sundance noticed the look and grunted. He took a leather pouch out of his pocket and threw a handful of double-eagles on the table. "We might not smell too good, ladies, but I'll bet the odor of this gold'll take your minds off that right quick."

The whores smiled, showing teeth that would have made a horse trader wince, and joined right in, throwing arms around any man they could reach. "Mescal for everybody, Roy," one called to the bartender. "Let's get this party going!"

Bull stood and swept the heavier of the two women up in his arms. He glared at the others. "I'm goin' first this time. Any objections?"

"Not as long as you don't take too long. I got me a powerful thirst for woman-flesh, and I don't aim to wait 'til tomorrow," yelled Lightning Jack, with a grin.

Toothpick smiled. "Don't you worry none, Lightnin'. Bull's a lot faster on the draw with a woman than he is with those two cannons he carries."

"His load's a mite smaller with that weapon, too," chimed in one of Jack's Southerners.

As Bull went through the door into a back room, he could be heard to say, "Yeah, but this one's good fer more'n two shots at a time."

While his men proceeded to get drunk and manhandle

the remaining whore, Sundance drew the sheriff to a quieter corner of the room for a private talk.

"What's your full name, Sheriff?"

"Jake Best."

"Well, Jake Best, I'm pleased to meet you. My men and me're on the way up north. I got me a score to settle with a town, and a feller up there." He poured Jake another slug of whiskey. "I was wonderin' if you got any men in this town who might like to make a little money. I need men that don't mind gettin' shot at, nor shootin' back when it comes right down to it."

Jake rubbed his chin whiskers, downed his drink in one quick swallow, then nodded. "There might be a few who'd be interested in a deal like that. We got a few hereabouts that're meaner than a polecat." He smirked and motioned for a refill. "Only not so smart."

Sundance tilted the bottle over his glass. "Brains ain't exactly what I'm lookin' for, Jake. I got enough brains for all of us. What I need is mean *hombres.*"

"Oh, they're plenty mean all right. Some of these boys'd shoot their mamma if she burnt their supper. Trouble is, they might be a mite hard to control."

Sundance's teeth flashed in the shadows. "That's not a problem. If'n money don't make 'em mind, then Mr. Colt will."

Jake's eyes shifted to the pistol tied down low on Sundance's hip. "Then I'll spread the word you're lookin' to hire some men. I'll tell 'em to meet you here in the saloon tomorrow after lunch." He looked around at the amount of whiskey the men were drinking. "I don't 'spect you'll be up and about much 'fore then."

Sundance glanced at the whore sitting on Lightning

Jack's lap. El Gato was standing between her legs with his hand stuck down her bodice. "No, Jake," Sundance mused, his lips curling in a slight smile. "We've all got some catchin' up to do, too."

The sun was directly overhead the next day when Sundance slouched into the saloon. His forehead was wrinkled and his eyes squinted against the power of the headache sending lightning bolts through his skull. His groin was sore and had begun to itch, adding worry about the health of his private parts to the agony of his hangover.

"Roy," he croaked, throat raw from whiskey and cigars he had consumed through the night, "bring me some coffee. As strong as you got."

"You want me to fetch some eggs or steak from the boardin' house across the street, Mr. Sundance?"

Stomach rolling at the thought of putting anything solid in it, Sundance shook his head and moaned as the motion caused pain to awaken behind his eyes. "No, just coffee, and water, if you got any worth drinkin'. My mouth's dry as Correo County back home in Texas."

After three cups of boiled bellywash, with pieces of eggshells used to settle the grounds still floating in it, Sundance was feeling more alive. His two trips to the outhouse out back had relieved his gut some and eased his poor disposition a little.

It wasn't long before some of the roughest looking men he had ever seen began to drift into the room. They all wore pistols tied down low, and several carried rifles or shotguns slung over their shoulders.

When seven men were seated at his table, Sundance

ordered beer all around, more to settle his stomach than to be sociable.

He rolled a cigarette and stuck it carelessly between his lips. Striking a lucifer on the hammer of his Colt, he lit his *cigarillo* and peered at the men through a cloud of smoke.

"Okay gents, here's the deal. My men and me are headed up into the mountains to a town name of Big Rock. I intend to tree that town and kill a man up there who did me dirt."

One of the cowboys, with eyes as old and hard as coal, raised his eyebrows. "Big Rock? Ain't that the town where Smoke Jensen hangs his hat?"

Sundance's eyes narrowed. "And who might you be, mister?"

"Name's Evans." He had one Colt in a low-slung holster, another stuck behind his belt, and an American Arms tengauge scattergun across his back on a rawhide sling.

"And I'll bet you be Sundance Morgan," he continued, the right side of his mouth curling in a sneer.

"What makes you say that?"

Evans picked up his mug of beer and drank, using his left hand. His right lay on his thigh, inches from his pistol. He sat the glass down and sleeved the foam off his moustache with his left forearm.

"I was down in Mexico last year, near Chihuahua, and ran into a Mex named Carbone. He told me 'bout an *hombre* who fancied himself a gunhawk, and how Smoke Jensen shot off his ear to teach him a lesson." Evans reached for his beer and took another swig, his eyes never leaving Sundance's. "He also said not to never turn my back on this particular gunslick—'cause he's a back-shooter."

"Why you . . ." Sundance grabbed for iron, only to find himself looking down the barrel of Evans's Colt before he could clear leather. He forced a sickly grin and put his hands flat on the table. "You got it wrong, mister. Smoke Jensen bushwhacked me when I wasn't lookin'. It weren't no fair fight."

"That's not the way I heard it, pilgrim, and I heard it from more'n one person." He grinned insolently. "You're more famous than you realize, Sundance. Folks're laughing at you and your one ear from Mexico to the Canadian border."

Evans stepped out of his chair, his gun barrel never wavering an inch. As he backed toward the door, he said, "I don't know 'bout you other fellers, but this is one galoot who'd rather go to bed with a grizzly than trust Sundance Morgan."

Sundance's face turned blotchy red as Evans backed through the batwings and disappeared into the sunlight. He slammed his fist on the table and asked. "Who was that asshole?"

The man sitting next to him said, "That there was Jessie Evans. Made himself quite a name in the Lincoln County war a few years back." The cowboy cut himself a chunk of tobacco from his plug and stuffed it in his mouth, then took a long drink of his beer. "Said to have killed more men than he has fingers and toes."

One of the others added, "He supposedly backed down Billy Bonney, but, since he's been dead, most everybody claims that nowadays."

Sundance took a deep breath, trying to calm his anger. "Hell, I don't need him anyway." He raised his eyebrows and looked around the table. "You men interested in makin' some money, and havin' some fun along the way?"

The man with the chewing tobacco leaned to the side and spit on the floor. "How much money we talkin' about?"

"We split up the take evenly among those that survive, but I'll personally guarantee you each a hundred dollars a month, and I pay all expenses."

"Including whiskey and women?"

"All you can stand of both."

The men looked at each other, thought a moment, then one by one they nodded. "Count us in. Hell, it's got to be better'n scrabbling on our knees tryin' to dig gold outta them mountains."

Sundance gave each of the men two double-eagle gold pieces. "Here's an advance, boys. We're gonna leave in the mornin', so see if you can round up any more men who want a few of these in their pockets and the chance to tree a town and kill a sonofabitch at the same time."

The next day, the gang gathered in the saloon. Sundance stood and banged the butt of his Colt on the table for attention. "Men, we've got some new partners who have agreed to come along to Big Rock with us."

He pointed to a table aside from the ones where the original members sat. "The man on the end, with the scalps hangin' from his belt, is Blackjack Walker." Sundance looked around the room, "He says he's not particular, he'll scalp anybody, red, brown, or black."

As the men laughed, Sundance said, "The black man next to Walker is Moses Washburn. Moses was a buffalo soldier for the North, but I don't want that to put your men off, Lightning Jack. He deserted 'fore killin' any Southerners. He came out here and spent most of the war killin' Injuns."

"Next to Moses is Slim Johnson, he's from over New Mexico way, but says he don't wanna go back there 'cause there's more'n one noose waitin' on him."

He inclined his head toward two men sitting off by themselves at another table. "Over there we have George Stalking Horse and Jeremiah Gray Wolf. They used to scout for the Army, but had to leave suddenly after killin' one of their officers. He walked up on 'em while they was enjoyin' a little white woman lovin'. Seems she wasn't enjoyin' it quite as much as they was. They claim to be able to track a sidewinder through a sandstorm." He smiled, "We'll see. We might just need some good trackers if Jensen's forted up in the mountains."

The gang stood and began to mill around the newcomers, introducing themselves and trading stories about mutual acquaintances. After a little while, Sundance said, "Okay boys, time to dust the trail. Load up on what you like to drink and eat, and let's saddle our mounts."

Chapter Sixteen

As dawn broke and the sun peered over peaks to the east, Cal and Pearlie walked their mounts up a narrow mountain trail. It was little more than a path, winding through dense ponderosa pines, with underbrush and small shrubs tugging at their legs on either side.

The air became thinner and colder the higher they climbed, and occasional small flurries of snow fell and dusted their hats and shoulders and their horses.

Cal sighed deeply, sending clouds of fog from his mouth to stir and mix with early morning ground mist still hanging low around them. "I swear, Pearlie," he said, "if'n we climb much higher, we're gonna have to look under rocks and such to find enough air to breathe."

Pearlie shook his head, flinging small flakes of snow off his hat. "Yeah, and we're only 'bout halfway to the top. It's gonna git worse 'fore it gits any better." He coughed as he shivered in his fur-lined coat. The dampness of the mist caused small beads of moisture to form in his moustache, glistening and sparkling in sunlight.

They rounded a bend, where tall pines thinned out into a small clearing next to a sheer drop-off. Pearlie, who was in the lead, leaned sideways and glanced over the edge at a two-hundred-foot drop straight down. His horse, nervous at being so close to the cliff, whinnied loudly and began to sidestep and dance away into the brush on the right side of the trail. "Whoa boy, easy there!" Pearlie cried, sweat popping out on his forehead as he fought his frightened animal.

When he finally had his mount under control, he swung his leg over the cantle and stepped out of his saddle. He spent a moment rubbing the horse's neck to calm its fear. "Cal, we'd better walk our mounts through this narrow place. Mine's actin' a mite skittish."

Cal reined up and jumped to the ground, only a few feet from the precipice. "Yep," he said, "that looks to be one helluva long fall."

Pearlie grunted. "It ain't the fall that kills 'ya, kid. It's the landin' that messes up your innards."

They stood there, looking across snowy mountains and enjoying the view. Emerald-green pines and junipers interspersed and mingled with brilliant, sun-brightened white snow on peaks and in the valleys.

Suddenly, without warning, a piece of bark on a nearby pine tree in front of them exploded with a resounding thump, followed seconds later by a booming echo of a gunshot from trees to their right.

"Holy shit!" yelled Pearlie, as he dove beneath the belly of his snorting, rearing horse. He scrabbled on his hands and knees into nearby bushes, followed closely by Cal.

"Jesus, Pearlie! Someone's shootin' at us!"

Pearlie crouched in thick weeds and grass and small shrubs, looking around, trying to get a fix on where the bullet had come from. "That sounds like a Sharps Big Fifty."

"What's that?" asked Cal, both hands full of Colts.

"It's a buffalo gun," Pearlie said. He sprang from cover and jerked his Henry rifle out of his saddle boot, then hurried back into the brush, panting, his chest heaving as he thumbed a shell into the chamber. "I ain't seen one since Smoke's mountain men friends came to the ranch two year ago. Those old coots are 'bout the onliest ones who still carry 'em."

Dirt next to Cal's boot erupted, spewing a geyser of soil and pine needles into the air, followed again by an explosion that made their ears ring as it reverberated off the mountainside.

A voice called from a distance, "Come on out, boys, or I'll put the next one up your nose."

Fear-sweat dripped off Cal's face and his eyes were wide. "What'll we do now, Pearlie?"

Pearlie swiveled his head, but could see nothing except trees and forest all around them. "Don't look like we have much choice, Cal. That Sharps will cut through this brush like a hot knife through lard." He sighed and laid his Henry on the grass. "Holster them Colts, kid. You can't hit what you can't see."

He stood and raised his hands, stepping into the clearing with the back of his neck tingling. Cal followed, looking around in hopes of catching sight of whoever fired at them.

"Grab some sky, fellers, or I'll ventilate your ribs," the voice cried.

As Cal and Pearlie stood there, hands lifted over their heads, a ghost-like figure appeared out of the mist. He was leading a pinto pony and carrying a rifle that looked to be as long as he was tall.

Cal whispered, "Jumpin' Jiminy." He had never met one of the special breed called mountain men. The oldtimer was clad in buckskin shirt and pants, moccasins, with leggings up to his knees, and wore what appeared to be a beaver-skin hat. His grizzled whiskers were snow white, and his grin revealed yellow stubs of teeth. The barrel of his Sharps ended in a hole that seemed big enough to put a fist in, and it was pointed straight at the two cowboys.

"Howdy gents. Name's Puma Buck." The mountain man's eyes narrowed to slits and his grin faded. "Just what the hell are you two pilgrims doin' up here in my backyard?"

Pearlie smiled with relief, removed his hat and sleeved sweat off his face.

Puma's Sharps moved to aim between his eyes. "Why're you grinnin' like a she-wolf in heat, boy? You starin' death plumb in the face."

"We're right glad to meet up with you, Mr. Buck. I met you 'bout two years ago at Smoke Jensen's ranch, when you and the other mountain men came down to Sugarloaf." He put his hat back on and lowered his hands. "Cal and me work for Smoke, an' we came up here to see if'n we could find him." Pearlie paused a moment, hoping the old man hadn't forgotten the occasion, then continued, "Seems Smoke's got hisself a little problem."

Puma lowered his long rifle and nodded. "I 'member now." He peered closely at Pearlie. "You be the puncher that eats anythin' that ain't tied down."

Pearlie blushed as Puma chuckled. "Smoke spoke right highly of you, boy. Said you was a lot like him when

Preacher took him to raise. Your name be Pearlie, if'n I recollect correctly."

"Yes sir, Mr. Buck."

Puma frowned and gave the men an irritated look. "My name be Puma, boy, but only my daddy was called Mr. Buck." He raised his eyebrows. "So you two pilgrims came traipsin' up here to see if'n you could help Smoke out, huh?"

"Yes sir."

Puma smirked, cocking his head. "'Pears you young'uns don't have much faith that ole Smoke can take care of hisself."

Cal blurted out, "That's not it at all, Mr. Puma! It's jest that there's thirty or more gunslicks on their way here, settin' out to kill Smoke."

Pearlie nodded. "We just figgered a couple more guns wouldn't do no harm."

Puma chuckled. "You boys've got it all wrong. It ain't the number of guns you got with ya' or agin ya' that counts in a business like this. It be what you got deep inside that makes the difference in who rides out and who gits carried out facedown across a horse." He rubbed his whiskers and leaned on his Sharps as he looked out over the mountains. "I been knowin' Smoke since he weren't nothin' more'n a tadpole, and I'm here to tell you boys somethin'. He had fire in his belly and steel in his spine even then."

Puma paused to fire up one of the stogies Smoke had given him. After a few puffs, with smoke trailing out of his nostrils, he continued, "Ole Preacher recognized that fact right off." The mountain wore a dreamy expression on his face as he remembered his old friend. "Preacher was tough and mean as a coon with rabies, but he had a soft spot in him for young'uns." He winked at Cal, "'Specially those with bark on 'em. Smoke must have got some of that particular weakness from his ol' teacher. He tole me the other day he and Sally had taken in a button that would be famouser than him someday." The old-timer smiled around his cigar. "I guess that'd be you be was talkin' 'bout, Cal."

Pearlie smothered a laugh by getting his makings out and rolling a cigarette, while Cal's face turned red as sunset.

"That's why I'm here, Mr. Puma. I owe Smoke an' Sally Jensen 'bout everything a body can, and I aim to pay 'em back by putting as much lead in Sundance Morgan's gang as I'm able."

Puma put his hand on Cal's shoulder. "Now, don't git your fur in a tangle, boy. Everybody was young onc't upon a time. Ain't no shame in bein' green as a new sapling when you's first startin' out." He picked a piece of tobacco off his lip. "Shame is not learnin' from those that can teach ya' what ya' need to know."

He leaned his head to the side and said, "Come on over here and follow me, both of you." He walked twenty yards up the trail and squatted, pointing at the ground. "Reason I shot at you boys wasn't to scare ya' . . ." he paused a moment, with a twinkle in his faded blue eyes, and said, "leastways, not the onliest reason."

He wrapped his gnarled, arthritic hand around a branch lying in the dirt, partially covered with leaves and pine boughs. When he raised it, the men could see where the trail had been dug away and the trap had been set.

"If'n your mounts had stepped on this," he said,

looking a few feet away to the edge of the cliff, "you'd be buzzard bait, splattered all over them rocks down there by now."

Pearlie whistled low under his breath as Puma reset the trap. "I didn't even see that." He looked back over his shoulder at the path they had been on. "It don't look no different from the rest of the trail."

Puma pinched the fire off his cigar and stuffed the rest into his mouth and began to chew. "Hellfire, boy, that's the whole idee! Don't do much good to set a trap fer an animal if'n the critter can see it."

Cal whispered in a hoarse voice, "That don't look like no animal trap to me."

Puma spit tobacco juice into the dirt. "It's fer the most dangerous and cunnin' animal there is, boy. The two-legged kind."

Puma stood up slowly and stretched, as if his old legs had stiffened in the short time he squatted. "Well, I guess if you young'uns are bound and determined to help your friend, the least I can do is make sure you survive long enough to pop a cap or two." Shaking his head in disgust, he climbed into his saddle. "You damn sure don't have enough trail-sense to make it on your own."

He turned his pinto into the woods and trotted off, avoiding the trail, without looking back. He called over his shoulder, "Follow me, boys, if'n you manage it without gittin' yourselves killed."

Puma led the men on a tortuous journey up the mountain. He rarely used trails or paths, winding in and out among trees and underbrush in no discernable pattern. When Cal and Pearlie would think they were at a dead end, Puma would pull a branch aside and there would be an opening just big enough for the horses and men to squeeze through.

Cal whispered, "Jiminy, Pearlie, he must know 'bout every tree and rock on this here mountain. I'd have sworn there weren't no way up this hill 'ceptin' the trail."

Pearlie grunted. "Yeah, but that old man's been roamin' these mountains since long 'fore either one of us was born. He oughta know his way 'round by now."

After two hours of climbing, just when the men thought their horses weren't going to be able to go any longer, Puma led them into a small clearing in front of his cabin. He twisted in his saddle and said, "Here be home, boys. Light and set and I'll git some *cafecito* goin'. Looks like you could use some."

As they stepped off their mounts, Puma disappeared into his lean-to. After a moment, he came out carrying a bag of Arbuckles' coffee and a pot that looked as old as the mountain man, and as black as if it hadn't been cleaned since he bought it.

He filled the pot half full of grounds, added a small amount of water, and hung it from a trestle over the camp-fire coals. Stirring the glowing embers with his moccasin, he threw some dry grass and twigs on top. After a moment, small flames began to flicker and then he added a couple of short logs.

Puma glanced at the sun, dimly visible through the snow-clouds overhead, and said, "Looks close enough to noon fer me to eat. How 'bout you boys?"

Pearlie grinned and rubbed his belly. "Sounds good to me, Mr. Puma. I'm so hungry my stomach thinks my throat's been cut."

Cal shook his head. "Boy, Puma sure had you pegged,

Pearlie. You'd fight a buzzard fer its leavin's if'n you ever missed a . . . which you sure as hell haven't since I've knowed ya'."

Puma raised his eyebrows. "I've got some two-day-old venison in the cabin, which should be okay since it's been so cold lately, or I can rustle up some quail eggs, fatback, and make some pan bread. It's your call, men."

Cal spoke up quickly, "If'n it's all the same to you, Mr. Puma, I'd like some of that venison." He glanced over at his friend. "Pearlie's a fine cook an' all, but I'm gittin' a mite tired of fatback and biscuits."

Pearlie frowned. "You sure as hell didn't seem to mind when it came time to dish it outta the pan, least not so's I noticed when ya' piled it so high it took both your hands to lift your plate."

Puma chuckled. "You boys make me miss havin' a woman 'round to jaw at." He rubbed his whiskers, "Huh, must be goin' on ten years or more since my last squaw died on me."

Cal's forehead wrinkled. "How'd she die, Mr. Puma? Killed by outlaws?"

"Naw, nothin' like that. Was in the middle of winter, and she got outta the blankets to go an' heat us up some coffee. One of those high-mountain squalls blew in kinda sudden-like, an' next thing I knowed, she was froze solid, squattin' in front of the fire with the coffeepot in her hand."

Pearlie said, "Jesus, that musta been awful."

With a twinkle in his eye, Puma nodded. "Yeah, it was. I had to wait fer the spring thaw to git the coffeepot outta her hand 'fore I could use it." He grinned, "It's a long winter without *cafecito,* let me tell ya'."

It was only when he laughed and slapped his knee

that the men knew he was funning with them. He went into the cabin to get the deer meat, and Pearlie jabbed Cal in the side with his elbow. "I knowed he was havin' us on all the time."

Cal laughed, "Sure you did, Pearlie, sure you did."

The men all pitched in to cook lunch. Cal peeled some wild potatoes and cleaned the dirt off onions Puma had in a burlap sack, and Pearlie poured coffee all around while Puma put the venison on a spit to heat it up.

Cal dumped the potatoes and onions in a pot to boil, then took a drink of coffee Pearlie handed him. After sucking in his breath and swallowing a couple of times, he said, "That's some bellywash."

Puma sipped his coffee and sighed. "Just 'bout right, I reckon." He looked over at Pearlie. "I wouldn't leave it in the cup too long, boy. It's liable to eat its way through the tin."

He drew one of the largest knives Cal and Pearlie had ever seen out of his scabbard and sliced off hunks of steaming meat and piled it on their plates, then speared potatoes and onions and added them to the venison. "Dig in men, 'fore the flies and mosquitoes carry it off."

As they ate, Cal said, "Mr. Puma, Pearlie's been tellin' me some stories 'bout when Smoke was first up here, when he was with Preacher."

Puma nodded. "Those were the good days. The only law up here then was the law a man carried in his holster or in his saddle boot. The rivers was full of beaver, the woods was full of wolves an' grizzlies, and the plains was full of Injuns. Hell, if'n I saw another white man more'n twice a year, I'd move 'cause the area was gittin' too civilized."

Pearlie spoke up. "I was tellin' Cal 'bout how Smoke went after Potter, Stratton, and Richards, the men who killed his brother and stole the Confederates' gold."

Puma held a large piece of deer meat in both hands, chewing it as fast as his stubby teeth would allow. "Yep. That was a right smart fracas, all right."

"Can you tell me about how he got 'em, Puma?"

The old man looked up, over his venison, and grinned. "Soon's I finish this here meat, boy. Never could eat 'an talk at the same time."

CHAPTER SEVENTEEN

The three men sat around the campfire eating quietly, enjoying their meal. Occasional small flurries of snow fell, hissing and crackling in the flames, while frigid mountain air ruffled fringe on the old man's buckskin shirt and caused the younger men to hunch their shoulders in their heavy coats.

Pearlie noticed the mountain man didn't seem to mind the cold. His blood must be as thick as molasses after all these years up here in the high lonesome, he thought.

Puma finished his venison, wiped his greasy hands on his buckskin shirt, and fished out a stogie out of his pocket. He lit it with a burning twig from the fire and laid back against a log, coffee tin in one hand and cigar in the other.

"That were the last battle fer some of ol' friends, Dupre, Greybull, and the midget, Audie. They'd come out of the mountains to help their friend, Preacher, and his young boy, Smoke, to git his revenge. T'was near the town of Bury, but the final fight took place at an ol' ghost town, name of Slate."

He took a few pulls on the cigar, getting it going just right, then sipped his coffee and began his tale.

* * *

The ever-shrinking band of outlaws and gunhands looked toward the west. Another cloud of black smoke filled the air.

Lansing began cursing. "How in the hell are those old men doin' it?" he yelled. "We're fightin' a damned bunch of ghosts."

"Are you stayin' or leavin'?" Stratton asked.

"Might as well see it through," the man said bitterly. Those were the last words he would speak. A Sharps barked, its big slug taking the rancher in the center of his chest, knocking him spinning from his saddle.

"I've had it!" a gunhand said. He spun his horse and rode away. A dozen men followed him. No one tried to stop them.

"Look around us," Brown said.

The riders examined the land. A mile away, in a semi-circle, ten mountain men sat their ponies. As if on signal, the mountain men lifted their rifles high above their heads.

Turkel, one of the most feared gunhawks in the territory, looked the situation over through field glasses. "That there's Preacher," he said, pointing. "That 'un over yonder is the Frenchman, Dupre, The one ridin' a mule is Greybull. That little bitty shithead is the midget, Audie. Boys, I don't want no truck with them old men. I'm tellin' you all flat-out."

The aging mountain men began waving their rifles.

"What are they tryin' to tell us?" Reese asked.

"That Smoke is waitin' in the direction they're pointing,"

Richards said. "They're telling us to tangle with him—if we've got the sand in us to do it."

Potter did some fast counting. Out of what was once a hundred and fifty men, only nineteen remained, including himself. "Hell, boys! He's only one man. There's nineteen of us!"

"There was about this many over at that minin' camp, too," Britt said. "Way I see it is this, we either fight ten of them ringtailed-tooters, or we fight Smoke Jensen."

"I'll take Smoke," Howard said. But he wasn't all that happy with his choice.

The mountain men began moving, tightening the circle. The gunhands turned their horses and moved out, allowing themselves to be pushed toward the west.

"They're pushin' us toward the ghost town," Williams said.

Richards smiled at Smoke's choice of a showdown spot.

As the abandoned town appeared on the horizon, located on flats between the Lemhi River and the Beaverhead Range, Turkel's buddy, Harris, reined up and pointed. "Goddamn place is full of people!"

"Miners," Brown said. "They come to see the show. Drinking and betting. Them mountain men spread the word."

"Just like it was at the camp on the Uncompahgre," Richards said with a grunt.

"Check your weapons. Stuff your pockets full of extra shells. I'm going back to talk with Preacher. I want to see how this deal is going down."

Richards rode back to the mountain men, riding with one hand in the air.

"That there's far enough," Lobo said. "Speak your piece."

"We win this fight, do we have to fight you men, too?"

"No," Preacher said quickly. "My boy Smoke done laid down rules."

His *boy*! Richards thought. Jesus God. "We win, do we get to stay in this part of the country?"

"If'n you win," Preacher said, "you leave with what you got on your backs. If'n we win, we pass the word, and here 'tis. If'n you or any of your people ever come west of Kansas, you dead men. That clear?"

"You're a hard man, Preacher."

"You wanna see just how hard?" Preacher challenged.

"No," Richards said, shaking his head. "We'll take chances with Smoke."

"You would be better off taking your chances with us," Audie suggested.

Richards looked at Nighthawk. "What do have to say about it?"

Nighthawk made no sound.

Richards looked pained.

"That means haul your ass back to your friends," Phew said.

Richards trotted his horse back to what was left of his band. He told them the rules of engagement.

Britt looked uphill toward a crumbling store. "There he is."

Smoke stood alone on the rotted boardwalk. The men could see his twin .44's belted around his waist. He held a

Henry repeating rifle in his right hand, a double-barreled express gun in his left hand. Smoke ducked into the building, leaving only a slight bit of dust to signal where he once stood.

"Two groups of six," Richards said, "one group of three, one group of four. Britt, take your men in from the rear. Turkel, take your boys in from the east. Reese, take your people in from the west. I'll take my hands in from this direction. Move out."

Smoke had removed his spurs, hanging them on the saddle horn of Drifter. As soon as he ducked out of sight, he ran from the building, staying in the alley. He stashed his express gun on one side of the street in an old store, his rifle across the road. He met up with Skinny Davis first, in the gloom of what had once been a saloon.

"Draw!" Davis hissed, hunkering down.

Smoke cleared leather and put two holes in the gunman's chest before Davis could cock his .44's. The thunder from his Colts echoed across the valley.

"In Pat's Saloon!" someone shouted farther down the street.

Williams jumped through an open, glassless window of the saloon. Just as his boots hit the floor, Smoke shot him, his .44 slug knocking the gunslick back out the window to the boardwalk. Williams was hurt, but not out of it yet. He crawled along the side of the building, one arm broken and dangling, useless, blood pouring from a gaping bullet wound in his shoulder.

"Smoke Jensen!" Cross yelled. "You ain't got the guts to face me!"

"That's one way of putting it," Smoke muttered savagely, taking careful aim and shooting the outlaw, feeling his pistol slam into his palm. A ball of lead struck Cross in the stomach, doubling him over and dropping him to the weed-grown, dusty road.

The miners had hightailed it to ridges surrounding the town. There they sat, drinking and betting and cheering. The mountain men stood and squatted and sat on an opposite ridge, watching.

A bullet dug a trench along a plank, sending tiny splinters flying, a few of them striking Smoke's face, stinging and bringing a few drops of blood from his cheeks.

Smoke ran out the back of the saloon and came face-to-face with Simpson, a gunhawk with both hands filled with .44's.

Smoke pulled the trigger on his own .44's, the double hammerblows of lead taking Simpson in his lower chest, slamming him to the ground, dying from two mortal wounds.

Quickly reloading, Smoke grabbed up Simpson's guns and tucked them behind his gun belt. He ran down the alley. The last of Richards's gunslicks stepped out of a gaping doorway just as Smoke cut to his right, leaping through an open window. A bullet burned Smoke's shoulder. Spinning, he fired both Colts, one bullet striking Martin in his throat, the second taking the gunnie just above his nose, almost tearing off the upper part of his right cheek.

Smoke caught a glimpse of someone running. He

dropped to one knee and fired. His slug shattered Rogers's hip, sending the big man sprawling in the dirt, howling and cursing. Reese spurred his horse and charged the building where Smoke was crouched. He smashed his horse's shoulder against a thin plank door and thundered in. The horse, wild-eyed and scared, lost its footing and fell, pinning Reese to the floor, crushing his belly and chest. Reese screamed in agony as blood filled his mouth and darkness clouded his eyes.

Smoke left the dying man and ran out a side door.

"Get him, Turkel!" Brown shouted.

Smoke glanced up. Turkel was on the roof of an old building, a rifle in his hand. Smoke flattened against a building as Turkel pulled the trigger, the slug plowing up dirt at Smoke's feet. Smoke snapped off a shot, getting lucky as the bullet hit the gunhand in his chest. Turkel dropped the rifle and fell to the street, crashing down to a rotted section of boardwalk. He did not move.

A bullet from nowhere nicked a small part of Smoke's right ear. Blood poured down the side of his face. He ran to the spot where he had hidden his shotgun, grabbing it and cocking it just as the door frame filled with men.

Firing both barrels, Smoke cleared the doorway of all living things, including Britt, Harris, and Smith, buckshot knocking men off the boardwalk, leaving them dead and dying in the street.

"Goddamn you, Jensen!" Brown screamed in rage, stepping out into the empty roadway.

Smoke dropped his shotgun and picked up a bloody rifle from the doorway. He aimed quickly and fired, catching

Brown in the stomach. Brown jerked and fell to the street, both hands holding his stomach.

Rogers leveled a pistol and fired, his bullet ricocheting off a support post, a chunk of lead striking Smoke's left leg, dropping him to the boardwalk. Smoke ended Roger's life with a single shot to his head.

White-hot pain lanced through Smoke's side as Williams shot him from behind. Smoke toppled off the boards, turning as he fell. He fired twice, his bullets taking Williams in the neck, causing Williams's head to twist at an unnatural angle.

Smoke scrambled painfully to his feet, grabbing a fallen scattergun with blood on the barrel. He checked the shotgun, then quickly examined his wounds. Bleeding, but not serious. Williams's slug had gone through the fleshy part of his side. Using the point of his knife, Smoke picked out a tiny piece of lead from Rogers's gun and tied a bandanna around the slight wound. He slipped farther into the darkness of the building as spurs jingled in an alley at the rear of the old store. Smoke thumbed back both hammers on the coach gun. He waited.

The spurs jingled once more. Smoke followed the sound with both barrels of the express gun. Carefully, silently, he slipped across the floor to a wall fronting the alley. He could hear heavy breathing somewhere in front of him.

He pulled both triggers, the charge blowing a bucket-sized hole in the weathered plank wall.

The gunslick was blown across the alley, hurled against an outhouse. The outhouse collapsed, while the gunhand fell into a pit where the outhouse had been.

Silently, Smoke reloaded the shotgun, then reloaded his own .44s and the ones taken from the dead gunman. He listened as Fenerty called for help from his companions.

There was no reply.

Fenerty was the last gunhawk left.

Smoke located the voice, just across the road in a decaying building. Laying aside the shotgun, he picked up a rifle and emptied its magazine into the storefront, explosions ending a brief moment of silence. Fenerty came staggering out, shot in chest and belly. He died facedown in a corpse-littered street.

"All right, you bastards!" Smoke yelled to Richards, Potter, and Stratton. "Holster your guns and step out where I can see you. Face me, if you've got the guts."

The sharp odor of sweat mingling with blood and gunsmoke filled the still summer air as four men walked out into the sunshine.

Richards, Potter, and Stratton stood at one end of the town. A tall, blood-smeared figure stood at the other. All their guns were in leather.

"You son of a bitch!" Stratton screamed, his voice as high-pitched as a woman's. "You ruined it all." He clawed for his .44.

Smoke drew and fired before Stratton's pistol could clear leather. Potter grabbed for his Colt. Smoke shot him dead, gunshots echoing off empty buildings, then he holstered his gun, waiting.

Richards had not moved. He stood with a faint smile on his lips, staring at Smoke.

"You ready to die?" Smoke asked, a sardonic grin creasing his face.

"As ready as I'll ever be, I reckon," Richards replied. There was no fear in his voice. His hands appeared steady. "Janey gone?"

"Took your money and pulled out."

"Been a long run, hasn't it, Jensen?"

"It's just about over now."

"What happens to all our holdings?"

"I don't care what happens to the mines. The miners can have them. I'm giving all your stock to decent, hard-working punchers and homesteaders. They've earned it."

A puzzled look spread over Richards's face. "I don't understand. You did . . . all this," he waved his hand, "for nothing?"

Someone moaned, the sound coming from up the street.

"I did it for my pa, my brother, my wife, and my baby son."

"But it won't bring them back!"

"I know."

"I wish I'd never heard the name Jensen."

"You'll never hear it again after this day, Richards."

"One way to find out," Richards said with a smile. He drew his Colt and fired. He was snake-quick, but hurried his shot, lead digging up dirt at Smoke's feet.

Smoke shot him in the right shoulder, spinning the gunman around. Richards grabbed for his lefthand gun and Smoke fired again, his slug striking Richards in the left side of his chest. He struggled to bring up his Colt. He managed to cock it before Smoke's third shot struck him in his belly. Richards sat down hard in the bloody dirt. He toppled over on his side and died instantly.

Smoke looked up at the ridge where the mountain men were gathered.

They were leaving as silently as the wind.

Puma finished his cigar at the same time he finished his story. He flicked it into the fire and stared silently at the flames, remembering his old friends and their last battle.

A voice called from the edge of the forest, startling the three men. "You boys believe anything that old coot has to say and you'll be sorry."

Smoke grinned and walked into the clearing, a Colt in each fist hanging at his side. "I heard you had company, Puma, so I slipped up here to see if they were friendly."

Cal and Pearlie both jumped to their feet and slapped Smoke on the back and shoulders. "Boy are we glad to see you, Smoke. We came up here lookin' for ya', to see if we could help out against Sundance and his gang," blurted Cal in a rush of words.

Smoke raised one eyebrow. "Uh-huh, and you end up listening to that old coot over there, the ugliest living mountain man in all Colorado Territory, tell you some of his lies."

Puma frowned. "Weren't no lies, Smoke Jensen." He paused and grinned at his friend. "Leastways, not too many anyway."

Smoke threw his arm around Puma's shoulder and said to his punchers, "Boys, would you run up that trail, just over the next ridge, and fetch me the buckboard I left back yonder?"

As Cal and Pearlie turned to go, Smoke added, "Oh, and be careful, it's got a couple of women in it who've had a hard time."

After the Aldritch women were brought to Puma's cabin and were given some venison and coffee, Smoke asked Pearlie if he would escort them down to Big Rock to see Doc Spalding.

Pearlie raised his eyebrows. "What about Cal?"

"I reckon be can stay up here for a while. Maybe Puma can teach him some trail-craft while I set my traps and prepare for the arrival of Sundance and his gang."

"But Smoke," Pearlie said, obviously not wanting to leave his friends.

Smoke held up his hand. "No buts, Pearlie. You know Cal can't manage that buckboard by himself, and you can. Now, the sooner you get gone, the sooner you can get back up here." He paused, then said, "I wouldn't want you to miss all the excitement."

Pearlie grinned. "Yes sir, Smoke. I'm on my way already."

Both the Aldritch women thanked Smoke, causing him to blush mightily. "You tell Doc Spalding to give you anything you need," he called to them, as Pearlie drove the wagon away.

Puma shook his head and spit into the campfire. "I ain't never had so much company at one time in all my born days. It's gettin' too damned crowded around here."

Chapter Eighteen

Sundance Morgan reined in his mount and sat with his palms resting on his saddle horn, staring ahead through the heat waves and dust devils on the trail, thinking about what lay before him. His gang pulled their horses to a halt and they gathered around him. The animals' sides heaved and they shook sweat from their necks, exhausted from the ride. El Gato took a long pull from his canteen, wiped his moustache with the back of his hand, and asked, "Señor Sundance, why we stop?"

Sundance removed his hat and sleeved trail dust and sweat off his forehead. "Just over that next ridge is the town of Big Rock. I'm decidin' how we should handle it."

Perro Muerte grinned, his brass tooth gleaming in the sunlight. He pulled a Colt from his holster and held it up, barrel pointed at the sky. "This be one way. It sure to get their attention."

Sundance frowned. "I don't think so, not just yet. I believe we oughta just ride in, peaceable as can be, and get the lay of the land first." He put his hat back on and settled it low. His eyes sparkled with hatred and remembered shame. "Then, if we don't get what we want, we'll have some fun and do some damage."

He spurred his bronc, and the others followed, raising a cloud of dust in still, dry air.

Matt and Timmy O'Leary, thirteen- and fourteen-year-old brothers, pulled their ponies up in front of Sheriff Monte Carson's jail in Big Rock.

"Sheriff Carson, Sheriff Carson, come quick," the younger boy cried from his saddle.

Monte stepped to the door of the jail, pipe in one hand and cup of coffee in the other. "Okay boys, calm down and tell me what's got you so riled up."

Matt, the older of the two, pointed over his shoulder toward the city limits. "Big cloud of dust, 'bout five or six miles out of town. Looks like it might be that gang we was watchin' for."

Monte's eyes narrowed as he looked south. "You boys did good. Ride on down to the blacksmith shop and ring the fire bell like we planned. That'll let everyone know the time has come."

"Gee, Mr. Carson, you're gonna let us ring the bell?"

Monte smiled. "Sure. You gave the warning, so you get to ring the bell. Tell Smitty I told you to do it. He'll understand." He pointed with the stem of his pipe. "Afterwards, you get your butts on home and stay off the street 'til I tell you it's okay to come out."

"Sure thing, Sheriff. Let's go, Timmy. I'll let you ring it first, then it's my turn." The rode off, kicking their ponies to a gallop.

Monte took a deep drag on his pipe, then he spoke to his deputy. "Jim, looks like it's about that time. Hand me my Greener, will ya'? We got to get to our stations as soon as we can."

Monte took his ten-gauge scattergun from Jim and sat in his chair on the boardwalk in front of the jail. He put his coffee cup down, loosened the rawhide thongs to his Colts, and leaned his chair back against the wall. He placed the Greener across his lap, both hammers jacked back, stuck his pipe in his mouth, and waited. I hope we're doing the right thing, he thought, worrying about what could happen to his town.

Louis Longmont drew three cards to a pair of queens. As he spread them out, he noticed he had drawn two sevens and another queen. Other than a shallow breath, he displayed no emotion at all over his good fortune. He picked up his cigar and fingered a stack of chips, ready to bet his hand, when he heard the fire bell begin to ring.

He rolled his eyes and swore softly to himself. Yet another reason to hate Sundance Morgan. He flipped the pasteboards to the table facedown and said to the man seated across from him, "Your pot, James. Game's over."

Coming to his feet, he motioned to his barkeeper and the women around his saloon to take their places. Two of the girls took small belly-guns out of their handbags and sat at tables on either side of the batwings. His young waiter took an old shotgun with rusted barrels off a rack and went upstairs, finding a spot next to a window overlooking the street below. Jonathan, the barkeep, put a .44 Colt in his waistband behind his back and stood, wiping the bar with a rag and whistling to himself.

Louis drew his pistol and opened the loading gate, spinning the cylinder to check his loads. After he finished, he holstered his gun and called, "André. Come out here please."

When the chef appeared, apron tied around his ample stomach, Louis said, "André, under no circumstances are you to come out of the kitchen. Do you understand?"

"But sir," André answered, "I want to do my part. What if you get shot? What will I do?"

Louis smiled. "André, the world can easily do without a gambler and roustabout like me, but civilization can ill afford to lose a master chef of your talent. Believe me, I will not abide you risking your life in this matter." Louis hesitated, sniffing the air. "Now, if my nose does not deceive me, you have a soufflé in the oven that needs your immediate attention."

André smiled at the compliment and departed to his beloved kitchen, swaggering as he walked away.

Sundance rode into Big Rock, his men spread out behind him, riding six abreast, forty-three men in all. They were a rough bunch and he knew it. All wore their guns tied down low, and most carried rifles or shotguns braced upright on their thighs or lying across saddle horns.

Something is terribly wrong in this place, he thought. He had ridden through dozens of Western towns in his years on the owlhoot trail. Some were big, and some small enough to throw a stone from one end to the other, but none was like this one. There were no people on the streets, no children or dogs, and no cowboys on horseback or folks in buckboards loading supplies.

George Stalking Horse spurred his mount up to trot side by side with Sundance. "Boss," he said out of the corner of his mouth, eyes narrowed and suspicious. "I'm beginnin' to feel like Custer must have felt ridin' into Little Bighorn."

"I know the feeling, George. Something ain't right here, that's for sure." Sundance looked to one side as they neared the jail, and saw the only sign of life in town. A man was sitting, his chair tilted back and legs outstretched on the hitching rail. His pipe was emitting a thin trail of smoke, and his hand was on the shotgun in his lap.

Bull, riding on Sundance's other side, whispered, "Boss, take a peek at his short-guns."

Sundance turned and saw the rawhide thongs pulled back from the hammers of a pair of Colts. He gritted his jaw. He didn't like the looks of things.

Pulling his mount to a halt, he thumbed his hat back and grinned at the man with a badge pinned to his shirt, the effort hurting his lips. "Howdy, Sheriff. How're things?"

The lawman raised his head, glaring at the riders from under his hat brim. "Hello, Sundance. Things are just fine. How about with you?"

Sundance was startled when the sheriff called him by name, and suddenly he realized that meant he probably had known they were on the way and the reason for his visit. He remembered the sheriff's name. "Tolerable, Sheriff. Carson's your handle, ain't it?"

Carson let his chair fall forward until all four legs were on the porch. While doing so, he slowly let the barrel of the shotgun lean over until it pointed directly at Sundance's belly. "Yep. I'm honored that you remember." He laughed derisively, low in his throat. "Last time you was here, you left in such a rush, I didn't get to give you your ear back."

Sundance sucked in his breath and his face blanched at the insult. His hand twitched and hovered over his Colt, but the end of the Greener never wavered an inch, and Carson's eyes burned a hole in his face.

Carson continued, a smirk on his lips. "I tried to save it for you, but a dog ate it before I could get to it."

Sundance did his best to bridle his temper. Those twin barrels of the scattergun looked like cannons. "Speakin' of that incident, Sheriff, where is Smoke Jensen these days? I'd kinda like to pay him a visit." His voice broke when he spoke, making him even more angry that he'd lost control.

Carson said, "I know you'd like to pay him a social call, Sundance, but I bet he'll like it a bunch more'n you will." He tilted his head toward the mountains. "He heard you were coming, so he went up into the high lonesome to wait for you. Said to give you his regards, and to tell you he'd be somewhere close to that tall peak to the east." Carson spat on the ground, as if talking to the gunman gave him a bad taste in his mouth. "Course, don't none of us who know you think you'll have the guts to go up after him." He glanced at the assortment of riders behind Sundance. "No matter how many men you have backin' you up."

Sundance turned his horse to face Carson and leaned forward in the saddle. "You know, Sheriff Carson," he muttered, venom in his voice, "you shouldn't let your mouth overrun your ass. I got over forty men with me here, and you got . . . what? Two shots in that express gun of yours?"

Carson continued to smile insolently at the outlaw. "I'm not worried. You see, the first barrel, the one on the right here, is loaded with buckshot. That's for you. I figger there won't be enough of you left to fill a coffee cup after I unload on your belly." His smile turned to a snarl when he saw sweat running down Sundance's cheeks, staining the bandanna around his neck. "The second barrel, the one on the left is also loaded with buckshot, but it's for that big, stupid-looking gent ridin' next to you, the one with the jug-handle ears."

Bull's eyes widened, and his hands clenched and un-clenched in helpless anger. He knew that if he drew, he'd be dead before he cleared leather. In his high, woman's voice, he spat, "What about the rest of these men, Sheriff? They'll kill you where you sit, before you reach for those pistols."

Carson laughed, infuriating Sundance even more, but clearly making the rest of his gang edgy. What was this man so confident about? Sundance wondered. He was facing forty men with guns.

"We've been ready," Carson said, continuing to chuckle over Bull's voice. He yawned elaborately, covering it with the back of his hand. "You asked about the rest of your men?" He put two fingers in his mouth and whistled shrilly.

Doorways all along the street filled with citizens armed to the teeth with rifles, shotguns, and pistols. Heads popped up on roofs and behind eaves and elevated storefronts, and gun-toting men appeared in alleys and between buildings.

From behind, Sundance heard a deep voice say, "Hey, back-shooter, remember me?"

Sundance twisted in his saddle to glance over his shoulder. He saw a tall, slim man, dressed in a black split-tail coat and a ruffle-front shirt, with two Colts slung low on his hips. Then he recognized him as Louis Longmont, hands hanging at his sides, fingers flexing in anticipation.

"That's correct, Lester Morgan, I'm calling you a coward," Louis shrugged his shoulders minutely, then the gambler proceeded to give the outlaw a solid cussing.

Sundance cursed under his breath, looking wildly around at all the townspeople and their guns. "Now's not the time, Longmont," he answered hoarsely, trying to control his jittery horse.

Longmont spread his arms. "When is the proper time for you, coward? How about those sons-of-whores who ride with you? Are they chickenshit like you? Don't any of you *men* have any balls?" he added sarcastically.

Several of the men on horseback yelled and cursed and drew their weapons, unable to take the insults any longer. Sundance held up his hands, trying to stop them, warning it was a trick, but his men were too angry to listen.

The street erupted with the sound of gunfire, booming and echoing off buildings while both men and horses screamed, some hit hard by flying lead. Clouds of gunsmoke billowed away from flaming gun barrels, filling the town with deafening noise.

Carson's scattergun exploded as he pulled both triggers and rolled out of his chair, scrambling quickly behind a nearby water trough. His shot cut one of the outlaws almost in half, blowing him out of his saddle.

Bull filled his hands with iron, sawed-off shotguns both firing at Carson, molten buckshot tearing into the water trough, sending water and splinters into the air. Pellets penetrated the wood to lodge in Carson's left arm and shoulder, knocking him backward. He grunted in pain and rolled on his side, clawing for his Colts.

Sundance leaned over his horse's neck and spurred hell-for-leather down the street, firing twice at Louis as he galloped by. One of his slugs took Louis's hat off, the other burning a path across his waist, cutting a shallow gouge in his flesh.

Louis did not flinch from the pain, standing calmly while he took careful aim, firing both his Colts at Sundance, one after the other. Shots came so fast they sounded like one continuous explosion. One of his .44 bullets sliced a chunk out of Sundance's butt, the only target he gave Louis as he spurred away. Sundance screamed in pain and dropped his Colt to grab his ass, although he managed to stay in his saddle.

Bull, his shotguns empty, reined his horse into an alleyway, hitting a man with the animal's shoulder, knocking him to the dirt. Bull jumped off his mount and grabbed the stunned man's rifle, then stood over him and shot him in the head. Wheeling, he grabbed his saddle horn in one huge hand and made a running vault onto the galloping horse's back. As he rode out of town, he fired the rifle one-handed at a figure silhouetted in a window, showering him with bits of glass and splinters, missing his target.

Perro Muerte was having his own troubles. Wounded in the arm and thigh in the initial volley of gunfire, his horse shot out from under him, he was kneeling in the dusty street, firing his Colt at anything that moved. When his hammers clicked on empty chambers, he reached down into the bloody mess that had been the man Carson blew to pieces. He picked up a blood-splattered rifle and wheeled around. A member of the gang, Charley Wilson, was riding by, firing pistols with both hands. Without hesitation, Perro Muerte swung the rifle in a horizontal arc, slamming Wilson backwards out of his saddle and shattering his jaw. Perro Muerte got lucky and managed to grab the mount's reins. Dropping his rifle, he stepped into the saddle and clung to the frightened animal's side for dear life as it galloped down the street.

Slim Johnson didn't have to worry about returning to New Mexico and being hanged. As he was riding out of town, firing over his shoulder, one of the ladies who sang in the church choir stepped out of a doorway, leveled her husband's Henry repeating rifle, and blew him to hell. The bullet entered the killer's left ear and exited his right, taking most of the side of his head with it. Johnson was dead before his body hit the ground, to bounce and tumble in the dirt like a rag doll.

As Toothpick spurred down the street, ducking and leaning to the side to avoid bullets, he saw Louis standing on the boardwalk shooting at Sundance. Toothpick drew his long knife from its scabbard and threw it at Louis with all his might as he passed. He laughed with delight when he saw the blade embed itself in Louis's chest, knocking him backward. He fell on the boardwalk.

The battle of Big Rock lasted only a few minutes, but

when it was over, twelve desperados lay dead or dying. Three townspeople were killed and six were wounded.

Monte Carson got to his knees, his Colts and express gun empty, and peered through the gunsmoke, nose wrinkling at the smell of cordite and blood and voided bowels. Moaning, crying, and pleas for help echoed down the street, but his attention was drawn to his friend, Louis, whose body he could see lying on the boards with a knife stuck in his chest.

"Oh no! God don't let this be," Monte cried as he stumbled and limped painfully around the bodies of men and horses, running to see if he was too late to help.

He bent over the body and grabbed Louis's shoulders, blood from his own wounds dripping onto his friend's chest. "Louis, Louis, can you hear me?" he yelled, shaking the unconscious man.

Slowly, after a moment, a hand came up and touched Monte on the shoulder. "Of course I can hear you, Monte. I'm wounded, not deaf."

"What . . . ?"

Louis grabbed Monte's arm and pulled himself to a sitting position. He grunted and jerked the knife out of his chest, then reached into his coat and removed a sterling silver flask with a knife hole in it. "Damn," he said with feeling, as amber liquid spilled in the dirt, "that was twelve-year-old scotch."

Monte grinned and sat down hard next to the gambler. "Well, Louis," he rasped though a raw throat, "how'd we do?"

Louis glanced at the number of bullet-ridden bodies lying in the street. "This town did fine, my old friend, just fine."

He gazed toward mountain peaks in the distance. "The rest is up to Smoke Jensen."

CHAPTER NINETEEN

Pearlie heard booming echoes of shotguns and higher pitched cracks and pops of short guns being fired in the distance while he was still several miles from Big Rock.

Jessica Aldritch, sitting next to him on the buckboard seat, cocked her head. The sky at these lower altitudes was a brilliant azure blue with small puffs of white clouds scattered from horizon to horizon like tufts of cotton waiting to be picked.

"Mr. Pearlie, what is that noise? It sounds like thunder, but I don't see any storm clouds."

Pearlie's eyes narrowed, a frown on his face. "'Tweren't thunder, Mrs. Aldritch. That there was gunfire . . . a lot of it, and it's coming from Big Rock:

"Big Rock? Isn't that where we're going?"

"Yes ma'am."

"Do you think it might be Indians?"

"Not likely, ma'am. What few Injuns we got left 'round here might attack a small party if they was hungry enough, but there ain't hardly a band anywhere in these parts big enough to try to take on a whole town."

He shook his head, torn between his desire to whip the

horses into a gallop and rush to help his friends in town, and his duty to protect the two women Smoke had entrusted to his care.

He hesitated a moment, unsure how much he should tell the widows about their present situation. He drew back on the reins and brought their wagon to a halt.

Aileen Aldritch, bundled in back under bearskins and wrapped in a buffalo robe Pearlie borrowed from Puma Buck, raised her head and looked around, a dazed expression on her face. She was not yet fully recovered from the ordeal she had endured at the hands of the men at the mine. "Jessica, why are we stopping? Have we arrived at our destination already?"

Jessica twisted in her seat. "No, Mamma Aldritch." She looked at Pearlie with a quizzical expression. "Mr. Pearlie is just giving the horses a rest. You go on back to sleep. We'll wake you when we get there."

Pearlie sat still, reins in his hands, forehead wrinkled in thought, considering his options. Finally, he decided his best course of action was to relate his concerns to Jessica.

"Mrs. Aldritch, I think those gunshots are from a band of desperados, a bad bunch from down South."

"You mean outlaws?"

"Yes, ma'am. We got word a couple of weeks ago they was on their way up here from Texas. They're lookin' fer Smoke Jensen, and intend to kill him."

"They want to kill Mr. Jensen? But . . . why?"

Pearlie shook his head in exasperation. He knew they didn't have much time. "It's a long story, ma'am. I'll tell ya' later, when I git you two to town safe and sound." He looked around, trying to find a suitable place to hide the buckboard and women.

"Trouble is, if'n those men survive the fightin' in town, they're gonna be comin' this way, headed up into the high country lookin' fer Smoke."

Jessica's eyes widened. "Oh, I see. You're concerned that if they see us, they might do us some harm."

Pearlie nodded, lips drawn tight. "You can near 'bout count on it, ma'am. Those men are some of the low-downest, meanest God ever put on this earth." He peered into her eyes, not wanting to frighten her, but knew he had to make her aware of the danger they were in. "If they see us," he said quietly, "they'll kill us sure." He hesitated, "At least, they'll kill me. I 'spect they'll have other plans fer you and mamma-in-law."

She put her hand to her mouth, face blanching at his implication. "Oh dear God!"

He touched her shoulder. "Not to worry, ma'am, they got to find us first." He surveyed the area again, eyes flicking back and forth.

They were near the boundary of the forest. Another quarter mile and they would be on the plains surrounding Big Rock, wide, sweeping expanses of short grass with no cover to conceal them.

He pulled hard on the reins, turning the team in a wide circle, and headed back the way they had come. After a hundred yards he came to an overgrown path leading off the main trail to the east. It wasn't much more than a mule trace, once used by miners to pack supplies from town up to their camps on the upper peaks.

It would be a tight fit, but he thought they might just be able to squeeze through the narrow spots.

He leaned over and whispered in Jessica's ear, "It's gonna git a mite bumpy. Why don't you git in the back with your mamma and help hold her while I try to git us outta sight?"

She nodded, and without another word scrambled into the rear of the wagon to wrap her arms around Aileen. "Mamma Aldritch, Mr. Pearlie is going to take a shortcut through the forest. Hold onto me, dear, because it may get a trifle rough."

Slowly, harness horses whinnying and shaking their heads in protest, he drove them up the path, holding his reins in one hand and the side of the buckboard with the other to keep from being thrown off as it tilted and rocked over rocks and mud holes along the trail. Branches scratched along the sides of the wagon, and twice he had to climb down and clear piles of brush and deadfall out of the way.

When he had gone a half-mile deeper into the piney woods, he pulled the team to a halt. Reaching behind the seat, he grabbed his Henry repeating rifle and jumped to the ground.

"I'm goin' back down the road to cover our back trail." He paused. "If'n anything happens, an' I don't come back . . ." He turned, pointing down the mountain, "Big Rock is 'bout three or four miles in that direction. Just unhitch the horses and ride on in." He smiled reassuringly. "Folks there'll take good care of you."

Jessica nodded. "Mr. Pearlie, don't you worry about us. We're miners' wives, we can take care of ourselves. But," she looked into his eyes, worry evident, "you be careful, you hear? We don't want anything to happen to you on our account."

"Oh, I'll be careful as a tomcat in a roomful of rockin' chairs, Mrs. Aldritch. An' I'll be back for you, I promise."

He turned, drew his knife from its scabbard, and cut a low-hanging branch off a nearby pine tree. Using it like a broom, he backed down the path, sweeping dirt with the branch to obliterate any signs of their passage.

When he got to a turn off the mountain trail, he piled dead branches and bushes over his wagon tracks, hiding them from sight. Finally satisfied the buckboard's prints were erased as well as they could be in such a short time, he walked to a bald knob and looked back toward Big Rock. Shading his eyes with his hand, he could see a dark blot of men on horseback in the distance, riding hard toward the mountain and raising a sizable dust cloud.

He moved a hundred yards farther up the trail and slipped into the forest, hiding himself behind a large bush. He worked the lever on his Henry, jacking a shell into the chamber, and loosened the thongs on his Colts. He intended to fire on the group only as a last resort, if they looked like they were about to find the road they had taken or if any of them turned toward the spot where he had hidden the Aldritch women.

After a short wait he peered through the branches and leaves covering his hiding place to watch riders slow their mounts to a walk as they entered the forest.

Pearlie's heart pounded and light sweat beaded his forehead, running down his cheeks when the band stopped and several of the gunhawks dismounted a few yards from the hidden turnoff the mule path.

He brought his Henry to his shoulder and drew a bead on a man who seemed to be the leader of the gang. As he prepared to give his life to protect the women Smoke entrusted to his care, he thought, if nothin' else, I can blow Sundance Morgan back to hell where he came from.

Maybe then the rest of his men'll go on back to Texas and leave Smoke alone.

Sundance, wincing in pain, eased off his mount, holding a blood-soaked bandanna to his butt. He limped over to El Gato's horse and jerked a bottle of tequila out of his saddlebag. Dropping his pants and longjohns to his knees, Sundance poured the fiery liquid over his wound.

"Goddamn that hurts!" he yelled, dancing around, drawing a few grins and smirks on the dusty, sweat-rimmed faces of several of his gunhands.

Lightning Jack helped Perro Muerte off his bronc and laid him on his back in the dirt. After a cursory examination of his thigh, Jack said, "You got lucky, Carlito. Looks like the bullet missed the bone."

He took Carlito's bandanna off his neck and tied it in a knot around his leg, slowing the flow of blood to a trickle. He grinned at the Mexican, who clamped his eyes shut in pain. "Good thing there ain't no Confederate sawbones with us, Carlito, or they'd try an' hack that leg off real quick."

The *bandido* rasped through pain-tightened lips, "Señor Sundance, give me tequila, *rapido*!"

Sundance splashed more tequila on his bandanna and poked it gingerly in his bullet wound, then handed the half-empty bottle to Carlito. "You want me to pour some on your leg?" he asked.

"No." Suarez raised himself on one elbow and tilted the bottle to the sky, draining the rest of the liquid in two large swallows. He gasped and sucked air in through his teeth, his face turning beet-red. "Works better from inside."

* * *

As the rest of the men attended to their wounds and reloaded their weapons, Pearlie silently lowered his Henry. "Come on you bastards, git a move on," he whispered to himself.

Even from this distance, he could see where ruts from the buckboard wheels and his team's hoofprints ended, just short of the path. He mouthed a silent prayer the gang wouldn't notice how the tracks suddenly disappeared.

After another ten minutes Sundance climbed on his horse, grunting at the pain his effort caused. "Let's go, men. We'll ride 'til we find a suitable place to make camp. I figure a day or so to heal up and lick our wounds, then we can plan on how to take care of Smoke Jensen." Pearlie could hear them talking at a distance.

One of the men cleared his throat. "Mr. Morgan, I didn't plan on gittin' the crap shot out of me when I joined up." The gunslick removed his hat and wiped his forehead as he looked around at the others. "I think I'll just mosey down the trail and look fer an easier way to make some money."

Sundance's eyes narrowed and his jaw clenched in anger. He shifted sideways in his saddle to take his weight off his backside. "Bull," he said, pointing his finger at the big man, "I want you to kill any sonofabitch who tries to leave!" He glared at his men. "You bastards took my money and agreed to do a job. Nobody quits 'til that job is done, an' that means 'til Smoke Jensen's been dusted, through and through. You got two choices. You can ride with me and maybe get shot later, or you can try to leave and damn sure get killed now." He whirled his mount, eyes glittering hate. "Any arguments?"

Bull sat rock-still, his hands on the butts of his sawed-off shotguns, watching closely as Sundance's men nodded agreement one by one.

"Okay," Sundance growled, teeth bared in a solemn grin, "let's go."

Pearlie sighed with relief and mopped his face with his bandanna as the gang rode off up the trail. He let the hammer down on his Henry when the outlaws disappeared from sight. He stood and stretched cramped legs, then walked along the path toward the spot where he left the women.

As he made a bend in the trail, he saw Jessica lying on her stomach in the buckboard, aiming a Colt over the side at him. He raised grinning. "It's okay, ma'am, it's jest me."

It took him almost an hour, sweating and fighting his team, to get the wagon turned around in the narrow passage. While on their way down the mountain, he had Jessica keep an eye on their back trail in case the outlaws returned. After another hour and a half, they drove up at the outskirts of town.

When Pearlie pulled his team into Big Rock, he found Monte Carson and Louis Longmont standing before a collection of bodies, lined up like cordwood on the boardwalk for viewing. Monte had his left arm in a sling, and Louis had his coat off, wearing a white shirt with a deep red stain in front.

Pearlie introduced Jessica and Aileen Aldritch to the men, and explained briefly what had happened to them in the mountains and how Smoke had sent them down to Big Rock for medical attention.

Louis removed his hat and bowed deeply. "Ladies, Doctor Spalding is busy now—he's removing some bullets from citizens injured in our little fracas. If you'll permit me, I'll escort you to my establishment and have my chef prepare you some nourishment. By the time you finish your meal, I'm sure the doctor will be able to see you."

Louis extended his hand to help the ladies off the wagon. Once they were down, he turned to Pearlie. "Monte can fill you in on what happened here. I'll take the ladies with me and see that they're cared for properly, then I'll arrange for them to stay at the boardinghouse." As he turned to go, he winked at Pearlie and said, "I'll also have André throw a couple of beefsteaks and some potatoes on the fire for you. You look like you could use some food."

He walked off, saying to Jessica, "Do you ladies care for French cuisine, by any chance?"

Pearlie eyed the corpses of the gunslicks. "'Pears y'all had a little excitement here."

Monte pulled his pipe out of his sling where he had stashed it and put it in his mouth. After he got it going to his satisfaction, clouds of smoke swirling around his head, he grunted, "Yep. These ole boys never knew what hit 'em." He cut his eyes to Pearlie. "I figure we softened 'em up a little for Smoke."

Pearlie nodded. "That you did, and he's gonna need it. I ran into the gang after you got through with them, and they look like some of the hardest lookin' men I ever see'd."

Montc's lips curled in a smirk. "As hard as Smoke?"

"Ain't nobody alive as hard as Smoke Jensen."

"What're you gonna do now, Pearlie?"

"I'm gonna eat those steaks Louis offered, then I'm headin' back up the mountain to see if I can be of any assistance to Smoke."

Monte's eyebrows raised. "You be careful, son. Try not to find Sundance 'fore you locate Smoke."

"Don't worry, I'm gonna take the back way up—Puma told me how to git up there without goin' by a clear trail."

"Well, you take care anyway. An' let Smoke know the whole town's prayin' for him."

Pearlie grinned wickedly as he turned toward Louis's place. "Y'all'd do better prayin' fer them outlaws. I've got a feelin' Smoke's gonna be doin' some fall planting, an' the crop's gonna be dead Texicans!"

CHAPTER TWENTY

Smoke and Cal rode side by side through a ponderosa pine forest, their mounts at an easy walk, discussing the upcoming battle. "Just how much do you know about Indians, Cal?" Smoke asked.

"I know they's dangerous, sneaky, and unpredictable as hell. One time they can be friendly and neighborly, and the next time you meet up with 'em, they'll try an' take your scalp."

Smoke remembered his past. "Yeah, they can be real changable. Preacher used to call it being 'notionable.'" He reined his mount to a stop and fished in his pocket for tobacco. As he began to build a cigarette, Cal coughed lightly and said, "Do ya' think I could have one of those myself?"

Smoke turned his head and regarded the teenager with raised eyebrows. "When did you take up smoking?"

"On the trail up here with Pearlie. He allowed as how if'n I was old enough to fight bandits and outlaws and carry firearms, I was old enough to smoke if'n I had a mind to."

Smoke frowned for a moment, then grinned and shook

his head. "Hell, I guess Pearlie's right. You're a man full grown in this country, Cal, and that means you got a right to make up your own mind how you're gonna live your life." He handed him his tobacco pouch and papers. As Smoke struck a lucifer and lit his cigarette, he said, "Course, that don't mean you're always gonna make the right decisions, but you sure as hell have the right to make your own mistakes." He exhaled a cloud of smoke. "The trick, my young friend, is to learn from mistakes and try never to make the same one twice."

Cal stuck a rumpled cigarette in his mouth and handed Smoke back his makings. "Yes sir, Smoke, that's what Pearlie said when he was drinkin' whiskey the other night."

Smoke broke into a laugh. "I can see I need to have a talk with Pearlie. Sometimes a good idea can be taken too far." He raised his canteen, pulled the cork, and took a long draught of cool water before passing it to Cal. "Sorry it ain't whiskey, but from now on, water and coffee are all we're gonna be drinking. Liquor and altitude don't mix. Here in the up-high, one drink is like two or three in flat-lands, an' we keep our senses sharp and our minds clear if we're to stand a chance against Sundance Morgan and his gang."

Smoke sat his horse, palms on his saddle horn, looking out over the high lonesome. "Cal, this country is perfect for the type of fighting Indians showed us."

A puzzled expression flitted across Cal's features. "What do ya' mean, Smoke? I thought Injuns fought just like everybody else, 'ceptin' they used bows an' arrows 'fore they had rifles."

Smoke shook his head. "No, Cal, that's where you're wrong. Indians and white men have completely different ideas about how to wage a war. The white man has always put his faith in superior numbers and better weapons to defeat an enemy." He took his cigarette from his mouth, pinched out the fire, and scattered remnants of tobacco and paper into the wind. "An Indian, on the other hand, uses stealth and fear, and knowledge of the countryside to make up for fewer numbers and more primitive weapons."

Cal frowned. "But isn't our way better? After all, we've managed to beat the Injun tribes and damn near wipe 'em out."

Smoke smiled, a sad expression on his face. "You're right, Cal. In the long run, larger numbers of soldiers and better guns and rifles will eventually win out. But, in the short run, the Indians' tactics of hit-and-run sneak attacks at night, avoiding pitched battles, exacts a horrible toll on the winners." He took a deep breath, thinking back to his early days in the mountains, when he and Preacher fought Indians on what seemed like a daily basis. "That's why, long ago, mountain men adopted the Indians' way of fighting. It was the only way to survive against them." He paused, then continued. "Hell, when you think on it, I'll bet red men have killed ten or more whites for every brave they lost in battle. If we didn't have a steady stream of settlers coming here from back East, the Indians would've run us off years ago."

Cal thought for a moment. "So, what you're sayin' is that to beat Sundance and his gang, we're gonna have to fight him like we was Injuns?"

Smoke's lips curled, teeth gleaming and eyes glittering in a fierce smile. "That's exactly what I mean, Cal. There's simply no way two or three of us stand a chance in a battle with thirty or forty experienced gunhands if we play by their rules. So, we fight this war like an Apache."

Cal interrupted. "What does that mean?"

"It's something an old Indian taught me last time I was up here fighting a bunch of bounty hunters who had us outmanned and outgunned. Me and Louis Longmont took them on, one by one and two by two, and managed to kill or run every one of them off. We fought smart and cautious and used these mountains and forests of the high lonesome to help us whip them."

"But Smoke, I don't know nothin' 'bout fightin' like some Injun."

"You'll learn, Cal, 'cause I'm going to teach you, just like the best Indian fighter who ever lived—Preacher, who taught me."

"When do we start?"

"We've already started. Did you notice what I did with my cigarette butt?"

"Uh . . . yeah."

"I did that for two reasons. One, we don't want any fires up here, they might trap us and leave us with nowhere to run, and second, we leave no traces of our passage. When we move through an area, no one can know we've been there, unless we want them to know."

"Oh, I see. You mean, like coverin' our tracks and such."

"Yeah, but it's more than just that. It's making sure that we don't break branches or twigs, we walk our mounts around boggy or muddy spots so we don't leave prints, and we never camp where we make our fires." He thought a moment, "Matter of fact, when the going gets hot and heavy, we'll probably be eating cold food more often than not and doing without fires."

Cal glanced at dark, snow-filled clouds overhead. "I guess that means bein' cold ourselves most of the time, too."

Smoke nodded. "If you're gonna wage war in the high lonesome, being cold is part of it. But you'll get used to it before those galoots from Texas do. They're more used to frying in the heat than shivering in the cold, and that'll be to our advantage when the time comes. Let's go, we're burnin' daylight."

Smoke wheeled his mount to ride up the mountain and began moving toward the peaks. "I'm gonna take you to where we'll make our last stand, assumin' we both live long enough to get there. On the way, I'll show you some of the traps and falls I've set up, and how to spot them if you have to get out of here on your own."

"I don't much like it when you talk like that, Smoke, 'bout us maybe not surviving and such."

Smoke agreed. "I can see where it'd bother you, Cal, but it's the truth of the matter." He looked at the boy. "I want you to understand what we're going up against here, 'cause this ain't no Sunday school picnic, and it sure as hell ain't no kid's game where you get up after you're shot bad to try again. This here's for real." He sighed deeply. "Cal, only a few men are gonna ride out of this fracas forked end down. I hope it's you and Pearlie and Puma and me, but it's liable to be Sundance who pisses on our graves, not the other way 'round."

"Smoke, I ain't afraid of dyin', I'm more afraid of not bein' good enough, or of doin' more harm than good by bein' up here with you. I don't want you to get hurt 'cause you're havin' to look after me."

Smoke chuckled. "Don't worry about that, son. Everybody gets a mite nervous 'fore a battle, but once the lead starts to flying, your natural instincts will take over and you'll do just fine. If I didn't believe you were up to what's gonna happen, I wouldn't let you stay—and I'm a damn good judge of character."

Cal sat a little straighter in his saddle and began to look for traps Smoke had set. He wanted to find some without Smoke having to show him where they were, to prove to his friend he was worthy of his trust.

After a few miles he reined up, asking, "What's that ahead of us?"

Smoke turned his head. "What are you lookin' at?"

"Right there, near the pine tree. That pile of leaves and pine needles don't look natural—kinda there on purpose." He stepped out of his saddle and walked slowly up to the tree, squatting before it, leaning down. "Uh-huh, here's a rope, covered with mud or something, wrapped 'round the trunk." He followed the rope with his hands where it ran along the ground across the trail to encircle another tree and finally to where it was tied to a branch, holding it back under tension. "Jumpin' Jiminy, Smoke. If we'd tripped this here rope, it would've let that branch go and it would've damn near taken our heads off!"

Smoke smiled. "You're learning, Cal. That's exactly what it's meant to do. Let's hope the gunslicks aren't as keen eyed as you."

Cal walked to his horse and swung into the saddle, blushing over the compliment. "I'd never have seen it if'n I weren't lookin' fer it," he said quietly.

"Don't let up," Smoke added, "there's a few more between us and our destination."

Cal managed to find two more of three traps on the way to where Smoke had left his supplies. Smoke had to stop him before he walked his mount onto a thin covering over a pit Smoke dug in the middle of a mountain path. Even after he was shown the trap, Cal stated he could not tell it from what looked natural.

They came to Smoke's fort, as he called it, at noon. Smoke figured it would be a good time to take their nooning.

"Want me to gather wood fer a campfire?" Cal asked.

Smoke frowned. "Remember what I told you. We don't make a fire where we're gonna camp."

"But Smoke, they ain't hardly had time to get up here yet," Cal protested.

Smoke shrugged. "You're probably right, Cal, but are you willing to bet your life they haven't sent a scout or a party of gunmen ridin' hard to try and catch us unawares?"

"When you say it like that, I reckon not."

"No, and I'm not, either. This is a game with high stakes, life or death, and it don't do to underestimate your opponent. We won't get any second chances, so we'd better be right every time."

They staked their horses on the trail below and hiked up the steep incline to a level spot at the top, stumbling some on loose soil. They surveyed the approach, and Smoke said, "I picked this place for its defense." He pointed down. "We got an unobstructed view in front and both sides, and our back is covered by those cliffs behind us. A rock slide some time back took out the trees and brush on the hill to the front, and there aren't any boulders or tree trunks big enough for our attackers to hide behind while working their way up here. We've got over a hundred and fifty yards of clear space they'll have to cross to get to us, on foot 'cause it's too steep for horses." He pointed left and right, "Not quite as good over on the sides, there's some good-sized rocks and a couple of fallen trees over there, but I'm gonna let you hide a few surprises in that cover there in case our friends decide to try and use 'em."

Cal's forehead wrinkled, "What kind of surprises?"

Smoke shook his head. "You'll get no help from me. I'll show you what we got to work with, and you let your imagination take it from there. Hell, if you can't cook up something mean, then I may have to change my opinion of the natural contrariness of young men."

Cal rubbed his chin a moment, thinking. "You say you got some extra dynamite and a few cans of black powder?"

"Yep, and there's a pile of gourds and small pumpkins and rocks I gathered the other day, if you're planning what I think you are."

Cal pointed to several areas and explained in detail what he had in mind to Smoke, causing the older man to grin in anticipation. "You know, Cal, you almost make me hope some of those outlaws make it this far, just so we can see if your plan works."

"Me too, boss," Cal said.

Smoke opened his saddlebags and broke out some jerked meat and biscuits he had saved from breakfast, along with a few dried apples. They washed their food down with water from canteens. After they finished eating,

Smoke gave Cal a tour of his caches of guns, rifles, and shotguns, ammunition, and explosives he had placed in various locations around his plateau. "I've spread the supplies around 'cause I don't know how many are going to be coming up after us and I don't have any way of knowing if we're gonna be wounded or able to move around much, if they're firing on us real heavy."

Cal followed Smoke as he showed him where everything was located, nodding his head at the meticulous planning that had gone into the arrangement. "Looks like you thought of most everything, Smoke," he said.

"I doubt it, because you can never anticipate all the possibilities, but I'm damned if I can think of anything else to do up here to prepare for an assault." Smoke packed up the remnants of their lunch and said, "Now, we set about making more tricks for Sundance and his gang. That's the other part of fightin' like Indians—instilling fear of the unknown in your adversaries."

They slipped and slid down the embankment to their horses and mounted up. Smoke inclined his head at his bedroll. "I've got an extra pair of moccasins and some buckskins in there, so remind me to give 'em to you later. We're gonna be doing some sneaking around and I want you to be as quiet as a mouse, and as close to invisible as I can make you in the dark. Get rid of your spurs, and anything else that jangles or clinks when you're crawling around on your hands and knees. We'll also get you some mud to put on your weapons, just in case the clouds clear and we get some moonlight. It won't do to have anything that'll cause a glare or reflection to give us away."

"You mean we're gonna go right into their camp?"

"Maybe. There's nothing makes a man more nervous than to wake up and find the gent next to him with his throat cut and his scalp gone." He grinned at Cal's wide-eyed expression. "Makes it a mite tough to get to sleep the next night, and tired men don't fight real well or think too clear."

The balance of the afternoon was spent setting more traps, undermining areas of the trail, and digging pits and placing sharpened stakes in the bottoms. Smoke was amazed at how quickly Cal grasped the ideas behind creating fear and terror in their enemies, and how innovative he was at thinking up his own surprises for the gang.

At dusk, Smoked called a halt to their preparations, and they made camp a few miles from Smoke's fort. The hat-sized fire was placed up against some rocks so the flames couldn't be seen from more than a few yards away. Smoke cooked the last of Puma's venison, made pan bread and a pot of boiled coffee, which Cal said was considerably weaker than Puma's.

Smoke's eyes twinkled in the firelight as he said, "I want you to get some sleep tonight, and real mountain man coffee will keep somebody who isn't used to it awake for a spell—like two or three days."

Cal asked, "Why'd you make so much? Ain't no way we're gonna drink all that."

"I brought a couple of spare canteens. What we don't drink tonight, we'll put in those. Cold coffee ain't high on my list of favorite things to drink, but it'll help keep us alert if we aren't able to make a fire to warm it."

Cal was about to answer, when suddenly Smoke held

up his hand. A Colt appeared in Smoke's fist as if by magic, so fast that Cal never saw him draw. "Keep talking, like I'm still here," Smoke whispered, and slipped out of camp as silently as the breeze.

Cal continued to talk, until a few minutes later when Smoke reappeared, leading Pearlie's horse by the reins, with a blushing Pearlie still in the saddle.

"Cal," Smoke said, barely visible at the edge of the fire-light, "we're coming in, so don't shoot."

Cal holstered the Colt Navy he was holding and stood up to welcome his friends back to camp. "Hey, Pearlie, glad you found us," he said.

"Shucks, I didn't find you. Smoke found me. I figgered if I rode around up here makin' enough noise, y'all'd hear me sooner or later."

Smoke said, "What if it'd been Sundance's gang who heard you?"

Pearlie shook his head. "Naw, I passed their camp over five miles down the mountain. You can't hardly miss it, since they got a fire big enough to roast a cow, although they seem to be drinkin' their supper instead of eatin' it."

"That's good—drunk and hungover men have a tendency to be careless about keeping their scalps in a fight. Did you get the Aldritch women down to Big Rock?" Smoke asked.

"Yes sir. Just missed meetin' up with the outlaws, though."

"Oh?"

"Yeah." Pearlie squatted before the fire, piled some deer meat and bread and beans on his plate, and poured a cup of coffee. While he ate, he told Smoke and Cal about the gunfight in Big Rock.

Smoke shook his head. "I can't believe those fools tried to tree that town."

Pearlie grinned. "I don't know if the fight was strictly the outlaws' idea, boss. 'Pears to me that Monte Carson and Louis Longmont set them up where they didn't exactly have any choice in the matter. Monte said the town wanted to soften 'em up a mite fer ya'."

"I'd certainly call killing a dozen hardcases softening 'em up," Smoke said, "though I wish my friends hadn't taken such a chance on my account."

"Turned out all right. Those gents will think twice 'bout ridin' back though Big Rock any time soon."

Smoke's eyes, reflected in the campfire, radiated hate. "I don't intend to give them that chance, Pearlie. Every one of the sorry sons of bitches is going to be planted right here, in the up-high, or I will."

Cal added softly, "You mean, *we* will, Smoke. Me an' Pearlie are in this with you to the very end."

CHAPTER TWENTY-ONE

As the sun rose above the eastern slopes of the Rockies, Sundance walked among his sleeping men, kicking them out of their bedrolls with the toe of his boot. Hungover gunfighters and outlaws moaned and groaned, holding their aching heads and complaining about the early hour.

The smell of frying fatback and coffee finally roused the unhappy gang. They crawled out of their bedrolls, shivering and shaking in the early morning chill as they gathered around a fire gulping coffee, waiting for Sundance to give them their orders.

He sat on a boulder, his hands wrapped around a steaming tin cup, elbows on knees. His gaze flicked over the rag-tag group of misfits and murderers he brought with him while he thought about their forthcoming battle with Smoke Jensen. He realized most of his men would be useless—they were too dumb or too slow to be a danger to a mountain man. Their only benefit to Sundance would be to draw attention to Smoke's location by drawing his fire.

Sundance knew the gang stood no chance at all if they stayed together. Thirty men on horseback would be noticed before they could get in range, and would make a tempting target for ambushes and long-range rifle fire from cliffs and overhangs. He didn't like the idea of breaking up his followers, but there wasn't any other way to proceed in this country. Its thick forests, steep and narrow trails and passes were ideal for bottling up a large group, or catching them in a crossfire if Smoke managed to bring help with him. Sundance had few options, thus he made the only decision he could.

"Boys, I'm going to divide us up into groups of four to six riders. Each group will have a leader. We'll arrange meeting places and signals, in the event anyone catches sight of Jensen or his trail. I'll also give each of you a password so we won't be shootin' each other in the dark, if it comes to that."

George Stalking Horse thumbed his hat back. "Boss, General Custer divided his troops and you remember what happened to him."

Sundance smirked. "You fool! Custer got his ass kicked 'cause he was facing several thousand Injuns with nothin' but a bunch of green soldiers, and most of 'em had never been in an Injun fight before." He waved his arm at thick pines and steep slopes around them. "George, just how do you expect thirty of us to cross these mountains and manage to sneak up on a man said to be one of the best mountain men in the territory?"

George lowered his head, mumbling under his breath, while Sundance snorted in derision. "Anyone else gonna try an' tell me how to run this outfit?"

When he got no answer, he continued. "Bull, I want you and Toothpick and El Gato to pick some men to ride with. You'll be the leaders, so pick boys you think you can work with who'll obey orders."

Lightning Jack narrowed his eyes and flexed his huge arms until the muscles bulged beneath his shirt. "What about me, Sundance?"

"I want you to ride with me. I need someone I can trust to watch my back. Besides, you're the meanest son of a bitch on the mountain and I want you between me and Smoke Jensen."

As chosen leaders began to pick their riders, it was only a few moments before Bull and Toothpick squared off in an argument over who would ride with them. Toothpick had the point of his knife at Bull's throat even as Bull stuck his sawed-off shotgun in the other's stomach and jacked back the hammers.

"Goddammit, hold on there!" Sundance yelled, quickly stepping between two angry men. He shook his head "If you can't pick your bunches then I'll do it for you." He surveyed the band of milling outlaws. "El Gato, you and Chiva and those three men ride together." He pointed to three Mexican *pistoleros.*

"Toothpick, you take George Stalking Horse and those three cowboys over there," he said, pointing to three of the Southerners.

"Perro Muerte, you take Curly Bill and those four men." He picked two Anglos and two Mexicans to join them.

"One-Eye Jordan, you and Blackjack Walker grab those men by that tree over yonder." A Mexican and two Texas gunmen looked up from saddling their mounts and nodded agreement.

"Bull, you take Moses Washburn and the four men standing next to that rock and make your plans."

He looked at his followers as they began to split into small groups. "I'm taking Lightning Jack, Jeremiah Gray Wolf, and the two remaining cowboys with me." He put his hands on his hips, his face stern and eyes narrowed. "I'm only gonna say this once. Either you take orders from your ramrods, or you die. By their hands, or mine, It won't make much difference, 'cause you'll be in hell before you're dead."

He stepped off to one side. "I want the men in charge over here and we'll decide who goes where, and what our signals will be if anybody runs across Jensen."

Sundance squatted next to the fire and refilled his cup. El Gato, Toothpick, Suarez, Jordan, and Bull gathered around him, warming their hands over the flames, stamping their feet to get blood flowing.

As Sundance looked up, sipping his coffee, snow-swollen clouds overhead emptied and flakes began to fall. Within a few minutes visibility was cut to less than ten feet and the temperature seemed to drop twenty degrees.

"Okay men, here's our situation. We got a lot of mountain to cover, and not a hell of a lot of time to do it if 'n we want to kill Jensen and get down to the flatlands 'fore full winter." He paused to roll a cigarette and drain his cup. "El Gato, you and Chiva and your *vaqueros* head up the mountain on the main trail. Take your time and watch out for ambushes. Fire three shots if you see anybody or need some help."

He pointed down their back trail. "One-Eye, you and Blackjack start down the trail behind us. After you make sure Jensen ain't back there, ride north and go straight up the slope through the trees. It'll be rough goin', but at least you won't have to worry about being bushwhacked.

"Toothpick, you and George Stalking Horse and your men head northeast toward the peak. See if that breed can manage to cut Jensen's tracks or pick up a trail on him. And don't try to take him alone if you find him. Give the signal and we'll all come ridin' hard as we can. I don't want that bastard gettin' away.

"Suarez, you and Curly Bill go upslope to the northwest and look for tracks or campfire smoke. Sing out if you see anything. Bull and Moses, take your men and head straight up the mountain. Spread out and cover as much territory as you can. Lightning Jack and Jeremiah Gray Wolf and I are goin' to roam, cuttin' back and forth across all of your back trails. With any luck at all, we'll bracket that son of a bitch and catch him between us, and he'll be dead meat if he shows himself."

Sundance drew his Colt and flipped open the loading gate, checking his loads. "Oh, and by the way, tell your men that the shooter who puts the first lead pill in Jensen's hide will get a bonus of five thousand dollars, paid when I see his body."

Smoke raised his head where he lay hidden in weeds and brush near the outlaws' encampment. He had heard every word of Sundance's plan and now he knew the positions and numbers of each bunch of men searching for him. Old hoss, he thought, you're in for a few surprises before you see my dead carcass.

The outlaws mounted up and began to leave, talking

quietly among themselves about their assignments and the five-thousand-dollar reward for Smoke's death.

Bull and Moses Washburn's group was the last to leave camp, four men trailing their leaders through tall pines, riding single file.

Moving silently through falling snow, his moccasins making no sound in the shallow drifts, Smoke pulled his knife from its scabbard and sprinted after the men. The last man in line leaned to the side to adjust his stirrup, and grunted in surprise when a tall figure wearing buckskins suddenly appeared at his side.

Smoke's teeth flashed in a savage grin. "Howdy, neighbor," he whispered. He grabbed the startled gunman by his shirtfront and growled. "Tell me, is this worth five thousand dollars?" In a lightning-quick move, Smoke's knife slashed through the gunslick's neck, severing both carotid arteries and cutting off his strangled yell. Smoke pushed the dying man over his saddle horn and slapped his horse's rump with the flat of his hand, causing it to bolt forward.

Smoke wiped his blade on his trouser leg and walked back through drifting snow, where he had left his rifle and mount.

Jack Robertson was surprised and almost jumped out of his saddle when Micah Jacob's horse galloped by him as he wound his way through thick stands of ponderosa pines. Robertson was trying to keep the riders in front of him in sight, squinting into driving snow flurries, as they followed Bull up a steep slope.

He glanced to one side as Jacob's mount brushed against his legs and could see the man leaning forward over his saddle horn as if he were too drunk to sit up. "Goddammit, Micah," he cried, "take it easy. You're gonna git us kilt ridin' like that in these here trees."

Jacob didn't appear to hear the shouted warning, and his bronc continued to lope ahead, blundering into the next horse in line.

Robertson spurred his mount and pulled up next to Jacob's, grabbing the frightened animal's reins and pulling it to a halt.

Jacob's horse crow-hopped a couple of times, causing its rider to slowly topple sideways out of the saddle, landing with a loud thump in shallow snow.

Robertson stepped out of his saddle, calling ahead, "Hey, Bull, you and Moses wait up a minute! Micah's hurt back here!"

He grabbed both horses' reins in one hand, calming the animals a moment, then walked to where Jacob lay facedown on the ground. "You stupid son of a bitch," he said, grabbing Jacob by the shoulder, rolling him over onto his back. "What's the matter with . . ."

Vomit rose in his throat and he almost threw up as the dead gunslick's head rolled back, exposing a neck slashed open to his spine, blood and gore splattered over the front of his shirt.

"Goddamn! Shit . . . shit!" He raised his head and put his hands around his mouth and screamed, "Bull, git over here quick! Micah's been kilt!"

Bull and the others appeared out of the driving snow like ghosts, further scaring the terrified cowboy. "What the hell's goin' on here?" Bull asked, as he swung his leg over his cantle and dropped to the ground.

Robertson's voice rose in pitch as he stammered, "Micah's gone and gotten his throat cut! That bastard Jensen's done kilt him deader'n hell!"

Bull squatted next to the corpse, looking at the gruesome wound. After a moment, he glance up at Robertson. "How'd this happen? He was right behind you . . ."

Robertson wagged his head, eyes wide as he looked around wildly. "I don't know, Bull. I didn't hear nothin'. I was just followin' along, an' then his horse came runnin' by with Micah dead in the saddle."

Bull's eyes narrowed. "He didn't call out or yell or nothin'?"

Robertson clenched his jaws to keep his teeth from chattering. "I told you, I didn't hear nothin'." He drew his pistol and whirled around when a clump of snow fell from a pine branch behind him with a soft plop. The Colt was shaking in his hand as he waved it around, aiming at nothing. "We're fightin' a ghost, boys, and we're all gonna end up like Micah if'n we don't git the hell outta here."

Bull quickly stepped over, grabbed Robertson by the shoulder, and spun him around. He slapped the hysterical man once across his face with an open palm, knocking his hat off and sending him sprawling on his back in the snow.

Bull stood over him, looking down in disgust. "Shut up, you sniveling coward!" He put his hands on his hips and swiveled his head slowly, examining his surroundings.

Moses Washburn sat on his mount, his palms on his saddle horn. "Jack's right, Bull." Moses pointed to the body on the ground. "This ain't no ordinary cowboy we're dealin' with here. Jensen's a hairy ole mountain grizzly, an' we're gonna take some heavy losses trackin' him here in his own country."

Bull scowled at the man. "You figgerin' on quittin' us too, Washburn?"

Moses's shoulders heaved in a deep sigh. "Nope. I took Sundance's money, so I'll stay." He pulled a shotgun from his saddle boot and eared back the hammers, resting it across his knee. His eyes flicked back and forth, trying to see through falling snow. "I'll stay," he repeated quietly, "but that don't mean I like it."

Bull stepped into a stirrup and swung a leg over his saddle, loosening thongs on his sawed-off shotguns. "All this means is, Jensen's drawn first blood. I still plan on collectin' that five-thousand-dollar reward fer killin' him."

Robertson swung into his saddle and looked over his shoulder at Jacob's body, stiffening in the frigid air. His dead, glazed eyes were slowly being covered with white flakes, and the gaping cavity in his neck was half-filled with pink-tinged snow. He shook his head sadly. "Bet that don't sound like near enough to Micah."

CHAPTER TWENTY-TWO

Cal was pouring himself a cup of coffee when he looked up through the falling snow and saw Smoke squatting by their small campfire, hands extended to get some warmth. He hadn't heard him approach, not a single sound.

He shook his head and wondered if maybe someday he'd be able to move through snow so quietly. "Want some coffee, Smoke?"

"Yeah. An' some breakfast if Pearlie left any."

Cal grinned. "There's a couple of sinkers and a hunk of fatback that Pearlie ain't had time to wolf down yet."

Pearlie looked at them over a plate of grub he was eating, hunched over, holding it against his chest to keep it from being covered by snow. "Only 'cause I didn't have no more room on this tin. Lucky you got here 'fore I went back for a second helpin', Smoke."

Cal grunted as he handed Smoke a steaming cup. "More like a third or fourth helpin', you mean." He shook his head. "Smoke, if'n this fracas lasts more'n a couple of days, we're gonna have to send to Big Rock fer more supplies. Pearlie goes through food like a grizzly bear fattenin' up fer the winter."

Pearlie gazed at them with an innocent look. "That's only natural. A body needs more food up here in this awful cold." He shivered and hunched his shoulders in the buffalo hide coat he was wearing. "Hell, if'n I don't eat, I'm liable to freeze plumb solid." Ice rimmed his moustache and turned his sparse beard white.

Smoke filled his plate and began to eat. "Don't gripe about the snow and cold, men. It's gonna help even up the odds if it keeps up. It's sure to bother those flatlanders a lot more than it does us, an' it'll cover our tracks and muffle any sounds we make when we sneak up on 'em." He nodded toward their horses standing nearby. "Did you cover your mounts' hooves with burlap like I told you?"

"Yes sir," Cal answered. "We're ready to ride soon as you give the word."

While he ate, Smoke smoothed a patch of snow with his hand, then took a twig and began to draw a crude map of the mountain in it. He made two small marks with the stick. "This here is where we are," he said, pointing to the one near the top of the mountain, "and this is where Sundance had his camp."

Pearlie and Cal ambled over to watch him draw. Smoke made six fine lines on the sketch, curving off from the camp location at angles to one other.

"Sundance divided his men up into groups of five or six men and sent them off in different directions."

Cal frowned. "Why'd he do that?"

Smoke shrugged. "It's not a bad plan, for a know-nothin' outlaw. He hopes to cover a lot of territory in a short time. He knows winter's coming and if his gang gets caught up in these slopes during a blizzard they won't stand a chance of getting us."

Pearlie made a cigarette and smoked as he studied the map. "'Pears to me it'll also make it a lot tougher on us to move around without one of those groups cuttin' our trail or seein' our sign, 'specially if'n this snow stays on the ground fer any length of time."

Smoke nodded. "You're right, Pearlie. It's mighty tough to cover your tracks in fresh snow. Sundance was shrewd enough to spread his men out in different sections, so any tracks they come up on will have to be ours."

Cal frowned. "Jiminy, Smoke. If that's so, then how are we gonna manage to sneak around and Injun up on them gunnies like you planned?"

Smoke grinned. "Don't you worry 'bout that, son. Tracks are like women. They can seem to say one thing, and mean exactly the opposite."

"Huh?"

Pearlie smiled, nodding his head. "I understand, Smoke. You mean the man bein' followed is in control. He can lead the ones following him anywhere he wants to."

"That's the idea, Pearlie. It's a situation made to order for setting up ambushes and traps. Our other advantage is that Sundance doesn't know about you and Cal—he thinks I'm up here without any help."

Smoke bent over his map. "Now, here's where I want you and Cal to go, and what I want you to do when you get there . . ."

For the next hour, the three men planned their campaign of terror against the Sundance Morgan gang. When Smoke was satisfied his allies understood, he got up and stretched cramped muscles. "Okay men, now I want you to crawl into those blankets and get some shut-eye. We can't do anything until dark, then we're gonna be busy most of the night, and I want you fresh and ready to go at sunset."

Cal looked around, a worried expression on his face. "What if one of those bunches chances upon our camp?"

"Don't worry about that. Those galoots will be lucky to make it more'n two or three miles in this storm. Let them wear themselves and their mounts out fighting drifts and wind and cold." Smoke grinned fiercely in the gloom of the storm. "That just means they'll be sleeping heavier when we come calling on 'em later."

As the day wore on the sun rose higher in the sky, but it couldn't penetrate snow clouds and the temperature stayed just above freezing. Flurries of wind-driven snow coated the outlaws' faces and entered their horses' nostrils, making their search a living hell. Several of the groups stopped their trek up the mountain and hobbled their mounts in the shelter of pines and made fires to try to keep hands and fingers from freezing.

El Gato rode hunched over in his saddle, fighting his way along the main trail up the mountain. His men, strung out behind him, were barely visible through the white cloud that surrounded them. Julio Valdez spurred his mount and pulled up next to El Gato.

His moustache and beard were coated with a thick layer of ice and snow, his face was wind-burned a bright red, and blood was trickling from chapped, cracked lips that had split open.

"Jefe, momentito!" he yelled through the wind.

El Gato peered out from under his hat brim as he reined his horse to a halt. *"Sí.* What is it, Julio?"

"We must stop, *Jefe*. This storm, she is killing us." He held up his hands, gloves covered with ice. "I no can feel my hands."

El Gato twisted in his saddle to look to the rear. His other men were waiting, hands stuffed under their armpits, shoulders hunched against windchill. He nodded, "Okay. Is time for food, and horses need rest." He pulled his bronc around and began to walk it toward a small clearing a few yards off the trail, Valdez grinning as he rode alongside him.

El Gato's mount stumbled over something buried in the snow, and a large pine branch suddenly whipped toward the pair of gunmen. The rushing tree limb took them both full in the chest, knocking El Gato backward off his horse to land flat on his back in a snowdrift, his left arm bent at an odd angle.

El Gato moaned and pulled himself up on his right elbow. He looked up to see Valdez sitting on his mount, leaning against the branch, head thrown back, screaming in agony. The other riders rode up and jumped out of their saddles. One helped El Gato to his feet, another walked over to Valdez, then turned away and vomited in the snow, gagging and choking and mumbling, *"Madre de Dios,"* over and over.

El Gato frowned, "What is matter?" He grabbed Valdez's shoulder and pulled him around. A two-foot-long sharpened stake was buried in his stomach, just below his rib cage. It was attached to the branch with strands of rawhide, and had speared Valdez hard enough that several inches of the stake were protruding from his back.

El Gato shouted, "Goddamn!" He turned to his men. "Cut him down. Now!"

Juan Gonzalez, Valdez's partner, said, "But *Jefe,* if we pull stake out, Julio die."

El Gato stared at the man for a moment, then reached into his coat and withdrew a long, black cigar. He stuck it in his mouth, struck a lucifer on his saddle horn, and lit it. He stared at Valdez as smoke trailed from his nostrils. "Juan," he said as he put his arm around the *bandido*'s shoulders, "what you want to do? Leave him there 'til a priest comes to give last rites?"

Gonzalez shrugged. El Gato scowled around his cigar and inclined his head toward Valdez. "Cut him down." He grabbed his saddlebags off his horse. "Make fire, *muchachos,* I am very hungry."

Chiva held Valdez's shoulders while Gonzalez jerked the branch back, pulling the stake free. Valdez screamed again, scarlet jets of blood pumping between his fingers as he grasped his stomach, trying to stanch the flow. The gunhawk choked, gasped, and fell from his horse face-down in the snow, dying as he hit the ground.

Gonzalez knelt beside his dead friend, laying a hand on his shoulder. After a moment, he sighed and reached into a pocket of Valdez's vest and pulled out a gold pocket watch. He studied it briefly, then stuck it in his own pocket and stood, brushing snow off his pants legs.

Chiva frowned and spat on the ground. "You gonna take his boots, too?"

Gonzalez glanced at the dead man's shoes. "No. His feet is too small."

El Gato dumped an armload of wood on a fire his men had started and said over his shoulder, "Take his *pistolas* and ammunition and put in my saddlebags."

Chiva asked, "You want us to bury him?"

"No. Drag him into bushes away from camp and leave him." El Gato pulled a coffeepot and burlap sack of supplies from his saddlebags and began to prepare food. "We make camp here and wait for this storm to pass. We begin looking again tomorrow."

El Gato built a roaring fire and everyone ate their fill of beans, tortillas, and jerked meat. After they ate, they sat in front of the fire, warming their hands and passing a bottle of tequila around until it was empty.

As the sky became darker and men settled down in bedrolls, Chiva asked, "El Gato, you want guards sent out *esta noche*?"

El Gato raised his blankets to his chin and pulled his *sombrero* low over his face. "No. No one can move in this storm in darkness. Get some sleep and we start fresh in morning."

Chiva grunted, staring out into the dark veil of blowing snow and wind. He shivered and moved his bedroll closer to the fire. As a final precaution, he drew his Colt and placed it on his chest under his blankets.

Smoke waited patiently for the outlaws' fire to die down, lying twenty yards from the sleeping men. Thick, fur-lined gloves kept his hands warm, and he shifted positions frequently to keep his legs and back from growing stiff in the frigid air. After two hours, when he could hear El Gato and his men snoring loudly, he started to move.

He crept silently among the horses, running his hands over their necks and backs to soothe them and keep them quiet. He cut their tether ropes and led them, one by one, away from the camp to the trail. Once there, he gently slapped their rumps, causing them to trot down the mountain. Before he sent the last horse off, he lifted Valdez's lifeless body and laid it over the animal's back, tying his hands and feet together under the gelding's belly.

As the horse and its dead rider moved away, Smoke grinned, his teeth flashing in the darkness, Now it was time to really put fear of the unknown into his adversaries.

Smoke walked softly into camp, sliding his feet so he would make no sound as he broke through crusty, frozen snowdrifts. Slipping his knife from its holster, he squatted between Gonzalez and the other Mexican. He placed his left hand over one *bandido*'s mouth and quickly slit his throat, holding tight while the dying man quivered and shook with death throes. When the body lay still, Smoke turned to Gonzalez and repeated the procedure.

As Gonzalez choked on his own blood, he spasmed and kicked out with his legs. One of his boots hit a coffeepot next to the fire, sending it spinning and tumbling and clanking against a nearby tree.

Chiva was startled awake by the sound and sat up, fumbling with his blanket to get his gun out and aim it at the ghostly figure squatting next to Gonzalez. Smoke saw the motion from the corner of his eye and looked over his shoulder as Chiva's Colt appeared from his blanket, pointing at him. Employing lightning reflexes, Smoke leaned to the side and lashed out with his right leg. The toe of his boot caught Chiva on his temple, knocking him unconscious, sending him spinning to one side.

Before Smoke could straighten up, a heavy weight landed on his back, driving him down in the snow. A beefy forearm wrapped around his neck, bending his head back and squeezing his throat, cutting off his air.

With a tremendous effort, Smoke arched his back and reached over his shoulder to grab a handful of hair. As his vision began to darken, he heaved with all his might, throwing El Gato over his shoulder to land on his back in the fire.

Smoke gasped for air, drawing in huge lungfuls with a heaving chest. El Gato rolled off the fire and stood up, shaking his head. Smoke pulled his Colt and aimed it at the outlaw's chest.

El Gato spread his arms and grinned insolently. "You going to shoot unarmed man? That not sound like Smoke Jensen."

Smoke glanced at the Colt .44 he held in his hand, then back to El Gato. He grinned, teeth white against his mud-blackened face. "You're right, outlaw. Though I don't usually hesitate to shoot snakes or rabid dogs, killing a man who has no weapon does kinda go against my grain." He holstered his pistol. "How about I just beat you to death? That sound better to you?"

El Gato's teeth glinted in the firelight. "Oh yes, *gringo,* that make El Gato very happy." He flexed his arms and tightened his hands into fists, muscles bulging under his shirt. "I gonna kill you, *gringo,* then I will cut out your heart and carry it with me to show how you died."

Smoke shook his head. "All I see you doin' is shootin' off your mouth. Now, you gonna fight or are you gonna try an' talk me to death?"

With a roar, El Gato bounded over the fire and charged Smoke, his massive hands reaching for the mountain man's throat. Smoke leaned to one side and planted the toe of his boot in his solar plexus, his boot sinking almost out of sight in El Gato's gut.

The *bandido* bent over with a loud "whoosh" and grabbed his stomach. Smoke straightened and swung his fist in a wide arc, ending behind El Gato's ear with a sickening crunch, driving him to his knees. Smoke stepped back, rubbing his fist and wincing at the pain in his knuckles.

He was amazed when El Gato shook his head and struggled to his feet. The outlaw's chin was canted to the side, indicating his jaw was dislocated or broken. He looked at Smoke with hate in his eyes. "Gonna kill you, *gringo*," he mumbled, spitting blood as he came at Smoke. More blood flowed from his ear, and his hands flexed with anticipation.

Smoke stood his ground, assuming a classic boxer's stance. El Gato swung his right hand at Smoke's head, but he ducked and hit El Gato twice under the chest with sharp left-right jabs, crushing his lower ribs. El Gato doubled over, gasping, hands on knees. Smoke danced back, fists up, in no hurry to finish the fight. He was thoroughly enjoying himself, and wanted to make El Gato suffer as much as possible.

Suddenly, without warning, El Gato dove forward, wrapping his arms around Smoke's back while burying his head against Smoke's chest. He locked his hands against Smoke's spine and grunted as he squeezed with all his might.

Smoke groaned in pain, thinking his back was going to break under the pressure of El Gato's arms. After a moment, getting short of breath and unable to take in air, Smoke seized one of El Gato's ears in each hand and twisted with all of his might. El Gato shrieked as his left ear came off with a wet, ripping sound. The outlaw loosened his grip to feel his head, and Smoke took the opportunity to plant his knee squarely in El Gato's crotch, again doubling him, a high keening sound like a gut-shot pig coming from his lips. Smoke took a deep breath and swung his right hand up in an uppercut with all of his two hundred and twenty pounds behind it. El Gato's neck snapped back with a noise like a dry twig breaking and he did a backward dive, arms outstretched, landing spread-eagled in the fire again. This time he didn't move, but lay there, eyes staring at eternity as his flesh sizzled and burned.

Smoke worked his hand, making sure it wasn't broken, then stepped over to the spot where he had left Chiva unconscious. The wiry Mexican was stirring, not fully awake yet. Smoke rolled him over onto his stomach and pulled his boots off. As Chiva began to struggle weakly, Smoke drew his knife and quickly slit the Achilles tendons of both ankles.

Chiva screamed and rolled over, grabbing his legs, eyes wide with fright. "What you do? Why you cut me, Jensen?"

Smoke sleeved sweat off his forehead and sheathed his knife while he stood before the writhing man. "I'm a mite tired of killin' just now, so you're gettin' off lucky."

Chiva struggled to his feet, then fell awkwardly when he tried to walk, his ankles flopping loosely at the end of his legs. His severed tendons prevented him from being able to move at all.

Smoke said, "I'm taking your guns, so you can't signal your friends, but I'm gonna leave you some food so you won't starve to death."

Chiva stammered, "But, I no can walk. I will freeze!"

Smoke shrugged. "There's that possibility, I suppose." He glared at Chiva through narrowed eyes. "If it happens, I suspect it won't be any great loss."

Chiva frowned, fear-sweat beading his forehead. "Why you not kill me?"

"Simple. Dead, you don't help me at all. Alive, it'll take at least one, maybe two of your friends to take care of you and keep you from dying. That's one or two who won't be gunnin' for me."

Smoke bent and picked up his hat off the ground. He smirked at Chiva as he prepared to leave. "I hope your friends don't think you're too much of a burden on them. Otherwise," he shrugged and settled his hat low on his head, "they're liable to kill you themselves and mess up my plans."

Chiva shook his fist at Smoke from where he lay on the ground, hate and pain clouding his eyes. *"Chinga tu madre, gringo!"*

Smoke grinned as he disappeared in the night. "You keep warm now, you hear," he said.

CHAPTER TWENTY-THREE

Smoke planned to cover the north part of the trail himself and to slow down or eliminate that bunch of paid assassins. He directed Cal and Pearlie farther down the mountain to harass and attack a second bunch headed up the mountain along a winding deer trail through tall timber.

By the time Cal and Pearlie made their way down the slopes to locate the gunmen's campfire, it was past ten o'clock at night and snow had stopped falling, dark skies beginning to clear.

Cal and Pearlie lay just outside the circle of light from the fire and listened to the outlaws as they prepared to turn in for the night.

One-Eye Jordan, his hand wrapped around a whiskey bottle and his speech slightly slurred, said, "Blackjack, I'll lay a side wager that I'm the one puts lead in Smoke Jensen first."

Blackjack Walker looked up from checking his Colt's loads, spun the cylinder, and answered, "You're on, One-Eye. I've got two double-eagle gold pieces that say I'll not only drill Jensen first, but that I'll be the one who kills him."

The Mexican and two Anglos who were watching from the other side of the fire chuckled and shook their heads. They apparently did not think much of their leaders' wager, or were simply tired and wanted them to quit jawing so they could turn in and get some rest.

Finally, when One-Eye finished his bottle and tossed it in the flames, the men quit talking and rolled up in their blankets under a dusting of light snow.

Pearlie and Cal waited until the gunnies were snoring loudly and then they stood, stretching muscles cramped from lying on the snow-covered ground. Being careful not to make too much noise, they circled the camp, noting the location and number of horses, the layout of surrounding terrain. They crept up on the group of sleeping gunhawks, moving slowly while counting bedrolls to make sure all of Sundance's men were accounted for.

Pearlie leaned over and cupped his hand around Cal's ear, whispering. "I count five bodies. That matches the number of horses."

Cal nodded, holding up five fingers to show he agreed. He took two sticks of dynamite from his pack and held them up so Pearlie could see, then he pointed to Pearlie and made a circular motion with his hand to indicate he wanted Pearlie to go around to the other side of camp and cover him.

Pearlie nodded and slipped a twelve-gauge shotgun off his shoulder. He broke it open and made sure both chambers were loaded, then snapped it shut gently so as not to make a sound. He gave Cal a wink as he slipped quietly into the darkness.

Cal waited five minutes to give Pearlie time to get into position. Taking a deep breath, he drew his Navy Colt with his right hand and held the dynamite in his left. He slowly made his way among sleeping outlaws, being careful not to step on anything that might cause noise. When he was near the fire, he tossed both sticks of dynamite into the dying flames and quickly stepped out of camp. He ducked behind a thick ponderosa pine just as the dynamite exploded with an earsplitting roar, blowing chunks of bark off the other side of the tree.

The screaming began before echoes from the explosion stopped reverberating off the mountainside, while flaming pieces of wood spiraled through the darkness, hissing when they fell into drifts of snow.

Cal swung around his tree, both hands full of iron. One of the outlaws, his hair and shirt on fire, ran toward him. He was yelling and shooting his pistol wildly.

Cal fired both Colts, thumbing back hammers, pulling triggers so quickly the roaring gunshots seemed like a single blast. Pistols jumped and bucked in his hands, belching flame and smoke toward the running gunnie.

The bandit, shot in his chest and stomach, was thrown backward to land like a discarded rag doll on his back, smoke curling lazily from his flaming scalp.

One-Eye Jordan threw his smoldering blanket aside and stood, dazed and confused. His eyepatch had been blown off, along with most of the left side of his face. He staggered a few steps, then pulled his pistol and aimed it at Cal, moving slowly as if in slow motion.

Twin explosions erupted from Pearlie's scattergun, taking Jordan low in the back, splitting his torso with molten pieces of lead. His lifeless body flew across the clearing where it landed atop another outlaw who had been killed in the dynamite blast.

One of the Mexican *bandidos,* shrieking curses in Spanish, crawled away from the fire on hands and knees. Scrabbling like a wounded crab toward the shelter of darkness, he looked over his shoulder to find Pearlie staring at him across the sights of a Colt .44.

"Aiyee . . . no . . ." he yelled, holding his hands in front of him as if they could stop the inevitable bullets. Pearlie shot him, the hot lead passing through his hand and entering the bandit's left eye, exploding his skull and sending brains and blood spurting into the air.

Blackjack Walker, who was thrown twenty feet in the air into a deep snowdrift, struggled to his feet. As be drew his pistol, he saw Pearlie shoot his *compadre.* Pearlie was turned away from Walker and did not see the stunned outlaw creep slowly toward him, drawing a bead on his back with a hogleg.

Cal glanced up, checking on bodies for signs of life. He saw Walker with his arm extended, about to shoot Pearlie in the back.

With no thought for his own safety, Cal yelled as he stood up, drawing his Navy Colt, triggering off a hasty shot.

Walker heard the shout and whirled, catching a bullet in his neck as he wheeled around. A death spasm curled his triggerfinger and his pistol fired as he fell.

Cal felt like a mule had kicked him in the chest as he was thrown backward. He lay in the snow, gasping for breath, staring at stars. In shock, he felt little pain—that would come much later. He knew he was hit hard and wondered briefly if he was going to die. His right arm was numb and wouldn't move, and his vision began to dim, as if snow clouds were again covering the stars.

Suddenly, Pearlie's face appeared above him, tears streaming down his cheeks. "Hey pardner, you saved my life," he said with worry pinching his forehead.

Cal gasped, trying to breathe. He felt as if the mule that had kicked him was now sitting on his chest. "Pearlie," he said in a hoarse whisper rasping through parched lips, "how're you doin'?"

Pearlie pulled Cal's shirt open and examined a blood-splattered hole in the right side of his ribs. He choked back a sob, then he muttered, "I'm fine, cowboy. How about you? You havin' much pain?"

Cal winced when suddenly, his wound began to throb. "I feel like someone's tryin' to put a brand on my chest, an' it hurts like hell."

Pearlie rolled him to the side, looking for an exit wound. The bullet had struck his fourth rib, shattering it, and traveled around the chest just underneath the skin, causing a deep, bloody furrow, then exited from the side, just under Cal's right arm. The wound was oozing blood, but there was none of the spurting that would signify artery damage, and it looked as if the slug had not entered his chest cavity.

Cal groaned, coughed, and passed out. Pearlie tore his own shirt off and wrapped it around Cal, tying it as tightly as he could to stanch the flow of blood from the bullet hole. He sat back on his haunches, trying to think of something else he could do to help his friend. "Goddammit kid," he whispered, sweat beading his forehead, "it shoulda been me lyin' there instead of you."

The sound of a twig snapping not far away caught

Pearlie's attention and he jerked his Colt, thumbing back the hammer.

"Hold on there, young'un," a voice called from the darkness, "it's jest me, ole Puma, come to see what all this commotion's about."

Pearlie released the hammer and holstered his gun with a sigh of relief. "Puma! Boy, am I glad to see you!"

Puma sauntered into the light, then he saw Cal lying wounded at Pearlie's feet. He squatted down, laying his Sharps Big Fifty rifle near his feet, and bent over the kid. He lifted Pearlie's improvised dressing and examined Cal's wound. Pursing his lips, he whistled softly. "Whew . . . this child's got him some hurt."

He pulled a large bowie knife from his scabbard and held it out to Pearlie. "Here. Put this in that fire and get me some fatback and lard out'n my saddlebag."

When Pearlie just stared at him, Puma's voice turned harsh. "Hurry, son, we don't have a lot of time if'n we want to save this'n."

Pearlie snatched the knife from Puma and hurried to carry out his request.

Puma took his bandanna and began wiping sweat from Cal's forehead, speaking to him in a low, soothing voice. "You just rest easy, young beaver, ole Puma's here now an' you're gonna be jest fine."

When Pearlie returned carrying a sack of fatback and a small tin of lard, Puma asked him if he had any whiskey.

"Some, in my saddlebags, but . . ."

"Git it, and don't dawdle now, you hear?"

After Pearlie handed Puma the whiskey, the old mountain man cradled Cal's head in his arms and slowly poured half the bottle down his throat, stopped to let him cough and gag, then gave him the rest of the liquor.

Without looking up, he said, "Git my blade outta the fire, it oughta be 'bout ready by now."

Pearlie fished the knife out of the coals, its blade glowing red-hot and steaming in the chilly air. He carried it to Puma and gave it to him, dreading what was to come next.

"Pearlie, you sit on the young'un's legs and try an' keep him from moving too much. I'll sit on his left arm and hold down his right."

When they were in position, Puma pulled a two-inch cartridge from his pocket and placed it between Cal's teeth. "Bite down on this, boy, an' don't worry none if'n you have to yell every now'n then. There ain't nobody left alive to hear you."

Cal nodded, fear in his eyes, jaws clenched around the bullet.

Puma laid the glowing knife blade sideways on Cal's wound and dragged it along his skin, cauterizing the flesh. It hissed and steamed, and the smell of burning meat caused Pearlie to turn his head and empty his stomach in the snow.

Cal's face turned blotchy red and every muscle in his body tensed, but he made no sound while the knife did its work.

When he was through, Puma stuck his blade in the snow to cool it, sleeving sweat off his forehead. He looked down at Cal, who was breathing hard through his nose, bullet sticking out of his lips like an unlit cigarette. "Smoke was right, Cal," Puma whispered. "You're one hairy little son of a bitch. You were born with the bark on, all right."

Cal spit the bullet out and mumbled, "Do you think you could move, Pearlie? You're about to break my legs."

Pearlie laughed. "Sure, Cal. I wouldn't want to cause you no extra amount of pain."

Cal chuckled, then he winced and moaned. "Oh. It hurts so bad when I laugh."

While they were talking, Puma gently washed the wound with snow, then packed the furrow with crushed chewing tobacco."

"What's that for?" Pearlie asked.

"Tabaccy will heal just about anything," Puma answered, as he dipped his fingers in the lard and spread a thin layer over the tobacco-covered wound.

Cal looked down at his chest, then up at Pearlie. "Would you build me a cigarette, Pearlie? I think I'd rather burn a twist of tobacco than wear it."

Puma sliced a hunk of fatback off a larger piece, laid it over Cal's chest, and tied it down with Pearlie's shirt. "There, that oughta keep you from bleedin' to death 'til you git down to Big Rock an' the doctor."

Pearlie handed Cal a cigarette and lit it for him. "How are we gonna git him down to town, Puma? I don't think he can sit a horse."

Puma stood up and walked off into the darkness, fetching two geldings back, leading them into the light. He tied a dallyrope from one to the other and then turned to the two younger men. "We'll sit Cal in the saddle, and you'll ride double behind him, with your arms around him holdin' the reins. That way, if'n he faints or passes out, you can hold him in the saddle. 'Bout halfway down, change horses when this'n gets tired." He glanced up at the stars. "I figure you'll make it to town about daylight."

Pearlie said, "But what about Smoke? How'll he know what happened to us? He's expectin' us back at camp in the morning."

Puma smiled. "Don't you worry none about that. I'll tell him what you done and where you're gone to. Now git goin' if'n you want to make it in time fer breakfast."

The two men lifted Cal into the saddle, and Pearlie climbed on behind, his arms around the younger man. "Just a minute," Cal said, feeling his empty holster. "Where's my Navy?"

"Don't worry about it," Pearlie said, "I'll get you another one."

Cal shook his head. "No. That was Smoke's gun when he came up here with Preacher. It means somethin' special to me, an' I won't leave without it."

Puma dug in the snow where Cal had fallen until he found the pistol. He brushed it off and handed it to the teenager. "Here ya' go, beaver. You might want to check your loads 'fore you put it in your holster." He glanced back, surveying the outlaws' bodies lying around camp. "Looks like you mighta used a few cartridges in the fracas earlier."

Pearlie grinned as they rode off. "That we did, Puma. That we did."

CHAPTER TWENTY-FOUR

Sundance stood in the middle of a small clearing, hands on his hips, surveying the carnage surrounding him. It was a little past dawn and he, Jeremiah Gray Wolf, Lightning Jack Warner, and two of his hired guns from the Mexican border came here when they heard an explosion and gunshots the previous night.

The two Texas cowboys riding with him were standing to one side, trying not to look at the mutilated bodies covered with a thin layer of snow, slowly rotting in early morning light despite low temperatures so high in the mountains. Their faces pale and drawn, both men appeared to be about to lose their breakfast over the grisly sight, bloody remains scattered everywhere, fire-blackened corpses sprawled in patches of pink snow.

"Gray Wolf," Sundance snarled, his voice thick with anger, "scout around camp to see if you can tell how many men did this."

"Okay, boss, but it's gonna be tough. The tracks're messed up and the snow's startin' to melt."

Sundance fixed him with a hard stare, "Don't give me any of your goddamn excuses, just do it!"

"Yes sir."

Lightning Jack squatted beside One-Eye Jordan's mutilated corpse. It lay atop that of another man who'd been blown into several pieces by the force of a dynamite explosion. Jordan's body, cut virtually in half by double-barrel shotgun loads, was intermingled with various parts of other bodies.

Lightning Jack thumbed back his hat and stood up. "These boys died hard, Sundance, real hard."

Sundance made a face. "You know any easy way to die, Jack?"

Lightning Jack grunted. "Sure. Shot in the back when I'm ninety years old by a mad husband while I'm humpin' his twenty-year-old wife." His eyes narrowed as he looked around at other bodies lying in the snow. "But that don't appear too likely if we stay on this mountain huntin' Smoke Jensen."

Sundance glared at his companion. "You figuring on leavin', Jack?"

Jack shrugged. "No. This Jensen's startin' to piss me off. I plan to dust him through and through, then piss on his lifeless carcass."

Sundance gave a tight smile. "Good." He glanced at the two Texas gunmen, talking quietly off by themselves. "How 'bout you two?" he asked. "You boys havin' any second thoughts 'bout the job I hired you to do?"

Both men shuffled their boots in the snow, refusing to meet Sundance's gaze. "Uh, no boss. We're in fer the duration," one of the cowboys mumbled, although he didn't sound all that convinced. "It's just that . . ." he hesitated, looking at his partner. "Well, this Jensen's done kilt some of the toughest men I ever rode with, an' it don't appear that any of them managed to get a shot into him while he was doin' it." He shrugged his shoulders, looking down at his feet. "Me and Josh here was just thinkin', maybe it'd be better if'n we went back down to the base of the mountain an' waited fer him to come outta these hills."

Sundance asked sarcastically, "An' just how long do you two think we'd have to wait?"

The other cowboy, Josh, said hopefully, "Not too long, boss. Winter's comin' an' he'll have to come down sometime fer supplies an' such. Nobody could live through a winter in these mountains without stockin' up on vittles and necessaries."

Sundance shook his head in disgust. "You idiots. Jensen is a mountain man. Do you know what that means?"

When they failed to answer, he went on. "You could stick Jensen buck naked in the middle of a blizzard without a horse or a gun and he'd be sittin' by a fire, covered with furs, eatin' deer meat before you could get back down the mountain."

Jeremiah Gray Wolf looked up, no longer studying tracks, and nodded. "He's right, boys. My people have a name for these old mountain men. They call them ghosts of the mountains, an' sing songs about them at tribal gatherings."

Lightning Jack frowned down at him. "You sayin' we don't stand a chance agin' him, Gray Wolf?"

Gray Wolf straightened, looking around at the heavy, snow-clad forests surrounding them. "No, they can be killed only if your heart is strong and your medicine is powerful." He pointed to bloodstained snow near his feet. "They're flesh and blood, just like us, an' they bleed if you manage to put a slug in one, like this one here did."

Sundance and Lightning Jack ambled over to where he stood, followed reluctantly by the pair of Texans. "What do you see?" Sundance asked.

Gray Wolf squatted, pointing to tracks and blood in the snow. "Looks like one of the attackers was hit hard, maybe even killed. He spilled a lot of blood before he was moved."

Sundance's forehead wrinkled. "You say one of the attackers. That mean there was more'n one?"

Gray Wolf pursed his lips as he studied the tracks. "Yeah. At least two, maybe three. Look here," he bent down and pointed at hoof prints. "This bronc's a pony, an' he ain't wearing any shoes."

"You mean an Injun is helpin' Jensen?" asked Lightning Jack, a puzzled expression on his face.

Gray Wolf shrugged. "Don't know. Could be an Indian, or could be another mountain man. Some of the ancient ones ride in the Indian way, on ponies without shoes."

"Damn!'" Sundance slapped his thigh with an open palm. "I was afraid of that! Jensen's got himself some help." Before he could say anything else, a shout rang out while a rider galloped down the trail toward them, waving his arms in the air.

As the rider's horse slid to a stop in mushy, melting snow, Lightning Jack stepped to Sundance's side and spoke softly in his ear. "That there's Jack Robertson, boss. He was ridin' with Bull and Moses Washburn's group."

The sweating cowboy, chest heaving, jumped out of his saddle and ran over to Sundance. His eyes bugged wide at the sight of the devastation around him and the mutilated bodies lying like so much cordwood. "Jesus and Mary . . ." he whispered, sleeving sweat off his forehead.

Sundance glanced over his shoulder at the corpses, then back at Robertson. "You've seen dead men before. Now, what's so all-fired important for you to leave your bunch and come runnin' up here like your tail's on fire?"

Robertson shook his head, gulping to swallow bile rising in his throat at the sight of his comrades blown to hell. "Well, Bull sent me down here to tell you what's happened farther up on the mountain."

An impatient Sundance frowned, "Okay, get on with it, what the hell's goin' on?"

"Micah Jacob had his throat cut an' he was ridin' no more'n ten feet behind me when it happened, an' I didn't see nor hear a damn thing!"

Sundance clenched his teeth. "So? Look around you, boy. We got a whole passel of men killed here, not just one rider." He spat disgustedly on the ground. "You mean Bull sent you down just to tell me that?"

"No sir, that's not all. We heard some gunfire last night over to the north trail, an' rode over there this mornin' after breakfast to see what was goin' on." He took a deep breath, looking at the other outlaws. "We found El Gato an' his three Mex's as dead as doornails."

Sundance cursed, "Goddammit! How'd they die?"

"One of the Mexicans had a stake through his gut, went all the way through him and stuck out the back. The other two had their throats cut while they were sleepin'. They was still in their bedrolls."

"How about El Gato and Chiva?" asked Lightning Jack.

Robertson's face paled as he remembered what he had seen at their camp. "El Gato had been beaten to death. His ear was torn plumb off and his face looked like he'd been kicked by a bee-stung stallion. His ribs was caved in and his privates was squashed and mashed 'til you couldn't hardly tell what they was. His jaw was drove up into his brain and his neck was broken half in two, hardly holdin' his head on at all."

The two Texans glanced at each other, eyebrows raised. One said softly, awe in his voice, "El Gato was one mean *hombre.*"

The other whispered, "It 'pears Jensen was a mite meaner."

"And Chiva?" reminded Lightning Jack impatiently.

Robertson shook his head. "Oh, he's alive all right, if'n you can call it that. The muscles in his ankles have been cut, and he cain't walk nor stand up. And . . ."

"Go on," urged Sundance.

"Well, it ain't my place to say so, but I think he's gone a little loco, scared crazy, you might say."

"Whatta ya' mean?"

"He just sits there, rockin' back and forth, kinda foamin' at the mouth, an' when he hears any kinda sound, he jumps like he's scared to death and starts to cry and wail in Spanish. If you ask me, I think Jensen done scared the hell outta that boy and he ain't never gonna be right in the head again."

Sundance said, "Damn! I can't believe Chiva saw something that scared him that bad . . ."

Before he could say another word, a loud thump sounded from Robertson. Blood and tissue erupted from the front of his shirt and he was thrown backwards to land spread-eagled in the snow. A hole as big as a fist tunneled through his chest. Just as he hit the ground, the loud, booming sound of a Sharps Big Fifty echoed across the slopes.

The remaining men all dove to the ground in the watery mush and melting snow. As they looked around, their guns drawn and ready, Lightning Jack yelled, "There he is, up yonder!" pointing up the mountain.

In the distance, a small figure dressed in buckskins could be seen holding his rifle up, and the faint sound of an Indian yell filtered down through early morning mist. "Yi-yi-yi-ahhh!"

"Goddamn," said Sundance, "that shot must've been almost fifteen hundred yards."

Lightning Jack scrambled up on hands and knees until he was behind a thick ponderosa pine. "Yeah, an' I don't think it was a lucky hit, neither."

The other men rolled and crawled and ran wildly until they were also behind cover, shoulders hunched against the next shot, hoping it would be one of the others and not them.

Sundance muttered, "Damn!" as he took a deep breath. He jumped to his feet and ran to his horse, pulling his Henry rifle out of its saddle boot and positioning himself behind his mount. He jacked a round into the chamber, aimed over the saddle, and began to fire.

The mountain man could be heard laughing as bullets dug up earth and mud less than a third of the way upslope. Puma Buck put his Sharps to his shoulder and fired, the .50 caliber bullet hitting Sundance's horse in its shoulder. The force of the slug knocked the horse sideways, killing it instantly, throwing it on top of Sundance, who began to scream for help from his followers.

No one moved. Lightning Jack peered cautiously

around his tree. "Maybe Bull or one of the others will hear the shots and come to help us."

Jeremiah Gray Wolf muttered under his breath without raising his head behind a fallen log. "Not if he's got any sense at all, he won't!"

One of the Texans, rattled by Sundance's cries for help, called out, "Hey, Lightning Jack, you think maybe we ought a clear on out an' head back down the mountain?"

Jack shook his head. "Ain't no use, boys. Jensen's bound to have our back trail covered." He paused, sweat pouring off his face despite the chill of the early morning air. "No . . . the only way off this mountain is over Jensen's dead body."

The Texan glanced at his partner, eyes wide. "Or stretched out facedown across a saddle!"

Smoke raised his head above a bush where he was hiding and peered through binoculars down the slope toward a group of men working their way up a trail toward him. They were headed north-east, toward the peak, and if he didn't stop them now, they would soon discover his fortress.

George Stalking Horse was leading, leaning over his saddle horn, studying the ground for any sign of tracks. He was followed by the Southerners, spread out three abreast, their rifles resting on saddle horns, eyes flickering back and forth for any sign of danger. Toothpick brought up the rear, the butt of his Greener ten-gauge resting on his thigh.

Through his glasses, Smoke could see they were almost even with one of his traps. He worked the lever on his

Henry repeating rifle, shucked a shell into the chamber, and brought it to his shoulder. The range was too far for an accurate shot, but close enough for what Smoke had in mind.

He elevated the barrel to forty-five degrees to give him maximum distance and squeezed the trigger gently. His big gun exploded and slammed back into his shoulder, spurting fire and smoke.

The .44 caliber slug plowed into a large boulder next to the trail, ringing loudly, sending sparks and rock chips flying.

At the sound, the outlaws' horses shied to the left, toward the edge of a cliff, whinnying and crow-hopping in fear.

A man on the outside shouted as his mount's legs broke through the thin layer of sticks and leaves Smoke had placed over his dug-out area, and pitched sideways off the mountain ledge. Both the man's and horse's screams could be heard echoing off nearby ridges for several seconds as they fell, pinwheeling in freefall. A loud crash from below silenced the horrible sounds.

One of the Southerners spurred his horse into a gallop, trying frantically to escape. The bronc's front leg sank into a hole, causing him to swallow his head and somersault forward. His rider sailed ahead, twisting and turning in midair. He landed on his head, the fall snapping his neck and breaking his back in two places, killing him instantly.

The remaining Southerner, enraged at his comrades' deaths, put the spurs to his mount and charged up the trail, firing his rifle from his waist as he rode, screaming a rebel yell at the top of his lungs.

Smoke stepped out from his bush, drew his Colt, and

took an unhurried shot while bullets from the charging man's rifle pocked dirt and mud at his feet.

The slug from Smoke's Colt took the gunnie in the middle of his forehead, blowing blood, brains, and hair into the air. The lifeless body slumped forward, remaining in the saddle as the horse galloped past.

Toothpick looked down at his Greener, useless at this range, even if his nearsighted eyes could see far enough to aim it. George Stalking Horse asked softly, "Toothpick, what'll we do now? That scattergun ain't no use to us an' I don't carry nothing but a pistol."

Toothpick grinned, shaking his head. "Only one thing to try. Follow my lead, and kill the sonofabitch if you git the chance."

He stood, walking out onto the trail in plain sight. When he was away from cover he threw the shotgun to the side and called out, "Hey, Jensen. I'm unarmed. Come on down and let's have a parley."

Smoke shouted back, "Have your Indian friend come out and throw down his weapons and we'll talk."

George Stalking Horse stepped from the bushes at one side of the trail and tossed his pistol out in front of him.

The two outlaws watched with hooded eyes as Smoke rode down toward them, Colts in each hand. He stopped his horse a short distance away and holstered his guns. "Okay gents, what's on your minds?"

Toothpick said, "The way I heard it, you never did shoot an unarmed man, so I guess that makes us your prisoners."

Smoke gave a slow smile and shook his head. "No, I don't think so. You got two choices. Fight or die where you stand."

Toothpick held out his arms and looked around, grinning. "Fight? With what? I done throwed my shotgun away."

Smoke nodded at the knife in Toothpick's scabbard. "I hear you think you're pretty good with that blade. Want to give me a try?"

"Sure, mister. I ain't never found nobody I couldn't cut to ribbons."

Smoke stepped out of his saddle. He pointed to the Indian. "You, stand in the middle of the trail. If you make a move, I'll kill you."

George Stalking Horse gulped, "Yes sir."

Toothpick pulled his knife slowly out of his belt, kissed the blade, and held it low in front of him in a classic knife-fighter's stance.

Smoke drew his own knife and began to circle Tooth-pick, shifting the knife from hand to hand, his eyes boring into the outlaw's.

The two men closed, arms and hands moving faster than the eye could follow, swiping and slashing, blades twanging and sparking as they hit. After a moment Smoke stepped back, breathing hard, blood flowing from a three-inch gash on his forearm.

"How'd you like that, Mister Smoke Jensen? I'm gonna cut you up, you bastard."

Smoke slowly raised his arm to his mouth and licked the wound, blood trickling from his lips. "If your blade was as fast as your mouth, I'd be worried. As it is, I can see I'm gonna have to give you a lesson in manners."

Toothpick's forehead wrinkled. "What? What's that mean?"

Smoke bared his bloody teeth. "It means I'm gonna

show you what it's like to be cut up, really cut up. Then I'm gonna scalp you and leave you alive to live with the shame of it for the rest of your days."

Toothpick's face screwed up in rage and he screamed as he ran at Smoke, knife slashing back and forth in front of him in a windmill motion.

Smoke parried the thrust with his left hand and flicked his right arm in a lightning fast back-and-forth movement as Toothpick rushed by. The outlaw stumbled and almost fell, then turned back to face the mountain man.

Toothpick's right wrist dangled limply, its tendons cut to the bone, his knife lying in the mud at his feet. He snarled and picked it up with his left hand and advanced on Smoke, but a bit more carefully this time.

Smoke took a quick step in and whipped his blade to and fro again, then danced lightly back. Toothpick's eyes were wide, both his cheeks flayed open, flaps hanging down exposing his teeth. He sleeved the blood off his face with his useless right arm, growling with hate. "You sonofabitch, I'm gonna—"

Before he could finish his thought, Smoke rushed in and swung his knife again, cutting the biceps tendon on Toothpick's left arm, leaving raw muscle edges dripping blood into the mud.

A low, mewing sound came from Toothpick's carved face. "I give up . . . you win." He let his knife fall to the ground.

Smoke shook his head and swung backhanded, catching Toothpick across his chin with the steel butt of his knife handle. Toothpick whirled around and fell facedown on the ground, semi-conscious, moaning and groaning in pain.

Smoke stepped over to him and knelt, putting his knee in the middle of Toothpick's back. He reached down, grabbed a handful of hair, and pulled the man's head back. He made a quick incision along the hairline on his forehead from ear to ear. With a loud grunt, Smoke jerked back with all his might, ripping hair and scalp off Toothpick's skull.

Toothpick screamed a bloodcurdling howl, his split cheeks flapping and blood spurting from his head, then he passed out.

Smoke held the dripping scalp in front of him as he approached a terrified George Stalking Horse. "Here," he flipped the bloody mess to the Indian, who caught it without thinking, then he quickly dropped it to the ground, gagging.

Smoke smiled gently, asking, "Have you had enough, or do you want to finish this now?"

The man held his hands out in front of him and began to back away, saying, "No . . . no . . . please, mister."

Smoke glanced down and noted that he wore his holster on his right hip. Without another word, Smoke drew his Colt and shot him through the right hand, blowing off his index and middle fingers at the first knuckle.

The outlaw yelled and grabbed his hand, holding it to his stomach while retching in the mud. After a moment, he looked up with tears streaming down his face. "Why'd you do that?"

"I want you out of this fight." He shrugged. "It was that, or kill you." Smoke pointed over his shoulder to an unconscious Toothpick. "Now, pick up your trash and get on down the mountain. If I can still see you in five minutes, I'll change my mind and kill you both." He hesitated, then added, "And, if I ever lay eyes on either of you again, no matter where we are, I will kill you without another thought."

Smoke walked to his horse, stepped into the saddle, and sat there until George Stalking Horse had revived Toothpick and they were both stumbling down the mountain as fast as they could move, leaking scarlet blood to mingle with the black mud on the trail.

"Adiós, boys," Smoke said to their backs. "Be sure to tell your friend Sundance Morgan I said hello."

CHAPTER TWENTY-FIVE

Bull and Moses Washburn drank coffee at their tiny campfire, leaving two remaining gunmen stationed on opposite sides of camp, standing guard.

Chiva, his ankles bandaged with bloodstained bandannas, sat rocking back and forth, mumbling "Jensen *es el diablo,"* over and over again. His fear-widened eyes took in every detail and he jumped, reaching for a gun when he heard the slightest noise in the surrounding forest.

Moses cut his eyes to Bull. "What're we gonna do, Bull? We can't just sit here all day waitin' fer Jensen to show up." He sighed and drained his cup. "We're sittin' ducks here."

Bull shrugged, his eyes staring into his coffee as if he might find some answers there.

Johnny Larson, the outlaw guarding one side of camp next to the trail cried, "Hey Bull! We got company comin'!"

Bull drew his sawed-off shotgun and got to his feet, followed by Washburn, who shucked a shell into his rifle.

They hurried over to a spot where Larson stood, hidden behind a pine tree, aiming his rifle upslope.

Two men could be seen, lurching, stumbling down the middle of the path, their arms around each other's shoulders for support. As they drew nearer, they were easy to identify as George Stalking Horse and Toothpick.

Bull cursed softly under his breath at the sight of both bloody men. "Goddamn, will ya' look at that?"

Toothpick's bare skull was covered with dark, crusted blood, shining blackly in the mid-morning sun. Scarlet liquid trailed from gashes in his flayed cheeks, running down his chin to soak his shirt all the way to his waist. His eyes were wide and he had a haunted look, as if he had danced with the devil and hadn't much enjoyed the experience.

George wore a bloody bandanna wrapped around his right hand, tucked tight against his stomach, and he hunched over in obvious pain.

Larson let the hammer down on his rifle and walked slowly to greet his comrades, motioning them back to camp.

As soon as they were settled in front of the fire, Toothpick whined, "Whiskey, give me whiskey."

Bull took a bottle out of his saddlebags and passed it to Toothpick, wincing over the gruesome sight of his scalped head and the flayed edges of his slashed cheeks dripping blood.

Toothpick grabbed the bottle, his only good hand trembling, and upended it, gulping, swallowing fiery liquid convulsively until the container was empty. He sucked air through broken stubs of teeth and gaping holes in his face, then pitched the bottle into the flames, choking and coughing up more blood.

Bull put his hand on Toothpick's shoulder, causing him to flinch and pull away. "What happened up there, Toothpick?" he asked gently in his high voice.

Toothpick shook his head and stared into the fire, unable to answer.

George Stalking Horse looked up through pain-slitted eyes. "Jensen ambushed us as we was ridin' up the trail. He kilt the others, then came after Toothpick an' me." He moaned, cradling his mutilated right hand. "Ya' got any more whiskey? Bastard shot two of my fingers off an' it's hurtin' like hell."

After Moses handed him another bottle and he gulped most of it down, George continued with his story. He told them about the deadly knife fight and how Jensen tortured Toothpick, inflicting terrible wounds before finally scalping him as he lay dazed on the ground.

"Jesus," whispered Moses as he listened to George's tale. "I never heard anything like that." He glanced at Chiva, then back to the men who'd tangled with Smoke. "The son of a bitch is worse than Apaches back home."

George Stalking Horse looked over his shoulder at Washburn, nodding his head. "Yeah, only I'd rather face ten Apaches than one Smoke Jensen. At least Apaches kill ya' 'fore they scalp ya'."

The sound of horses approaching caused the outlaws to grab their guns and jump to their feet. All except Chiva, who covered his head with his arms and lay on the ground, whispering, *"Este el diablo . . . aiyee . . . este el diablo!"*

"Hello, the camp! It's me, Sundance, so hold your fire!"

Bull and Moses holstered their weapons as Sundance and his men rode into the clearing. Coffee had been brewed and while beans and tortillas were passed around, the outlaws wolfed food down as if they hadn't eaten for days. As they ate, Sundance told them how he and his men had been fired on and forced to stay under cover for several hours by an old mountain man with a large-bore rifle. He'd finally grown tired of making them cower behind trees and logs and disappeared into thick forest.

After they were sure he was gone, they got their horses and rode upslope, hoping to meet with remnants of Sundance's band.

Sundance looked around at the wounded, beaten men sitting with Bull and Washburn. "I guess the time for sneakin' around is over. I think we'll do better ridin' together. Maybe a large bunch of riders will have better luck against Jensen and his friends."

Bull frowned. "We sure as hell ain't done too good so far." He inclined his head toward Chiva, Toothpick, and George Stalking Horse. Lowering his voice, he told Sundance and Lightning Jack what had happened to the three of them, pausing now and then to emphasize a point.

Sundance nodded. "Yeah, Jensen's a mean bastard, all right. But there's no way he can stand agin' all of us at once." He got to his feet and approached the wounded men. "You boys gonna be able to fight, or are ya' gonna lay here lickin' your wounds like whipped dogs?"

Chiva didn't answer or bother to look up. Toothpick and George glanced at each other, then lowered their heads.

"I'm done, boss," said George Stalking Horse. "Jensen shot off two fingers on my gun hand. I ain't got the stomach fer any more of this, an' I'm headin' back down the mountain soon as I finish this grub."

Sundance raised his eyebrows. "How 'bout you, Tooth-pick? You done, too?"

Toothpick shrugged without raising his eyes. The hot coffee had started his cheeks bleeding again, blood trickling over his chin in fat, red drops onto his shirt

Without another word, Sundance drew his Colt and fired three times in rapid succession, putting a slug into each man's forehead. Their bodies were slammed into the ground to quiver and spasm in grotesque dances of death as they died.

Bull's and Washburn's eyes widened in horror, while Lightning Jack's teeth bared in a fierce grin of satisfaction.

Sundance whirled, his smoking Colt pointed at his other followers. "There ain't no room in my outfit for quitters or slackers. Either you ride with me, or you die by my hand right now! Any questions?"

As the echoes of his gunfire died, and gunsmoke slowly drifted away on a gentle mountain breeze, his men were silent. None dared speak out against him.

Sundance broke open the Colt's loading gate and punched out empty brass casings one by one. "Now, here's what we're gonna do . . ."

Smoke was dozing, conserving his energy for the fight he knew was coming later. He had made a small camp and ground-reined his horse, then walked seventy-five yards into thick ponderosa pines. He lay down, covering himself with pine boughs and branches so as to be invisible, should any of the outlaws chance upon him.

He was resting there, half asleep, his Colt in his hand, when a soft voice whispered in his ear. "Wake up, son, we gotta palaver."

Smoke was startled into full wakefulness in an instant, his thumb automatically earing back the hammer of his pistol as he sat up. He was astonished that anyone could have approached him without him hearing it.

Puma Buck sat squatted on his haunches, baring stubby teeth in a wide grin. "Don't look so damn surprised, Smoke, this ole beaver's been Injunin' up on critters with better hearin' than you longer than you been alive."

Smoke shook his head, a rueful expression on his face. "How'd you find me, Puma? I thought I was pretty well hid."

"Same way a squirrel finds nuts fer the winter, child. 'Cause he knows where to look." He cut his eyes toward Smoke's camp nearby. "Ya' got any *cafecito* over there? I be a mite parched."

Smoke scrambled to his feet and led the mountain man to his fire, mostly embers now. He scattered dry twigs and pine needles over the coals, then added larger pieces of wood when flames began to lick at the tinder.

While Smoke was building the fire, Puma got canteens and Arbuckles' coffee out of his saddlebags and prepared the tin pot with an abundance of coffee and a sparse amount of water.

Smoke cut strips of meat and grabbed a handful of dried apples and a tin of peaches out of his bags. As they ate, Puma informed Smoke of Cal's wound, and told him how he had sent the younger men down to Big Rock to see Doc Spalding.

Smoke's brow furrowed with concern. "Is Cal gonna be all right, Puma? Do you think he'll make it?"

Puma smacked his lips after draining his cup of the thick, black brew. His faded blue eyes softened as he glanced at Smoke, knowing he thought of Cal as his son. "Don't you worry 'bout that'un, Smoke. That boy's got the heart of a mountain grizzly." Puma pulled a cartridge from his pocket and handed it to Smoke, showing him tooth marks in the brass casing. "He never made a sound when I scorched his wound." Puma nodded, his eyes twinkling in the afternoon sun. "He's a natural-born mountain man, an' he'll have some impressive scars to show an' tales to tell about his experiences in the high lonesome, fightin' *bandidos* with Smoke Jensen an' Puma Buck."

Smoke grinned. "That's good, 'cause Sally'd have my hide if I let anything happen to that boy."

Puma topped off their cups with more coffee. He took two stogies from his buckskin shirt and handed one to Smoke, then lit them both with a burning twig from the fire. After puffing his cigar to life, filling the air with thick blue smoke, he asked, "What's your plan, Smoke? Best I can figger it, you still got over a dozen hardcases on your trail."

Smoke thought about it a moment, drinking coffee and smoking while he considered his options. "I'm gonna end it tonight." He glanced at the cloudless sky. "There won't be any snow tonight, an' the moon's still almost full, so there'll be plenty of light to shoot by."

Puma nodded.

"I plan to hit and run, takin' a few of 'em from ambush, an' leading the rest up the slope, to a spot where I have a forting-up place ready. I'll make my stand there."

Puma pursed his lips, staring at the glowing end of his cigar. "Ya' want some help?"

Smoke put his hand on Puma's shoulder. "This is my fight, old friend. I don't want anyone else hurt on my account."

Puma started to argue, "But—"

"No, you've done more than enough already." Smoke hesitated, then added, "However, if you could cover my left flank with your Sharps, you could keep 'em from sending a party to circle around to my rear."

Puma chuckled deep in his throat. "They've had a small taste of my Sharps once. I guess another bite or two will keep 'em in line."

Smoke's face got serious. "Puma, there's one more thing. If something happens . . . if things don't go as I plan, I got two more favors to ask."

Puma's eyebrows raised.

"One, make sure Sundance Morgan doesn't leave the mountain alive."

"Done. An' the other?"

"Take me home to Sugarloaf, and tell Sally what happened."

Puma stuck out his hand. "You got my word on it, partner."

Smoke took his friend's hand. "Now, it's time to do some serious damage. There's some stinkweed on this mountain that needs pruning."

CHAPTER TWENTY-SIX

Smoke was loaded for bear. He had his two Colt .44 pistols, a knife in his scabbard, a tomahawk in his belt against the small of his back, a Henry repeating rifle in one saddle boot, and a heavy Greener ten-gauge shotgun on a rawhide thong over his shoulder. He was ready to hunt, and to kill anything that got in his way.

He rode through thick ponderosa pines, making no sound that could be heard from more than a few feet away. By late afternoon he located the party of gunmen looking for him. Unused to traveling in the mountains, they were making so much noise they were easy to find.

Smoke stepped out of his saddle, leaving his horse ground-reined for a quick getaway should it be necessary, and slipped down a snowy slope toward a ribbon of trail the gang was following.

As the last man in line came abreast of his hiding place, Smoke took a running jump and leaped on the rider's horse behind him. Before the startled man could make a sound, Smoke slit his throat with his knife. Smoke pulled the dying man's gun from its holster and a knife hidden beneath his mackinaw as he slumped over his horse's withers.

He pushed the dead body out of the saddle and threw the knife at the next rider in line. The blade buried itself in the gunman's back, causing him to arch forward, screaming in pain.

Smoke thumbed back the Colt's hammer and began to fire. Two more of Sundance's hired killers were mortally wounded before any had time to clear leather.

Smoke whirled the dead man's horse in a tight circle and galloped into the brush, leaning over the saddle to avoid low-hanging branches and limbs.

Sundance's gang jerked their reins and tried to turn around to give chase, but the trail was narrow and all they managed to do was get in each other's way. Two men were knocked from their mounts, one sustaining a broken arm in the process.

Only minutes after the attack began, Smoke had disappeared and the gunhawks counted four dead and one injured, while not a shot had been fired at the mountain man.

Sundance was furious as he rode among his followers. "Goddammit! You worthless bastards didn't fire a single round!" He leaned to the side and spat on one of the bodies lying in the dirt. "Hell, I thought I was ridin' with some tough gunslicks." He shook his head in disgust. "I might as well have hired schoolmarms, for all the help you galoots have been."

"Fuck it!" yelled Curly Bill Cartwright. "I'm gonna kill that son of a bitch!" He filled his hand with iron and spurred his horse into the brush after Smoke.

Three other men pulled guns and started to follow Cartwright.

"Hold on there," yelled Sundance. "That's just what Jensen wants us to do." He waved the gang toward him. "Circle up and get ready in case he comes back. We'll stay here and see what happens. Maybe Cartwright'll get lucky."

Lightning Jack chuckled. "I doubt that, boss. He's goin' into Jensen's territory now, an' I'll bet a double-eagle he don't come out."

A loud double explosion came from the forest, startling the outlaws' mounts, causing one of the Mexicans to begin shooting wildly toward the noise while shouting curses in Spanish.

The gang waited expectantly, every gun trained on the spot where Smoke and Cartwright entered a stand of dense trees. After a few moments the sound of a horse moving through brush could be heard.

The men cocked pistols and rifles as a horse walked out of the trees onto the trail. In its saddle was the decapitated body of Curly Bill Cartwright. His head and upper shoulders had been blown off by a double load of ten-gauge buckshot. A tree branch had been stuck down the back of his shirt and his feet were tied together under the animal's belly to keep him upright in his saddle.

Lightning Jack spoke quietly. "You think maybe Jensen's sending us a message, boss?"

Sundance said, "Damn! I want to kill that bastard so bad I can taste it!"

Perro Muerte walked his horse over to Sundance. "What now, *jefe*? We go into trees, or stay on trail?"

Sundance said, "Stay on the trail. If we can locate his

camp, we can keep him from gettin' to his supplies and ammunition. Sooner or later he'll run low, and then we can take him." He pointed to Jeremiah Gray Wolf, "Take the point, Gray Wolf, and see if'n you can find some tracks or a sign showing which way his camp might be."

Moses Washburn spoke in a low voice to Bull, "I don't like this, Bull. I don't like it one bit."

Bull shook his head. "Me either, partner, me either."

Jeremiah Gray Wolf leaned over his saddle and began to walk his pony up the trail, followed twenty yards back by the rest of the group.

After a quarter of a mile, he held up his hand and called over his shoulder, "I've found some tracks. Let's go."

The Indian straightened in his saddle and spurred his mount into a trot, disappearing around a bend in the trail. The others drew weapons and followed him from a distance.

Sundance rounded the bend and stopped short when he saw Gray Wolf's pony standing riderless by the side of the trail, grazing on the short grass partially hidden by melting snow. "Crap," he whispered under his breath. He hadn't heard a sound, not even a call for help.

When the rest of his men rode up to him, Sundance slowly urged his horse forward, scanning trees and brush on either side for a sign of Gray Wolf.

From behind him, Sundance heard a sharp intake of breath, and the words *"Madre de Dios,"* spoken in a hoarse whisper. He turned to see Perro Muerte crossing himself and staring up at a nearby tree.

He followed Perro Muerte's gaze, and found Jeremiah Gray Wolf hanging from a limb, a rope around his neck, his legs still kicking, quivering in death throes. The Indian's bowels had let loose and the stench was overpowering.

Sundance held his bandanna across his nose and rode over to examine the area under the body. Horse tracks showed that Smoke had probably roped the man while hiding in the tree, then dropped to his horse, pulling Gray Wolf out of his saddle by a rope he'd looped over the branch.

Bull said, "He never knew what hit him."

"Shut up!" yelled Sundance. "Come on, he can't be more'n a few hundred feet away. Let's go!"

The group cocked their weapons and started to follow Sundance up a steep slope past the tree with the body hanging from it. It was a steep grade, covered with loose gravel and small stones, and they were only about halfway up the incline when a gunshot from above caught their attention.

They looked up to see Smoke standing next to a large pile of boulders, grinning, holding something in one hand and a smoking cigar in the other. He cried, "Howdy, gents," and put his cigar against the object in his other hand. As a fuse began to sputter and sparkle, he dropped the bundle among the rocks and ducked out of sight.

"Holy shit, it's dynamite," yelled Moses Washburn, as he jerked his reins and tried to turn his horse around. The men all panicked and reined their horses to turn in different directions, running into each other, knocking men and animals to the ground.

The explosion was strangely muffled, yet the pile of boulders shifted. Slowly at first, then with gathering speed, huge rocks rolled and tumbled, racing down the slope, bounding as they descended toward the trapped riders milling about on the trail.

A huge dust cloud enveloped the area, covering screaming men and horses as rocks crushed bones and flattened bodies and ended life.

When dust had settled, the only men left alive were Sundance, Lightning Jack, Bull, and Perro Muerte. The slide had killed four Texas gunfighters and Moses Washburn, who could only be identified by his hand showing from beneath a huge boulder.

In the sudden quiet of dusk, the remaining men could hear the sounds of Jensen's horse in the distance galloping up the mountain.

"Moses," Bull said through gritted teeth, "I'm gonna kill him for you."

Sundance took a deep breath, looking around at all that was left of his band. "Okay, boys. He's headed straight up the mountain. There ain't much cover up there, an' there ain't nowhere to run to once he gits to the top."

He pulled his pistol and checked his loads. "Let's go git him!"

The moon had risen and in the cloudless sky made the area as bright as day. Smoke was hidden in his natural fortress leaning over the edge, peering below through his binoculars, waiting for Sundance and his men. It was time to end it, and he was ready.

There was movement below, and Smoke could see Bull and Perro Muerte crawling on hands and knees off to his right. They were going to try to inch up the slope, using small logs and rocks on that side for cover. Smoke grinned, remembering tricks Cal had devised for just that eventuality.

Smoke waited until they were halfway up the incline. Bull, panting heavily in the thin air, motioned for Perro Muerte to stop so he could catch his breath.

Smoke worked the lever on his Henry and sighted down the barrel. "Hey Bull!" he cried.

The big man squinted in semi-darkness. trying to see where Jensen's voice was coming from, hoping to get off a lucky shot. "Yeah, whatta ya' want, Jensen? You wanna know how I'm gonna kill you?"

Smoke grinned. "No, I was just wondering if you'd noticed all those gourds and pumpkins down there."

Bull and Perro Muerte glanced around them and saw for the first time a number of small squash and pumpkins resting on the ground. Bull looked up the slope. "Yeah, what about it? You hungry?"

Smoke laughed out loud, his voice echoing off surrounding ridges. "Did you ever wonder, you ignorant bastard, how gourds could grow on bare rock?"

Bull's eyes widened in horror and he opened his mouth to scream as he realized the trap they had fallen into.

Smoke squeezed his trigger, firing into the pumpkin directly in front of them. Molten lead entered the gourd, igniting black powder. The object exploded, blasting hundreds of small stones hurtling outward. Bull's and Perro Muerte's bodies were riddled, shredded, blown to pieces. They died instantly.

Below, Sundance sleeved sweat off his forehead and turned to Lightning Jack. "Maybe we oughta head down the mountain and come back later, with more men."

Lightning Jack looked at the gunfighter with disgust.

"You coward. You got over thirty good men killed lookin' fer your vengeance. You ain't backin' out now."

Sundance dropped his hand to his Colt, but froze when a voice behind them said, "Hold it right there, gents."

Lightning Jack and Sundance turned to see a small, wiry man in buckskins pointing a shotgun at their heads. "Ease them irons outta those holsters and grab some sky."

As they dropped their pistols to the ground, Puma called out, "Hey Smoke. I got me a couple of polecats in my sights. What do you want me to do with 'em?"

"Bring 'em up here."

Puma pointed up the hill with his scattergun. "Git."

As the outlaws struggled uphill, the mountain man, more than twice their age, walked nimbly up the slope with never a misstep, nor was he breathing hard when they reached the top.

Smoke stood there, hands on hips, shaking his head at Puma. "It's easier to tree a grizzly than to keep you ornery old-timers out of a good fight."

Puma nodded. "Yeah, I'd rather bed down with a skunk than miss a good fracas." He cut his eyes over at Smoke. "You want me to dust 'em now, or just stake 'em out over an anthill?"

Sundance's eyes widened. "You wouldn't do that . . . would you, you son of a bitch?"

Smoke pursed his lips, rubbing his chin. "Well, I'm feelin' real generous tonight. How about you boys picking your own way to die? Guns, knives, fists, or boots, it makes no difference to me."

Lightning Jack grinned, flexing his muscles while clenching his fists. "You man enough to take me on hand to hand?" He inclined his head toward Puma. "Winner goes free?"

Smoke removed belt and holsters and took a pair of padded black gloves out of his pants and began to pull them on. "Puma, if this loudmouth beats me, take his left ear as a souvenir and let him go."

Puma grunted and spat on the ground. "How 'bout I take his top-knot instead?"

"Wait a minute . . ." began Lightning Jack, until Puma jacked back the hammers on his shotgun, shutting his mouth for the moment.

Smoke stepped into the middle of a level area at the top of the plateau. He bowed slightly and said, "Let's dance!"

Lightning Jack worked his shoulders, loosening up. "Any rules?"

Smoke grinned, but his eyes held no warmth. "Yeah, the man left alive at the end is the winner."

"Just the way I like it. Say good-bye to your friend, mountain man."

The two men circled slowly, bobbing and weaving and throwing an occasional feint to test their opponent's reflexes. Lightning Jack suddenly rushed at Smoke, swinging roundhouse blows with both arms. Smoke ducked his chin into his chest, hunched his shoulders, and took two heavy blows on his arms. He grunted with pain, and thought, this man can hit like a mule! As Jack drew back to swing again, Smoke unloaded two short, sharp left jabs, both landing on Jack's nose, flattening it, snapping his head back hard enough so that Puma could hear his neck crack.

Jack shook his head, flinging blood and snot in the air,

a dazed look on his face. Smoke stood, spread-eagled, his fists in front of him, waiting patiently.

After a pause Jack sleeved blood off his lip and felt his flattened nose. He glared at Smoke, hate in his eyes. Growling like an animal, he advanced toward the mountain man, pumping his arms while swinging his fists.

Smoke stepped lightly to one side and swung a left cross against Jack's chin, stopping him in his tracks. Smoke followed with a straight right to the middle of his chest, knocking him backward, rocking him back on his heels. Another left jab to the forehead to straighten him up, and then a mighty uppercut to his solar plexus, just under his sternum, lifted him up on his toes before he fell to one knee. Jack remained there a few moments, catching his breath.

He looked up at Smoke, blood pouring from his ruined nose. He grinned wickedly, then snatched a slender knife from his boot and rushed at Smoke with the blade extended.

Smoke took the blade in the outer part of his left shoulder, bent to his right, and swung with all his might. His fist hit Jack in the throat, crushing his larynx with a sharp crunching sound. The knife slipped from Jack's numb fingers and he fell to his knees, grabbing his neck with both hands. A loud whistling wheeze came from his mouth as he tried to pull air in through his broken trachea, and his eyes widened, bugging out like those of a frightened frog. His skin turned dusky blue, then black as he ran out of air. His eyes glazed over and he died, falling on his face in the dirt.

Smoke took the knife handle in his right hand, closed his eyes and set his jaw, and yanked it free with a jerk. He staggered at the pain, then straightened, a steely glint in his eyes as blood seeped from the wound to stain his shirt.

Puma started toward him, but Smoke waved him away. "Not yet, Puma. We got one more snake to stomp 'fore we're through."

Sundance stuttered, "But, I'm not much good with my fists. I ain't no prizefighter."

"You fancy yourself a gunfighter?"

"Yeah, and I'm a hell of a lot better'n I was last time you bushwhacked me, Jensen. I been practicing for years."

Smoke, his left arm hanging limp at his side, bent down and picked up his belt and holsters. "Buckle this on for me, would you, Puma?"

Puma placed the guns around Smoke's waist and snapped the buckle shut, then tied the righthand holster down low on his thigh. Smoke slipped the hammer thongs off both guns using his right hand, stepping over to the center of the plateau. "Give the lowlife his pistol, Puma, then watch your back. Sundance is famous for shooting people from the north when they're facing south."

Sundance put his hand on the handle of his Colt. "You're gonna die for that, Jensen."

The two men squared off, thirty yards apart, hands hanging loose, fingers flexing in anticipation. "You called this play, Sundance. Now it's time for you to pay the band. Fill your damn hand!"

Sundance snarled and grabbed for his pistol, crouching and turning slightly sideways to give Smoke less of a target. Smoke waited a second, giving the gunfighter time to get his gun halfway out of his holster. In a move that was so fast Puma blinked and missed it, Smoke cleared leather and fired. His bullet took Sundance in the right wrist, snapping it, flinging his Colt into the dirt.

Sundance howled, cradling his right hand with his left, hunched over, tears running down his cheeks. "Okay, you bastard. You win," he sobbed.

Smoke shook his head. "No, I don't think so. You've got another gun and another hand. Use 'em."

Sundance looked up in astonishment. "My left hand against your right? That ain't fair!"

Smoke shook his head, twirled his righthand Colt once, and then he settled it in his holster. "I'll cross-draw my left gun, if that's more to your liking."

Sundance's lips curled in a tight smile. The cross-draw wasn't a speed draw. No one could beat him with a cross-draw, even lefthanded, he thought. "Okay. It's your call, Jensen."

He stood up, threw his shoulders back, and went for his iron.

Smoke's right hand flashed across his belly, drawing and firing again before Sundance could fist his weapon. This time, Smoke's slug took the outlaw in his left shoulder, shattering it while spinning him around to land facedown on the ground.

Smoke looked at Puma. "Bring me a rope from that bag over yonder."

He took the rope from Puma, formed a large loop, and passed it over Sundance's arms to tie it around his chest. He dragged the sobbing, sniffling gunman across the plateau to the edge of the cliff on the east side of the clearing.

"Help me lower him down onto that ledge down there, Puma."

"What . . . what are you doing? No . . . no . . . please . . ."

The two mountain men lowered the crying outlaw twenty feet down the side of the sheer cliff, letting him down gently on a three-foot ledge that stuck out over a drop of two hundred feet.

Smoke leaned over the edge and called down, "I'm gonna do something for you that you never did for your victims, Sundance. I'm gonna give you a choice about the way you want to die. You can lay there on that ledge and slowly starve to death, or you can jump and fall two hundred feet so you'll die quickly. It's all up to you."

"Wait, you can't do this to me. It ain't right . . ."

Smoke and Puma slowly walked away, ignoring cries from the coward below. Neither one much cared how he chose to die, just so long as he died, and that was a certainty.